Praise for #1 *New York Times* bestselling author

NORA ROBERTS

"America's favorite writer."
—*The New Yorker*

"When Roberts puts her expert fingers on the pulse of romance, legions of fans feel the heartbeat."
—*Publishers Weekly*

"Nora Roberts is among the best."
—*The Washington Post*

"Roberts' bestselling novels are some of the best in the romance genre."
—*USA TODAY*

"Roberts' style has a fresh, contemporary snap."
—*Kirkus Reviews*

"You can't bottle wish fulfillment, but Nora Roberts certainly knows how to put it on the page."
—*New York Times*

NORA ROBERTS

KEEP YOU CLOSE

Published by Silhouette Books
America's Publisher of Contemporary Romance

SILHOUETTE BOOKS

Keep You Close

ISBN-13: 978-1-335-54776-7

Recycling programs
for this product may
not exist in your area.

Copyright © 2018 by Harlequin Books S.A.

The publisher acknowledges the copyright holder
of the individual works as follows:

Night Shift
Copyright © 1990 by Nora Roberts

Night Moves
Copyright © 1985 by Nora Roberts

This edition published by arrangement with Harlequin Books S.A.

For questions and comments about the quality of this book, please contact us at CustomerService@Harlequin.com.

Visit Silhouette Books at www.Harlequin.com

Printed in U.S.A.

CONTENTS

NIGHT SHIFT

To Kay in Denver
And with appreciation to the staff of WQCM

Chapter 1

"All right, night owls, it's coming up on midnight, and you're listening to KHIP. Get ready for five hits in a row. This is Cilla O'Roarke, and, darling, I'm sending this one straight out to you."

Her voice was like hot whiskey, smooth and potent. Rich, throaty, touched with the barest whisper of the South, it might have been fashioned for the airwaves. Any man in Denver who was tuned in to her frequency would believe she was speaking only to him.

Cilla eased up on the pot on the mixer, sending the first of the five promised hits out to her listeners. Music slid into the booth. She could have pulled off her headphones and given herself three minutes and twenty-two seconds of silence. She preferred the sound. Her affection for music was only one of the reasons for her success in radio.

Her voice was a natural attribute. She'd talked herself into her first job—at a low-frequency, low-budget station in rural Georgia—with no experience, no résumé and a brand-new high school diploma. And she was perfectly aware that it was her voice that had landed her that position. That and her willingness to work for next to nothing, make coffee and double as the station's receptionist. Ten years later, her voice was hardly her only qualification. But it still often turned the tide.

She'd never found the time to pursue the degree in communications she still coveted. But she could double—and had—as engineer, newscaster, interviewer and program director. She had an encyclopedic memory for songs and recording artists, and a respect for both. Radio had been her home for a decade, and she loved it.

Her easygoing, flirtatious on-air personality was often at odds with the intense, organized and ambitious woman who rarely slept more than six hours and usually ate on the run. The public Cilla O'Roarke was a sexy radio princess who mingled with celebrities and had a job loaded with glamour and excitement. The private woman spent an average of ten hours a day at the station or on station business, was fiercely determined to put her younger sister through college and hadn't had a date in two years of Saturday nights.

And didn't want one.

Setting the headphones aside, she rechecked her daily log for her next fifteen-minute block. For the space of time it took to play a top 10 hit, the booth was silent. There was only Cilla and the lights and gauges on the control board. That was how she liked it best.

When she'd accepted the position with KHIP in

Denver six months before, she'd wrangled for the 10:00-p.m.-to-2-a.m. slot, one usually reserved for the novice deejay. A rising success with ten years' experience behind her, she could have had one of the plum day spots when the listening audience was at its peak. She preferred the night, and for the past five years she'd carved out a name for herself in those lonely hours.

She liked being alone, and she liked sending her voice and music out to others who lived at night.

With an eye on the clock, Cilla adjusted her headphones. Between the fade-out of hit number four and the intro to hit number five, she crooned out the station's call letters and frequency. After a quick break when she popped in a cassette of recorded news, she would begin her favorite part of her show. The request line.

She enjoyed watching the phones light up, enjoyed hearing the voices. It took her out of her booth for fifty minutes every night and proved to her that there were people, real people with real lives, who were listening to her.

She lit a cigarette and leaned back in her swivel chair. This would be her last quiet moment for the next hour.

She didn't appear to be a restful woman. Nor, despite the voice, did she look like a smoldering femme fatale. There was too much energy in her face and in her long, nervous body for either. Her nails were unpainted, as was her mouth. She rarely found time in her schedule to bother with polish and paint. Her dark brandy-brown eyes were nearly closed as she allowed her body to charge up. Her lashes were long, an inheritance from her dreamy father. In contrast to the silky lashes and the pale, creamy complexion, her features were strong and angular. She had been blessed with a cloud of rich, wavy black hair that she ruthlessly pulled back, clipped back or twisted up in deference to the headphones.

With an eye on the elapsed-time clock, Cilla crushed out the cigarette and took a sip of water, then opened her mike. The On Air sign glowed green.

"That was for all the lovers out there, whether you've got someone to cuddle up with tonight or you wish you did. Stay tuned. This is Cilla O'Roarke, Denver. You're listening to KHIP. We're coming back with our request line."

As she switched on the tape for a commercial run, she glanced up. "Hey, Nick. How's it going?"

Nick Peters, the college student who served as an intern at the station, pushed up his dark-framed glasses and grinned. "I aced the Lit test."

"Way to go." She gratefully accepted the mug of steaming coffee he offered. "Is it still snowing?"

"Stopped about an hour ago."

She nodded and relaxed a little. She'd been worrying about Deborah, her younger sister. "I guess the roads are a mess."

"Not too bad. You want something to go with that coffee?"

She flicked him a smile, her mind too busy with other things to note the adoration in his eyes. "No, thanks. Help yourself to some stale doughnuts before you sign out." She hit a switch and spoke into the mike again.

As she read the station promos, he watched her. He knew it was hopeless, even stupid, but he was wildly in love with her. She was the most beautiful woman in the world to him, making the women at college look like awkward, gangling shadows of what a real woman should be. She was strong, successful, sexy. And she barely knew he was alive. When she noticed him at all, it was with a distractedly friendly smile or gesture.

For over three months he'd been screwing up his courage to ask her for a date. And fantasizing about what it would be like to have her attention focused on him, only him, for an entire evening.

She was completely unaware. Had she known where his mind had led him, Cilla would have been more amused than flattered. Nick was barely twenty-one, seven years her junior chronologically. And decades younger in every other way. She liked him. He was unobtrusive and efficient, and he wasn't afraid of long hours or hard work.

Over the past few months she'd come to depend on the coffee he brought her before he left the station. And to enjoy knowing she would be completely alone as she drank it.

Nick glanced at the clock. "I'll, ah, see you tomorrow."

"Hmm? Oh, sure. Good night, Nick." The moment he was through the door, she forgot about him. She punched one of the illuminated buttons on the phone. "KHIP. You're on the air."

"Cilla?"

"That's right. Who's this?"

"I'm Kate."

"Where are you calling from, Kate?"

"From home—over in Lakewood. My husband's a cabdriver. He's working the late shift. We both listen to your show every night. Could you play 'Peaceful, Easy Feeling' for Kate and Ray?"

"You got it, Kate. Keep those home fires burning." She punched the next button. "KHIP. You're on the air."

The routine ran smoothly. Cilla would take calls, scribbling down the titles and the dedications. The small studio was lined with shelves crammed with albums, 45s, CDs, all labeled for easy access. After a handful of calls she would break to commercials and station promos to give herself time to set up for the first block of songs.

Some of the callers were repeaters, so she would chat a moment or two. Some were the lonely, calling just to hear the sound of another voice. Mixed in with them was the occasional loony that she would joke off the line or simply disconnect. In all her years of handling live phones, she couldn't remember a moment's boredom.

She enjoyed it tremendously, chatting with callers, joking. In the safety of the control booth she was able, as she had never been able face-to-face, to relax and develop an easy relationship with strangers. No one hearing her voice would suspect that she was shy or insecure.

"KHIP. You're on the air."

"Cilla."

"Yes. You'll have to speak up, partner. What's your name?"

"That doesn't matter."

"Okay, Mr. X." She rubbed suddenly damp palms on the thighs of her jeans. Instinct told her she would have trouble with this one, so she kept her finger hovering over the seven-second-delay button. "You got a request?"

"I want you to pay, slut. I'm going to make you pay. When I'm finished, you're going to thank me for killing you. You're never going to forget."

Cilla froze, cursed herself for it, then cut him off in the midst of a rage of obscenities. Through strict control she kept her voice from shaking. "Wow. Sounds like somebody's a little cranky tonight. Listen, if that was Officer Marks, I'm going to pay those parking tickets. I swear. This one goes out to Joyce and Larry."

She shot in Springsteen's latest hit single, then sat back to remove the headphones with trembling hands.

Stupid. She rose to pluck out the next selection. After all these years she should have known better than to freak over a crank call. It was rare to get through a shift without at least one. She had learned to handle the odd, the angry, the propositions and the threats as skillfully as she had learned to handle the control board.

It was all part of the job, she reminded herself. Part of being a public personality, especially on the night shift, where the weird always got weirder.

But she caught herself glancing over her shoulder, through the dark glass of the studio to the dim corridor beyond. There were only shadows, and silence. Beneath her heavy sweater, her skin was shivering in a cold sweat. She was alone. Completely.

And the station's locked, she reminded herself as she cued up the next selection. The alarm was set. If it went off, Denver's finest would scream up to the station within minutes. She was as safe here as she would be in a bank vault.

But she stared down at the blinking lights on the phone, and she was afraid.

The snow had stopped, but its scent lingered in the chill March air. As she drove, Cilla kept the window down an inch and the radio up to the maximum. The combination of wind and music steadied her.

Cilla wasn't surprised to find that Deborah was waiting up for her. She pulled into the driveway of the house she'd bought only six months before and noted with both annoyance and relief that all the lights were blazing.

It was annoying because it meant Deborah was awake and worrying. And it was a relief, because the quiet suburban street seemed so deserted and she felt so vulnerable. She switched off the ignition, cutting the engine and the sounds of Jim Jackson's mellow all-night show. The instant of total silence had her heart leaping into her throat.

Swearing at herself, she slammed the car door and, hunched in her coat against the wind, dashed up the stairs. Deborah met her at the door.

"Hey, don't you have a nine-o'clock class tomorrow?" Stalling, Cilla peeled off her coat and hung it in the closet. She caught the scent of hot chocolate and furniture polish. It made her sigh. Deborah always resorted to housecleaning when she was tense. "What are you doing up at this hour?"

"I heard. Cilla, that man—"

"Oh, come on, baby." Turning, Cilla wrapped her arms around her sister. In her plain white terry-cloth robe, Deborah still seemed twelve years old to her. There was no one Cilla loved more. "Just one more harmless nut in a fruitcake world."

"He didn't sound harmless, Cilla." Though several inches shorter, Deborah held Cilla still. There was a resemblance between them—around the mouth. Both their mouths were full, passionate and stubborn. But Deborah's features were softer, curved rather than angular. Her eyes, thickly lashed, were a brilliant blue. They were drenched now with concern. "I think you should call the police."

"The police?" Because this option had simply not occurred to her, Cilla was able to laugh. "One obscene call and you have me dashing to the cops. What kind of nineties woman do you take me for?"

Deborah jammed her hands in her pockets. "This isn't a joke."

"Okay, it's not a joke. But, Deb, we both know how little the police could do about one nasty call to a public radio station in the middle of the night."

With an impatient sigh, Deborah turned away. "He really sounded vicious. It scared me."

"Me, too."

Deborah's laugh was quick, and only a little strained. "You're never scared."

I'm always scared, Cilla thought, but she smiled. "I was this time. It shook me enough that I fumbled the delay button and let it broadcast." Fleetingly she wondered how much flak she'd get for that little lapse the next day. "But he didn't call back, which proves it was a one-shot deal. Go to bed," she said, passing a hand over her sister's dark, fluffy hair. "You're never going to be the best lawyer in Colorado if you stay up pacing all night."

"I'll go if you go."

Knowing it would be hours before her mind and body settled down, Cilla draped an arm over her sister's shoulders. "It's a deal."

He kept the room dark, but for the light of a few sputtering candles. He liked the mystic, spiritual glow of them, and their dreamy religious scent. The room was small, but it was crammed with mementos—trophies from his past. Letters, snapshots, a scattering of small china animals, ribbons faded by time. A long-bladed hunting knife rested across his knees, gleaming dully in the shifting light. A well-oiled .45 automatic rested by his elbow on a starched crocheted doily.

In his hand he held a picture framed in rosewood. He stared at it, spoke to it, wept bitter tears over it. This was the only person he had ever loved, and all he had left was the picture to press to his breast.

John. Innocent, trusting John. Deceived by a woman. Used by a woman. Betrayed by a woman.

Love and hate entwined as he rocked. She would pay. She would pay the ultimate price. But first she would suffer.

The call—one single ugly call—came every night. By the end of a week, Cilla's nerves were frazzled. She wasn't able to make a joke of it, on or off the air. She was just grateful that now she had learned to recognize the voice, that harsh, wire-taut voice with that undercurrent of fury, and she would cut him off after the first few words.

Then she would sit there in terror at the knowledge that he would call back, that he was there, just on the other side of one of those blinking lights, waiting to torment her.

What had she done?

After she dropped in the canned news and commercial spots at 2:00 a.m., Cilla rested her elbows on the table and dropped her head into her hands. She rarely slept well or deeply, and in the past week she had managed only a few snatches of real sleep. It was beginning to tell, she knew, on her nerves, her concentration.

What had she done?

That question haunted her. What could she possibly have done to make someone hate her? She had recognized the hate in the voice, the deep-seated hate. She knew she could sometimes be abrupt and impatient with people. There were times when she was insensitive. But she had never deliberately hurt anyone. What was it she would have to pay for? What crime, real or imagined, had she committed that caused this person to focus in on her for revenge?

Out of the corner of her eye she saw a movement. A shadow amid the shadows in the corridor. Panic arrowed into her, and she sprang up, jarring her hip against the console. The voice she had disconnected barely ten minutes before echoed in her head. She watched, rigid with fright, as the knob on the studio door turned.

There was no escape. Dry-mouthed, she braced for a fight.

"Cilla?"

Heart thudding, she lowered slowly into her chair, cursing her own nerves. "Mark."

"Sorry, I must have scared you."

"Only to death." Making an effort, she smiled at the station manager. He was in his middle thirties, and he was drop-dead gorgeous. His dark hair was carefully styled and on the long side, adding more youth to his smooth and tanned face. As always, his attire was carefully hip. "What are you doing here at this hour?"

"It's time we did more than talk about these calls."

"We had a meeting just a couple of days ago. I told you—"

"You told me," he agreed. "You have a habit of telling me, and everybody else."

"I'm not taking a vacation." She spun around in her chair to face him. "I've got nowhere to go."

"Everybody's got somewhere to go." He held up a hand before she could speak. "I'm not going to argue about this anymore. I know it's a difficult concept for you, but I am the boss."

She tugged at the hem of her sweatshirt. "What are you going to do? Fire me?"

He didn't know that she held her breath on the challenge. Though he'd worked with her for months, he hadn't scratched deep enough beneath the surface to understand how precarious was her self-esteem. If he had threatened her then, she would have folded. But all he knew was that her show had pumped new life into the station. The ratings were soaring.

"That wouldn't do either of us any good." Even as she let out the pent-up breath, he laid a hand on her shoulder. "Look, I'm worried about you, Cilla. All of us are."

It touched her, and, as always, it surprised her. "All he does is talk." For now. Scooting her chair toward the turntables, she prepared for the next music sweep.

"I'm not going to stand by while one of my people is harassed. I've called the police."

She sprang up out of her chair. "Damn it, Mark. I told you—"

"You told me." He smiled. "Let's not go down that road again. You're an asset to the station. And I'd like to think we were friends."

She sat down again, kicking out her booted feet. "Sure. Hold on." Struggling to concentrate, she went on-air with a station plug and the intro for the upcoming song. She gestured toward the clock. "You've got three minutes and fifteen seconds to convince me."

"Very simply, Cilla, what this guy's doing is against the law. I should never have let you talk me into letting it go this long."

"If we ignore him, he'll go away."

"Your way isn't working." He dropped his hand onto her shoulder again, patiently kneading the tensed muscles there. "So we're going to try mine. You talk to the cops or you take an unscheduled vacation."

Defeated, she looked up and managed a smile. "Do you push your wife around this way?"

"All the time." He grinned, then leaned down to press a kiss on her brow. "She loves it."

"Excuse me."

Cilla jerked back in what she knew could easily be mistaken for guilt. The two people in the doorway of the booth studied her with what she recognized as professional detachment.

The woman looked like a fashion plate, with a flow of dark red hair cascading to her shoulders and small, elegant sapphires at her ears. Her complexion was the delicate porcelain of a true redhead. She had a small, compact body and wore a neatly tailored suit in wild shades of blue and green.

The man beside her looked as if he'd just spent a month on the range driving cattle. His shaggy blond hair was sun-streaked and fell over the collar of a denim work shirt. His jeans were worn and low at the hips, snug over what looked to Cilla to be about three feet of leg. The hems were frayed. Lanky, he slouched in the doorway, while the woman stood at attention. His boots were scuffed, but he wore a classically cut tweed jacket over his scruffy shirt.

He didn't smile. Cilla found herself staring, studying his face longer than she should have. There were hollows beneath his cheekbones, and there was the faintest of clefts in his chin. His tanned skin was taut over his facial bones, and his mouth, still unsmiling, was wide and firm. His eyes, intent enough on her face to make her want to squirm, were a clear bottle green.

"Mr. Harrison." The woman spoke first. Cilla thought there was a flicker of amusement in her eyes as she stepped forward. "I hope we gave you enough time."

Cilla sent Mark a killing look. "You told me you'd called them. You didn't tell me they were waiting outside."

"Now you know." He kept a hand on her shoulder, but this time it was more restraining than comforting. "This is Ms. O'Roarke."

"I'm Detective Grayson. This is my partner, Detective Fletcher."

"Thank you again for waiting." Mark gestured her, then her partner, in. The man lazily unfolded himself from the doorjamb.

"Detective Fletcher and I are both used to it. We could use a bit more information."

"As you know, Ms. O'Roarke has been getting some disturbing calls here at the station."

"Cranks." Cilla spoke up, annoyed at being talked around. "Mark shouldn't have bothered you with it."

"We're paid to be bothered." Boyd Fletcher eased a lean hip down on the table. "So, this where you work?"

There was just enough insolence in his eyes to raise her hackles. "I bet you're a hell of a detective."

"Cilla." Tired and wishing he was home with his wife, Mark scowled at her. "Let's cooperate." Ignoring her, he turned to the detectives again. "The calls started during last Tuesday's show. None of us paid much attention, but they continued. The last one came in tonight, at 12:35."

"Do you have tapes?" Althea Grayson had already pulled out her notebook.

"I started making copies of them after the third call." At Cilla's startled look, Mark merely shrugged. "A precaution. I have them in my office."

Boyd nodded to Althea. "Go ahead. I'll take Ms. O'Roarke's statement."

"Cooperate," Mark said to Cilla, and led Althea out.

In the ensuing silence, Cilla tapped a cigarette out of her dwindling pack and lit it with quick, jerky movements. Boyd drew in the scent longingly. He'd quit only six weeks, three days and twelve hours ago.

"Slow death," he commented.

Cilla studied him through the haze of smoke. "You wanted a statement."

"Yeah." Curious, he reached over to toy with a switch. Automatically she batted his fingers aside.

"Hands off."

Boyd grinned. He had the distinct feeling that she was speaking of herself, as well as her equipment.

She cued up an established hit. After opening her mike, she did a backsell on the song just fading—the title, the artist, the station's call letters and her name. In an easy rhythm, she segued into the next selection.

"Let's make it quick," she told him. "I don't like company during my shift."

"You're not exactly what I expected."

"I beg your pardon?"

No, indeed, he thought. She was a hell of a lot more than he'd expected. "I've caught your show," he said easily. "A few times." More than a few. He'd lost more than a few hours' sleep listening to that voice. Liquid sex. "I got this image, you know. Five-seven." He took a casual glance from the top of her head, down her body, to the toe of her boots. "I guess I was close there. But I took you for a blonde, hair down to your waist, blue eyes, lots of…personality." He grinned again, enjoying the annoyance in her eyes. Big brown eyes, he noted. Definitely different, and more appealing than his fantasy.

"Sorry to disappoint you."

"Didn't say I was disappointed."

She took a long, careful drag, then deliberately blew the smoke in his direction. If there was one thing she knew how to do, it was how to discourage an obnoxious male.

"Do you want a statement or not, Slick?"

"That's what I'm here for." He took a pad and the stub of a pencil out of his jacket pocket. "Shoot."

In clipped, dispassionate terms, she ran through every call, the times, the phrasing. She continued to work as she spoke, pushing in recorded tapes of commercials, cuing up a CD, replacing and selecting albums.

Boyd's brow rose as he wrote. He would check the tapes, of course, but he had the feeling that she was giving him word-for-word. In his job he respected a good memory.

"You've been in town, what? Six months?"

"More or less."

"Make any enemies?"

"A salesman trying to hawk encyclopedias. I slammed the door on his foot."

Boyd spared her a glance. She was trying to make light of it, but she had crushed out her cigarette and was now gnawing on her thumbnail. "Dump any lovers?"

"No."

"Have any?"

Temper flashed in her eyes again. "You're the detective. You find out."

"I would—if it was personal." His eyes lifted again in a look that was so direct, so completely personal, that her palms began to sweat. "Right now I'm just doing my job. Jealousy and rejection are powerful motivators. According to your statements, most of the comments he made to you had to do with your sexual habits."

Bluntness might be her strong suit, but she wasn't about to tell him that her only sexual habit was abstinence. "I'm not involved with anyone at the moment," she said evenly.

"Good." Without glancing up, he made another note. "That was a personal observation."

"Look, Detective—"

"Cool your jets, O'Roarke," he said mildly. "It was an observation, not a proposition." His dark, patient eyes took her measure. "I'm on duty. I need a list of the men you've had contact with on a personal level. We'll keep it to the past six months for now. You can leave out the door-to-door salesman."

"I'm not involved." Her hands clenched as she rose.

"I haven't been involved. I've had no desire to be involved."

"No one ever said desire couldn't be one-sided." At the moment he was damn sure his was.

She was suddenly excruciatingly tired. Dragging a hand through her hair, she struggled for patience. "Anyone should be able to see that this guy is hung up on a voice over the radio. He doesn't even know me. He's probably never seen me. An image," she said, tossing his own words back at him. "That's all I am to him. In this business it happens all the time. I haven't done anything."

"I didn't say you had."

There was no teasing note in his voice now. The sudden gentleness in it had her spinning around, blinking furiously at threatening tears. Overworked, she told herself. Overstressed. Overeverything. With her back to him, she fought for control.

Tough, he thought. She was a tough lady. The way her hands balled at her sides as she fought with her emotions was much more appealing, much sexier, than broken sighs or helpless gestures could ever be.

He would have liked to go to her, to speak some word of comfort or reassurance, to stroke a hand down her hair. She'd probably bite it off at the wrist.

"I want you to think about the past few months, see if you can come up with anything, however small and unimportant, that might have led to this." His tone had changed again. It was brisk now, brisk and dispassionate. "We can't bring every man in the greater Denver area in for questioning. It doesn't work that way."

"I know how cops work."

The bitterness in her voice had his brows drawing

together. There was something else here, but this wasn't the time to dig into it.

"You'd recognize the voice if you heard it again."

"Yes."

"Anything familiar about it?"

"Nothing."

"Do you think it was disguised?"

She moved her shoulders restlessly, but when she turned back to him she had herself under control. "He keeps it muffled and low. It's, ah…like a hiss."

"Any objections to me sitting in on tomorrow night's show?"

Cilla took another long look at him. "Barrels of them."

He inclined his head. "I'll just go to your boss."

Disgusted, she reached for her cigarettes. He closed his firm hard-palmed hand over hers. She stared down at the tangled fingers, shocked to realize that her pulse had doubled at the contact.

"Let me do my job, Cilla. It'll be easier all around if you let Detective Grayson and me take over."

"Nobody takes over my life." She jerked her hand away, then jammed it into her pocket.

"Just this small part of it, then." Before she could stop him, he reached out and tucked her hair behind her ear. "Go home and get some sleep. You look beat."

She stepped back, made herself smile. "Thanks, Slick. I feel a lot better now."

Though she grumbled, she couldn't prevent him waiting until she signed off and turned the studio over to the all-night man. Nor did her lack of enthusiasm discourage him from walking her out to her car, reminding her to lock her door and waiting until she'd driven away. Disturbed by the way he'd looked at her—and the way she'd reacted—she watched him in the rearview mirror until he was out of sight.

"Just what I needed," she muttered to herself. "A cowboy cop."

Moments later, Althea joined Boyd in the parking lot. She had the tapes in her bag, along with Mark's statement. "Well, Fletcher—" she dropped a friendly hand on his shoulder "—what's the verdict?"

"She's tough as nails, hardheaded, prickly as a briar patch." With his hands in his pockets, he rocked back on his heels. "I guess it must be love."

Chapter 2

She was good, Boyd thought as he downed his bitter coffee and watched Cilla work. She handled the control board with an automatic ease that spoke of long experience—switching to music, to recorded announcements, to her own mike. Her timing was perfect, her delivery smooth. And her fingernails were bitten to the quick.

She was a package full of nerves and hostility. The nerves she tried to hide. She didn't bother with the hostility. In the two hours they'd been in the booth together, she had barely spoken a word to him. A neat trick, since the room was barely ten by ten.

That was fine. As a cop, he was used to being where he wasn't wanted. And he was just contrary enough to enjoy it.

He liked his job. Things like annoyance, animosity and belligerence didn't concern him. The simple fact was that negative emotions were a whole lot easier to deal with than a .45 slug. He'd had the opportunity to be hit with both.

Though he would have been uncomfortable with the term philosopher, he had a habit of analyzing everything down to its most basic terms. At the root of this was an elemental belief in right and wrong. Or—though he would have hesitated to use the phrase—good and evil.

He was savvy enough to know that crime often did pay, and pay well. Satisfaction came from playing a part in seeing that it didn't pay for long. He was a patient man. If a perpetrator took six hours or six months to bring down, the results were exactly the same. The good guys won.

Stretching out his long legs, he continued to page through his book while Cilla's voice washed over him. Her voice made him think of porch swings, hot summer nights and the sound of a slow-moving river. In direct contrast was the tension and restless energy that vibrated from her. He was content to enjoy the first and wonder about the second.

He was driving her crazy. Just being there. Cilla switched to a commercial, checked her playlist and deliberately ignored him. Or tried to. She didn't like company in the booth. It didn't matter that when she had coolly discouraged conversation he had settled back with his book—not the Western or men's adventure she had expected, but a dog-eared copy of Steinbeck's *East of Eden*. It didn't matter that he had been patiently quiet for nearly two hours.

He was there. And that was enough.

She couldn't pretend that the calls had stopped, that

they meant nothing, that her life was back on its normal track. Not with this lanky cowboy reading the great American novel in the corner of the booth, so that she had to all but climb over him to get to the albums stored on the back wall. He brought all her nerves swimming to the surface.

She resented him for that, for his intrusion and for the simple fact that he was a cop.

But that was personal, she reminded herself. She had a job to do.

"That was INXS taking you to midnight. It's a new day, Denver. March 28, but we're not going out like a lamb. It's eighteen degrees out there at 12:02, so tune in and heat up. You're listening to KHIP, where you get more hits per hour. We've got the news coming up, then the request line. Light up those phones and we'll rock and roll."

Boyd waited until she'd run through the news and moved to a commercial before he marked his place in his book and rose. He could feel the tension thicken as he sat in the chair next to Cilla.

"I don't want you to cut him off."

She stiffened and struggled to keep her voice carelessly sarcastic. "My listeners don't tune in for that kind of show, Slick."

"You can keep him on the line, on the studio speakers, without sending it on air, right?"

"Yes, but I don't want to—"

"Cut to a commercial or some music," Boyd said mildly, "but keep him on the line. We might get lucky and trace the call. And if you can, keep the request line open until the end of shift, to give him enough time to make his move."

Her hands were balled into fists in her lap as she stared at the lights that were already blinking on the phone. He was right. She knew he was right. And she hated it.

"This is an awful lot of trouble for one loose screw."

"Don't worry." He smiled a little. "I get paid the same whether the screws are loose or tight."

She glanced down at the clock, cleared her throat, then switched on her mike. "Hello, Denver, this is Cilla O'Roarke for KHIP. You're listening to the hottest station in the Rockies. This is your chance to make it even hotter. Our request lines are open. I'll be playing what you want to hear, so give me a call at 555-KHIP. That's 555-5447."

Her finger trembled slightly as she punched the first lit button.

"This is Cilla O'Roarke. You're on the air."

"Hi, Cilla, this is Bob down in Englewood."

She closed her eyes on a shudder of relief. He was a regular. "Hey, Bob. How's it going?"

"Going great. My wife and I are celebrating our fifteenth anniversary tonight."

"And they said it wouldn't last. What can I play for you, Bob?"

"How about 'Cherish' for Nancy from Bob."

"Nice choice. Here's to fifteen more, Bob."

With her pen in one hand, she took the second call, then the third. Boyd watched her tighten up after each one. She chatted and joked. And grew paler. At the first break, she pulled a cigarette out of the pack, then fumbled with a match. Silently Boyd took the matches from her and lit one for her.

"You're doing fine."

She took a quick, jerky puff. Patient, he waited in silence for her to respond. "Do you have to watch me?"

"No." Then he smiled. It was a long, lazy smile that had her responding in spite of herself. "A man's entitled to some fringe benefits."

"If this is the best you can do, Slick, you ought to look for another line of work."

"I like this one." He rested the ankle of his boot on his knee. "I like it fine."

It was easier, Cilla decided, to talk to him than to stare at the blinking lights on the phone and worry. "Have you been a cop long?"

"Going on ten years."

She looked at him then, struggling to relax by concentrating on his face. He had calm eyes, she thought. Dark and calm. Eyes that had seen a lot and learned to live with it. There was a quiet kind of strength there, the kind women—some women—were drawn to. He would protect and defend. He wouldn't start a fight. But he would finish one.

Annoyed with herself, she looked away again, busying herself with her notes. She didn't need to be protected or defended. She certainly didn't need anyone to fight for her. She had always taken care of herself. And she always would.

"It's a lousy job," she said. "Being a cop."

He shifted. His knee brushed her thigh. "Mostly."

Instinctively she jiggled her chair for another inch of distance. "It's hard to figure why anyone would stick with a lousy job for ten years."

He just grinned. "I guess I'm in a rut."

She shrugged, then turned to her mike. "That was for Bill and Maxine. Our request lines are still open.

That's 555-5447." After one quick breath, she punched a button. "KHIP. You're on the air."

It went smoothly, so smoothly that she began to relax. She took call after call, falling into her old, established rhythm. Gradually she began to enjoy the music again, the flow of it. The pulsing lights on the phone no longer seemed threatening. By 1:45 she was sure she was going to make it through.

Just one night, she told herself. If he didn't call tonight, it would be over. She looked at the clock, watched the seconds tick by. Eight more minutes to go and she would turn the airwaves over to Jackson. She would go home, take a long, hot bath and sleep like a baby.

"KHIP, you're on the air."

"Cilla."

The hissing whisper shot ice through her veins. She reached over reflexively to disconnect, but Boyd clamped a hand over her wrist and shook his head. For a moment she struggled, biting back panic. His hand remained firm on hers, his eyes calm and steady.

Boyd watched as she fought for control, until she jammed in a cassette of commercials. The bright, bouncy jingles transmitted as she put the call on the studio speaker.

"Yes." Pride made her keep her eyes on Boyd's. "This is Cilla. What do you want?"

"Justice. I only want justice."

"For what?"

"I want you to think about that. I want you to think and wonder and sweat until I come for you."

"Why?" Her hand flexed under Boyd's. In an instinctive gesture of reassurance, he linked his fingers with hers. "Who are you?"

"Who am I?" There was a laugh that skidded along her skin. "I'm your shadow, your conscience. Your executioner. You have to die. When you understand, only when you understand, I'll end it. But it won't be quick. It won't be easy. You're going to pay for what you've done."

"What have I done?" she shouted. "For God's sake, what have I done?"

He spit out a stream of obscenities that left her dazed and nauseated before he broke the connection. With one hand still covering hers, Boyd punched out a number on the phone.

"You get the trace?" he demanded, then bit off an oath. "Yeah. Right." Disgusted, he replaced the receiver. "Not long enough." He reached up to touch Cilla's pale cheek. "You okay?"

She could hardly hear him for the buzzing in her ears, but she nodded. Mechanically she turned to her mike, waiting until the commercial jingle faded.

"That about wraps it up for this morning. It's 1:57. Tina Turner's going to rock you through until two. My man Jackson's coming in to keep all you insomniacs company until 6:00 a.m. This is Cilla O'Roarke for KHIP. Remember, darling, when you dream of me, dream good."

Light-headed, she pushed away from the console. She only had to stand up, she told herself. Walk to her car, drive home. It was simple enough. She did it every morning of her life. But she sat where she was, afraid her legs would buckle.

Jackson pushed through the door and stood there, hesitating. He was wearing a baseball cap to cover his healing hair transplant. "Hey, Cilla." He glanced from her to Boyd and back again. "Rough night, huh?"

Cilla braced herself, pasted on a careless smile. "I've had better." With every muscle tensed, she shoved herself to her feet. "I've got them warmed up for you, Jackson."

"Take it easy, kid."

"Sure." The buzzing in her ears was louder as she walked from the booth to snatch her coat from the rack. The corridors were dark, catching only a faint glow from the lobby, where the security lights burned. Disoriented, she blinked. She didn't even notice when Boyd took her arm and led her outside.

The cold air helped. She took big, thirsty gulps of it, releasing it again in thin plumes of white smoke. "My car's over there," she said when Boyd began to pull her toward the opposite end of the lot.

"You're in no shape to drive."

"I'm fine."

"Great. Then we'll go dancing."

"Look—"

"No, you look." He was angry, furious. He hadn't realized it himself until that moment. She was shaking, and despite the chill wind, her cheeks were deathly pale. Listening to the tapes hadn't been the same as being there when the call came through, seeing the blood drain out of her face and her eyes glaze with terror. And not being able to do a damn thing to stop it. "You're a mess, O'Roarke, and I'm not letting you get behind the wheel of a car." He stopped next to his car and yanked open the door. "Get in. I'll take you home."

She tossed the hair out of her eyes. "Serve and protect, right?"

"You got it. Now get in before I arrest you for loitering."

Because her knees felt like jelly, she gave in. She wanted to be asleep, alone in some small, quiet room. She wanted to scream. Worse, she wanted to cry. Instead, she rounded on Boyd the second he settled in the driver's seat.

"You know what I hate even more than cops?"

He turned the key in the ignition. "I figure you're going to tell me."

"Men who order women around just because they're men. I don't figure that as a cultural hang-up, just stupidity. The way I look at it, that's two counts against you, Detective."

He leaned over, deliberately crowding her back in her seat. He got a moment's intense satisfaction out of seeing her eyes widen in surprise, her lips part on a strangled protest. The satisfaction would have been greater, he knew, if he had gone on impulse and covered that stubborn, sassy mouth with his own. He was certain she would taste exactly as she sounded—hot, sexy and dangerous.

Instead, he yanked her seat belt around her and fastened it.

Her breath came out in a whoosh when he took the wheel again. It had been a rough night, Cilla reminded herself. A tense, disturbing and unsettling night. Otherwise she would never have sat like a fool and allowed herself to be intimidated by some modern-day cowboy.

Her hands were shaking again. The reason didn't seem to matter, only the weakness.

"I don't think I like your style, Slick."

"You don't have to." She was getting under his skin,

Boyd realized as he turned out of the lot. That was always a mistake. "Do what you're told and we'll get along fine."

"I don't do what I'm told," she snapped. "And I don't need a second-rate cop with a John Wayne complex to give me orders. Mark's the one who called you in, not me. I don't need you and I don't want you."

He braked at a light. "Tough."

"If you think I'm going to fall apart because some creep calls me names and makes threats, you're wrong."

"I don't think you're going to fall apart, O'Roarke, any more than you think I'm going to pick up the pieces if you do."

"Good. Great. I can handle him all by myself, and if you get your kicks out of listening to that kind of garbage—" She broke off, appalled with herself. Lifting her hands, she pressed them to her face and took three deep breaths.

"I'm sorry."

"For?"

"For taking it out on you." She dropped her hands into her lap and stared at them. "Could you pull over for a minute?"

Without a word, he guided the car to the curb and stopped.

"I want to calm down before I get home." In a deliberate effort to relax, she let her head fall back and her eyes close. "I don't want to upset my sister."

It was hard to hold on to rage and resentment when the woman sitting next to him had turned from barbed wire to fragile glass. But if his instincts about Cilla were on target, too much sympathy would set her off again.

"Want some coffee?"

"No thanks." The corners of her mouth turned up for the briefest instant. "I've poured in enough to fuel an SST." She let out a long, cleansing breath. The giddiness was gone, and with it that floating sense of unreality. "I am sorry, Slick. You're only doing your job."

"You got that right. Why do you call me Slick?"

She opened her eyes, made a brief but comprehensive study of his face. "Because you are." Turning away, she dug in her bag for a cigarette. "I'm scared." She hated the fact that the admission was shaky, that her hand was unsteady as she struck a match.

"You're entitled."

"No, I'm really scared." She let out smoke slowly, watching a late-model sedan breeze down the road and into the night. "He wants to kill me. I didn't really believe that until tonight." She shuddered. "Is there any heat in this thing?"

He turned the fan on full. "It's better if you're scared."

"Why?"

"You'll cooperate."

She smiled. It was a full flash of a smile that almost stopped his heart. "No, I won't. This is only a momentary respite. I'll be giving you a hard time as soon as I recover."

"I'll try not to get used to this." But it would be easy, he realized, to get used to the way her eyes warmed when she smiled. The way her voice eased over a man and made him wonder. "Feeling better?"

"Lots. Thanks." She tapped out her cigarette as he guided the car back on the road. "I take it you know where I live."

"That's why I'm a detective."

"It's a thankless job." She pushed her hair back from

her forehead. They would talk, she decided. Just talk. Then she wouldn't have to think. "Why aren't you out roping cattle or branding bulls? You've got the looks for it."

He considered a moment. "I'm not sure that's a compliment, either."

"You're fast on the draw, Slick."

"Boyd," he said. "It wouldn't hurt you to use my name." When she only shrugged, he slanted her a curious look. "Cilla. That'd be from Priscilla, right?"

"No one calls me Priscilla more than once."

"Why?"

She sent him her sweetest smile. "Because I cut out their tongues."

"Right. You want to tell me why you don't like cops?"

"No." She turned away to stare out the side window. "I like the nighttime," she said, almost to herself. "You can do things, say things, at three o'clock in the morning that it's just not possible to do or say at three o'clock in the afternoon. I can't even imagine what it's like to work in the daylight anymore, when people are crowding the air."

"You don't like people much, do you?"

"Some people." She didn't want to talk about herself, her likes and dislikes, her successes, her failures. She wanted to talk about him—to satisfy her curiosity, and to ease her jangled nerves. "So, how long have you had the night shift, Fletcher?"

"About nine months." He glanced at her. "You meet an…interesting class of people."

She laughed, surprised that she was able to. "Don't you just? Are you from Denver?"

"Born and bred."

"I like it," she said, surprising herself again. She hadn't given it a great deal of thought. It had simply been a place that offered a good college for Deborah and a good opportunity for her. Yet in six months, she realized, she had come close to sinking roots. Shallow ones, but roots nonetheless.

"Does that mean you're going to stick around?" He turned down a quiet side street. "I did some research. It seems two years in one spot's about your limit."

"I like change," she said flatly, closing down the lines of communication. She didn't care for the idea of anyone poking into her past and her private life. When he pulled up in her driveway, she was already unsnapping her seat belt. "Thanks for the ride, Slick."

Before she could dash to her door, he was beside her. "I'm going to need your keys."

They were already in her hand. She clutched them possessively. "Why?"

"So I can have your car dropped off in the morning."

She jingled them, frowning, as she stood under the front porch light. Boyd wondered what it would be like to walk her to her door after an ordinary date. He wouldn't keep his hands in his pockets, he thought ruefully. And he certainly would scratch this itch by kissing her outside the door.

Outside, hell, he admitted. He would have been through the door with her. And there would have been more to the end of the evening than a good-night kiss.

But it wasn't a date. And any fool could see that there wasn't going to be anything remotely ordinary between them. Something. That he promised himself. But nothing remotely resembling the ordinary.

"Keys?" he repeated.

After going over her options, Cilla had decided his was best. Carefully she removed a single key from the chain, which was shaped like a huge musical note. "Thanks."

"Hold it." He placed the palm of his hand on the door as she unlocked it. "You're not going to ask me in for a cup of coffee?"

She didn't turn, only twisted her head. "No."

She smelled like the night, he thought. Dark, deep, dangerous. "That's downright unfriendly."

The flash of humor came again. "I know. See you around, Slick."

His hand dropped onto hers on the knob, took a firm hold. "Do you eat?"

The humor vanished. That didn't surprise him. What did was what replaced it. Confusion. And—he could have sworn—shyness. She recovered so quickly that he was certain he'd imagined it.

"Once or twice a week."

"Tomorrow." His hand remained over hers. He couldn't be sure about what he'd thought he saw in her eyes, but he knew her pulse had quickened under his fingers.

"I may eat tomorrow."

"With me."

It amazed her that she fumbled. It had been years since she'd experienced this baffling reaction to a man. And those years had been quiet and smooth. Refusing a date was as simple as saying no. At least it always had been for her. Now she found herself wanting to smile and ask him what time she should be ready. The words were nearly out of her mouth before she caught herself.

"That's an incredibly smooth offer, Detective, but I'll have to pass."

"Why?"

"I don't date cops."

Before she could weaken, she slipped inside and closed the door in his face.

Boyd shuffled the papers on his desk and scowled. The O'Roarke case was hardly his only assignment, but he couldn't get his mind off it. Couldn't get his mind off O'Roarke, he thought, wishing briefly but intensely for a cigarette.

The veteran cop sitting two feet away from him was puffing away like a chimney as he talked to a snitch. Boyd breathed in deep, wishing he could learn to hate the smell like other nonsmokers.

Instead, he continued to torture himself by drawing in the seductive scent—that, and the other, less appealing aromas of a precinct station. Overheated coffee, overheated flesh, the cheap perfume hovering around a pair of working girls who lounged resignedly on a nearby bench.

Intrusions, he thought, that he rarely noticed in the day-to-day scheme of things. Tonight they warred with his concentration. The smells, the sound of keyboards clicking, phones ringing, shoes scuffing along the linoleum, the way one of the overhead lights winked sporadically.

It didn't help his disposition that for the past three days Priscilla Alice O'Roarke had stuck fast to his mind like a thick, thorny spike. No amount of effort could shake her loose. It might be because both he and his partner had spent hours at a time with her in the booth during her show. It might be because he'd seen her with her defenses down. It might be because he'd felt, fleetingly, her surge of response to him.

It might be, Boyd thought in disgust. Then again, it might not.

He wasn't a man whose ego was easily bruised by the refusal of a date. He liked to think that he had enough confidence in himself to understand he didn't appeal to every woman. The fact that he'd appealed to what he considered a healthy number of them in his thirty-three years was enough to satisfy him.

The trouble was, he was hung up on one woman. And she wasn't having any of it.

He could live with it.

The simple fact was that he had a job to do now. He wasn't convinced that Cilla was in any immediate danger. But she was being harassed, systematically and thoroughly. Both he and Althea had started the ball rolling, questioning men with priors that fit the M.O., poking their fingers into Cilla's personal and professional life since she had come to Denver, quietly investigating her coworkers.

So far the score was zip.

Time to dig deeper, Boyd decided. He had Cilla's résumé in his hand. It was an interesting piece of work in itself. Just like the woman it belonged to. It showed her bouncing from a one-horse station in Georgia—which accounted for that faint and fascinating Southern drawl—to a major player in Atlanta, then on to Richmond, St. Louis, Chicago, Dallas, before landing—feetfirst, obviously—in Denver at KHIP.

The lady likes to move, he mused. Or was it that she needed to run? That was a question of semantics, and he intended to get the answer straight from the horse's mouth.

The one thing he could be sure of from the bald facts typed out in front of him was that Cilla had pulled herself along the road to success with a high school diploma and a lot of guts. It couldn't have been easy for a woman—a girl, really, at eighteen—to break into what was still a largely male-dominated business.

"Interesting reading?" Althea settled a hip on the corner of his desk. No one in the station house would have dared whistle at her legs. But plenty of them looked.

"Cilla O'Roarke." He tossed the résumé down. "Impressions?"

"Tough lady." She grinned as she said it. She'd spent a lot of time razzing Boyd about his fascination with the sultry voice on the radio. "Likes to do things her own way. Smart and professional."

He picked up a box of candy-coated almonds and shook some into his hand. "I think I figured all that out myself."

"Well, figure this." Althea took the box and carefully selected one glossy nut. "She's scared down to the bone. And she's got an inferiority complex a mile wide."

"Inferiority complex." Boyd gave a quick snort and kicked back in his chair. "Not a chance."

With the same careful deliberation, Althea chose another candied almond. "She hides it behind three feet of steel, but it's there." Althea laid a hand on the toe of his boot. "Woman's intuition, Fletcher. That's why you're so damn lucky to have me."

Boyd snatched the box back, knowing Althea could,

and would, methodically work her way through to the last piece. "If that woman's insecure, I'll eat my hat."

"You don't have a hat."

"I'll get one and eat it." Dismissing his partner's instincts, he gestured toward the files. "Since our man isn't letting up, we're going to have to go looking elsewhere for him."

"The lady isn't very forthcoming about her past."

"So we push."

Althea considered a moment. Then she shifted her weight gracefully, recrossed her legs. "Want to flip a coin? Because the odds are she'll push back."

Boyd grinned. "I'm counting on it."

"It's your turn in the booth tonight."

"Then you start with Chicago." He handed her the file. "We got the station manager, the landlord." He scanned the sheet himself. He intended to go far beyond what was printed there, but he would start with the facts. "Use that sweet, persuasive voice of yours. They'll spill their guts."

"Thousands have." She glanced over idly as an associate shoved a swearing suspect with a bloody nose into a nearby chair. There was a brief tussle, and a spate of curses followed by mumbled threats. "God, I love this place."

"Yeah, there's no place like home." He snatched up what was left of his coffee before his partner could reach for it. "I'll work from the other end, the first station she worked for. Thea, if we don't come up with something soon, the captain's going to yank us."

She rose. "Then we'll have to come up with something."

He nodded. Before he could pick up the phone, it rang. "Fletcher."

"Slick."

He would have grimaced at the nickname if he hadn't heard the fear first. "Cilla? What is it?"

"I got a call." A quick bubble of laughter worked its way through. "Old news, I guess. I'm at home this time, though, and I— Damn, I'm jumping at shadows."

"Lock your doors and sit tight. I'm on my way. Cilla," he said when there was no response. "I'm on my way."

"Thanks. If you could break a few traffic laws getting here, I'd be obliged."

"Ten minutes." He hung up. "Thea." He caught her before she could complete the first call. "Let's move."

Chapter 3

She had herself under control by the time they got to her. Above all, she felt foolish to have run to the police—to him—because of a phone call.

Only phone calls, Cilla assured herself as she paced to the window and back. After a week of them she should have a better handle on it. If she could tone down her reaction, convince the caller that what he said and how he said it left her unaffected, they would stop.

Her father had taught her that that was the way to handle bullies. Then again, her mother's solution had been a right jab straight to the jaw. While Cilla saw value in both viewpoints, she thought the passive approach was more workable under the circumstances.

She'd done a lousy job of it with the last call, she admitted. Sometime during his tirade she'd come uncomfortably close to hysteria, shouting back, pleading, meeting threats with threats. She could only be grateful that Deborah hadn't been home to hear it.

Struggling for calm, she perched on the arm of a chair, her body ruler-straight, her mind scrambling. After the call she had turned off the radio, locked the doors, pulled the drapes. Now, in the glow of the lamplight, she sat listening for a sound, any sound, while she scanned the room. The walls she and Deborah had painted, the furniture they had picked out, argued about. Familiar things, Cilla thought. Calming things.

After only six months there was already a scattering of knickknacks, something they hadn't allowed themselves before. But this time the house wasn't rented, the furniture wasn't leased. It was theirs.

Perhaps that was why, though they'd never discussed it, they had begun to fill it with little things, useless things. The china cat who curled in a permanent nap on the cluttered bookshelf. The foolishly expensive glossy white bowl with hibiscus blossoms painted on the rim. The dapper frog in black tie and tails.

They were making a home, Cilla realized. For the first time since they had found themselves alone, they were making a home. She wouldn't let some vicious, faceless voice over the phone spoil that.

What was she going to do? Because she was alone, she allowed herself a moment of despair and dropped her head into her hands. Should she fight back? But how could she fight someone she couldn't see and didn't understand? Should she pretend indifference? But how long could she keep up that kind of pretense, especially if he continued to invade her private hours, as well as her public ones?

And what would happen when he finally wearied of talk and came to her in person?

The brisk knock on the door had her jolting, had her pressing a hand between her breasts to hold in her suddenly frantic heart.

I'm your executioner. I'm going to make you suffer. I'm going to make you pay.

"Cilla. It's Boyd. Open the door."

She needed a moment more, needed to cover her face with her hands and breathe deep. Steadier now, she crossed to the door and opened it.

"Hi. You made good time." She nodded to Althea. "Detective Grayson." Cilla gestured them inside, then leaned her back against the closed door. "I feel stupid for calling you all the way out here."

"Just part of the job," Althea told her. The woman was held together by very thin wires, she decided. A few of them had already snapped. "Would you mind if we all sat down?"

"No. I'm sorry." Cilla dragged a hand through her hair. She wasn't putting on a very good show, she thought. And she prided herself on putting on a good show. "I could, ah, make some coffee."

"Don't worry about it." He sat on an oatmeal-colored couch and leaned back against sapphire-blue pillows. "Tell us what happened."

"I wrote it down." The underlying nerves showed in her movements as she walked to the phone to pick up a pad of paper. "A radio habit," she said. "The phone rings and I start writing." She wasn't ready to admit that she didn't want to repeat the conversation out loud. "Some of it's in O'Roarke shorthand, but you should get the drift."

He took the pad from her and scanned the words. His gut muscles tightened in a combination of fury and revulsion. Outwardly calm, he handed the note to his partner.

Cilla couldn't sit. Instead, she stood in the center of the room, twisting her fingers together, dragging them apart again to tug at her baggy sweatshirt. "He's pretty explicit about what he thinks of me, and what he intends to do about it."

"Is this your first call at home?" Boyd asked her.

"Yes. I don't know how he got the number. I— We're not listed."

Althea put the pad aside and took out her own. "Who has your home number?"

"The station." Cilla relaxed fractionally. This was something she could deal with. Simple questions, simple answers. "It would be on file at the college. My lawyer—that's Carl Donnely, downtown. There are a couple of guys that Deb sees. Josh Holden and Darren McKinley. A few girlfriends." She ran through the brief list. "That's about it. What I'm really concerned about is—" She spun around as the door opened behind her. "Deb." Relief and annoyance speared through her. "I thought you had evening classes."

"I did." She turned a pair of big, smoldering blue eyes on Boyd and Althea. "Are you the police?"

"Deborah," Cilla said, "you know better than to cut classes. You had a test—"

"Stop treating me like a child." She slapped the newspaper she was carrying into Cilla's hand. "Do you really expect me to go along like nothing's wrong? Damn it, Cilla, you told me it was all under control."

So she'd made the first page of section B, Cilla

thought wearily. Late-night radio princess under siege. Trying to soothe a growing tension headache, she rubbed her fingers at her temple. "It is under control. Stuff like this makes good copy, that's all."

"No, that's not all."

"I've called the police," she snapped back as she tossed the paper aside. "What else do you want?"

There was a resemblance between the two, Boyd noted objectively. The shape of the mouth and eyes. While Cilla was alluring and sexy enough to make a man's head turn a 360, her sister was hands-down gorgeous. Young, he thought. Maybe eighteen. In a few years she'd barely have to glance at a man to have him swallow his tongue.

He also noted the contrasts. Deborah's hair was short and fluffed. Cilla's was long and untamed. The younger sister wore a deep crimson sweater over tailored slacks that were tucked into glossy half boots. Cilla's mismatched sweats bagged and hit on a variety of colors. The top was purple, the bottoms green. She'd chosen thick yellow socks and orange high-tops.

Their tastes might clash, he mused, but their temperaments seemed very much in tune.

And when the O'Roarke sisters were in a temper, it was quite a show.

Shifting only slightly, Althea whispered near his ear. "Obviously they've done this before."

Boyd grinned. If he'd had popcorn and a beer, he would have been content to sit through another ten rounds. "Who's your money on?"

"Cilla," she murmured, crossing one smooth leg. "But the sister's a real up-and-comer."

Apparently weary of beating her head against a

brick wall, Deborah turned. "Okay." She poked a finger at Boyd. "You tell me what's going on."

"Ah…"

"Never mind." She zeroed in on Althea. "You."

Biting back a smile, Althea nodded. "We're the investigating officers on your sister's case, Miss O'Roarke."

"So there is a case."

Ignoring Cilla's furious look, Althea nodded again. "Yes. With the station's cooperation, we have a trace on the studio line. Detective Fletcher and I have already interrogated a number of suspects who have priors for obscene or harassing phone calls. With this latest development, we'll put a tap on your private line."

"Latest development." It only took Deborah a moment. "Oh, Cilla, not here. He didn't call you here." Temper forgotten, she threw her arms around her sister. "I'm sorry."

"It's nothing for you to worry about." When Deborah stiffened, Cilla drew back. "I mean it, Deb. It's nothing for either of us to worry about. We've got the pros to do the worrying."

"That's right." Althea rose. "Detective Fletcher and I have over fifteen years on the force between us. We intend to take good care of your sister. Is there a phone I can use to make some arrangements?"

"In the kitchen," Deborah said before Cilla could comment. She wanted a private interview. "I'll show you." She paused and smiled at Boyd. "Would you like some coffee, Detective?"

"Thanks." He watched her—what man wouldn't?—as she walked from the room.

"Don't even think about it," Cilla mumbled.

"Excuse me?" But he grinned. It didn't take a detective to recognize a mother hen. "Your sister— Deborah, right?—she's something."

"You're too old for her."

"Ouch."

Cilla picked up a cigarette and forced herself to settle on the arm of a chair again. "In any case, you and Detective Grayson seem well suited to each other."

"Thea?" He had to grin again. Most of the time he forgot his partner was a woman. "Yeah, I'm one lucky guy."

Cilla ground her teeth. She hated to think she could be intimidated by another woman. Althea Grayson was personable enough, professional enough. Cilla could even handle the fact that she was stunning. It was just that she was so *together.*

Boyd rose to take the unlit cigarette from her fingers. "Jealous?"

"In your dreams, Slick."

"We'll get into my dreams later." He lifted her chin up with a fingertip. "Holding on?"

"I'm fine." She wanted to move, but she had the feeling he wouldn't give her room if she stood. And if she stood it would be much too easy to drop her head on his shoulder and just cave in. She had responsibilities, obligations. And her pride. "I don't want Deb mixed up in this. She's alone here at night while I'm at work."

"I can arrange to have a cruiser stationed outside."

She nodded, grateful. "I hate it that somewhere along the line I've made a mistake that might put her in danger. She doesn't deserve it."

Unable to resist, he spread his fingers to cup her cheek. "Neither do you."

It had been a long time since she'd been touched, allowed herself to be touched, even that casually. She managed to shrug. "I haven't figured that out yet." She gave a little sigh, wishing she could close her eyes and turn her face into that strong, capable hand. "I've got to get ready to go to the station."

"Why don't you give that a pass tonight?"

"And let him think he's got me running scared?" She stood then. "Not on a bet."

"Even Wonder Woman takes a night off."

She shook her head. She'd been right about him not giving her room. Her escape routes were blocked by the chair on one side and his body on the other. Tension quivered through her. Pride kept her eyes level. He was waiting, damn him. And unless he was blind or stupid, he would see that this contact, this connection with him, left her frazzled.

"You're crowding me, Fletcher."

In another minute, just one more minute, he would have given in to impulse and pulled her against him. He would have seen just how close to reality his fantasy was. "I haven't begun to crowd you, O'Roarke."

Her eyes sharpened. "I've had enough threats for one day, thanks."

He wanted to strangle her for that. Slowly, his eyes on hers, he hooked his thumbs in his pockets. "No threat, babe. Just a fact."

Deborah decided she'd eavesdropped long enough and cleared her throat. "Coffee, Detective Fletcher." She passed him a steaming mug. "Thea said black, two sugars."

"Thanks."

"I'm going to hang around," she said, silently daring

Cilla to argue with her. "They should be here in an hour or so to hook up the phone." Then, she put her hands on Cilla's shoulders and kissed both of her cheeks. "I haven't missed a class this semester, Simon."

"Simon?" Boyd commented.

"Legree." With a laugh, Deborah kissed Cilla again. "The woman's a slave driver."

"I don't know what you're talking about." Cilla moved aside to gather up her purse. "You ought to catch up on your reading for U.S. studies. Your political science could use a boost. It wouldn't hurt to bone up on Psychology 101." She pulled her coat from the closet. "While you're at it, the kitchen floor needs scrubbing. I'm sure we have an extra toothbrush you could use on it. And I'd like another cord of wood chopped."

Deborah laughed. "Go away."

Cilla grinned as she reached for the doorknob. Her hand closed over Boyd's. She jolted back before she could stop herself. "What are you doing?"

"Hitching a ride with you." He sent Deborah a quick wink as he pulled Cilla out the door.

"This is ridiculous," Cilla said as she strode into the station.

"Which?"

"I don't see why I have to have a cop in the studio with me night after night." She whipped off her coat as she walked—a bit like a bullfighter swirling a cape, Boyd thought. Still scowling, she reached for the door of a small storage room, then shrieked and stumbled back against Boyd as it swung open. "Jeez, Billy, you scared the life out of me."

"Sorry." The maintenance man had graying hair,

toothpick arms and an apologetic grin. "I was out of window cleaner." He held up his spray bottle.

"It's okay. I'm a little jumpy."

"I heard about it." He hooked the trigger of the bottle in his belt, then gathered up a mop and bucket. "Don't worry, Cilla. I'm here till midnight."

"Thanks. Are you going to listen to the show tonight?"

"You bet." He walked away, favoring his right leg in a slight limp.

Cilla stepped inside the room and located a fresh bottle of stylus cleaner. Taking a five-dollar bill out of her bag, she slipped it into a pile of cleaning rags.

"What was that for?"

"He was in Vietnam," she said simply, and closed the door again.

Boyd said nothing, knowing she was annoyed he'd caught her. He chalked it up to one more contradiction.

To prep for her shift, she went into a small lounge to run over the daily log for her show, adding and deleting as it suited her. The program director had stopped screaming about this particular habit months before. Another reason she preferred the night shift was the leeway it gave her.

"This new group," she muttered.

"What?" Boyd helped himself to a sugared doughnut.

"This new group, the Studs." She tapped her pencil against the table. "One-shot deal. Hardly worth the airtime."

"Then why play them?"

"Got to give them a fair shake." Intent on her work, she took an absent bite of the doughnut Boyd held to her lips. "In six months nobody will remember their names."

"That's rock and roll."

"No. The Beatles, Buddy Holly, Chuck Berry, Springsteen, Elvis—that's rock and roll."

He leaned back, considering her. "Ever listen to anything else?"

She grinned, then licked a speck of sugar from her top lip. "You mean there *is* something else?"

"Have you always been one-track?"

"Yeah." She pulled a band of fabric out of her pocket. With a couple of flicks of the wrist she had her hair tied back. "So what kind of music do you like?"

"The Beatles, Buddy Holly, Chuck—"

"Well, there's hope for you yet," she interrupted.

"Mozart, Lena Horne, Beaujolais, Joan Jett, Ella Fitzgerald, B.B. King..."

Her brow lifted. "So, we're eclectic."

"We're open-minded."

She leaned back a moment. "You're a surprise, Fletcher. I guess I figured you for the loving-and-hurting, drinking-and-cheating type."

"In music appreciation or personality?"

"Both." She glanced at the clock. "It's showtime."

Wild Bob Williams, who had the six-to-ten slot, was just finishing up his show. He was short, paunchy and middle-aged, with the voice of a twenty-year-old stud. He gave Cilla a brief salute as she began sorting through 45s and albums.

"Mmm, the long-legged filly just walked in." He hit a switch that had an echoing heartbeat pounding. "Get ready out there in KHIP land, your midnight star's rising. I'm leaving you with this blast from the past." He potted up "Honky Tonk Woman."

He swung out of his chair and stretched his rubbery leg muscles. "Hey, honey, you okay?"

"Sure." She set her first cut on the turntable and adjusted the needle.

"I caught the paper."

"No big deal, Bob."

"Hey, we're family around here." He gave her shoulder a quick squeeze. "We're behind you."

"Thanks."

"You're the cop?" he asked Boyd.

"That's right."

"Get this guy soon. He's got us all shaking." He gave Cilla another squeeze. "Let me know if you need anything."

"I will. Thanks."

She didn't want to think about it, couldn't afford to think about it, with thirty seconds to air. Taking her seat, she adjusted the mike, took a series of long, deep breaths, ran a one-two-three voice check, then opened her mike.

"All right, Denver, this is Cilla O'Roarke coming to you on number one, KHIP. You've got me from ten till two in the a.m. We're going to start off giving away one hundred and nine dollars. We've got the mystery record coming up. If you can give me the title, the artist and the year, you've got yourself a fistful of cash. That number is 555-5447. Stand by, 'cause we're going to rock."

The music blasted out, pleasing her. She was in control again.

"Elton John," Boyd said from behind her. "'Honky Cat.' Nineteen seventy...two."

She turned in her chair to face him. He was looking damned pleased with himself, she thought. That half grin on his face, his hands in his pockets. It was a shame he was so attractive, a bloody crying shame. "Well, well, you surprise me, Slick. Remind me to put you down for a free T-shirt."

"I'd rather have a dinner."

"And I'd rather have a Porsche. But there you go— Hey," she said when he took her hand.

"You've been biting your nails." He skimmed a thumb over her knuckles and watched her eyes change. "Another bad habit."

"I've got lots more."

"Good." Instead of sitting back in the corner, he chose a chair beside her. "I didn't have time to get a book," he explained. "Why don't I watch you work?"

"Why don't you—" She swore, then punched a button on the phone. He'd nearly made her miss her cue. "KHIP. Can you name the mystery record?"

It took five calls before she had a winner. Trying to ignore Boyd, she put on another cut while she took the winner's name and address.

As if she didn't have enough on her mind, she thought. How was she supposed to concentrate on her show when he was all but sitting on top of her? Close enough, she realized, that she could smell him. No cologne, just soap—something that brought the mountains to mind one moment and quiet, intimate nights the next.

She wasn't interested in either, she reminded herself. All she wanted was to get through this crisis and get her life back on an even keel. Attractive men came and went, she knew. But success stayed—as long as you were willing to sweat for it.

She shifted, stretching out to select a new record. Their thighs brushed. His were long and as hard as rock. Determined not to jolt, she turned her head to look into his eyes. Inches apart, challenge meeting challenge. She watched as his gaze dipped down to linger on her mouth. And it lifted again, desire flickering. Music pulsed in her ears from the headphones she stubbornly wore so that she wouldn't have to speak to him. They were singing of hot nights and grinding needs.

Very carefully, she moved away. When she spoke into the mike again, her voice was even huskier.

He rose. He'd decided it was his only defense. He'd meant to annoy her, to distract her from the inevitable phone call that would come before the night was over. He'd wanted her mind off it, and on him. He wouldn't deny that he'd wanted her to think of him. But he hadn't known that when he'd succeeded, she would tie him up in knots.

She smelled like midnight. Secret and sinful. She sounded like sex. Hot and inviting. Then you looked into her eyes, really looked, and saw simple innocence. The man that combination wouldn't drive mad either had never been born or was already dead.

A little distance, Boyd told himself as he moved quietly out of the studio. A lot of objectivity. It wouldn't do either one of them any good to allow his emotions to get so tangled up with a woman he was supposed to protect.

When she was alone, Cilla made a conscious effort to relax, muscle by muscle. It was just because she was already on edge. It was a comfort to believe that. Her reaction to Boyd was merely an echo of the tension she'd lived with for more than a week. And he was trying to goad her.

She blew the hair out of her eyes and gave her listeners a treat—two hits in a row. And herself another moment to calm.

She hadn't figured him out yet. He read Steinbeck and recognized Elton John. He talked slow and lazy—and thought fast. He wore scarred boots and three-hundred-dollar jackets.

What did it matter? she asked herself as she set up for the next twenty minutes of her show. She wasn't interested in men. And he was definitely a man. Strike one. She would never consider getting involved with a cop. Strike two. And anyone with eyes could see that he had a close, even intimate relationship with his knockout partner. She'd never been one to poach on someone else's property.

Three strikes and he's out.

She closed her eyes and let the music pour through her. It helped, as it always did, to calm her, or lift her up, or simply remind her how lucky she was. She wasn't sharp and studious like Deborah. She wasn't dedicated, as their parents had been. She had little more than the education required by law, and yet she was here, just where she wanted to be, doing just what she wanted to do.

Life had taught her one vital lesson. Nothing lasted forever. Good times or bad, they passed. This nightmare, however horrid it was at this point in time, would be over eventually. She only had to get through it, one day at a time.

"That was Joan Jett waking you up as we head toward eleven-thirty. We've got a news brief coming up for you, then a double shot of Steve Winwood and Phil Collins to take us into the next half hour. This is KHIP, and the news is brought to you by Wildwood Records."

She punched in the prerecorded cassette, then scanned the printout of the ads and promos she would read. By the time Boyd came back, she was into the next block of music and standing up to stretch her muscles.

He stopped where he was, trying not to groan as she lifted her arms to the ceiling and rotated her hips. In time to the music, he was sure, as she bent from the waist, grabbed her ankles and slowly bent and straightened her knees.

He'd seen the routine before. It was something she did once or twice during her four-hour stint. But she thought she was alone now, and she put a little more rhythm into it. Watching her, he realized that the ten-minute break he'd taken hadn't been nearly long enough.

She sat again, pattered a bit to the audience. Her headphones were around her neck now, as she'd turned the music up for her own pleasure. As it pulsed, she swayed.

When he put a hand on her shoulder, she bolted out of the chair. "Easy, O'Roarke. I brought you some tea."

Her heart was like a trip-hammer in her chest. As it slowed, she lowered to the table. "What?"

"Tea," he repeated, offering her a cup. "I brought you some tea. You drink too much coffee. This is herbal. Jasmine or something."

She'd recovered enough to look at the cup in distaste. "I don't drink flowers."

"Try it. You might not hit the ceiling the next time someone touches you." He sipped a soft drink out of the bottle.

"I'd rather have that."

He took another sip, a long one, then passed the bottle to her. "You're almost halfway there."

Like Boyd, she looked at the clock. It was nearing midnight. This had once been her favorite leg of the show. Now, as she watched the second hand tick away, her palms began to sweat.

"Maybe he won't call tonight, since he got me at home."

He settled beside her again. "Maybe."

"But you don't think so."

"I think we take it a step at a time." He put a soothing hand at the back of her neck. "I want you to try to keep calm, keep him on the line longer. Ask questions. No matter what he says, just keep asking them, over and over. He may just answer one and give us something."

She nodded, then worked her way through the next ten minutes. "There's a question I want to ask you," she said at length.

"All right."

She didn't look at him, but drained the last swallow of the cold drink to ease her dry throat. "How long will they let me have a baby-sitter?"

"You don't have to worry about it."

"Let's just say I know something about how police departments work." It was there in her voice again, that touch of bitterness and regret. "A few nasty calls don't warrant a hell of a lot of attention."

"Your life's been threatened," he said. "It helps that

you're a celebrity, and that there's already been some press on it. I'll be around for a while."

"Mixed blessings," she muttered, then opened the request line.

The call came, as she had known it would, but quickly this time. On call number five, she recognized the voice, battled back the urge to scream and switched to music. Without realizing it, she groped for Boyd's hand.

"You're persistent, aren't you?"

"I want you dead. I'm almost ready now."

"Do I know you? I like to think I know everyone who wants to kill me."

She winced a little at the names he spewed at her and tried to concentrate on the steady pressure of Boyd's fingers at the base of her neck.

"Wow. I've really got you ticked off. You know, buddy, if you don't like the show, you've just got to turn it off."

"You seduced him." There was a sound of weeping now, fueled with fury. "You seduced him, tempted him, promised him. Then you murdered him."

"I…" She was more shocked by this than by any of the gutter names he had called her. "Who? I don't know what you're talking about. Please, who—"

The line went dead.

As she sat there, dazed and silent, Boyd snatched up the phone. "Any luck? Damn it." He rose, stuffed his hands in his pockets and began pacing. "Another ten seconds. We'd have had him in another ten seconds. He has to know we've got it tapped." His head snapped around when Nick Peters entered, his hands full of sloshing coffee. "What?"

"I—I—I—" His Adam's apple bobbed as he swallowed. "Mark said it was okay if I stayed through the show." He swallowed again. "I thought Cilla might want some coffee."

Boyd jerked a thumb toward the table. "We'll let you know. Can you help her get through the rest of the show?"

"I don't need help." Cilla's voice was icy-calm. "I'm fine, Nick. Don't worry about it." She put a steady hand on the mike. "That was for Chuck from Laurie, with all her love." She aimed a steady look at Boyd before she punched the phone again. "KHIP, you're on the air."

She got through it. That was all that mattered. And she wasn't going to fall apart the way she had the other night. Cilla was grateful for that. All she needed to do was think it all through.

She hadn't objected when Boyd took the wheel of her car. Relinquishing the right to drive was the least of her worries.

"I'm coming in," Boyd said after he parked the car. She just shrugged and started for the door.

Very deliberately she hung up her coat and pried off her shoes. She sat, still without speaking, and lit a cigarette. The marked cruiser outside had relieved her mind. Deborah was safe and asleep.

"Look," she began once she'd marshaled her thoughts. "There really isn't any use going into this. I think I have it figured out."

"Do you?" He didn't sit down. Her icy calm disturbed him much more than hysterics or anger would have. "Fill me in."

"It's obvious he's made a mistake. He has me mixed up with someone else. I just have to convince him."

"Just have to convince him," Boyd repeated. "And how do you intend to do that?"

"The next time he calls, I'll make him listen." She crossed an arm across her body and began to rub at the chill in her shoulder. "For God's sake, Fletcher, I haven't murdered anyone."

"So you'll tell him that and he'll be perfectly reasonable and apologize for bothering you."

Her carefully built calm was wearing thin. "I'll make him understand."

"You're trying to make yourself believe he's rational, Cilla. He's not."

"What am I supposed to do?" she demanded, snapping the cigarette in two as she crushed it out. "Whether he's rational or not, I have to make him see he's made a mistake. I've never killed anyone." Her laugh was strained as she pulled the band from her hair. "I've never seduced anyone."

"Give me a break."

Anger brought her out of the chair. "What do you see me as, some kind of black widow who goes around luring men, then knocking them off when I'm finished? Get the picture, Fletcher. I'm a voice, a damn good one. That's where it ends."

"You're a great deal more than voice, Cilla. We both know that." He paused, waiting for her to look at him again. "And so does he."

Something trembled inside her—part fear, part longing. She wanted neither. "Whatever I am, I'm no temptress. It's an act, a show, and it has nothing to do with reality. My ex-husband would be the first to tell you I don't even have a sex drive."

His eyes sharpened. "You never mentioned you'd been married."

And she hadn't intended to, Cilla thought as she wearily combed a hand through her hair. "It was a million years ago. What does it matter?"

"Everything applies. I want his name and address."

"I don't know his address. We didn't even last a year. I was twenty years old, for God's sake." She began to rub at her forehead.

"His name, Cilla."

"Paul. Paul Lomax. I haven't seen him for about eight years—since he divorced me." She spun to the window, then back again. "The point is, this guy's on the wrong frequency. He's got it into his head I—what?—used my wiles on some guy, and that doesn't wash."

"Apparently he thinks it does."

"Well, he thinks wrong. I couldn't even keep one man happy, so it's a joke to think I could seduce legions."

"That's a stupid remark, even for you."

"Do you think I like admitting that I'm all show, that I'm lousy in bed?" She bit off the words as she paced. "The last man I went out with told me I had ice water for blood. But I didn't kill him." She calmed a little, amused in spite of herself. "I thought about it, though."

"I think it's time you start to take this whole business seriously. And I think it's time you start taking yourself seriously."

"I take myself very seriously."

"Professionally," he agreed. "You know exactly

what to do and how to do it. Personally…you're the first woman I've met who was so willing to concede she couldn't make a man dance to her tune."

"I'm a realist."

"I think you're a coward."

Her chin shot up. "Go to hell."

He wasn't about to back off. He had a point to prove, to both of them. "I think you're afraid to get close to a man, afraid to find out just what's inside. Maybe you'd find out it's something you can't control."

"I don't need this from you. You just get this man off my back." She started to storm past him but was brought up short when he grabbed her arm.

"What do you say to an experiment?"

"An experiment?"

"Why don't you give it a try, O'Roarke—with me? It should be safe, since you can barely stand the sight of me. A test." He took her other arm. "Low-risk." He could feel the anger vibrate through her as he held her. Good. For reasons he couldn't have begun to name, he was just as angry. "Five-to-one I don't feel a thing." He drew her inches closer. "Want to prove me wrong?"

Chapter 4

They were close. She had lifted one hand in an unconscious defensive gesture and now her fingers were splayed across his chest. She could feel his heartbeat, slow and steady, beneath her palm. She focused her resentment on that even rhythm as her own pulse jerked and scrambled.

"I don't have to prove anything to you."

He nodded. The barely banked fury in her eyes was easier for him to handle than the glaze of fear it replaced. "To yourself, then." Deliberately he smiled, baiting her. "What's the matter, O'Roarke? Do I scare you?"

He'd pushed exactly the right button. They both knew it. He didn't give a damn if it was temper that pushed her forward. As long as she moved.

She tossed her hair back and slowly, purposefully slid her hand from his chest to his shoulder. She wanted a reaction, hang him. He only lifted a brow and, with that faint smile playing around his mouth, watched her.

So he wanted to play games, she thought. Well, she was up for it. Tossing common sense aside, she pressed her lips to his.

His were firm, cool. And unresponsive. With her eyes open, she watched his remain patient, steady and hatefully amused. As her hand balled into a fist on his shoulder, she snapped her head back.

"Satisfied?"

"Not hardly." His eyes might have been calm. That was training. But if she had bothered to monitor his heartbeat she would have found it erratic. "You're not trying, O'Roarke." He slid a hand down to her hip, shifting her balance just enough to have her sway against him. "You want me to believe that's the best you can do?"

Angry humiliation rippled through her. Cursing him, she dragged his mouth to hers and poured herself into the kiss.

His lips were still firm, but they were no longer cool. Nor were they unresponsive. For an instant the urge to retreat hammered at her. And then needs, almost forgotten needs, surged. A flood of longings, a storm of desires. Overwhelmed by them, she strained against him, letting the power and the heat whip through her, reminding her what it was like to sample passion again.

Every other thought, every other wish, winked out. She could feel the long, hard length of him pressed against her, the slow, deliberate stroke of his hands as they moved up her back and into her hair. His mouth, no longer patient, took and took from hers until the blood pounded like thunder in her head.

He'd known she would pack a punch. He'd thought he was prepared for it. In the days he'd known her he'd imagined tasting her like this dozens of times. He'd imagined what it would be like to hold her against him, to hear her sigh, to catch the fevered scent of her skin as he took his mouth over her.

But reality was much more potent than any dream had been.

Chain lightning. She was every bit as explosive, as turbulent, as potentially lethal. The current sparked and sizzled from her into him, leaving him breathless, dazed and churning. Even as he groaned against the onslaught, he felt her arch away from the power that snapped back into her.

She shuddered against him and made a sound—part protest, part confusion—as she tried to struggle away.

He'd wrapped her hair around his hand. He had only to tug gently to have her head fall back, to have her eyes dark and cloudy on his.

He took his time, letting his gaze skim over her face. He wanted to see in her eyes what he had felt. The reflection was there, that most elemental yearning. He smiled again as her lips trembled open and her breath came fast and uneven.

"I'm not finished yet," he told her, then dragged her against him again and plundered.

She needed to think, but her thoughts couldn't fight their way through the sensations. Layers of them, thin and silky, seemed to cover her, fogging the reason, drugging the will. Before panic could slice through, she was rocketing up again, clinging to him, opening for him, demanding from him.

He knew he could feast and never be full. Not when

her mouth was hot and moist and ripe with flavor. He knew he could hold yet never control. Not when her body was vibrating from the explosion they had ignited together. The promise he had heard in her voice, seen in her eyes, was here for the taking.

Unable to resist, he slid his hands under her sweatshirt to find the warmed satin skin beneath. He took, possessed, exploited, until the ache spreading through his body turned to pain.

Too fast, he warned himself. Too soon. For both of them. Holding her steady, he lifted his head and waited for her to surface.

She dragged her eyes open and saw only his face. She gulped in air and tasted only his flavor. Reeling, she pressed a hand to her temple, then let it fall to her side. "I… I want to sit down."

"That makes two of us." Taking her arm, he led her to the couch and sat beside her.

She worked on steadying her breathing, focused on the dark window across the room. Maybe with enough time, enough distance, she would be able to convince herself that what had just happened had not been life-altering.

"That was stupid."

"It was a lot of things," he pointed out. "Stupid doesn't come to mind."

She took one more deep breath. "You made me angry."

"It isn't hard."

"Listen, Boyd—"

"So you *can* say it." Before she could stop him, he stroked a hand down her hair in a casually intimate gesture that made her pulse rate soar again. "Does that mean you don't use a man's name until you've kissed him?"

"It doesn't mean anything." She stood up, hoping she'd get the strength back in her legs quicker by pacing. "Obviously we've gotten off the track."

"There's more than one." He settled back, thinking it was a pleasure to watch her move. There was something just fine and dandy about watching the swing of long feminine legs. As she paced, nervous energy crackling, he tossed an arm over the back of the couch and stretched out his legs.

"There's only one for me." She threw him a look over her shoulder. "You'd better understand that."

"Okay, we'll ride on that one for a while." He could afford to wait, since he had every intention of switching lines again, and soon. "You seem to have some kind of screwy notion that the only thing that attracts men to you is your voice, your act. I think we just proved you wrong."

"What just happened proved nothing." If there was anything more infuriating than that slow, patient smile of his, she had yet to see it. "In any case, that has nothing to do with the man who's calling me."

"You're a smart woman, Cilla. Use your head. He's fixed on you, but not for himself. He wants to pay you back for something you did to another man. Someone you knew," he continued when she stopped long enough to pick up a cigarette. "Someone who was involved with you."

"I've already told you, there's no one."

"No one now."

"No one now, no one before, no one for years."

Having experienced that first wave of her passion, he found that more than difficult to believe. Still, he nodded. "So it didn't mean as much to you. Maybe that's the problem."

"For God's sake, Fletcher, I don't even date. I don't have the time or the inclination."

"We'll talk about your inclinations later."

Weary, she turned away to stare blindly through the glass. "Damn it, Boyd, get out of my life."

"It's your life we're talking about." There was an edge to his voice that had her holding back the snide comment she wanted to make. "If there's been no one in Denver, we'll start working our way back. But I want you to think, and think hard. Who's shown an interest in you? Someone who calls the station more than normal. Who asks to meet you, asks personal questions. Someone who's approached you, asked you out, made a play."

She gave a short, humorless laugh. "You have."

"Remind me to run a make on myself." His voice was deceptively mild, but she caught the underlying annoyance and frustration in it. "Who else, Cilla?"

"There's no one, no one who's pushed." Wishing for a moment's, just a moment's, peace of mind, she pressed the heels of her hands against her eyes. "I get calls. That's the idea. I get some that ask me for a date, some that even send presents. You know, candy-and-flower types. Nothing very sinister about a bunch of roses."

"There's a lot sinister about death threats."

She wanted to speak calmly, practically, but she couldn't keep the nastiness out of her voice. "I can't remember everyone who's called and flirted with me on the air. Guys I turn down stay turned down."

He could only shake his head. It was a wonder to him that such a sharp woman could be so naive in certain situations. "All right, we'll shoot for a different angle. You work with men—almost all men—at the station."

"We're professionals," she snapped, and began biting her nails. "Mark's happily married. Bob's happily married. Jim's a friend—a good one."

"You forgot Nick."

"Nick Peters? What about him?"

"He's crazy about you."

"What?" She was surprised enough to turn around. "That's ridiculous. He's a kid."

After a long study, he let out a sigh. "You really haven't noticed, have you?"

"There's nothing to notice." More disturbed than she wanted to admit, she turned away again. "Look, Slick, this is getting us nowhere, and I'm..." Her words trailed off, and her hand crept slowly toward her throat.

"And you're what?"

"There's a man across the street. He's watching the house."

"Get away from the window."

"What?"

Boyd was already up and jerking her aside. "Stay away from the windows and keep the door locked. Don't open it again until I get back."

She nodded and followed him to the door. Her lips pressed together as she watched him take out his weapon. That single gesture snapped her back to reality. It had been a smooth movement, not so much practiced as instinctive. Ten years on the force, she remembered. He'd drawn and fired before.

She wouldn't tell him to be careful. Those were useless words.

"I'm going to take a look. Lock the door behind me."

Gone was the laid-back man who had taunted her into an embrace. One look at his face and she could see that he was all cop. Their eyes changed, she thought. The emotion drained out of them. There was no room for emotion when you held a gun. "If I'm not back in ten minutes, call 911 for backup. Understood?"

"Yes." She gave in to the need to touch his arm. "Yes," she repeated.

After he slipped out, she shoved the bolt into place and waited.

He hadn't buttoned his coat, and the deep wind of the early hours whipped through his shirt. His weapon, warmed from sitting in its nest against his side, fitted snug in his hand. Sweeping his gaze right, then left, he found the street deserted, dark but for the pools of light from the street lamps spaced at regular intervals. It was only a quiet suburban neighborhood, cozily asleep in the predawn hours. The night wind sounded through the naked trees in low moans.

He didn't doubt Cilla's words—wouldn't have doubted it even if he hadn't caught a glimpse through her window of a lone figure on the opposite sidewalk.

Whoever had been there was gone now, probably alerted the moment Cilla had spotted him.

As if to punctuate Boyd's thoughts, there was the sound of an engine turning over a block or two away. He swore but didn't bother to give chase. With that much of a lead, it would be a waste of time. Instead, he walked a half block in each direction, then carefully circled the house.

Cilla had her hand on the phone when he knocked. "It's okay. It's Boyd."

In three hurried strides, she was at the door. "Did

you see him?" she demanded the moment Boyd stepped inside.

"No."

"He was there. I swear it."

"I know." He relocked the door himself. "Try to relax. He's gone now."

"Relax?" In the past ten minutes she'd had more than enough time to work herself from upset to frantic. "He knows where I work, where I live. How in God's name am I ever supposed to relax again? If you hadn't scared him off, he might have—" She dragged her hands through her hair. She didn't want to think about what might have happened. Didn't dare.

Boyd didn't speak for a moment. Instead, he watched as she slowly, painfully brought herself under control. "Why don't you take some time off, stay home for a few days? We'll arrange for a black-and-white to cruise the neighborhood."

She allowed herself the luxury of sinking into a chair. "What difference does it make if I'm here or at the station?" She shook her head before he could speak. "And if I stayed home I'd go crazy thinking about it, worrying about it. At least at work I have other things on my mind."

He hadn't expected her to agree. "We'll talk about it later. Right now you're tired. Why don't you go to bed? I'll sleep on the couch."

She wanted to be strong enough to tell him it wasn't necessary. She didn't need to be protected. But the wave of gratitude made her weak. "I'll get you a blanket."

It was almost dawn when he dragged himself home. He'd driven a long time—from one sleepy suburb to another, into an eerily quiet downtown. Covering his trail. The panic had stayed with him for the first hour, but he'd beaten it, made himself drive slowly, carefully. Being stopped by a roving patrol car could have ruined all of his plans.

Under the heavy muffler and cap he was wearing, he was sweating. In the thin canvas tennis shoes, his feet were like ice. But he was too accustomed to discomfort to notice.

He staggered into the bathroom, never turning on a light. With ease he avoided his early-warning devices. The thin wire stretched from the arm of the spindly chair to the arm of the faded couch. The tower of cans at the entrance to his bedroom. He had excellent night vision. It was something he'd always been proud of.

He showered in the dark, letting the water run cold over his tensed body. As he began to relax, he allowed himself to draw in the fragrance of soap—his favorite scent. He used a rough, long-handled brush to violently scrub every inch of his skin.

As he washed, the dark began to lessen with the first watery light of dawn.

Over his heart was an intricate tattoo of two knives, blades crossed in an X. With his fingers he caressed them. He remembered when it had still been new, when he had shown it to John. John had been so impressed, so fascinated.

The image came so clearly. John's dark, excited eyes. His voice—the way he spoke so quickly that the words tumbled into each other. Sometimes they had sat in the dark and talked for hours, making plans and promises. They were going to travel together, do great things together.

Then the world had interfered. Life had interfered. The woman had interfered.

Dripping, he stepped from the shower. The towel was exactly where he had placed it. No one came into this room, into any of his rooms, to disturb his carefully ordered space. Once he was dry, he pulled on faded pajamas. They reminded him of the childhood he'd been cheated out of.

As the sun came up, he made two enormous sandwiches and ate them standing in the kitchen, leaning over the sink so that the crumbs wouldn't fall to the floor.

He felt strong again. Clean and fed. He was outwitting the police, making fools of them. And that delighted him. He was frightening the woman, bringing terror into every day of her life. That excited him. When the time was right, he would do everything he'd told her he would do.

And still it wouldn't be enough.

He went into the bedroom, shut the door, pulled the shades and picked up the phone.

Deborah strolled out of her room in a white teddy, a thin blue robe that reached to mid-thigh, flapping open. Her toenails were shocking pink. She'd painted them the night before to amuse herself as she'd crammed for an exam.

She was muttering the questions she thought would be on the exam she had scheduled at nine. The questions came easily enough, but the answers continued to bog down at some crossroads between the conscious and the unconscious. She hoped to unblock the answers with a quick shot of coffee.

Yawning, she stumbled over a boot, pitched toward the couch, then let out a muffled scream as her hand encountered warm flesh.

Boyd sat up like a shot, his hand already reaching for his weapon. With their faces close, he stared at Deborah—the creamy skin, the big blue eyes, the tumble of dark hair—and relaxed.

"Good morning."

"I— Detective Fletcher?"

He rubbed a hand over his eyes. "I think so."

"I'm sorry. I didn't realize you were here." She cleared her throat and belatedly remembered to close her robe. Still fumbling, she glanced up the stairs and automatically lowered her voice. Her sister wasn't a sound sleeper under the best of circumstances. "Why are you here?"

He flexed a shoulder that had stiffened during his cramped night on the couch. "I told you I was going to look after Cilla."

"Yes, you did." Her eyes narrowed as she studied him. "You take your job seriously."

"That's right."

"Good." Satisfied, she smiled. In the upheaval and confusion of her nineteen years, she had learned to make character judgments quickly. "I was about to make some coffee. I have an early class. Can I get you some?"

If she was anything like her sister, he wouldn't get any more sleep until he'd answered whatever questions were rolling around in her head. "Sure. Thanks."

"I imagine you'd like a hot shower, as well. You're about six inches too long to have spent a comfortable night on that couch."

"Eight," he said, rubbing the back of his stiff neck. "I think it's more like eight."

"You're welcome to all the hot water you want. I'll start on the coffee." As she turned toward the kitchen, the phone rang. Though she knew Cilla would pick it up before the second ring, she stepped toward it automatically. Boyd shook his head. Reaching over, he lifted the receiver and listened.

With her hands clutching the lapels of her robe, Deborah watched him. His face remained impassive, but she saw a flicker of anger in his eyes. Though brief, it was intense enough to make her certain who was on the other end of the line.

Boyd disconnected mechanically, then punched in a series of numbers. "Anything?" He didn't even bother to swear at the negative reply. "Right." After hanging up, he looked at Deborah. She was standing beside the couch, her hands clenched, her face pale. "I'm going upstairs," he said. "I'll take a rain check on that coffee."

"She'll be upset. I want to talk to her."

He pushed aside the blanket and rose, wearing only his jeans. "I'd appreciate it if you'd let me handle it this time."

She wanted to argue, but something in his eyes stopped her. She nodded. "All right, but do a good job of it. She isn't as tough as she likes people to think."

"I know."

He climbed the stairs to the second floor, walked past an open door to a room where the bed was tidily made. Deborah's, he decided, noting the rose-and-white decor and the feminine bits of lace. Pausing at the next door, he knocked, then entered without waiting for an answer.

She was sitting in the middle of the bed, her knees drawn up close to her chest and her head resting on them. The sheets and blankets were tangled, a testimony to the few hours of restless sleep she'd had.

There were no bits of feminine lace here, no soft, creamy colors. She preferred clean lines rather than curves, simplicity rather than flounces. In contrast, the color scheme was electric, and anything but restful. In the midst of the vibrant blues and greens, she seemed all the more vulnerable.

She didn't look up until he sat on the edge of the bed and touched her hair. Slowly she lifted her head. He saw that there were no tears. Rather than the fear he'd expected, there was an unbearable weariness that was even more disturbing.

"He called," she said.

"I know. I was on the extension."

"Then you heard." She looked away, toward the window, where she could see the sun struggling to burn away a low bank of clouds. "It was him outside last night. He said he'd seen me, seen us. He made it sound revolting."

"Cilla—"

"He was watching!" She spit out the words. "Nothing I say, nothing I do, is going to make him stop. And if he gets to me, he's going to do everything he said he'd do."

"He's not going to get to you."

"How long?" she demanded. Her fingers clenched and unclenched on the sheets as her eyes burned into his. "How long can you watch me? He'll just wait. He'll wait and keep calling, keep watching." Something snapped inside her, and she picked up the bedside phone and heaved it across the room. It bounced against the wall, jangling as it thudded to the floor. "You're not going to stop him. You heard him. He said nothing would stop him."

"This is just what he wants." Boyd took her by the arms and gave her one quick shake. "He wants you to fall apart. He wants to know he's made you fall apart. If you do, you're only helping him."

"I don't know what to do," she managed. "I just don't know what to do."

"You've got to trust me. Look at me, Cilla." Her breath was hitching, but she met his eyes. "I want you to trust me," he said quietly, "and believe me when I say I won't let anything happen to you."

"You can't always be there."

His lips curved a little. He gentled his hold to rub his hands up and down her arms. "Sure I can."

"I want—" She squeezed her eyes shut. How she hated to ask. Hated to need.

"What?"

Her lips trembled as she fought for one last handhold on control. "I need to hold on to something." She let out an unsteady breath. "Please."

He said nothing, but he gathered her close to cradle her head on his shoulder. Her hands, balled into fists, pressed against his back. She was trembling, fighting off a wild bout of tears.

"Take five, O'Roarke," he murmured. "Let loose."

"I can't." She kept her eyes closed and held on. He was solid, warm, strong. Dependable. "I'm afraid once I do I won't be able to stop."

"Okay, let's try this." He tilted her head up and touched his lips gently to hers. "Think about me. Right here." His mouth brushed hers again. "Right now." Easy, patient, he stroked her rigid back. "Just me."

Here was compassion. She hadn't known a kiss from a man could hold it. More than gentle, more than tender, it soothed frayed nerves, calmed icy fears, cooled hot despair. Her clenched hands relaxed, muscle by muscle. There was no demand here as his lips roamed over her face. Just understanding.

It became so simple to do as he'd asked. She thought only of him.

Hesitant, she brought a hand to his face, letting her fingers skim along his beard-roughened cheek. Her stomach unknotted. The throbbing in her head quieted. She said his name on a sigh and melted against him.

He had to be careful. Very careful. Her complete and total surrender had his own needs drumming. He ignored them. For now she needed comfort, not passion. It couldn't matter that his senses were reeling from her, the soft give of her body, the rich taste of her mouth. It couldn't matter that the air had thickened so that each breath he took was crowded with the scent of her.

He knew he had only to lay her back on the bed among the tangled sheets. And cover her. She wouldn't resist. Perhaps she would even welcome the heat and the distraction. The temporary respite. He intended to be much more to her.

Battling his own demons, he pressed his lips to her forehead, then rested his cheek on her hair.

"Better?"

On one ragged breath, she nodded. She wasn't sure she could speak. How could she tell him that she wanted only to stay like this, her arms around him, his heart beating against hers? He'd think she was a fool.

"I, uh…didn't know you could be such a nice guy, Fletcher."

He wanted to sigh, but he found himself grinning. "I have my moments."

"Yeah. Well, that was certainly above and beyond."

Maybe, just maybe, she wasn't really trying to needle him. He pulled back, put a hand under her chin and held it steady. "I'm not on duty. When I kiss you, it's got nothing to do with my job. Got it?"

She'd meant to thank him, not annoy him. There was a warning in his eyes that had her frowning. "Sure."

"Sure," he repeated, then rose to jam his hands in his pockets in disgust.

For the first time she noted that he wore only his jeans, unsnapped and riding low. The sudden clutching in her stomach had nothing to do with fear and left her momentarily speechless.

She wanted him. Not just to hold, not just for a few heated kisses. And certainly not just for comfort. She wanted him in bed, the way she couldn't remember ever wanting a man before. She could look at him—the long, lean, golden line of torso, the narrow hips, the dance of muscle in his arms as he balled his hands—and she could imagine what it would be like to touch and be touched, to roll over the bed in one tangled heap of passion. To ride and be ridden.

"What the hell's wrong with you now?"

"What?"

Eyes narrowed, he rocked back on his heels as she blinked at him. "Taking a side trip, O'Roarke?"

"I, ah…" Her mouth was dry, and there was a hard knot of pressure in her gut. What would he say if she told him where her mind had just taken her, taken them? She let her eyes close. "Oh, boy," she whispered. "I think I need some coffee." And a quick dip in a cold lake.

"Your sister was fixing some." He frowned as he studied her. He thought of Deborah for a moment, of how she had nearly fallen on top of him wearing hardly more than a swatch of white lace. He'd appreciated the long, lissome limbs. What man wouldn't? But looking at her hadn't rocked his system.

And here was Cilla—sitting there with her eyes shadowed, wearing a Broncos football jersey that was two sizes too big. The bright orange cotton was hardly seductive lingerie. If he stood there one more moment, he would be on his knees begging for mercy.

"How about breakfast?" His voice was abrupt, not even marginally friendly. It helped to bring her thoughts to order.

"I never eat it."

"Today you do. Ten minutes."

"Look, Slick—"

"Do something with your hair," he said as he walked out of the room. "You look like hell."

He found Deborah downstairs in the kitchen, fully dressed, sipping a cup of coffee. That she was waiting for him was obvious. The moment he stepped into the room, she was out of her chair.

"She's fine," he said briefly. "I'm going to fix her some breakfast."

Though her brow lifted at this information, she nodded. "Look, why don't you sit down? I'll fix some for both of you."

"I thought you had an early class."

"I'll skip it."

He headed for the coffee. "Then she'll be mad at both of us."

She had to smile as he poured a cup, then rooted through a drawer for a spoon for the sugar. "You already know her very well."

"Not well enough." He drank half the cup and felt nearly human again. He had to think of Cilla. It would be safe enough, he hoped, if he kept those thoughts professional. "How much time do you have?"

"About five minutes," she said as she glanced at her watch.

"Tell me about the ex-husband."

"Paul?" There was surprise in her eyes, in her voice. "Why?" She was shaking her head before he could answer. "You don't think he has anything to do with what's going on here?"

"I'm checking all the angles. The divorce...was it amicable?"

"Are they ever?"

She was young, Boyd thought, nodding, but she was sharp. "You tell me."

"Well, in this case, I'd say it was as amicable—or as bland as they get." She hesitated, torn. If it was a question of being loyal to Cilla or protecting her, she had to choose protection. "I was only about twelve, and Cilla was never very open about it, but my impression was, always has been, that he wanted it."

Boyd leaned back against the counter. "Why?"

Uncomfortable, Deborah moved her shoulders. "He'd fallen in love with someone else." She let out a hiss of breath and prayed Cilla wouldn't see what she was doing as a betrayal. "It was pretty clear that they were having problems before I came to live with them.

It was right after our parents had died. Cilla had only been married a few months, but…well, let's say the honeymoon was over. She was making a name for herself in Atlanta, and Paul—he was very conservative, a real straight arrow. He'd decided to run for assemblyman, I think it was, and Cilla's image didn't suit."

"Sounds like it was the other way around to me."

She smiled then, beautifully, and moved over to top off his coffee. "I remember how hard she was working, to hold her job together, to hold everything together. It was a pretty awful time for us. It didn't help matters when the responsibility for a twelve-year-old was suddenly dumped on them. The added strain—well, I guess you could say it hastened the inevitable. A couple of months after I moved in, he moved out and filed for divorce. She didn't fight it."

He tried to imagine how it would have been. At twenty, she'd lost her parents, accepted the care and responsibility of a young girl and watched her marriage crumble. "Sounds to me like she was well rid of him."

"I guess it doesn't hurt to say I never liked him very much. He was inoffensive. And dull."

"Why did she marry him?"

"I think it would be more appropriate to ask me," Cilla said from the doorway.

Chapter 5

The something she had done with her hair was to pull it back in a ponytail. It left her face unframed, so the anger in her eyes was that much easier to read. Along with the jersey she'd slept in, she'd pulled on a pair of yellow sweatpants. It was a deceptively sunny combination. Her hands were thrust into their deep pockets as she stood, directing all her resentment at Boyd.

"Cilla." Knowing there was a time to argue and a time to soothe, Deborah stepped forward. "We were just—"

"Yes, I heard what you were just." She shifted her gaze to Deborah. The edge of her temper softened. "Don't worry about it. It's not your fault."

"It's not a matter of fault," Deborah murmured. "We care what happens to you."

"Nothing's going to happen. You'd better get going, Deb, or you'll be late. And it appears that Detective Fletcher and I have things to discuss."

Deborah lifted her hands and let them fall. She shot one sympathetic glance toward Boyd, then kissed her sister's cheek. "All right. You'd never listen to reason at this hour anyway."

"Get an A," was all Cilla said.

"I intend to. I'm going to catch a burger and a movie with Josh, but I'll be back before you get home."

"Have a good time." Cilla waited, not moving an inch until she heard the front door close. "You've got a hell of a nerve, Fletcher."

He merely turned and slipped another mug off the hook behind the stove. "Want some coffee?"

"I don't appreciate you grilling my sister."

He filled the mug, then set it aside. "I left my rubber hose in my other suit."

"Let's get something straight." She walked toward him, deliberately keeping her hands in her pockets. She was dead sure she'd hit him if she took them out. "If you have any questions about me, you come to me. Deborah is not involved in any of this."

"She's a lot more forthcoming than her sister. Got any eggs?" he asked as he opened the refrigerator.

She managed to restrain the urge to kick the door into his head. "You know, for a minute upstairs you had me fooled. I actually thought you had some heart, some compassion."

He found a half-dozen eggs, some cheese and a few miserly strips of bacon. "Why don't you sit down, O'Roarke, and drink your coffee?"

She swore at him, viciously. Something shot into his eyes, something dangerous, but he picked up a skillet and calmly began to fry the bacon. "You'll have to do better than that," he said after a moment. "After ten years on the force there's not much you could call me and get a rise."

"You had no right." Her voice had quieted, but the emotion in it had doubled. "No right to dredge all that up with her. She was a child, devastated, scared to death. That entire year was nothing but hell for her, and she doesn't need you to make her remember it."

"She handled herself just fine." He broke an egg into a bowl, then crushed the shell in his hand. "It seems to me you're the one with the problem."

"Just back off."

He had her arm in a tight grip so quickly that she had no chance to evade. His voice was soft, deadly, with temper licking around the edges. "Not a chance."

"What happened back then has nothing to do with what's happening now, and what's happening now is the only thing that concerns you."

"It's my job to determine what applies." With an effort, he reeled himself in. He couldn't remember when anyone had pushed him so close to the edge so often. "If you want me to put it to rest, then spell it out for me. Ex-spouses are favored suspects."

"It was eight years ago." She jerked away and, needing something to do with her hands, snatched up her coffee. It splattered over the rim and onto the counter.

"I find out from you or I find out from someone else. The end result's the same."

"You want me to spell it out? You want me to strip bare? Fine. It hardly matters at this point. I was twenty, I was stupid. He was beautiful and charming and smart—all the things stupid twenty-year-old girls think they want."

She took a long sip of hot coffee, then automatically

reached for a washcloth to mop up the spill. "We only knew each other a couple of months. He was very persuasive, very romantic. I married him because I wanted something stable and real in my life. And I thought he loved me."

She was calmer now. She hadn't realized that the anger had drained away. Sighing, she turned, mechanically reaching for plates and flatware. "It didn't work—almost from day one. He was disappointed in me physically and disillusioned when he saw that I believed my work was as important as his. He'd hoped to convince me to change jobs. Not that he wanted me to quit altogether. He wasn't against my having a career, even in radio—as long as it didn't interfere with his plans."

"Which were?" Boyd asked as he set the bacon aside to drain.

"Politics. Actually, we met at a charity event the station put on. He was trying to charm up votes. I was promoting. That was the basic problem," she murmured. "We met each other's public personalities."

"What happened?"

"We got married—too fast. And things went wrong—too fast. I was even considering his idea that I go into marketing or sales. I figured I should at least give it a shot. Then my parents… I lost my parents, and brought Deborah home."

She stopped speaking for a moment. She couldn't talk of that time, couldn't even think of the fears and the grief, the pain and the resentments.

"It must have been rough."

She shrugged the words away. "The bottom line was, I couldn't handle another upheaval. I needed to work. The strain ate away at what shaky foundation we had. He found someone who made him happier, and he left me." She filled her mug with coffee she no longer wanted. "End of story."

What was he supposed to say? Boyd wondered. Tough break, kid? We all make mistakes? You were better off without the jerk? No personal comments, he warned himself. They were both edgy enough.

"Did he ever threaten you?"

"No."

"Abuse you?"

She gave a tired laugh. "No. No. You're trying to make him into the bad guy, Boyd, and it won't play. We were simply two people who made a mistake because we got married before we knew what we wanted."

Thoughtful, Boyd scooped eggs onto her plate. "Sometimes people hold resentments without even being aware of it. Then one day they bust loose."

"He didn't resent me." Sitting, she picked up a piece of bacon. She studied it as she broke it in two. "He never cared enough for that. That's the sad, sad truth." She smiled, but there wasn't a trace of humor in her eyes. "You see, he thought I was like the woman he heard on the radio—seductive, sophisticated, sexy. He wanted that kind of woman in bed. And outside the bedroom he wanted a well-groomed, well-mannered, attentive woman to make his home. I was neither." She shrugged and dropped the bacon on her plate again. "Since he wasn't the attentive, reliable and understanding man I thought he was, we both lost out. We had a very quiet, very civilized divorce, shook hands and went our separate ways."

"If there was nothing more to it, why are you still raw?"

She looked up then, eyes somber. "You've never been married, have you?"

"No."

"Then I couldn't begin to explain. If you want to run a check on Paul, you go ahead, but it's a waste of time. I can guarantee he hasn't given me a thought since I left Atlanta."

He doubted that any man who had ever been close to her would be able to push her completely out of his mind, but he would let that ride for the moment. "You're letting your eggs get cold."

"I told you I don't eat breakfast."

"Humor me." He reached over, scooped up a forkful of eggs from her plate and held them to her lips.

"You're a pest," she said after she swallowed them. "Don't you have to check in or something?"

"I already did—last night, after you went up to bed."

She toyed with the food on her plate, eating a bite or two to keep him from nagging her. He had stayed, she reminded herself, long after his duty shift was over. She owed him for that. And she always paid her debts.

"Look, I appreciate you hanging around, and I know it's your job to ask all kinds of personal and embarrassing questions. But I really want you to leave Deb out of it."

"As much as I can."

"Spring break's coming up. I'm going to try to convince her to head for the beach."

"Good luck." He sipped, watching her over the rim of his mug. "You might pull it off if you went with her."

"I'm not running from this." After pushing her half-eaten breakfast aside, she rested her elbows on the table. "After the call this morning, I was pretty close to doing just that. I thought about it—and after I did I realized it's not going to stop until I figure it out. I want my life back, and that's not going to happen until we know who he is and why he's after me."

"It's my job to find him."

"I know. That's why I've decided to cooperate."

He set his mug aside. "Have you?"

"That's right. From now on, my life's an open book. You ask, I'll answer."

"And you'll do exactly what you're told?"

"No." She smiled. "But I'll do exactly what I'm told if it seems reasonable." She surprised them both by reaching over to touch his hand. "You look tired, Slick. Rough night?"

"I've had better." He linked his fingers with hers before she could withdraw them. "You look damn good in the morning, Cilla."

There it was again—that fluttering that started in her chest and drifted down to her stomach. "A little while ago you said I looked like hell."

"I changed my mind. Before I clock in I'd like to talk to you about last night. About you and me."

"That's not a good idea."

"No, it's not." But he didn't release her hand. "I'm a cop, and you're my assignment. There's no getting around that." She nearly managed a relieved breath before he continued. "Any more than there's any getting around the fact that I want you so much it hurts."

She went very still, so still she could hear the sound of her own heartbeat drumming in her head. Very slowly she moved her eyes, only her eyes, until they met his. They were not so calm now, she thought. There was a fire there, barely banked. It was exciting, terrifyingly exciting.

"Lousy timing," he continued when she didn't speak. "But I figure you can't always pick the right time and the right place. I'm going to do my job, but I think you should know I'm having trouble being objective. If you want someone else assigned to you, you'd better say so now."

"No." She answered too quickly, and she forced herself to backtrack. "I don't think I'm up to breaking in a new cop." Keep it light, she warned herself. "I'm not crazy about having one at all, but I'm almost used to you." She caught herself gnawing on her thumbnail and hastily dropped her hand into her lap. "As for the rest, we're not children. We can…handle it."

He knew he shouldn't expect her to admit the wanting wasn't all one-sided. So he would wait a little while longer.

When he rose, she sprang up so quickly that he laughed. "I'm going to do the dishes, O'Roarke, not jump on you."

"I'll do them." She could have kicked herself. "One cooks, one cleans. O'Roarke rules."

"Fine. You've got a remote at noon, right?"

"How did you know?"

"I checked your schedule. Leave enough time for us to drop by my place so I can shower and change."

"I'm going to be in a mall with dozens of people," she began. "I don't think—"

"I do." With that, he left her alone.

Boyd was lounging on the couch with the paper and a last cup of coffee when Cilla came downstairs. He glanced over, and the casual comment he'd been about to make about her being quick to change died before it reached his tongue. He was glad he was sitting down.

She wore red. Vivid, traffic-stopping red. The short leather skirt was snug at the hips and stopped at midthigh. The jeans she usually wore hadn't given him a true measure of how long her legs were, or how shapely. The matching jacket crossed over her body to side snaps at the waist. It made him wonder what she was wearing beneath it.

She'd done something to her hair. It was still tumbled, but more artfully, and certainly more alluringly. And her face, he noted as he finally stood. She'd fiddled with that, as well—enough to highlight her cheekbones, accent her eyes, slicken her lips.

"Stupid," she muttered as she struggled with an earring. "I can never figure out why hanging things from your ears is supposed to be attractive." On a sigh, she stared down at the dangling columns and the little gold back in her palm. "Either these are defective or I am. Are you any good at this?"

She walked over to him, her hand held out. Her scent was wheeling in his head. "At what?"

"Putting these in. I don't wear them for weeks at a time, so I've never really gotten the hang of it. Give me a hand, will you?"

He was concentrating on breathing, nice, slow, even breaths. "You want me to put that on for you?"

She rolled her eyes impatiently. "You catch on fast, Slick." She thrust the earring into his hand, then tucked the hair behind her right ear. "You just slide the post through, then fasten the little doodad on the back. That's the part I have trouble with."

He muttered something, then bent to the task. There

was a pressure in his chest, and it was building. He knew he would never get that scent out of his system. Swearing softly, he struggled to pinch the tiny fastening with his fingertips.

"This is a stupid system."

"Yeah." She could barely speak. She'd known the minute he touched her that she'd made an enormous mistake. Bursts of sensations, flashes of images, were rushing into her. All she could do was stand still and pray he'd hurry up and finish.

The back of his thumb brushed up and down over her jaw. His fingertips grazed the sensitive area behind her ear. His breath fluttered warm against her skin until she had to bite back a moan.

She lifted an unsteady hand. "Listen, why don't we just forget it?"

"I've got it." Letting out a long breath, he stepped back an inch. He was a wreck. But some of the tension eased when he looked at her and saw that she was far from unaffected. He managed to smile then and flicked a finger over the swaying gold columns. "We'll have to try that again…when we've got more time."

Since no response she could think of seemed safe, she gave none. Instead, she retrieved his coat and her own from the closet. She set his aside and waited while he slipped into his shoulder holster. Watching him give his weapon a quick, routine check brought back memories she wanted to avoid, so she looked away. Pulling open the door, she stepped into the sunlight and left him to follow when he was ready.

He made no comment when he joined her.

"Do you mind if I tune the station in?" she asked as they settled into his car.

"It's on memory. Number three."

Pleased, she turned it on. The morning team was chattering away, punctuating their jokes with sound effects. They plugged an upcoming concert, promised to give another pair of tickets away during the next hour, then invited the listening audience to the mall to see Cilla O'Roarke live and in person.

"She'll be giving away albums, T-shirts and concert tickets," Frantic Fred announced.

"Come on, Fred," his partner broke in. "You know those guys out there don't care about a couple of T-shirts. They want to—" he made loud, panting noises "—see Cilla." There was a chorus of wolf whistles, growls and groans.

"Cute," Boyd muttered, but Cilla only chuckled.

"They're supposed to be obnoxious," she pointed out. "People like absurdity in the morning when they're dragging themselves out of bed or fighting traffic. Last quarter's Arbitron ratings showed them taking over twenty-four percent of the target audience."

"I guess you get a kick out of hearing some guy pant over you."

"Hey, I live for it." Too amused to be offended, she settled back. He certainly had a nice car for a cop. Some sporty foreign job that still smelled new. She was never any good with makes and models. "Come on, Slick, it's part of the act."

He caught himself before he could speak again. He was making a fool of himself. His own investigation had verified that both morning men were married, with tidy homes in the suburbs. Frantic Fred and his wife were expecting their first child. Both men had been with KHIP for nearly three years, and he'd found no cross-reference between their pasts and Cilla's.

Relaxing as the music began, Cilla gazed out the window. The day promised to be warm and sunny. Perhaps this would be the first hint of spring. And her first spring in Colorado. She had a weakness for the season, for watching the leaves bud and grow, the flowers bloom.

Yet in spring she would always think of Georgia. The magnolias, the camellias, the wisterias. All those heady scents.

She remembered a spring when she'd been five or six. Planting peonies with her father on a warm Saturday morning while the radio counted down the Top 40 hits of the week. Hearing the birds without really listening, feeling the damp earth under her hands. He'd told her they would bloom spring after spring and that she would be able to see them from her window.

She wondered if they were still there—if whoever lived in that house cared for them.

"Cilla?"

She snapped back. "What?"

"Are you all right?"

"Sure, I'm fine." She focused on her surroundings. There were big trees that would shade in the summer, trimmed hedges for privacy. A long, gently sloping hill led to a graceful three-story house fashioned from stone and wood. Dozens of tall, slender windows winked in the sunlight. "Where are we?"

"My house. I've got to change, remember?"

"Your house?" she repeated.

"Right. Everyone has to live somewhere."

True enough, she thought as she pushed the door

open. But none of the cops she had ever known had lived so well. A long look around showed her that the neighborhood was old, established and wealthy. A country-club neighborhood.

Disconcerted, she followed Boyd up a stone path to an arched door outlined in etched glass.

Inside, the foyer was wide, the floors a gleaming cherry, the ceilings vaulted. On the walls were paintings by prominent twentieth-century artists. A sweep of stairway curved up to the second floor.

"Well," she said. "And I thought you were an honest cop."

"I am." He slipped the coat from her shoulders to toss it over the railing.

She had no doubts as to his honesty, but the house and all it represented made her nervous. "And I suppose you inherited all this from a rich uncle."

"Grandmother." Taking her arm, he led her through a towering arch. The living room was dominated by a stone fireplace topped with a heavy carved mantel. But the theme of the room was light, with a trio of windows set in each outside wall.

There was a scattering of antiques offset by modern sculpture. She could see what she thought was a dining room through another arch.

"That must have been some grandmother."

"She was something. She ran Fletcher Industries until she hit seventy."

"And what is Fletcher Industries?"

He shrugged. "Family business. Real estate, cattle, mining."

"Mining." She blew out a breath. "Like gold?"

"Among other things."

She linked her fingers together to keep from biting her nails. "So why aren't you counting your gold instead of being a cop?"

"I like being a cop." He took her restless hand in his. "Something wrong?"

"No. You'd better change. I have to be there early to prep."

"I won't be long."

She waited until he had gone before she sank onto one of the twin sofas. Fletcher Industries, she thought. It sounded important. Even prominent. After digging in her bag for a cigarette, she studied the room again.

Elegant, tasteful, easily rich. And way out of her league.

It had been difficult enough when she'd believed they were on fairly equal terms. She didn't like to admit it, but the thought had been there, in the back of her mind, that maybe, just maybe, there could be a relationship between them. No, a friendship. She could never be seriously involved with someone in law enforcement.

But he wasn't just a cop now. He was a rich cop. His name was probably listed on some social register. People who lived in houses like this usually had Roman numerals after their names.

Boyd Fletcher III.

She was just Priscilla Alice O'Roarke, formerly from a backwater town in Georgia that wasn't even a smudge on the map. True, she had made something of herself, by herself. But you never really pulled out your roots.

Rising, she walked over to toss her cigarette in the fireplace.

She wished he would hurry. She wanted to get out

of this house, get back to work. She wanted to forget about the mess her life was suddenly in.

She had to think about herself. Where she was going. How she was going to get through the long days and longer nights until her life was settled again. She didn't have the time, she couldn't afford the luxury of exploring her feelings for Boyd. Whatever she had felt, or thought she was feeling, was best ignored.

If ever there were two people more mismatched, she couldn't imagine them. Perhaps he had stirred something in her, touched something she'd thought could never be touched again. It meant nothing. It only proved that she was alive, still functioning as a human being. As a woman.

It would begin and end there.

The minute whoever was threatening her was caught, they would go their separate ways, back to their separate lives. Whatever closeness they had now was born of necessity. When the necessity passed, they would move apart and forget. Nothing, she reminded herself, lasted forever.

She was standing by the windows when he came back. The light was in her hair, on her face. He had never imagined her there, but somehow, when he looked, when he saw her, he knew he'd wanted her there.

It left him shaken, it left him aching to see how perfectly she fit into his home. Into his life. Into his dreams.

She would argue about that, he thought. She would struggle and fight and run like hell if he gave her the chance. He smiled as he crossed to her. He just wouldn't give her the chance.

"Cilla."

Startled, she whirled around. "Oh. I didn't hear you. I was—"

The words were swallowed by a gasp as he yanked her against him and imprisoned her mouth.

Earthquakes, floods, wild winds. How could she have known that a kiss could be grouped with such devastating natural disasters?

She didn't want this. She wanted it more than she wanted to breathe. She had to push him away. She pulled him closer. It was wrong, it was madness. It was right, it was beautifully mad.

As she pressed against him, as her mouth answered each frenzied demand, she knew that everything she had tried to convince herself of only moments before was a lie. What need was there to explore her feelings when they were all swimming to the surface?

She needed him. However much that might terrify her, for now the knowledge and the acceptance flowed through her like wine. It seemed she had waited a lifetime to need like this. To feel like this. Trembling and strong, dazed and clear-eyed, pliant and taut as a wire.

His hands whispered over the leather as he molded her against him. Couldn't she see how perfectly they fitted? He wanted to hear her say it, to hear her moan it, that she wanted him as desperately as he wanted her.

She did moan as he drew her head back to let his lips race down her throat. The thudding of her pulse heated the fragrance she'd dabbed there. Groaning as it tangled in his senses, he dragged at the snaps of her jacket. Beneath he found nothing but Cilla.

She arched back, her breath catching in her throat as he captured her breasts. At his touch it seemed they filled with some hot, heavy liquid. When her knees buckled, she gripped his shoulders for balance, shuddering as his thumbs teased her nipples into hard, aching peaks.

Mindlessly she reached for him, diving into a deep, intimate kiss that had each of them swaying. She tugged at his jacket, desperate to touch him as he touched her. Her hand slid over the leather of his holster and found his weapon.

It was like a slap, like a splash of ice water. As if burned, she snatched her hand away and jerked back. Unsteady, she pressed the palm of her hand against a table and shook her head.

"This is a mistake." She paced her words slowly, as if she were drunk. "I don't want to get involved."

"Too late." He felt as if he'd slammed full tilt into a wall.

"No." With deliberate care, she snapped her jacket again. "It's not too late. I have a lot on my mind. So do you."

He struggled for the patience that had always been part of his nature. For the first time in days he actively craved a cigarette. "And?"

"And nothing. I think we should go."

He didn't move toward her or away, but simply held up a hand. "Before we do, are you going to tell me you don't feel anything?"

She made herself look at him. "It would be stupid to pretend I'm not attracted to you. You already know you affect me."

"I want to bring you back here tonight."

She shook her head. She couldn't afford, even for an instant, to imagine what it would be like to be with him. "I can't. There are reasons."

"You've already told me there isn't anyone else." He stepped toward her now, but he didn't touch her. "If there was, I wouldn't give a damn."

"This has nothing to do with other men. It has to do with me."

"Exactly. Why don't you tell me what you're afraid of?"

"I'm afraid of picking up the phone." It was true, but it wasn't the reason. "I'm afraid of going to sleep, and I'm afraid of waking up."

He touched her then, just a fingertip to her cheek. "I know what you're going through, and believe me, I'd do anything to make it go away. But we both know that's not the reason you're backing away from me."

"I have others."

"Give me one."

Annoyed, she walked over to grab her purse. "You're a cop."

"And?"

She tossed her head up. "So was my mother." Before he could speak, she was striding back into the foyer to get her coat.

"Cilla—"

"Just back off, Boyd. I mean it." She shoved her arms into her coat. "I can't afford to get churned up like this before a show. For God's sake, my life's screwed up enough right now without this. If you can't let it alone, I'll call your captain and tell him I want someone else assigned. Now you can take me to the mall or I can call a cab."

One more push and she'd be over the edge, he thought. This wasn't the time for her to take that tumble. "I'll take you," he said. "And I'll back off. For now."

Chapter 6

He was a man of his word, Cilla decided. For the rest of that day, and all of the next, they discussed nothing that didn't relate directly to the case.

He wasn't distant. Far from it. He stuck with her throughout her remote at the mall, subtly screening all the fans who approached her for a word or an autograph, all the winners who accepted their T-shirts or their albums.

It even seemed to Cilla that he enjoyed himself. He browsed through the record racks, buying from the classical, pop and jazz sections, chatted with the engineer about baseball and kept her supplied with a steady supply of cold soft drinks in paper cups.

He talked, but she noted that he didn't talk *to* her, not the way she'd become accustomed to. They certainly had conversations, polite and impersonal conversations.

And not once, not even in the most casual of ways, did he touch her.

In short, he treated her exactly the way she'd thought she wanted to be treated. As an assignment, and nothing more.

While he seemed to take the afternoon in stride, even offering to buy her a burger between the end of the remote and the time she was expected back in the studio, she was certain she'd never spent a more miserable afternoon in her life.

It was Althea who sat with her in the booth over her next two shifts, and it was Althea who monitored the calls. Why Boyd's silence, and his absence, made it that much more difficult for her to concentrate, Cilla couldn't have said.

It was probably some new strategy, she decided as she worked. He was ignoring her so that she would break down and make the first move. Well, she wouldn't. She hit her audience with Bob Seger's latest gritty rock single and stewed.

She'd wanted their relationship to be strictly professional, and he was accommodating her. But he didn't have to make it seem so damned easy.

Undoubtedly what had happened between them—or what had almost happened between them—hadn't really meant that much to him. That was all for the best. She would get over it. Whatever it was. The last thing she needed in her life was a cop with a lazy smile who came from a moneyed background.

She wished to God she could go five minutes without thinking about him.

While Cilla juggled turntables, Althea worked a crossword puzzle. She had always been able to sit for hours at a time in contented silence as long as she could exercise her mind. Cilla O'Roarke, she mused, was a different matter. The woman hadn't mastered the fine art of relaxation. Althea filled the squares with her neat, precise printing and thought that Boyd was just the man to teach her how it was done.

Right now, Cilla was bursting to talk. Not to ask questions, Althea thought. She hadn't missed the quick disappointment on Cilla's face when Boyd hadn't been the one to drive her to the station for her night shift.

She's dying to ask me where he is and what he's doing, Althea thought as she filled in the next word. But she doesn't want me to think it matters.

It wasn't possible for her not to smile to herself. Boyd had been pretty closemouthed himself lately. Althea knew he had run a more detailed check on Cilla's background and that he had found answers that disturbed him. Personally, she thought. Whatever he had discovered had nothing to do with the case or he would have shared it with his partner.

But, no matter how close they were, their privacy was deeply respected. She didn't question him. If and when he wanted to talk it through, she would be there for him. As he would be there for her.

It was too bad, she decided, that when sexual tension reared its head, men and women lost that easy camaraderie.

Abruptly Cilla pushed away from the console. "I'm going to get some coffee. Do you want some?"

"Doesn't Nick usually bring some in?"

"He's got the night off."

"Why don't I get it?"

"No." Restlessness seemed to vibrate from her. "I've

got nearly seven minutes before the tape ends. I want to stretch my legs."

"All right."

Cilla walked to the lounge. Billy had already been there, she noted. The floor gleamed, and the coffee mugs were washed and stacked. There was the lingering scent of the pine cleaner he always used so lavishly.

She poured two cups and as an afterthought stuck one leftover and rapidly hardening pastry in her pocket.

With a cup in each hand, she turned. In the doorway she saw the shadow of a man. And the silver gleam of a knife. With a scream, she sent the mugs flying. Crockery smashed and shattered.

"Miss O'Roarke?" Billy took a hesitant step into the light.

"Oh, God." She pressed the heel of one hand to her chest as if to force out the air trapped there. "Billy. I thought you were gone."

"I—" He stumbled back against the door when Althea came flying down the hallway, her weapon drawn. In an automatic response, he threw his hands up. "Don't shoot. Don't. I didn't do nothing."

"It's my fault," Cilla said quickly. She stepped over to put a reassuring hand on Billy's arm. "I didn't know anyone was here, and I turned around—" She covered her face with her hands. "I'm sorry," she managed, dropping them again. "I overreacted. I didn't know Billy was still in the station."

"Mr. Harrison had a lunch meeting in his office." He spoke quickly, his eyes darting from Althea to Cilla. "I was just getting to it." He swallowed audibly. "Lots of—lots of knives and forks left over."

Cilla stared at the handful of flatware he held and

felt like a fool. "I'm sorry, Billy. I must have scared you to death. And I've made a mess of your floor."

"That's okay." He grinned at her, relaxing slowly as Althea holstered her weapon. "I'll clean it right up. Good show tonight, Miss O'Roarke." He tapped the headphones that he'd slid around his neck. "You going to play any fifties stuff? You know I like that the best."

"Sure." Fighting nausea, she made herself smile. "I'll pick something out just for you."

He beamed at her. "You'll say my name on the air?"

"You bet. I've got to get back."

She hurried back to the booth, grateful that Althea was giving her a few moments alone. Things were getting pretty bad when she started jumping at middle-aged maintenance men holding dinner knives.

The best way to get through the nerves was to work, she told herself. Keeping her moves precise, she began to set up for what she called the "power hour" between eleven and midnight.

When Althea came back, bearing coffee, Cilla was inviting her audience to stay tuned for more music. "We've got ten hits in a row coming up. This first one's for my pal Billy. We're going back, way back, all the way back to 1958. It ain't Dennis Quaid. It's the real, the original, the awesome Jerry Lee Lewis with 'Great Balls of Fire.'"

After pulling off her headphones, she gave Althea a wan smile. "I really am sorry."

"In your place I probably would have gone through the roof." Althea offered her a fresh mug. "Been a lousy couple of weeks, huh?"

"The lousiest."

"We're going to get him, Cilla."

"I'm hanging on to that." She chose another record, took her time cuing it up. "What made you become a cop?"

"I guess I wanted to be good at something. This was it."

"Do you have a husband?"

"No." Althea wasn't sure where the questions were leading. "A lot of men are put off when a woman carries a gun." She hesitated, then decided to take the plunge. "You might have gotten the impression that there's something between Boyd and me."

"It's hard not to." Cilla lifted a hand for silence, then opened the mike to link the next song. "You two seem well suited."

As if considering it, Althea sat and sipped at her coffee. "You know, I wouldn't have figured you for the type to fall into the clichéd, sexist mind-set that says that if a man and woman work together they must be playing together."

"I didn't." Outraged, Cilla all but came out of her chair. At Althea's bland smile, she subsided. "I did," she admitted. Then her lips curved. "Kind of. I guess you've had to handle that tired line quite a bit."

"No more than you, I imagine." She gestured, both hands palms out, at the confines of the studio. "An attractive woman in what some conceive of as a man's job."

Even that small patch of common ground helped her to relax. "There was a jock in Richmond who figured I was dying to, ah…spin on his turntable."

Understanding and amusement brightened Althea's eyes. "How'd you handle it?"

"During my show I announced that he was hard up for dates and anyone interested should call the station during his shift." She grinned, remembering. "It cooled him off." She turned to her mike to plug the upcoming request line. After an update on the weather, a time check and an intro for the next record, she slipped her headphones off again. "I guess Boyd wouldn't be as easily discouraged."

"Not on your life. He's stubborn. He likes to call it patience, but it's plain mule-headed stubbornness. He can be like a damn bulldog."

"I've noticed."

"He's a nice man, Cilla, one of the best. If you're really not interested, you should make it clear up front. Boyd's stubborn, but he's not obnoxious."

"I don't want to be interested," Cilla murmured. "There's a difference."

"Like night and day. Listen, if the question's too personal, tell me to shut up."

A smile tugged at Cilla's mouth. "You don't have to tell me that twice."

"Okay. Why don't you want to be interested?"

Cilla chose a compact disc, then backed it up with two 45s. "He's a cop."

"So if he was an insurance salesman you'd want to be interested?"

"Yes. No." She let out a huff of breath. Sometimes it was best to be honest. "It would be easier. Then there's the fact that I made a mess of the one serious relationship I've had."

"All by yourself?"

"Mostly." She sent out the cut from the CD. "I'm more comfortable concentrating on my life, and Deborah's. My work and her future."

"You're not the type that would be happy for long with comfortable."

"Maybe not." She stared down at the phone. "But I'd settle for it right now."

So she was running scared, Althea thought as she watched Cilla work. Who wouldn't be? It had to be terrifying to be hounded and threatened by some faceless, nameless man. Yet she was handling it, Althea thought, better than she was handling Boyd and her feelings about him.

She had them, buckets of them. Apparently she just didn't know what to do with them.

Althea kept her silence as the calls began to come in. Cilla was afraid of the phone, afraid of what might be on the other end. But she answered, call after call, moving through them with what sounded like effortless style. If Althea hadn't been in the studio, watching the strain tighten Cilla's face, she would have been totally fooled.

She gave them their music and a few moments of her time. If her hand was unsteady, her finger still pushed the illuminated button.

Boyd had entered her life to protect it, not threaten it. Yet she was afraid of him. With a sigh, Althea wondered why it was that women's lives could be so completely turned upside down by the presence of a man.

If she ever fell in love herself—which so far she'd had the good sense to avoid—she would simply find a way to call the shots.

The tone of Cilla's voice had her snapping back. Recognizing the fear, sympathizing with it, Althea rose to massage her rigid shoulders.

"Keep him talking," she whispered. "Keep him on as long as you can."

Cilla blocked out what he said. She'd found it helped her keep sane if she ignored the vicious threats, the blood-chilling promises. Instead she kept her eye on the elapsed-time clock, grimly pleased when she saw that the one-minute mark had passed and he was still on the line.

She questioned him, forcing herself to keep her voice calm and even. He liked it best when she lost control, she knew. He would keep threatening until she began to beg. Then he would cut her off, satisfied that he had broken her again.

Tonight she struggled not to hear, just to watch the seconds tick away.

"I haven't hurt you," she said. "You know I haven't done anything to you."

"To him." He hissed the words. "He's dead, and it's because of you."

"Who did I hurt? If you'd tell me his name, I—"

"I want you to remember. I want you to say his name before I kill you."

She shut her eyes and tried to fill her head with sound as he described exactly how he intended to kill her.

"He must have been very important to you. You must have loved him."

"He was everything to me. All I had. He was so young. He had his whole life. But you hurt him. You betrayed him. An eye for an eye. Your life for his. Soon. Very soon."

When he cut her off, she turned quickly to send out the next record. She would backsell it, Cilla told herself. Her voice would be strong again afterward. Ignoring the other blinking lights, she pulled out a cigarette.

"They got a trace." Althea replaced the receiver,

then moved over to put a hand on Cilla's shoulder. "They got a trace. You did a hell of a job tonight, Cilla."

"Yeah." She closed her eyes. Now all she had to do was get through the next hour and ten minutes. "Will they catch him?"

"We'll know soon. This is the first real break we've had. Just hang on to that."

She wanted to be relieved. Cilla leaned back as Althea drove her home and wondered why she couldn't accept this step as a step forward. They had traced the call. Didn't that mean they would know where he lived? They would have a name, and they would put a face, a person, together with that name.

She would go and see him. She would make herself do that. She would look at that face, into those eyes, and try to find a link between him and whatever she had done in the past to incite that kind of hate.

Then she would try to live with it.

She spotted Boyd's car at the curb in front of her house. He stood on the walk, his coat unbuttoned. Though the calendar claimed it was spring, the night was cold enough for her to see his breath. But not his eyes.

Cilla took a firm grip on the door handle, pushed it open. He waited as she moved up the walk toward him.

"Let's go inside."

"I want to know." She saw his eyes now and understood. "You didn't get him."

"No." He glanced toward his partner. Althea saw the frustration held under grim control.

"What happened?"

"It was a phone booth a couple miles from the station. No prints. He'd wiped it clean."

Struggling to hold on for a few more minutes, Cilla nodded. "So we're no closer."

"Yes, we are." He took her hand to warm it in his. "He made his first mistake. He'll make another."

Weary, she looked over her shoulder. Was it just her overworked nerves, or was he out there somewhere, in the shadows, close enough to see? Near enough to hear?

"Come on, let me take you inside. You're cold."

"I'm all right." She couldn't let him come with her. She needed to let go, and for that she needed privacy. "I don't want to talk about any of this tonight. I just want to go to bed. Althea, thanks for the ride, and everything else." She walked quickly to the front door and let herself inside.

"She just needs to work this out," Althea said, placing a hand on his arm.

He wanted to swear, to smash something with his hands. Instead, he stared at the closed door. "She doesn't want to let me help her."

"No, she doesn't." She watched the light switch on upstairs. "Want me to call for a uniform to stake out the house?"

"No, I'll hang around."

"You're off duty, Fletcher."

"Right. We can consider this personal."

"Want some company?"

He shook his head. "No. You need some sleep."

Althea hesitated, then let out a quiet sigh. "You take the first shift. I sleep better in a car than a bed, anyway."

There was a light frost that glittered like glass on the lawn. Cilla sighed as she studied it through her bedroom window. In Georgia the azaleas would be blooming. It had been years, more years than she could remember, since she had yearned for home. In that chill Colorado morning she wondered if she had made a mistake traveling more than halfway across the country and leaving all those places, all those memories of her childhood, behind.

Letting the curtain fall again, she stepped back. She had more to think about than an April frost. She had also seen Boyd's car, still parked at the curb.

Thinking of him, she took more time and more care dressing than was her habit. Not for a moment had she changed her mind about it being unwise to become involved with him. But it seemed it was a mistake she'd already made. The wisdom to face up to her mistakes was something she'd learned very early.

She smoothed her plum-colored cashmere sweater over her hips. It had been a Christmas present from Deborah, and it was certainly more stylish, with its high neck and its generous sleeves, than most of the clothes Cilla chose for herself. She wore it over snug black leggings and on impulse struggled with a pair of star-shaped earrings in glossy silver.

He was spread comfortably over her couch, the newspaper open, a mug of coffee steaming in his hand. His shirt was carelessly unbuttoned to the middle of his chest and wrinkled from being worn all night. His jacket was tossed over the back of the couch, but he still wore his shoulder holster.

She had never known anyone who could melt into his surroundings so easily. At the moment he looked as though he spent every morning of his life in that spot, in her spot, lazily perusing the sports page and drinking a second cup of coffee.

He looked up at her. Though he didn't smile, his utter relaxation was soothing. "Good morning."

"Good morning." Feeling awkward, she crossed to him. She wasn't certain whether she should begin with an apology or an explanation.

"Deborah let me in."

She nodded, then immediately wished she'd worn trousers with pockets. There was nothing to do with her hands but link them together. "You've been here all night."

"Just part of the service."

"You slept in your car."

He tilted his head. Her tone was very close to an accusation. "It wasn't the first time."

"I'm sorry." On a long, shaky breath, she sat on the coffee table across from him. Their knees bumped. He found it a friendly gesture. One of the friendliest she'd made with him. "I should have let you inside. I should have known you would stay. I guess I was—"

"Upset." He passed her his coffee. "You were entitled, Cilla."

"Yeah." She sipped, wincing a bit at the added sugar. "I guess I'd talked myself into believing that you were going to catch him last night. It even—it's weird, but it even unnerved me a bit thinking about finally seeing him, finally knowing the whole story. Then, when we got here and you told me… I couldn't talk about it. I just couldn't."

"It's okay."

Her laugh was only a little strained. "Do you have to be so nice to me?"

"Probably not." Reaching out, he touched her cheek. "Would you feel better if I yelled at you?"

"Maybe." Unable to resist, she lifted a hand to his. "I have an easier time fighting than I do being reasonable."

"I've noticed. Have you ever considered taking a day, just to relax?"

"Not really."

"How about today?"

"I was going to catch up with my paperwork. And I have to call a plumber. We've got a leak under the sink." She let her hand fall to her knees, where it moved restlessly. "It's my turn to do the laundry. Tonight I'm spinning records at this class reunion downtown. Bob and Jim are splitting my shift."

"I heard."

"These reunion things…they can get pretty wild." She was groping, feeling more foolish by the minute. He'd taken the empty cup and set it aside, and was now holding both of her hands lightly in his. "They can be a lot of fun, though. Maybe you'd like to come and… hang around."

"Are you asking me to come and…hang around, like on a date?"

"I'll be working," she began, then subsided. She was getting in deep. "Yes. Sort of."

"Okay. Can I sort of pick you up?"

"By seven," she said. "I have to be there early enough to set up."

"Let's make it six, then. We can have some dinner first."

"I…" Deeper and deeper. "All right. Boyd, I have to tell you something."

"I'm listening."

"I still don't want to get involved. Not seriously."

"Mmm-hmm."

"You're completely wrong for me."

"That's just one more thing we disagree on." He held her still when she started to rise. "Don't pace, Cilla. Just take a couple of deep breaths."

"I think it's important we understand up front how far this can go, and what limitations there are."

"Are we going to have a romance, Cilla, or a business arrangement?"

He smiled. She frowned.

"I don't think we should call it a romance."

"Why not?"

"Because it's…because a romance has implications."

He struggled against another smile. She wouldn't appreciate the fact that she amused him. "What kind of implications?" Slowly, watching her, he brought her hand to his lips.

"Just…" His mouth brushed over her knuckles, and then, when her fingers went limp, he turned her palm up to press a kiss to its center.

"Just?" he prompted.

"Implications. Boyd—" She shivered when his teeth grazed over her wrist.

"Is that all you wanted to tell me?"

"No. Can you stop that?"

"If I really put my mind to it."

She found that her own lips had curved. "Well, put your mind to it. I can't think."

"Dangerous words." But he stopped nibbling.

"I'm trying to be serious."

"So am I." Once again he stopped her from rising. "Try that deep breath."

"Right." She did, then plunged on. "Last night, when

I lay down in the dark, I was afraid. I kept hearing him, hearing that voice, everything he'd said to me. Over and over. I knew I couldn't think of it. If I did, I'd go crazy. So I thought of you." She paused, waiting for the courage to go on. "And when I thought of you, it blocked out everything else. And I wasn't afraid."

His fingers tightened on hers. Her eyes were steady, but he saw that her lips trembled once before she pressed them together. She was waiting, he knew. To see what he would do, what he would say. She couldn't have known, couldn't have had any idea, that at that moment, at that one instant of time, he teetered off the edge he'd been walking and tumbled into love with her.

And if he told her that, he thought as he felt the shock of the emotions vibrate through him, she would never believe it. Some women had to be shown, convinced, not merely told. Cilla was one of them.

Slowly he rose, drawing her up with him. He gathered her close, cradling her head on his shoulder, wrapping his arms around her. He could feel her shiver of relief as he kept the embrace quiet and undemanding.

It was just what she needed. How was it he seemed always to know? To be held, only held, without words, without promises. To feel the solid warmth of his body against her, the firm grip of his hands, the steady beat of his heart.

"Boyd?"

"Yeah." He turned his head just enough to kiss her hair.

"Maybe I don't mind you being nice to me after all."

"We'll give it a trial run."

She thought she might as well go all the way with it. "And maybe I've missed having you around."

It was his turn to take a deep breath and steady himself. "Listen." He slid his hands up to her shoulders. "I've got some calls to make. After, why don't I take a look at that leak?"

She smiled. "I can look at it, Slick. What I want is to have it fixed."

He leaned forward and bit her lower lip. "Just get me a wrench."

Two hours later, Cilla had her monthly finances spread out over the secondhand oak desk in the den that doubled as her office. There were two dollars and fifty-three cents lost somewhere in her checkbook, an amount she was determined to find before she paid the neat stack of bills to her right.

Her sense of order was something she'd taught herself, something she'd clung to during the lean years, the unhappy years, the stormy years. If amid any crisis she could maintain this small island of normalcy, however bland, she believed she would survive.

"Ah!" She found the error, pounced on it. Making the correction, she scrupulously ran her figures again. Satisfied, she filed away her bank statement, then began writing checks, starting with the mortgage.

Even that gave her an enormous sense of accomplishment. It wasn't rent, it was equity. It was hers. The house was the first thing she had ever owned other than the clothes on her back and the occasional secondhand car.

She'd never been poor, but she had learned, growing up in a family where the income was a combination of a cop's salary and the lean monthly earnings of a public defender, to count pennies carefully. She'd grown up in a rented house, and she'd never known the luxury of riding in a new car. College wouldn't have been impossible, but because of the strain it would have added to her parents' income at a time when their marriage was rocky, Cilla had decided to bypass her education in favor of a job.

She didn't regret it often. She resented it only a little, at odd times. But her ability to subsidize Deborah's partial scholarship made her look back to the time when she had made the decision. It had been the right one.

Now they were slowly creeping their way up. The house wasn't simply an acquisition, it was a statement. Family, home, roots. Every month, when she paid the mortgage, she was grateful she'd been given the chance.

"Cilla?"

"What? Oh." She spotted Boyd in the doorway. She started to speak again, then focused. He still had the wrench she'd given him. His hair was mussed and damp. Both his shirt and his slacks were streaked with wet. He'd rolled his sleeves up to the elbows. Water glistened on his forearms. "Oh," she said again, and choked on a laugh.

"I fixed it." His eyes narrowed as he watched her struggle to maintain her dignity. "Problem?"

"No. No, not a thing." She cleared her throat. "So, you fixed it."

"That's what I said."

She had to bite down on her lip. She recognized a frazzled male ego when she heard it. "That's what you said, all right. And since you've just saved me a bundle, the least I can do is fix you lunch. What do you think about peanut butter and jelly?"

"That it belongs in a plastic lunch box with Spider-man on the outside."

"Well, I've got to tell you, Slick, it's the best thing I cook." Forgetting the bills, she rose. "It's either that or a can of tuna fish." She ran a fingertip down his shirt experimentally. "Did you know you're all wet?"

He held up one grimy hand, thought about it, then went with the impulse and rubbed it all over her face. "Yeah."

She laughed, surprising him. Seducing him. He'd heard that laugh before, over the radio, but not once since he'd met her. It was as low and rich and arousing as black silk.

"Come on, Fletcher, we'll throw that shirt in the wash while you eat your sandwich."

"In a minute." He kept his hand cupped on her chin, pulling her to him with that subtle pressure alone. When his mouth met hers, her lips were still curved. This time, she didn't stiffen, she didn't protest. With a sigh of acceptance, she opened for him, allowing herself to absorb the taste of his mouth, the alluring dance of his tongue over hers.

There was a warmth here that she had forgotten to hope for. The warmth of being with someone who understood her. And cared, she realized as his fingers skimmed over her cheek. Cared, despite her flaws.

"I guess you were right," she murmured.

"Damn right. About what?"

She took a chance, an enormous one for her, and brushed at the hair on his forehead. "It is too late."

"Cilla." He brought his hands to her shoulders again, battling back a clawing need, a ragged desire. "Come upstairs with me. I want to be with you."

His words sent the passion leaping. He could see the fire of it glow in her eyes before she closed them and shook her head. "Give me some time. I'm not playing games here, Boyd, but the ground's pretty shaky and I need to think it through." On a steadying breath, she opened her eyes, and nearly smiled. "You're absolutely everything I swore I'd never fall for."

He brought his hands down to hers and gripped. "Talk to me."

"Not now." But she laced her fingers with his. It was a sign of union that was rare for her. "I'm not ready to dig it all up right now. I'd just like to spend a few hours here like real people. If the phone rings, I'm not going to answer it. If someone comes to the door, I'm going to wait until they go away again. All I want to do is fix you a sandwich and wash your shirt. Okay?"

"Sure." He pressed a kiss to her brow. "It's the best offer I've had in years."

Chapter 7

There was a wall of noise—the backbeat, the bass, the wail of a guitar riff. There were spinning lights, undulating bodies, the clamor of feet. Cilla set the tone with her midnight voice and stood back to enjoy the results. The ballroom was alive with sound—laughter, music, voices raised in spurts of conversation. Cilla had her finger on the controls. She didn't know any of the faces, but it was her party.

Boyd sipped a club soda and politely avoided a none-too-subtle invitation from a six-foot blonde in a skimpy blue dress. He didn't consider this a trial. He'd spent a large portion of his career watching people, and he'd never gotten bored with it.

It was a hell of a party, and he wouldn't have minded a turn on the dance floor. But he preferred keeping his eye on Cilla. There were worse ways to spend the evening.

She presided over a long table at the front of the ballroom, her records stacked, her amps turned up high. She glittered. Her silver-sequined jacket and black stovepipe pants were a whole new look in tuxedos. Her hair was full and loose, and when she turned her head the silver stars at her ears glistened.

She'd already lured dozens of couples onto the dance floor, and they were bopping and swaying elbow to elbow. Others crowded around the edges in groups or loitered at the banquet tables, lingering over drinks and conversation.

The music was loud, hot and fast. He'd already learned that was how she liked it best. As far as he could tell, the class of '75 was having the time of their lives. From all appearances, Cilla was, too.

She was joking with a few members of the graduating class, most of them male. More than a few of them had imbibed freely at the cash bar. But she was handling herself, Boyd noted. Smooth as silk.

He didn't particularly like it when a man with a lineman's chest put a beefy arm around her and squeezed. But Cilla shook her head. Whatever brush-off she used, she sent the guy off with a smile on his face.

"There's more where that came from, boys and girls. Let's take you back, all the way back to prom night, 1975." She cued up the Eagles' "One Of These Nights," then skimmed the crowd for Boyd.

When she spotted him, she smiled. Fully, so that even with the room between them he could see her eyes glow. He wondered if he could manage to get her to look at him like that when they didn't have five hundred people between them. He had to grin when she put a hand to her throat and mimed desperate thirst.

Lord, he looked wonderful, Cilla thought as she watched him turn toward the bar. Strange, she would have thought a smoke-gray jacket would look too conservative on a man for her tastes. On him, it worked. So well, she mused with a wry smile, that half the female portion of the class of '75 had their eye on him.

Tough luck, ladies, she thought. He's mine. At least for tonight.

A little surprised by where her thoughts had landed, she shook herself back and chose a slip from the pile of requests next to the turntable. A nostalgic crowd, she decided and plucked another fifteen-year-old hit from her stack.

She liked working parties, watching people dance and flirt and gossip. The reunion committee had done a top-notch job on this one. Red and white streamers dripped from the ceiling, competing with a hundred matching balloons. The dance floor glittered from the light of a revolving mirror ball. When the music or the mood called for it, she could flick a switch on a strobe light and give them a touch of seventies psychedelia.

Mixed with the scents of perfume and cologne was the fragrance of the fresh flowers that adorned each table.

"This is for Rick and Sue, those high school sweeties who've been married for twelve years. And they said it was only puppy love. We're 'Rockin' All Over The World.'"

"Nice touch," Boyd commented.

She twisted her head and smiled. "Thanks."

He handed her a soft drink heaped with ice. "I've got a reunion coming up next year. You booked?"

"I'll check my schedule. Wow." She watched as a

couple cut loose a few feet away. Other couples spread out as they put the dirty in dirty dancing. "Pretty impressive."

"Mmm. Do you dance?"

"Not like that." She let out a little breath. "I wish I did."

He took her hand before she could reach for another request slip. "Why don't you play one for me?"

"Sure. Name it."

When he poked through her discs, she was too amused to be annoyed. She could reorganize later. After choosing one, he handed it to her.

"Excellent taste." She shifted her mike. "We've got ourselves a wild group tonight. Y'all having fun?" The roar of agreement rolled across the dance floor. "We're going to be here until midnight, pumping out the music for you. We've got a request here for Springsteen. 'Hungry Heart.'"

Fresh dancers streamed onto the floor. Couples twined around each other to sway. Cilla turned to speak to Boyd and found herself molded against him.

"Want to dance?" he murmured.

They already were. Body fitted to body, he took her on a long, erotically slow circle. "I'm working."

"Take five." He lowered his head to catch her chin between his teeth. "Until I make love with you, this is the next best thing."

She was going to object. She was sure of it. But she was moving with him, her body fine-tuned to his. In silent capitulation, she slid her arms around his neck. With their faces close, he smiled. Slowly, firmly, he ran his hands over her hips, up, lazily up to the sides of her breasts, then down again.

She felt as though she'd been struck by lightning. "You've, ah, got some nice moves, Slick."

"Thanks." When their lips were a whisper apart, he shifted, leaving hers hungry as he nuzzled into her neck. "You smell like sin, Cilla. It's just one of the things about you that's been driving me crazy for days."

She wanted him to kiss her. Craved it. She moaned when his hands roamed into her hair, drawing her head back. Her eyes closed in anticipation, but he only brushed those tempting lips over her cheekbone.

Breathless, she clung to him, trying to fight through the fog of pleasure. There were hundreds of people around them, all moving to the erotic beat of the music. She was working, she reminded herself. She was— had always been—a sensible woman, and tonight she had a job to do.

"If you keep this up, I won't be able to work the turntable."

He felt her heart hammering against his. It wasn't enough to satisfy him. But it was enough to give him hope. "Then I guess we'll have to finish the dance later."

When he released her, Cilla turned quickly and chose a record at random. A cheer went up as the beat pounded out. She lifted the hair from the back of her neck to cool it. The press of bodies—or the press of one body—had driven the temperature up. She'd never realized what a dangerous pastime dancing could be.

"Want another drink?" Boyd asked when she drained her glass.

"No. I'm okay." Steadying herself, she reached for the request sheet on top of her pile. "This is a nice group," she said as she glanced across the room. "I like reunions."

"I think I figured that out."

"Well, I do. I like the continuity of them. I like seeing all these people who shared the same experience, the same little block of time. 1975," she mused, the paper dangling from her fingers. "Not the greatest era for music, with the dreaded disco onslaught, but there were a few bright lights. The Doobie Brothers were still together. So were the Eagles."

"Do you always measure time in rock and roll?"

She had to laugh. "Occupational hazard. Anyway, it's a good barometer." Tossing her hair back, she grinned at him. "The first record I spun, as a professional, was the Stones' 'Emotional Rescue.' That was the year Reagan was elected the first time, the year John Lennon was shot—and the year the Empire struck back."

"Not bad, O'Roarke."

"It's better than not bad." She considered him. "I bet you remember what was playing on the radio the first time you talked a girl into the back seat of your car."

"'Dueling Banjos.'"

"You're kidding."

"You asked."

She was chuckling as she opened the request sheet. Her laughter died. She thought for a moment her heart had stopped. Carefully she squeezed her eyes shut. But when she opened them again the boldly printed words remained.

I want you to scream when I kill you.

"Cilla?"

With a brisk shake of her head, she passed the note to Boyd.

He was here, she thought, panic clawing as she searched the room. Somewhere in this crowd of laughing, chattering couples, he was watching. And waiting.

He'd come close. Close enough to lay that innocent-looking slip of paper on her table. Close enough to look into her eyes, maybe to smile. He might have spoken to her. And she hadn't known. She hadn't recognized him. She hadn't understood.

"Cilla."

She jolted when Boyd put a hand to her shoulder, and she would have stumbled backward if he hadn't balanced her. "Oh, God. I thought that tonight, just this one night, he'd leave me alone."

"Take a break."

"I can't." Dazed, she clamped her hands together and stared around the room. "I have to—"

"I need to make a call," he told her. "I want you where I can see you."

He could still be here, she thought. Close enough to touch her. Did he have the knife? The long-bladed knife he'd so lovingly described to her? Was he waiting for the moment when the music was loud, when the laughter was at a peak, so that he could plunge it into her?

"Come on."

"Wait. Wait a minute." With her nails biting into her palms, she leaned into the mike. "We're going to take a short break, but don't cool down. I'll be back in ten to start things rocking again." Mechanically she shut off her equipment. "Stay close, will you?" she whispered.

With an arm snug around her waist, he began to lead her through the crowd. Every time they were bumped she shuddered. When a man pushed through the throng and grabbed both of her hands, she nearly screamed.

"Cilla O'Roarke." He had a pleasant, affable face dampened with sweat from a turn on the dance floor. He was beaming as Cilla stood as still as a statue and Boyd tensed beside her. "Tom Collins. Not the drink," he said, still beaming. "That's my name. I'm chairman of the reunion committee. Remember?"

"Oh." She forced her lips to curve. "Yes. Sure."

"Just wanted to tell you how thrilled we are to have you. Got a lot of fans here." He released one of her hands to sweep his arm out. "I'm about the biggest. There's hardly a night goes by I don't catch at least a part of your show. Lost my wife last year."

"I…" She cleared her throat. "I'm sorry."

"No, I mean I lost her. Came home one night and she and the furniture were gone. Never did find her— or the sectional sofa." He laughed heartily while Cilla searched for something to say. "Fact is, your show got me through some pretty lonely nights. Just wanted to thank you and tell you you're doing a hell of a job here tonight." He pressed a business card into her hand. "I'm in appliances. You just call me whenever you need a new refrigerator." He winked. "Give you a good deal."

"Thanks." It should be funny, she thought. Later it would be funny. "Nice seeing you, Tom."

"Pleasure's mine." He watched her walk away and beamed again.

Boyd steered her out of the ballroom and toward the nearest pay phone. "Hang on. Okay?"

She nodded, even managed to smile at a group of women herding toward the ladies' lounge. "I'm better now. I'm going to sit down right over there." She pointed to an arrangement of chairs and a potted plant.

Leaving Boyd digging for change, she walked over, then let her legs collapse under her.

It was a nightmare. She wished it was as simple as a nightmare so that she could wake up with the sun shining in her face. She had nearly gotten through an entire day without thinking of him.

Shaky, she pulled out a cigarette.

Perhaps it had been foolish to let herself believe he would give her a day of peace. But to have come here. The odds of him actually being one of the alumni were slim. Yet he'd gotten inside.

With her back pressed into the chair, she watched people file in and out of the ballroom. It could be any one of them, she thought, straining for some spark of recognition. Would she know him if she saw him, or would he be a complete stranger?

He could be someone standing behind her at the market, someone sitting across from her at a gas pump. He might be the man in front of her at the bank, or the clerk at the dry cleaners.

Anyone, she thought as she closed her eyes. He could be any one of the nameless, faceless people she passed in the course of a day.

Yet he knew her name. He knew her face. He had taken away her peace of mind, her freedom. He wouldn't be satisfied until he'd taken her life.

She watched Boyd hang up the phone and waited until he crossed to her. "Well?"

"Thea's coming by to pick up the paper. We'll send it to the lab." His hand found the tensed muscle at the curve of her neck and soothed. "I don't think we'll get prints."

"No." She appreciated the fact that he didn't give her any false hope. "Do you think he's still here?"

"I don't know." That was its own frustration. "It's a big hotel, Cilla. There's no security to speak of for this event. It wouldn't be very effective to try to close it off and interrogate everyone in it. If you want to take off early, I can tell them you're sick."

"No, I don't want to do that." She took a long last drag on her cigarette. "The only satisfaction I can get is from finishing out. Proving I'm not ready to fold. Especially if he *is* still around, somewhere."

"Okay. Remember, for the next hour, I'm never going to be more than a foot away."

She put a hand in his as she rose. "Boyd, he changed his approach, writing a note. What do you think it means?"

"It could mean a lot of things."

"Such as?"

"Such as it was the most convenient way to contact you tonight. Or he's starting to get sloppy."

"Or impatient," she added, turning to him at the doorway. "Be honest with me."

"Or impatient." He cupped her face in his hands. "He has to get through me first, Cilla. I can promise that won't be an easy job."

She made herself smile. "Cops like to think they're tough."

"No." He kissed her lightly. "Cops have to be tough. Come on. Maybe you've got 'Dueling Banjos' in there. You can play it for me for old times' sake."

"Not on a bet."

* * *

She got through it. He'd never doubted that she would, and yet the way she held on despite her fears amazed and impressed him. Not once did she bog down, break down or falter. But he saw the way she studied the crowd, searched the faces as the music raged around her.

Her hands moved constantly, tapping out the beat on the table, sifting through records, fiddling with the sequined studs on her pleated shirt.

She would never be serene, he thought. She would never be soothing. She would pace her way through life driven by nerves and ambition. She would make a demanding and unsettling companion.

Not what he'd had in mind on the rare occasions he'd considered marriage and family. Not even close, he realized with a faint smile. But she was exactly what he wanted and intended to have.

He would protect her with his life. That was duty. He would cherish her for a lifetime. That was love. If the plans he'd made ran smoothly, she would understand the difference very soon.

He, too, was searching the crowd, studying the faces, watching for any sign, any movement, that would bring that quick tensing of the gut called instinct. But the music raged on. The partygoers laughed.

He saw Althea enter. And so, he thought with a shake of his head, did most of the men in the room. He had to chuckle when he saw one woman jab her husband in the ribs as he gawked at the redhead skirting the dance floor.

"You always make an entrance, Thea."

She only shrugged. She was wearing a simple off-the-shoulder cocktail dress in basic black. "I should thank you for getting me out of what turned into an annoying evening. My date had a toothbrush in his pocket and a night of wild sex on his mind."

"Animal."

"Aren't they all?" She glanced past him to Cilla. Amusement faded, to be replaced by concern. "How's she holding up?"

"She's incredible."

She lifted one arched brow. "Partner, my sharp investigative skills lead me to believe that you are seriously infatuated with our assignment."

"I passed infatuation. I'm in love with her."

Thea's lips formed a thoughtful pout. "Is that with a lowercase or uppercase *L*?"

"That's in all caps." He looked away from Cilla to his partner. There were few others with whom he would share his private thoughts. "I'm thinking marriage, Thea. Want to be my best man?"

"You can count on me." Still, she laid a hand on his arm. "I don't want to be a drag, Boyd, but you've got to keep some perspective on this. The lady's in trouble."

He struggled against annoyance. "I can function as a cop and as a man." Because it wasn't something he wanted to discuss at length, he reached in his pocket. "Here's the note, for what it's worth."

She skimmed the message, then slipped it into her bag. "We'll see what the lab boys can do."

He only nodded. "The ex-husband looks clean." An enormous disappointment. "I finished running him through tonight. State Senator Lomax has been married for seven years, and has one point six children. He hasn't been out of Atlanta for three months."

"I finally got ahold of the station manager in Chicago. He had nothing but good things to say about Cilla. I checked out his story about being in Rochester the past week visiting his daughter. It pans. She had a girl. Seven pounds, six ounces. He faxed me the personnel files on the jocks and staff who were at the station when Cilla worked there. So far nothing."

"When I come in Monday, we'll take a closer look."

"I figured I'd go over the file this weekend. Stick close to our girl."

"I owe you one, Thea."

"You owe me more than one, but who's counting?" She started out, pausing once, then twice, to refuse the offer of a dance. Then, again, to decline a more intimate offer.

Because a party was appreciated more when it ended on a fever pitch, Cilla chose the last three songs for their beat rather than their sentiment. Jackets were off, ties were undone and careful hairstyles were limp. When the last song ended, the dance floor was jammed.

"Thank you, class of '75, you've been great. I want to see all of you back here for your twentieth."

"Good job," Boyd told her.

She was already stacking records as the crowd split off into groups. Phone numbers and addresses would be exchanged. A few of the goodbyes would be tearful. "It's not over yet."

It helped to work. She had to break down the equipment, and with the help of the hotel staff she would load it into Boyd's car. Then there would be a trip back to the station and the unloading. After that, maybe she would allow herself to think again.

"It *was* a good job."

She looked up, surprised. "Mark? What are you doing here?"

"I could say I was checking up on one of my jocks." He picked up one of the 45s and laughed. "God, don't tell me you actually played this."

"It was pretty hot in '75." Suspicious, she took it back from him. "Now, why don't you tell me what you're really doing here?"

Feeling nostalgic himself, he glanced around. He and his wife had met in high school. "I'm here to get my equipment."

"Since when does the station manager load equipment?"

"I'm the boss," he reminded her. "I can do whatever I want. And as of now…" he glanced casually at his watch "…you're on sick leave."

It was suddenly very clear. She shot an accusing look at Boyd. "I'm not sick."

"You are if I say you are," Mark countered. "If I see you at the station before your shift Monday night, you're fired."

"Damn it, Mark."

"Take it or leave it." Softening the blow, he put his hands on her shoulders. "It's business, Cilla. I've had jocks burn out from a lot less pressure than you're under. I want you for the long haul. And it's personal. You've got a lot of people worried about you."

"I'm handling it."

"Then you should be able to handle a couple of free days. Now get out of here."

"But who's going to—"

Boyd took her arm. "You heard the man."

"I hate being bullied," she muttered as he dragged her along.

"Too bad. I guess you figure KHIP is going to fall apart without you there for a weekend."

Without turning her head, she shifted her eyes and aimed a killing look at him. "That's not the point."

"No, the point is you need a rest, and you're going to get it."

She grabbed her coat before he could help her on with it. "Just what the hell am I supposed to do with myself?"

"We'll think of something."

Seething with resentment, she stalked out to the parking lot. A few stragglers from the reunion loitered around their cars. She plopped into the passenger's seat and scowled.

"Since when did *we* come into it?"

"Since, by an odd coincidence, I've also got the weekend off."

Eyes narrowed, she studied him as he conscientiously buckled her seat belt. "It smells like a conspiracy."

"You haven't seen anything yet."

He deliberately chose a cassette of classical music and popped it into the tape player before driving out of the lot.

"Mozart?" she said with a sneer.

"Bach. It's called cleansing the palate."

On a heavy sigh, she reached for a cigarette. She didn't want people worried about her, didn't want to admit she was tired. Wasn't ready to admit she was relieved. "This stuff always puts me to sleep."

"You could use the rest."

She had her teeth clenched as she punched in the lighter. "I don't appreciate you running to Mark this way."

"I didn't run to Mark. I simply called him and suggested you could use some time."

"I can take care of myself, Slick."

"Your taxes are being used to see that I take care of you."

"Have I mentioned lately how much I dislike cops?"

"Not in the past twenty-four hours."

Apparently he wasn't going to rise to any of the bait she dangled and allow her to purge her annoyance with a fight. Maybe it was for the best after all, she decided. She could use the time to catch up on her reading. The last two issues of *Radio and Records* were waiting for her attention. She also wanted to look through one of the garden magazines that had come in the mail. It would be nice to plant some summer flowers around the house, maybe some bushes. She hadn't a clue what sort of thing suited Denver's climate.

The idea made her smile. She would buy a window box, and maybe one of those hanging baskets. Perhaps that was why she didn't notice they were heading in the wrong direction until Boyd had been driving for twenty minutes.

"Where are we?" She sat up quickly, blinking.

"On 70, heading west."

"Highway 70? What the devil are we doing on 70?"

"Driving to the mountains."

"The mountains." Groggy, she pushed back her tumbled hair. "What mountains?"

"I think they're called the Rockies," he said dryly. "You might have heard of them."

"Don't get smart with me. You're supposed to be driving me home."

"I am—in a manner of speaking. I'm driving you to my home."

"I've seen your home." She jerked her thumb. "It's back that way."

"That's where I live in Denver. This is the place I have in the mountains. It's a very comfortable little cabin. Nice view. We're going for the weekend."

"*We* are not going anywhere for the weekend." She shifted in her seat to glare at him. "I'm spending the weekend at home."

"We'll do that next weekend," he said, perfectly reasonable.

"Look, Fletcher, as a cop you should know when you take somebody somewhere against their will it's considered a crime."

"You can file charges when we get back."

"Okay, this has gone far enough." It wouldn't do any good to lose her temper, she reminded herself. He was immune. "You might think you're doing this for my own good, but there are other people involved. There's no way I'm going to leave Deborah in that house alone while this maniac is running loose looking for me."

"Good point." He glided off at an exit and nearly had her relaxing. "That's why she's spending a couple of days with Althea."

"I—"

"She told me to tell you to have a good time. Oh," he continued while Cilla made incoherent noises, "she packed a bag for you. It's in the trunk."

"Just when did you plan all this?" That fabulous

voice of hers was quiet. Too quiet, Boyd decided, bracing for the storm.

"I had some free time today. You'll like the cabin. It's peaceful, not too remote, and like I said, it has a nice view."

"As long as there's a nice high cliff I can throw you off of."

He slowed to navigate the winding road. "There's that, too."

"I knew you had nerve, Fletcher, but this goes beyond. What the hell made you think you could just put me in a car, arrange my sister's life and drive me off to some cabin?"

"Must've had a brainstorm."

"Brain damage is more like it. Get this straight. I don't like the country, I don't like rustic. I am not a happy camper, and I won't go."

"You're already going."

How could he stay so irritatingly calm? "If you don't take me back, right now, I'm going to——"

"What?"

She ground her teeth. "You have to sleep sometime." Her own words made her take a quantum leap. "You creep," she began on a fresh wave of fury. "If this is your way of getting me into bed, you miscalculated. I'll sit in the car and freeze first."

"There's more than one bedroom in the cabin," he said mildly. "You're welcome to share mine, or take any of the others. It's your choice."

She slumped back in her seat, finally speechless.

Chapter 8

She didn't intend to romanticize it. Being swept away was fine in books about titled ladies and swaggering buccaneers. But it didn't play well in twentieth-century Denver.

She didn't intend to change her attitude. If the only revenge available to her was keeping a frosty distance, she would keep it very well. He wouldn't get one smile or one kind word until the entire ridiculous weekend was over.

That was why it was a shame that her first glimpse of the house was in the moonlight.

He called this a cabin? Cilla was grateful the music masked her surprised gasp. Her idea of a cabin was a squat little log structure in the middle of nowhere lacking all possible conveniences. The kind of place men went when they wanted to grow beards, drink beer and complain about women.

It was built of wood—a soft, aged wood that glowed warm in the dappled moonlight. But it was far from little. Multileveled, with interesting juts of timber and windows, it rested majestically amid the snow-dusted pine. Decks, some covered, some open, promised a breathtaking view from any direction. The metal roof glinted, making her wonder how it would be to sit inside and listen to rain falling.

But she stubbornly bit back all the words of praise and pushed out of the car. The snow came up to mid-calf and clogged in her shoes.

"Great," she muttered. Leaving him to deal with whatever luggage they had, she trudged up to the porch.

So it was beautiful, she thought. It didn't make any difference. She still didn't want to be there. But since she was, and hailing a cab wasn't a possibility, she would keep her mouth shut, choose the bedroom farthest away from his and crawl into bed. Maybe she'd stay there for forty-eight hours.

Cilla kept the first part of the vow when he joined her on the porch. The only sounds were the planks creaking under his weight and the calling of something wild in the woods. After setting their bags aside, he unlocked the door and gestured her inside.

It was dark. And freezing. Somehow that made her feel better. The more uncomfortable it was, the more justified her foul temper. Then he switched on the lights. She could only gape.

The main room at the cabin's center was huge, an open gabled structure with rough-hewn beams and a charming granite fireplace. Thick, cushy furniture was arranged around it. Its freestanding chimney rose up through the high, lofted ceiling. Above, a balcony swept the width of the room, keeping with the theme of open space and wood. In contrast, the walls were a simple white, accented with glossy built-in shelves and many-paned doors and windows.

This was nothing like the arches and curves of his house in Denver. The cabin was all straight lines and simplicity. The wide planked floors were bare. A set of gleaming steps marched straight to the next level. Beside the fireplace was an open woodbox stacked with split logs. A touch of whimsy was added by grinning brass dragons that served as andirons.

"It warms up pretty quick," Boyd said, figuring she would start talking to him again when she was ready. He flipped on the heat before he shucked off his coat and hung it on a mirrored rack just inside the door. Leaving her where she was, he crossed to the fireplace and proceeded to arrange kindling and logs.

"The kitchen's through there." He gestured as he touched a match to some crumpled newspaper. "The pantry's stocked, if you're hungry."

She was, but she'd be damned if she'd admit it. She'd been getting a perverse pleasure in watching her breath puff out in front of her. Sulking, she watched the flames rise up to lick at the logs. He even did that well, she thought in disgust. He'd probably been an Eagle Scout.

When she didn't respond, he stood up, brushing off his hands. As stubborn as she was, he figured he could outlast her. "If you'd rather just go to bed, there are four bedrooms upstairs. Not counting the sleeping porch. But it's a little cold yet to try that."

She knew when she was being laughed at. Setting

her chin, she snatched up her bag and stalked up the stairs.

It was hard to tell which room was his. They were all beautifully decorated and inviting. Cilla chose the smallest. Though she hated to admit it, it was charming, with its angled ceiling, its tiny paneled bath and its atrium doors. Dropping her bag on the narrow bed, she dug in to see just what her sister—a partner in this crime—had packed.

The big, bulky sweater and thick cords met with approval, as did the sturdy boots and rag socks. The bag of toiletries and cosmetics was a plus, though she doubted she'd waste her time with mascara or perfume. Instead of her Broncos jersey and frayed chenille robe, there was a swatch of black silk with a matching—and very sheer—peignoir. Pinned to the bodice was a note.

Happy birthday a few weeks early. See you Monday.
Love,
Deborah

Cilla blew out a long breath. Her own sister, she thought. Her own baby sister. Gingerly she held up the transparent silk. Just what had Deborah had in mind when she'd packed an outfit like this? she wondered. Maybe that question was best left unanswered. So she'd sleep in the sweater, Cilla decided, but she couldn't resist running her fingertips over the silk.

It felt…well, glorious, she admitted. Rarely did she indulge herself with anything so impractical. A small section of her closet was devoted to outfits like the one she'd worn to the reunion. She thought of them more as costumes than as clothes. The rest were practical, comfortable.

Deborah shouldn't have been so extravagant, she thought. But it was so like her. With a sigh, Cilla let the silk slide through her hands.

It probably wouldn't hurt just to try it on. After all, it was a gift. And no one was going to see it.

Heat was beginning to pour through the vents. Grateful, she slipped out of her coat and kicked off her shoes. She'd indulge herself with a hot bath in that cute claw-footed tub, and then she'd crawl under that very comfortable-looking quilt and go to sleep.

She meant to. Really. But the hot water lulled her. The package of bubble bath Deborah had tucked in the case had been irresistible. Now the night-spice fragrance enveloped her. She nearly dozed off, dreaming, with the frothy, perfumed water lapping over her skin.

Then there was the skylight over the tub, that small square of glass that let the stardust sprinkle through. Indulgent, Cilla thought with a sigh as she sank deeper in the tub. Romantic. Almost sinfully soothing.

It had probably been silly to light the pair of candles that sat in the deep windowsill instead of using the overhead lamp. But it had been too tempting. And as she soaked and dreamed, their scent wafted around her.

She was just making the best of a bad situation, she assured herself as she rose lazily from the tub. Unpinning her hair, she let it swing around her shoulders as she slipped into the teddy Deborah had given her.

It had hardly any back at all, she noted, just a silly little flounce that barely covered the essentials. It laced up the front, thin, glossy ribbons that crisscrossed and ended in a small bow in the center, just below her breasts. Though it barely covered them, as well, some clever structural secret lifted them up, made them look fuller.

Despite her best intentions, she traced a fingertip down the ribbons, wondering what it would be like to have Boyd unlace them. Imagining what it might be like to have his fingers brush over her just-pampered skin. Would he go slowly, one careful hook at a time, or would he simply tear at them until—

Oh Lord.

Cursing herself, she yanked open the door and dashed out of the steamy bath.

It was ridiculous to daydream that way, she reminded herself. She had never been a daydreamer. Always, always, she had known where she was going and how to get there. Not since childhood had she wasted time with fantasies that had no connection with ambition or success.

She certainly had no business fantasizing about a man, no matter how attracted she was to him, when she knew there was no possible way they could become a comfortable reality.

She would go to bed. She would shut off her mind. And she would pray that she could shut off these needs that were eating away at her. Before she could shove her bag on the floor, she saw the glass beside the bed.

It was a long-stemmed crystal glass, filled with some pale golden liquid. As she sampled it, she shut her eyes. Wine, she realized. Wonderfully smooth. Probably French. Turning, she saw herself reflected in the cheval glass in the corner.

Her eyes were dark, and her skin was flushed. She looked too soft, too yielding, too pliant. What was he doing to her? she asked herself. And why was it working?

Before she could change her mind, she slipped the thin silk over her shoulders and went to find him.

He'd been reading the same page for nearly an hour. Thinking about her. Cursing her. Wanting her. It had taken every ounce of self-possession he had to set that wine beside her bed and leave the room when he could hear her splashing lazily in the tub just one narrow door away.

It wasn't as if it were all one-sided, he thought in disgust. He knew when a woman was interested. It wasn't as if it were all physical. He was in love with her, damn it. And if she was too stupid to see that, then he'd just have to beat her over the head with it.

Laying the book on his lap, he listened to the bluesy eloquence of Billie Holiday and stared into the fire. The cheerful flames had cut the chill in the bedroom. That was the practical reason he had built a fire in here, as well as one on the main floor. But there was another, a romantic one. He was annoyed that he had daydreamed of Cilla as he set the logs and lit the kindling.

She had come to him, wearing something thin, flowing, seductive. She had smiled, held out her hands. Melted against him. When he had lifted her into his arms, carried her to the bed, they had...

Keep dreaming, he told himself. The day Cilla O'Roarke came to him of her own free will, with a smile and an open hand, would be the day they built snowmen in hell.

She had feelings for him, damn it. Plenty of them. And if she weren't so bullheaded, so determined to lock up all that incredible passion, she wouldn't spend so much time biting her nails and lighting cigarettes.

Resentful, restrictive and repressed, that was Priscilla Alice O'Roarke, he thought grimly. He picked up his wine for a mock toast. It nearly slid out of his hand when he saw her standing in the doorway.

"I want to talk to you." She'd lost most of her nerve on the short trip down the hall, but she managed to step into the room. She wasn't going to let the fact that he was sitting in front of a sizzling fire wearing nothing but baggy sweats intimidate her.

He needed a drink. After a gulp of wine, he managed a nod. He was almost ready to believe he was dreaming again—but she wasn't smiling. "Yeah?"

She was going to speak, she reminded herself. Say what was on her mind and clear the air. But she needed a sip of her own wine first. "I realize your motives in bringing me here tonight were basically well-intentioned, given the circumstances of the last couple of weeks. But your methods were unbelievably arrogant." She wondered if she sounded like as much of a fool to him as she did to herself. She waited for a response, but he just continued to stare blankly at her. "Boyd?"

He shook his head. "What?"

"Don't you have anything to say?"

"About what?"

A low sound of frustration rumbled in her throat as she stepped closer. She slammed the glass down on a table, and the remaining wine lapped close to the rim. "The least you can do after dragging me all the way up here is to listen when I complain about it."

He was barely capable of breathing, much less listening. In self-defense he took another long sip of wine.

"If you had any legs—brains," he corrected, gnashing his teeth, "you'd know that a couple days away from everything would be good for you."

Anger flared in her eyes, making her all the more arousing. Behind her the flames shot high, and the light rippled through the thin silk she wore. "So you just took it on yourself to make the decision for me."

"That's right." In one jerky movement, he set the glass aside to keep it from shattering in his fingers. "If I had asked you to come here for a couple of days, you would have made a dozen excuses why you couldn't."

"We'll never know what I would have done," she countered, "because you didn't give me the option of making my own choice."

"I'm doing my damnedest to give you the option now," he muttered.

"About what?"

On an oath, he stood up and turned away. Hands braced on the wall, he began, none too gently, to pound his forehead against it. As she watched him, confusion warred with anger.

"What are you doing?"

"I'm beating my head against the wall. What does it look like I'm doing?" He stopped, letting his forehead rest against the wood.

Apparently she wasn't the only one under too much strain, Cilla mused. She cleared her throat. "Boyd, why are you beating your head against the wall?"

He laughed and, rubbing his hands over his face, turned. "I have no idea. It's just something I've felt obliged to do since I met you." She was standing, a little uncertain now, running nervous fingertips up and down her silk lapel. It wasn't easy, but after a deep breath he found a slippery hold on control. "Why don't you go on to bed, Cilla? In the morning you can tear apart what's left of me."

"I don't understand you." She snapped out the words, then began to pace. Boyd opened his mouth but couldn't even manage a groan as he stared at the long length of her back, bare but for the sheerest of black silk, at the agitated swing of her hips, accented by the sassy little flounce. She was talking again, rapid-fire and irritated, but it was all just a buzzing in his head.

"For God's sake, don't pace." He rubbed the heel of his hand against his heart. In another minute, he was sure, it would explode out of his chest. "Are you trying to kill me?"

"I always pace when I'm mad," she tossed back. "How do you expect me to go quietly to bed after you've got me worked up this way?"

"Got you worked up?" he repeated. Something snapped—he would have sworn he heard it boomerang in his head as he reached out and snatched her arms. "I've got you worked up? That's rich, O'Roarke. Tell me, did you wear this thing in here tonight to make me suffer?"

"I…" She looked down at herself, then shifted uncomfortably. "Deborah packed it. It's all I've got."

"Whoever packed it, it's you who's packed into it. And you're driving me crazy."

"I just thought we should clear all this up." She was going to start stuttering in a minute. "Talk it through, like grown-ups."

"I'm thinking very much like a grown-up at the moment. If you want to talk, there's a chestful of big, thick wool blankets. You can wrap yourself up in one."

She didn't need a blanket. She was already much too warm. If he continued to rub his hands up and down the silk on her arms, the friction was going to cause her skin to burst into flame.

"Maybe I wanted to make you suffer a little."

"It worked." His fingers toyed with the excuse of a robe as it slid from her right shoulder. "Cilla, I'm not going to make this easy on you and drag you to that bed. I'm not saying the idea doesn't appeal to me a great deal. But if we make love, you're going to have to wake up in the morning knowing the choice was yours."

Wasn't that why she had come to him? Hoping he'd take matters out of her hands? That made her a coward—and, in a miserable way, a cheat.

"It's not easy for me."

"It should be." He slid his hands down to hers. "If you're ready."

She lifted her head. He was waiting—every bit as edgy as she, but waiting. "I guess I've been ready since I met you."

A tremor worked through him, and he struggled against his self-imposed leash. "Just say yes."

Saying it wasn't enough, she thought. When something was important, it took more than one simple word.

"Let go of my hands, please."

He held them another long moment, searching her face. Slowly his fingers relaxed and dropped away from hers. Before he could back up, she moved into him, wrapping her arms around his neck. "I want you, Boyd. I want to be with you tonight."

She brought her lips to his. There had already been enough words. Warm and willing, she sank into him.

For a moment, he couldn't breathe. The onslaught on his senses was too overwhelming. Her taste, her scent, the texture of silk against silk. There was her sigh as she rubbed her lips over his.

He remembered taking a kick in the solar plexus from one of his father's prized stallions. This left him just as debilitated. He wanted to savor, to drown, to lose himself, inch by glorious inch. But even as he slipped the robe from her shoulders she was pulling him to the bed.

She was like a whirlwind, hands racing, pressing, tugging, followed by the mad, erotic journey of her mouth. The pressure was building too fast, but when he reached for her she shimmied out of the silk and rushed on.

She didn't want him to regret wanting her. She couldn't have borne it. If she was to throw every shred of caution to the winds for this one night, she needed to know that it would matter. That he would remember.

His skin was hot and damp. She wished she could have lingered over the taste of it, the feel of it under her fingers. But she thought men preferred speed and power.

She heard him groan. It delighted her. When she tugged off his sweats, his hands were in her hair. He was murmuring something—her name, and more—but she couldn't tell. She thought she understood his urgency, the way he pulled her up against him. When he rolled over her, she whispered her agreement and took him inside her.

He stiffened. On an oath, he tried to level himself

and draw back. But her hips arched and thrust against him, leaving his body no choice.

Her lips were curved when he lay over her, his face buried in her hair, his breath still shuddering. He wouldn't regret this, she thought, rubbing a soothing hand over his shoulder. And neither would she. It was more than she had ever had before. More than she had ever expected. There had been a warmth when he filled her, and a quiet contentment when she felt him spill into her. She thought how nice it would be to close her eyes and drift off to sleep with his body still warm on hers.

He was cursing himself, steadily. He was enraged by his lack of control, and baffled by the way she had rushed them both from kiss to completion. He'd barely touched her—in more ways than one. Though it was she who had set the pace at a sprint, he knew she hadn't come close to fulfillment.

Struggling for calm, he rolled away from her to stare at the ceiling. She'd set off bombs inside him, and though they had exploded, neither of them had shared the joy.

"Why did you do that?" he asked her.

Her hand paused on its way to stroke his hair. "I don't understand. I thought you wanted to make love."

"I did." He sat up, dragging the hair back from his face. "I thought you did, too."

"But I thought men liked…" She let her eyes close as the warmth drained out of her. "I told you I wasn't very good at it."

He swore, ripely enough to have her jolting. Moving quickly, she scrambled out of bed to struggle back into the peignoir.

"Where the hell are you going?"

"To bed." Because her voice was thick with tears, she lowered it. "We can just chalk this up to one more miscalculation." She reached down for her robe and heard the door slam. Bolting up, she saw Boyd turning a key in the lock, then tossing it across the room. "I don't want to stay here with you."

"Too bad. You already made your choice."

She balled up the robe, hugging it to her chest. So he was angry, she thought. And it was the real thing this time. It wouldn't be the first fight she had had about her inadequacies in bed. Old wounds, old doubts, trickled through her until she stood rigid with embarrassment.

"Look, I did the best I could. If it wasn't good enough, fine. Just let me go."

"Wasn't good enough," he repeated. As he stepped forward, she backed up, ramming into the carved footboard. "Somebody ought to bounce you on your head and knock some sense into it. There are two people in a bed, Cilla, and what happens in it is supposed to be mutual. I wasn't looking for a damn technician."

The angry flush died away from her face until it was marble white. Her eyes filled. Pressing his fingers against his own eyes, he swore. He hadn't meant to hurt her, only to show her that he'd wanted a partner.

"You didn't feel anything."

"I did." She rubbed tears from her cheek, infuriated. No one made her cry. No one.

"Then that's a miracle. Cilla, you barely let me touch you. I'm not blaming you." He took another step, but she evaded him. Searching for patience he stood where he was. "I didn't exactly fight you off. I thought— Let's just say by the time I understood, it was too late to do anything about it. I'd like to make it up to you."

"There's nothing to make up." She had herself under control again, eyes dry, voice steady. She wanted to die. "We'll just forget it. I want you to unlock the door."

He let out a huff of breath, then shrugged. When he turned to the door, she started to follow. But he only turned off the lights.

"What are you doing?"

"We tried it your way." In the moonlight, he moved across the room to light a candle, then another and another. He turned over the record that sat silent on the turntable, engaged the needle. The trembling cry of a tenor sax filled the room. "Now we try it mine."

She was starting to tremble now, from embarrassment and from fear. "I said I wanted to go to bed."

"Good." He swept her up into his arms. "So do I."

"I've had enough humiliation for one night," she said between her teeth.

She saw something in his eyes, something dark, but his voice was quiet when he spoke. "I'm sorry. I never meant to hurt you."

Though she held herself rigid, he lowered her gently to the bed. With his eyes on hers, he spread out her hair, letting his fingers linger. "I've imagined you here, in the candlelight, with your hair on my pillow." He lowered his lips to brush them across hers. "Moonlight and firelight on your skin. With nothing and no one else but you for miles."

Moved, she turned her head away. She wouldn't be seduced by words and make a fool of herself again. He only smiled and pressed his lips to her throat.

"I love a challenge. I'm going to make love with you, Cilla." He slipped the strap of the peignoir from her shoulder to cruise the slope with his mouth. "I'm going to take you places you've never even dreamed of." He took her hand, pleased that her pulse had quickened. "You shouldn't be afraid to enjoy yourself."

"I'm not."

"You're afraid to relax, to let go, to let someone get close enough to find out what's inside you."

She tried to shift away, but his arms wrapped around her. "We already had sex."

"Yes, we did." He kissed one corner of her mouth, then the other. "Now we're going to make love."

She started to turn her head again, but he cupped her face with his hands. When his mouth came to hers again, her heart leaped into her throat. It was so soft, so tempting. As his fingertips glided across her face, she gave a strangled sigh. He dipped into her parted lips to tease her tongue with his.

"I don't want—" She moaned as his teeth nipped into her bottom lip.

"Tell me what you do want."

"I don't know." Her mind was already hazy. She lifted a hand to push him away, but it only lay limp on his shoulder.

"Then we'll make it multiple-choice." To please himself, and her, he ran a trail of kisses down her throat. "When I'm finished, you can tell me what you like best."

He murmured to her, soft, dreamy words that floated in her head. Then he drugged her with a kiss, long, lazy, luxurious. Though her body had begun to tremble, he barely touched her—just those fingertips stroking along her shoulders, over her face, into her hair.

His tongue slid over the tops of her breasts, just above the fringe of black lace. Her skin was like honey there, he thought, laving the valley between. Her heart jackhammered against him, but when she reached out, he took her hands in his.

Taking his time, his devastating time, he inched the lace down with his teeth. She arched up, offering herself, her fingers tensing like wires against his. He only murmured and, leaving a moist trail, eased the other curve of lace down.

His own breathing was short and shallow, but he fought back the urge to take greedily. With teasing openmouthed kisses he circled her, flicking his hot tongue over her rigid nipple until she shuddered and sobbed out his name. On a groan of pleasure, he suckled.

She felt the pressure deep inside, clenching, unclenching, to the rhythm of his clever mouth. Building, layering, growing, until she thought she would die from it.

Her breath was heaving as she writhed beneath him. Her nails dug hard into the backs of his hands as her body bowed, driven up by a knot of sensation. She heard her own cry, her gasp of relief and torment as something shattered inside her. Hot knives that turned to silky butterfly wings. A pain that brought unreasonable pleasure.

As every muscle in her body went lax, he covered her mouth with his. "Good Lord. You're incredible."

"I can't." She brought a hand up to press a palm to her temple. "I can't think."

"Don't. Just feel."

He straddled her. She was prepared for him to take her. He had already given her more than she had ever had. Shown her more than she had ever imagined. He began to unlace the peignoir with infinite care, infinite patience. His eyes were on her face. He loved being able to see everything she felt as it flickered there. Every new sensation, every new emotion. He heard the whisper of silk against her skin as he drew it down. He felt passion vibrate from her as he pressed his mouth to the quivering flesh of her stomach.

Floating, she stroked his hair, let her mind follow where her body so desperately wanted to go. This was heaven, more demanding, more exciting, more erotic, than any paradise she could have dreamed. She could feel the sheets, hot from her own body, tangled beneath her. And the shimmer of silk as it slipped slowly, slowly away. His skin, dampened from pleasure, slid over hers. When her lips parted on a sigh, she could still taste him there, rich and male. Candlelight played against her closed lids.

There was so much to absorb, so much to experience. If it went on forever, it would still end too soon.

She was his now, he knew. Much more his than she had been when he had been plunged inside her. Her body was like a wish, long and slim and pale in the moonlight. Her breath was quick and quiet. And it was his name, only his name, she spoke when he touched her. Her hands flexed on his shoulders, urging him on.

He slid down her legs, taking the silk with him, nibbling everywhere as he went. The scent of her skin was a tormenting delight he could have lingered over endlessly. But her body was restless, poised. He knew she must be aching, even as he was.

He stroked a fingertip up her thigh, along that sensitive flesh, close, so close, to where the heat centered. When he slipped inside her, she was wet and waiting.

The breathless moan came first, and then the magic of his hands had her catapulting up, over a new and higher crest. Stunned by the power of it, she arched against him, shuddering again and again as she climbed. Though her hands clutched at him, he continued to drive her with his mouth, with his clever and relentless fingers, until she shot beyond pleasure to delirium.

Then her arms were around him and they were spinning off together, rolling over on the bed like lightning and thunder. The time for patience was over. The time for greed had begun.

He fought for breath as her hands raced over him. As she had the first time, she ripped away his control. But now she was with him, beat for beat and need for need. He saw her eyes glow, dark with passion, depthless with desire. Her slick skin shimmered with it in the shadowy light.

One last time he brought his mouth down on hers, swallowing her stunned cry, as he thrust himself into her. On a half sob she wrapped her arms and legs around him, locking tight so that they could race toward madness together.

He was exhausted. Weak as a baby. And he was heavy. Using what strength he could find, Boyd rolled, taking Cilla with him so that their positions were reversed. Satisfied, he cradled her head and decided he very much liked the sensation of her body sprawled over his.

She shuddered. He soothed.

"Cold?"

She just shook her head.

Lazy as a cat, he stroked a hand down her naked back. "I might, in an hour or so, find the strength to look for the blankets."

"I'm fine."

But her voice wasn't steady. Frowning, Boyd cupped a hand under her chin and lifted it. He could see a tear glittering on her lashes. "What's this?"

"I'm not crying," she said, almost fiercely.

"Okay. What are you?"

She tried to duck her head again, but he held it firm. "You'll think I'm stupid."

"Probably the only time I couldn't think you were stupid is right after you've turned me inside out." He gave her a quick kiss. "Spill it, O'Roarke."

"It's just that I…" She let out an impatient breath. "I didn't think it was supposed to be that way. Not really."

"What way?" His lips curved. Funny, but it seemed he was getting his strength back. Maybe it was the way she was looking at him. Dazed. Embarrassed. Beautiful. "You mean, like good?" He slid his hands down to caress her bottom casually. "Or very good? Maybe you mean terrific. Or astounding."

"You're making fun of me."

"Uh-uh. I was hoping for a compliment. But you don't want to give me one. I figure you're just too stubborn to admit that my way was better than your way. But that's okay. I also figure I can keep you locked in here until you do."

"Damn it, Boyd, it's not easy for me to explain myself."

"You don't have to." There was no teasing note in his voice now. The look in his eyes made her weak all over again.

"I wanted to tell you that I never…no one's ever made me…" She gave up. "It was terrific."

"Yeah." He cupped a hand on the back of her head and brought her mouth to his. "Now we're going to shoot for astounding."

Chapter 9

Cilla wrapped her arms across her body to ward off the chill and stared out over the pine and rock. Boyd had been right again. The view was incredible.

From this angle she could see the jagged, snow-capped peaks of the circling mountains. Closer, yet still distant, she caught the faint mist of smoke from a chimney. Evergreens stood, sturdy winter veterans, their needles whistling in the rising wind. There was the harsh whisper of an icy stream. She could catch glimpses of the water, just the glint of it in the fading sun.

The shadows were long, with late afternoon casting a cool blue light over the snow. Earlier she had seen a deer nuzzling her nose into it in search of the grass beneath. Now she was alone.

She'd forgotten what it was to feel so at peace. In

truth, she wondered if she had ever known. Certainly not since earliest childhood, when she had still believed in fairy tales and happy endings. It had to be too late, when a woman was nearly thirty, to start believing again.

And yet she doubted things would ever be quite the same again.

He had kept his promise. He had taken her places she had never dreamed of. In one exquisitely long night, he had shown her that love meant you could accept as well as offer, take as well as give. She had learned more than the power of lovemaking in Boyd's bed. She had learned the power of intimacy. The comfort and the glory of it. For the first time in years, she had slept deeply and dreamlessly.

She hadn't felt awkward or uncomfortable on waking with him that morning. She had felt calm. Wonderfully calm. It was almost impossible to believe that there was another world apart from this spot. A world of pain and danger and fear.

Yet there was. And it was a world she would have to face again all too soon. She couldn't hide here—not from a man who wanted her dead, nor from her own miserable memories. But wasn't she entitled to a little more time to pretend that nothing else mattered?

It wasn't right. On a sigh, she lifted her face to the dying sun. No matter how she felt—or perhaps because she had come to feel so deeply—she had to be honest with herself, and with Boyd. She wouldn't let what had started between them go any further. Couldn't, she thought, squeezing her eyes tight. It had to be better to let her heart break a little now than to have it smashed later.

He was a good man, she thought. An honest one, a caring one. He was patient, intelligent and dedicated. And he was a cop.

She shivered and held herself more tightly.

There was a scar just under his right shoulder. Front and back, she remembered. From a bullet—that occupational hazard of law enforcement. She hadn't asked, and wouldn't, how he had come by it, when it had happened, or how near death it had taken him.

But neither could she hide from the fact that the scars she bore were as real as his.

She simply could not delude either of them into believing there was a future for them. She should never have allowed it to progress as far as it had. But that was done. They were lovers. And though she knew that was a mistake, she would always be grateful for the time she had had with him.

The logical thing to do would be to discuss the limitations of their relationship. No strings, no obligations. In all likelihood he would appreciate that kind of practicality. If her feelings had grown too far too fast, she would just have to get a grip on them.

She would simply have to talk herself out of being in love.

He found her there, leaning out on the railing as if she were straining to fly out above the pines, above the snowcapped peaks. The nerves were coming back, he noted with some frustration. He wondered if she knew how relaxed she had been that morning when she had stretched against him, waking gradually, turning to him so that they could make slow, lazy love.

Now, when he touched her hair, she jolted before she leaned back against his hand.

"I like your place, Slick."

"I'm glad." He intended to come back here with her, year after year.

Her fingers danced over the railing, then groped in her pockets. "I never asked you if you bought it or had it built."

"Had it built. Even hammered a few nails myself."

"A man of many talents. It's almost a shame to have a place like this only for weekends."

"I've been known to break away for more than that from time to time. And my parents use it now and again."

"Oh. Do they live in Denver?"

"Colorado Springs." He began to massage the tensing muscles in her shoulders. "But they travel a lot. Itchy feet."

"I guess your father was disappointed when you didn't go into the family business."

"No. My sister's carrying on the family tradition."

"Sister?" She glanced over her shoulder. "I didn't know you had a sister."

"There's a lot you don't know." He kissed her lips when they formed into a pout. "She's a real go-getter. Tough, high-powered businesswoman. And a hell of a lot better at it than I would have been."

"But aren't they uneasy about you being a cop?"

"I don't think it's a day-to-day worry. You're getting chilled," he said. "Come on inside by the fire."

She went with him, moving inside and down the rear steps into the kitchen. "Mmm… What's that smell?"

"I threw some chili together." He walked over to the center island, where copper pots hung from the ceiling. Lifting the lid on a pan simmering on the range, he sniffed. "Be ready in about an hour."

"I would have helped you."

"That's okay." He selected a Bordeaux from the wine rack. "You can cook next time."

She made a feeble attempt at a smile. "So you did like my peanut-butter-and-jelly special."

"Just like Mom used to make."

She doubted that his mother had ever made a sandwich in her life. People who had that kind of money also had a houseful of servants. As she stood feeling foolish, he set the wine on the counter to breathe.

"Aren't you going to take off your coat?"

"Oh. Sure." She shrugged out of it and hung it on a hook by the door. "Is there anything you want me to do?"

"Yes. Relax."

"I am."

"You were." Selecting two glasses from above the rack, he examined them. "I'm not sure what has you tied up again, Cilla, but we're going to talk it through this time. Why don't you go sit by the fire? I'll bring out the wine."

If he read her this easily after a matter of weeks, Cilla thought as she went into the living room, how much would he see in a year? She settled on a low cushion near the fire. She wasn't going to think of a year. Or even a month.

When he came in, she offered him a much brighter smile and reached for her wine. "Thanks. It's a good thing I didn't come here before I went house hunting. I never would have settled on a house without a fireplace."

In silence, he settled beside her. "Look at me," he said at length. "Are you worried about going back to work?"

"No." Then she sighed. "A little. I trust you and Thea, and I know you're doing what you can, but I am scared."

"Do you trust me?"

"I said I did." But she didn't meet his eyes.

He touched a fingertip to her cheek until she faced him again. "Not just as a cop."

She winced, looked away again. "No, not just as a cop."

"And that's the trigger," he mused. "The fact that I am a cop."

"It's none of my business."

"We both know better."

"I don't like it," she said evenly. "I don't expect you to understand."

"I think I do understand." He leaned back against a chair, watching her as he sipped his wine. "I've done some checking, Cilla—necessary to the investigation. But I won't pretend that's the only reason I looked."

"What do you mean?"

"I looked into your background because I need to protect you. And I need to understand you. You told me your mother was a cop. It wasn't hard to track down what happened."

She clutched her glass in both hands and stared straight ahead, into the flames. After all these years, the pain was just as deadly. "So you punched some buttons on your computer and found out my mother was killed. Line of duty. That's what they call it. Line of duty," she repeated, her voice dull. "As if it were part of a job description."

"It is," he said quietly.

There was a flicker of fear in her eyes when she looked at him, then quickly away again. "Yeah. Right. It was just part of her job to be shot that day. Too bad about my father, though. He just happened to be in the wrong place at the wrong time. The old innocent bystander."

"Cilla, nothing's as black-and-white as that. And nothing's that simple."

"Simple?" She laughed and dragged her hair back from her face. "No, the word's *ironic*. The cop and the public defender, who just happen to be married, are going head-to-head over a case. They never agreed. Never once can I remember them looking at any one thing from the same angle. When this happened, they were talking about a separation—again. Just a trial one, they said." With a thoughtful frown, she studied her glass. "Looks like I'm out of wine."

Saying nothing, Boyd poured her more.

"So I guess you read the official report." She swirled the wine, then drank. "They brought this little creep in for interrogation. Three-time loser—armed robbery, assault, drugs. He wanted his lawyer present while the investigating officer questioned him. Talked about making a deal. He knew there wouldn't be any deal. They had him cold, and he was going to do hard time. He had two people to blame for it—in his head, anyway. His lawyer, and the cop who had collared him."

It was painful, still so painful, to remember, to try to picture an event she hadn't seen, one that had so drastically altered her life.

"They caught the guy who smuggled him the gun," she said softly. "He's still doing time." Taking a moment, she soothed her throat with wine. "There they were, sitting across from each other at the table—just as they might have been in our own kitchen—arguing about the law. The sonofabitch took out that smuggled snub-nosed .22 and shot them both."

She looked down at her glass again. "A lot of people lost their jobs over that incident. My parents lost their lives."

"I'm not going to tell you that cops don't die by mistake, unnecessarily, even uselessly."

When she looked at him, her eyes were eloquent. "Good. And I don't want the crap about how proud we're supposed to be of our valiant boys in blue. Damn it, she was my mother."

He hadn't just read the reports, he'd pored over them. The papers had called it a disgrace and a tragedy. The investigation had lasted more than six months, and when it was over eight officials had resigned or been replaced.

But over and above the facts, he remembered a file picture. Cilla, her face blank with grief, standing by the two graves, clutching Deborah's hand in hers.

"It was a horrible way to lose them," he said.

She just shook her head. "Yes. But in most ways I'd already lost my mother the day she joined the force."

"She had an impressive record," Boyd said carefully. "It wasn't easy for a woman back then. And it's always tough on a cop's family."

"How do you know?" she demanded. "You're not the one who sits at home and sweats. From the day I was old enough to understand, I waited for her captain to come to the door and tell us she was dead."

"Cilla, you can't live your life waiting for the worst."

"I lived my life waiting for a mother. The job always came first—it came before Dad, before me, before Deb. She was never there when I needed her." She snatched her hand aside before he could grasp it. "I didn't care if she baked cookies or folded my socks. I just wanted her to be there when I needed her. But her family was never as important as the masses she'd sworn to serve and protect."

"Maybe she was too focused on her career," he began.

"Don't you compare me with her."

His brow rose. "I wasn't going to." Now he took her hand despite her resistance. "It sounds like you are."

"I've had to be focused. She had people who loved her, who needed her, but she never took time to notice. Cops don't have regular hours, she'd say. Cops don't have regular lives."

"I didn't know your mother, and I can't comment on the choices she made, but don't you think it's time to cut it loose and get on with your life?"

"I have. I've done what I had to do. I've done what I've wanted to do."

"And you're scared to death of what you're feeling for me because of my job."

"It's not just a job," she said desperately. "We both know it's not just a job."

"Okay." He nodded. "It's what I do, and what I am. We're going to have to find a way to deal with it."

"It's your life," she said carefully. "I'm not asking

you to change anything. I didn't intend to get this involved with you, but I don't regret it."

"Thanks," he muttered, and drained his own glass.

"What I'm trying to say is that if we're reasonable I think we can keep it uncomplicated."

He set his glass aside. "No."

"No what?"

"No, I don't want to be reasonable, and it's already complicated." He gave her a long look that was very close to grim. "I'm in love with you."

He saw the shock. It flashed into her eyes an instant before she jerked back. The color drained away from her face.

"I see that thrills the hell out of you," he muttered. Rising, he heaved a log on the fire and cursed as he watched the sparks fly.

Cilla thought it best to stay exactly where she was. "Love's a real big word, Boyd. We've only known each other a couple of weeks, and not under the most ideal circumstances. I think—"

"I'm damn tired of you thinking." He turned back to face her. "Just tell me what you feel."

"I don't know." That was a lie, one she knew she would hate herself for. She was terrified. And she was thrilled. She was filled with regrets, and hammered by longings. "Boyd, everything that's happened has happened fast. It's as if I haven't had any control, and that makes me uneasy. I didn't want to be involved with you, but I am. I didn't want to care about you, but I do."

"Well, I finally managed to pry that out of you."

"I don't sleep with a man just because he makes me tingle."

"Better and better." He smiled as he lifted her hand

to kiss her fingers. "I make you tingle, and you care about me. Marry me."

She tried to jerk her hand free. "This isn't the time for jokes."

"I'm not joking." Suddenly his eyes were very intense. "I'm asking you to marry me."

She heard a log shift in the grate. Saw the flicker of a new flame as it cast light and shadow over his face. His hand was warm and firm on hers, holding, waiting. Her breath seemed to be blocked somewhere beneath her heart. The effort of dragging in air made her dizzy.

"Boyd—"

"I'm in love with you, Cilla." Slowly, his eyes steady on hers, he pulled her closer. "With every part of you." Soft, persuasive, his lips cruised over hers. "I only want fifty or sixty years to show you." His mouth skimmed down her throat as he lowered her to the hearth rug. "Is that too much to ask?"

"No… Yes." Struggling to clear her mind, she pressed a hand against his chest. "Boyd, I'm not going to marry anyone."

"Sure you are." He nibbled lightly at her lips as his hands began to stroke—soothing and exciting at the same time. "You just have to get used to the fact that it's going to be me." He deepened the kiss, lingering over it until her hand lost its resistance and slid to his back. "I'm willing to give you time." His lips curved as her murmured protest hummed against them. "A day or two. Maybe a week."

She shook her head. "I've already made one mistake. I'm not ever going to repeat it."

He caught her chin in his hand in a movement so quick that her eyes flew open. In his eyes was a ripe, raging fury that was rare for him, and all the more dangerous.

"Don't ever compare me with him."

She started to speak, but his fingers tightened once, briefly, and silenced her.

"Don't ever compare what I feel for you with what anyone else has felt."

"I wasn't comparing you." Her heart was hammering against his chest. "It's me. It was my mistake, mine alone. And I'm never going to make another one like it."

"It takes two people, damn it." Enraged, he braced himself over her, then took both her hands in his. "If you want to play it that way, fine. Ask yourself one question, Cilla. Has anyone else made you feel like this?"

His mouth swooped down to take hers in a hot, rough, frantic kiss that had her arching against him. In protest? In pleasure? Even she couldn't tell. Sensations swarmed through her like thousands of swirling stars, all heat and light. Before she could draw and release a breath, she was tossed into the storm.

No. Her mind all but screamed it. No one. Never. Only he had ever caused a hunger so sharp and a need so desperate. Even as her body strained against his, she struggled to remember that it wasn't enough to want. It wasn't always enough to have.

Whipped by fury and frustration, he crushed his mouth to hers, again, and then again. If only for this moment, he would prove to her that what they had together was unique to them. She would think of no one, remember nothing. Only him.

Her response tore through him, so complete, so

right. The small, helpless sound that purred up from her throat shuddered into him. Like the flames that rose beside them, what they created burned and consumed. The gentle loving that had initiated them both during the night was replaced by a wild and urgent hunger that left no room for tender words and soft caresses.

She didn't want them. This was a new, a frenetic storm of needs that demanded speed and pushed for power. *Hurry.* She tore her hands from his to drag at his shirt. *Touch me.* Twin groans tangled as flesh met flesh. *More.* With a new aggression, she rolled onto him to take her mouth on a frantic race over his body. And still it wasn't enough.

His breath ragged, he stripped the layers of clothing from her, not caring about what he tore. One driving need was prominent. To possess. Hands gripped. Fingers pressed. Mouths devoured.

Agile and electric, she moved over him. Her face glowed, fragile porcelain in the firelight. Her body arched, magnificent in its new power, sheened with passion, shuddering from it, strengthened by it.

For one glorious moment she rose, witchlike, over him, her hands lifting up into her hair, her head thrown back as she lost herself in the wonder. Her body shuddered once, twice, as separate explosions burst within her. Even as she gasped, he gripped her hips and sheathed himself inside her.

He filled her. Not just physically. Even through the wracking pleasure she understood that. He, and only he, had found the key that opened every part of her. He, and only he, had found the way inside her heart, her mind. And somehow, without trying, she had found the way into his.

She didn't want to love him. She reached for his hands and gripped them tight. She didn't want to need him. Opening her eyes, she looked down at him. His eyes were dark and direct on hers. She knew, though she didn't speak, that he understood every thought in her head. On a sigh that was as much from despair as from delight, she bent down to press her mouth to his.

He could taste both the needs and the fears. He was determined to exploit the first and drive away the second. Staying deep inside her, he pushed up so that he could wrap his arms around her. He watched her eyes widen, stunned with pleasure, glazed with passion. Her fingers dug into his back. Her cry of release was muffled against his mouth seconds before he let himself go.

Bundled in a large, frayed robe, her feet covered with thick rag socks, Cilla sampled the chili. She liked sitting in the warm golden light in the kitchen, seeing the blanket of snow outside the windows, hearing the quiet moan of the wind through the pines. What surprised her, and what she wasn't ready to consider too carefully, was this feeling of regret that the weekend was almost over.

"Well?"

At Boyd's question, she looked back from the window. He sat across from her, his hair still mussed from her hands. Like her, he wore only a robe and socks. Though it made no sense, Cilla found the meal every bit as intimate as their loving in front of the fire.

Uneasy, she broke a piece of the hot, crusty bread on her plate. She was afraid he was going to bring up marriage again.

"Well what?"

"How's the chili?"

"The— Oh." She spooned up another bite, not sure if she was relieved or disappointed. "It's great. And surprising." Nervous again, she reached for her wine. "I'd have thought someone in your position would have a cook and wouldn't know how to boil an egg."

"My position?"

"I mean, if I could afford to hire a cook I wouldn't hassle with making sandwiches."

It amused him that his money made her uncomfortable. "After we're married we can hire one if you want."

Very carefully she set down her spoon. "I'm not going to marry you."

He grinned. "Wanna bet?"

"This isn't a game."

"Sure it is. The biggest in town."

She made a low sound of frustration. Picking up her spoon again, she began to tap it against the wood. "That's such a typically male attitude. It's all a game. You Tarzan, me stupid." His laughter only enraged her further. "Why is it men think women can't resist them—for sex, for companionship, for handling the details of life? Oh, Cilla, you need me. Oh, Cilla, I just want to take care of you. I want to show you what life's all about."

He considered a moment. "I don't remember saying any of those things. I think what I said is I love you and I want to marry you."

"It's the same thing."

"Not even close." He continued to eat, undisturbed.

"Well, I don't want to marry you, but I'm sure that won't make a difference. It never does."

He shot her one brief and dangerous look. "I warned you not to compare me to him. I meant it."

"I'm not just talking about Paul. I wasn't even thinking about Paul." After pushing her bowl aside, she sprang up to find a cigarette. "I hadn't given him a thought in years before all of this." She blew out an agitated stream of smoke. "And if I want to compare you to other men, I will."

He topped off his wine, then hers. "How many others have asked you to marry them?"

"Dozens." It was an exaggeration, but she didn't give a damn. "But somehow I've found the strength to resist."

"You weren't in love with them," he pointed out calmly.

"I'm not in love with you." Her voice had a desperate edge to it, and she had the sinking feeling that they both knew she was lying.

He knew, but it still hurt. The hurt settled into a dull, grinding ache in his belly. Ignoring it, he finished off his chili. "You're crazy about me, O'Roarke. You're just too pigheaded to admit it."

"I'm pigheaded?" Stifling a scream, she crushed out the cigarette. "I'm amazed that even you have the nerve to toss that one out. You haven't listened to a simple no since the day I met you."

"You're right." His gaze skimmed down her. "And look where it's got me."

"Don't be so damn smug. I'm not going to marry you, because I don't want to get married, because you're a cop and because you're rich."

"You are going to marry me," he said, "because we both know you'd be miserable without me."

"Your arrogance is insufferable. It's just as irritating—and just as pathetic—as moon-eyed pleading."

"I'd rather be smug," he decided.

"You know, you're not the first jerk I've had to shake off." She snatched up her wine before she began to pace. "In my business, you get good at it." She whirled back, stabbing a finger at him. "You're almost as bad as this kid I had to deal with in Chicago. Up to now, he's taken the prize for arrogance. But even he didn't sit there with a stupid grin on his face. With him it was flowers and poetry. He was just as much of a mule, though. I was in love with him, too. But I wouldn't admit it. I needed him to take care of me, to protect me, to make my life complete." She spun in a quick circle. "What nerve! Before you, I thought he couldn't be topped. Hounding me at the station," she muttered. "Hounding me at the apartment. Sending me an engagement ring."

"He bought you a ring?"

She paused long enough for a warning look. "Don't get any ideas, Slick."

Boyd kept his voice very cool, very even. "You said he bought you a ring. A diamond?"

"I don't know." She dragged a hand through her hair. "I didn't have it appraised. I sent it back."

"What was his name?"

She waved a hand dismissively. "I don't know how I got off on this. The point I'm trying to make is—"

"I said, what was his name?"

He rose as he asked. Cilla took a confused step back. He wasn't just Boyd now. He was every inch a cop. "I— It was John something. McGill... No, McGillis,

I think. Look, he was just a pest. I only brought it up
because—"

"You didn't work with a John McGillis in Chicago."

"No." Annoyed with herself, she sat down again.
"We're getting off the subject, Boyd."

"I told you to tell me about anyone you were involved with."

"I wasn't involved with him. He was just a kid. Star-
struck or something. He listened to the show and got
hung up. I made the mistake of being nice to him, and
he misunderstood. Eventually I set him straight, and
that was that."

"How long?" Boyd asked quietly. "Just how long
did he bother you?"

She was feeling more foolish by the minute. She
could barely remember the boy's face. "Three or four
months, maybe."

"Three or four months," he repeated. Taking her by
the arms, he lifted her to her feet. "He kept this up for
three or four months and you didn't mention it to me?"

"I never thought of it."

He resisted the temptation to give her a good shake,
barely. "I want you to tell me everything you remember about him. Everything he said, everything he did."

"I can't remember."

"You'd better." Releasing her, he stepped back. "Sit
down."

She obeyed. He had shaken her more than he realized. She tried to comfort herself with the fact that
they were no longer arguing about marriage. But he
had reminded her of something she'd allowed herself
to forget for hours.

"All right. He was a night stocker at a market, and

he listened to the show. He'd call in on his break, and we'd talk a little. I'd play his requests. One day I did a remote—I can't remember where—and he showed up. He seemed like a nice kid. Twenty-three or four, I guess. Pretty," she remembered. "He had a pretty, sort of harmless face. I gave him an autograph. After that he started to write me at the station. Send poems. Just sweet, romantic stuff. Nothing suggestive."

"Go on."

"Boyd, really—"

"Go on."

The best she could do was a muttered oath. "When I realized he was getting in too deep, I pulled back. He asked me out, and I told him no." Embarrassed, she blew out a breath. "A couple of times he was waiting out in the parking lot when I got off my shift. He never touched me. I wasn't afraid of him. He was so pathetic that I felt sorry for him, and that was another mistake. He misunderstood. I guess he followed me home from work, because he started to show up at the apartment. He'd leave flowers and slip notes under the door. Kid stuff," she insisted.

"Did he ever try to get in?"

"He never tried to force his way in. I told you he was harmless."

"Tell me more."

She rubbed her hands over her face. "He'd just beg. He said he loved me, that he would always love me and we were meant to be together. And that he knew I loved him, too. It got worse. He would start crying when he called. He talked about killing himself if I didn't marry him. I got the package with the ring, and I sent it back with a letter. I was cruel. I felt I had to be. I'd already accepted the job here in Denver. It was only a few weeks after the business with the ring that we moved."

"Has he contacted you since you've been in Denver?"

"No. And it's not him who's calling. I know I'd recognize his voice. Besides, he never threatened me. Never. He was obsessed, but he wasn't violent."

"I'm going to check it out." He rose, then held out a hand. "You'd better get some sleep. We're going to head back early."

She didn't sleep. Neither did he. And they lay in the dark, in silence; there was another who kept vigil through the night.

He lit the candles. New ones he'd just bought that afternoon. Their wicks were as white as the moon. They darkened and flared as he set the match against them. He lay back on the bed with the picture pressed against his naked breast—against the twin blades of the tattooed knives.

Though the hour grew late, he remained alert. Anger fueled him. Anger and hate. Beside him the radio hummed, but it wasn't Cilla's voice he heard.

She had gone away. He knew she was with that man, and she would have given herself to that man. She'd had no right to go. She belonged to John. To John, and to him.

She was beautiful, just as John had described her. She had deceptively kind eyes. But he knew better. She was cruel. Evil. And she deserved to die. Almost lovingly, he reached down a hand to the knife that lay beside him.

He could kill her the way he'd been taught. Quick and clean. But there was little satisfaction in that, he knew. He wanted her to suffer first. He wanted her to beg. As John had begged.

When she was dead, she would be with John. His brother would rest at last. And so would he.

Chapter 10

The heat was working overtime in the precinct, and so was Boyd. While Maintenance hammered away at the faulty furnace, he pored over his files. He'd long since forsaken his jacket. His shoulder holster was strapped over a Denver P.D. T-shirt that had seen too many washings. He'd propped open a window in the conference room so that the stiff breeze from outside fought with the heat still pouring through the vents.

Two of his ongoing cases were nearly wrapped, and he'd just gotten a break in an extortion scam he and Althea had been working on for weeks. There was a court appearance at the end of the week he had to prepare for. He had reports to file and calls to make, but his attention was focused on O'Roarke, Priscilla A.

Ignoring the sweat that dribbled down his back, he read over the file on Jim Jackson, KHIP's all-night man. It interested and annoyed him.

Cilla hadn't bothered to mention that she had worked with Jackson before, in Richmond. Or that Jackson had been fired for drinking on the job. Not only had he broadcast rambling streams of consciousness, but he had taken to nodding off at the mike and leaving his audience with that taboo of radio. Dead air.

He'd lost his wife, his home and his prime spot as the morning jock and program director on Richmond's number-two Top 40 station.

When he'd gotten the ax, Cilla had taken over his duties as program director. Within six months, the number-two station had been number one. And Jackson had been picked up for drunk and disorderly.

As Althea stepped into the conference room carrying two dripping cans of soda, Boyd tossed the Jackson file across the table. Saying nothing, she passed one can to Boyd, popped the top on the second, then glanced at the file.

"He's clean except for a couple of D and D's," Althea commented.

"Revenge is high on the list for this kind of harassment. Could be he's carrying a grudge because she replaced him in Richmond and outdid him." Boyd took a swig of the warming soda. "He's only had the night spot in Denver for three months. The station manager in Richmond claims Jackson got pretty bent when they let him go. Tossed around some threats, blamed Cilla for undermining his position. Plus, you add a serious drinking problem to the grudge."

"You want to bring him in?"

"Yeah. I want to bring him in."

"Okay. Why don't we make it a doubleheader?" She picked up the file on Nick Peters. "This guy looks harmless—but then I've dated harmless-looking guys before and barely escaped with my skin. He doesn't date at all." She shrugged out of her turquoise linen jacket and draped it carefully over her chair back. "It turns out that Deborah has a couple of classes with him. Over the weekend she mentioned that he pumps her for information on Cilla all the time. Personal stuff. What kind of flowers does she like? What's her favorite color? Is she seeing anyone?"

She reached in her skirt pocket and drew out a bag of jelly beans. Carefully, and after much thought, she selected a yellow one. "Apparently he got upset when Deborah mentioned that Cilla had been married before. Deborah didn't think much of it at the time— put it down to his being weird. But she was worried enough to mention it over the weekend. She's a nice kid," Althea put in. "Real sharp. She's totally devoted to Cilla." Althea hesitated. "Over the course of the weekend, she told me about their parents."

"We've already covered that ground."

"I know we did." Althea picked up a pencil, ran it through her fingers, then set it aside again. "Deborah seems to think you're good for her sister." She waited until Boyd looked up. "I just wonder if her sister's good for you."

"I can take care of myself, partner."

"You're too involved, Boyd." She lowered her voice, though it couldn't have carried over the noise outside of the closed door. "If the captain knew you were hung up, personally, with an assignment, he'd yank you. He'd be right."

Boyd kicked back in his chair. He studied Althea's face, a face he knew as well as his own. Resentment simmered in him, but he controlled it. "I can still do my job, Thea. If I had any doubts about that, I'd yank myself."

"Would you?"

His eyes narrowed. "Yeah, I would. My first priority is my assignment's safety. If you want to go to the captain, that's your right. But I'm going to take care of Cilla, one way or the other."

"You're the one who's going to get hurt," she murmured. "One way or the other."

"My life. My problem."

The anger she'd hoped to control bubbled to the surface. "Damn it, Boyd, I care about you. It was one thing when you were infatuated by her voice. I didn't even see it as a problem when you met her and had a few sparks flying. But now you're talking serious stuff like marriage, and I know you mean it. She's got trouble, Boyd. She *is* trouble."

"You and I are assigned to take care of the trouble she's got. As for the rest, it's my business, Thea, so save the advice."

"Fine." Irked, she flipped open another file. "Bob Williams—Wild Bob—is so clean he squeaks. I haven't turned up a single connection with Cilla other than the station. He has a good marriage, goes to church, belongs to the Jaycees and for the last two weeks has been accompanying his wife to Lamaze classes."

"Nothing's turned up on the morning guys." Boyd took another swallow of the soda and wished it was an ice-cold beer.

"KHIP's just one big happy family."

"So it seems," Boyd mumbled. "Harrison looks solid, but I'm still checking. He's the one who hired her, and he actively pursued her, offering her a hefty raise and some tidy benefits to persuade her to move to Denver and KHIP."

Althea meticulously chose a red jelly bean. "What about the McGillis guy?"

"I'm expecting a call from Chicago." He opened another file. "There's the maintenance man. Billy Lomus. War veteran—Purple Heart and a Silver Star in Nam. Did two tours of duty before the leg mustered him out. He seems to be a loner. Never stays in one place more than a year or so. He did drop down in Chicago for a while a couple years back. No family. No close friends. Settled in Denver about four months ago. Foster homes as a kid."

Althea didn't look up. "Rough."

"Yeah." Boyd studied her bent head. There weren't many who knew that Althea Grayson had been shuffled from foster home to foster home as a child. "It doesn't look like we're going to have much luck inside the station."

"No. Maybe we'll do better with McGillis." She looked up, face calm, voice even. Only one who knew her well would have seen that she was still angry. "You want to start with Jackson or Peters?"

"Jackson."

"Okay. We'll try it the easy way first. I'll call and ask him to come in."

"Thanks. Thea," he added before she could rise, "you have to be hit before you can understand. I can't turn off my feelings, and I can't turn back from what I've been trained to do."

She only sighed. "Just watch your step, partner."

He intended to. And while he was watching his step,

he was going to watch Cilla's. She wouldn't care for that, Boyd thought as he continued to study the files. From the moment he had told her that he loved her, she'd been trying to pull back.

But she wasn't afraid of him, he mused. She was afraid of herself. The deeper her feelings for him went, the more afraid she became to acknowledge them. Odd, but he hadn't known he would need the words. Yet he did. More than anything he could remember, he needed to have her look at him and tell him that she loved him.

A smile, a touch, a moan in the night—it wasn't enough. Not with Cilla. He needed the bond, and the promise, that verbal connection. Three words, he thought. A simple phrase that came easily, often too easily—and could change the structure of people's lives.

They wouldn't come easily to Cilla. If she ever pushed them through the self-doubts, the barrier of defense, the fear of being hurt, she would mean them with all of her heart. It was all he needed, Boyd decided. And he would never let her take them back.

For now he had to put aside his own wants and needs and be a cop. To keep her safe, he had to be what she feared most. For her sake, he couldn't afford to think too deeply about where their lives would go once he closed the files.

"Boyd?" Althea poked her head back in the door. "Jackson's on his way in."

"Good. We should be able to catch Peters before he checks in at the station. I want to—" He broke off when the phone rang beside him. "Fletcher." He held up a hand to wave Althea inside. "Yeah. I appreciate you checking into it for me." He muffled the phone for a moment. "Chicago P.D. That's right," he continued into the receiver. "John McGillis." Taking up a pencil, he began making notes on a legal pad. In midstroke he stopped, fingers tightening. "When?" His oath was strong and quiet. "Any family? He leave a note? Can you fax it? Right." On the legal pad he wrote in bold letters: Suicide.

In silence, Althea lowered a hip to the table.

"Anything you can get me. You're sure he didn't have a brother? No. I appreciate it, Sergeant." He hung up and tapped the pencil against the pad. "Son of a bitch."

"We're sure it's the same McGillis?" Althea asked.

"Yeah. Cilla gave me the information she had on him, plus a physical description. It's the same guy. He cashed himself in almost five months ago." He let out a long breath. "Slit his wrists with a hunting knife."

"It fits, Boyd." Althea leaned over to check his notes. "You said McGillis was obsessing on Cilla, that he'd threatened to kill himself if she didn't respond. The guy over the phone is blaming her for the death of his brother."

"McGillis didn't have a brother. Only child, survived by his mother."

"Brother could be an emotional term. A best friend."

"Maybe." He knew it fit. What worried him was how Cilla would react. "The Chicago police are cooperating. They're sending us what information they've got. But I think it might be worth a trip east. We might get a lead from the mother."

Althea nodded. "Are you going to tell Cilla?"

"Yeah, I'm going to tell her. We'll talk to Jackson and Peters first, see if we can make a connection to McGillis."

* * *

Across town, Cilla dashed from the shower to the phone. She wanted it to be Boyd. She wanted him to tell her that he'd found John McGillis happily stocking shelves in Chicago. With her hair dripping down her back, she snatched up the phone.

"Hello."

"Did you sleep with him? Did you let him touch you?"

Her damp hands shook as she gripped the receiver. "What do you want?"

"Did you make promises to him the way you made promises to my brother? Does he know you're a whore and a murderer?"

"No. I'm not. I don't know why—"

"He'll have to die, too."

Her blood froze. The fear she thought she'd come to understand clawed viciously at her throat. "No! Boyd has nothing to do with this. It's—it's between you and me, just as you've said all along."

"He's involved now. He made his choice, like you made yours when you killed my brother. When I'm finished with him, I'm coming for you. Do you remember what I'm going to do to you? Do you remember?"

"You don't have to hurt Boyd. Please. Please, I'll do anything you want."

"Yes, you will." There was laughter, too, long, ee-rily lilting. "You'll do anything."

"Please. Don't hurt him." She continued to shout into the phone long after the connection went dead. With a sob tearing at her throat, she slammed the receiver down and raced to the bedroom to dress.

She had to talk to Boyd. To see him, face-to-face.

To make certain he was unharmed. And to warn him, she thought frantically. She wouldn't, couldn't, lose someone else she loved.

With her hair still streaming wet, she dashed down the stairs and yanked open the door. She nearly ran over Nick Peters.

"Oh, God." Her hands clutched at her chest. "Nick."

"I'm sorry." With fumbling hands, he pushed up his glasses. "I didn't mean to scare you."

"I have to go." She was already digging in her purse for her keys. "He called. I have to get to Boyd. I have to warn him."

"Hold on." Nick picked up the keys, which she'd dropped on the stoop. "You're in no shape to drive."

"I've got to get to Boyd," she said desperately, gripping Nick by his coat. "He said he would kill him."

"You're all worked up about the cop." Nick's mouth thinned. "He looks like he can handle himself."

"You don't understand," she began.

"Yeah, I understand. I understand just fine. You went away with him." The note of accusation surprised her, and unnerved her enough that she glanced toward the black-and-white sitting at her curb. Then she shook herself. It was foolish, absolutely foolish, to be afraid of Nick.

"Nick, I'm sorry, but I don't have time to talk right now. Can we get into this later, at the station?"

"I quit." He bit off the words. "I quit this morning."

"Oh, but why? You're doing so well. You have a future at KHIP."

"You don't even know," he said bitterly. "And you don't care."

"But I do." When she reached out to touch his arm, he jerked back.

"You let me make a fool of myself over you."

Oh, God, not again. She shook her head. "Nick, no."

"You wouldn't even let me get close, and then he comes along and it's all over before you let it begin. Now they want me to come down to the police station. They want to question me." His lips trembled. "They think I'm the one who's been calling you."

"There has to be a mistake—"

"How could you?" he shouted. "How could you believe I'd want to hurt you?" He dropped the keys back into her hand. "I just came by to let you know I'd quit, so you don't have to worry about me bothering you again."

"Nick, please. Wait." But he was already striding off to his car. He didn't look back.

Because her knees were weak, Cilla lowered herself to the stoop. She needed a moment, she realized. A moment to steady herself before she got behind the wheel of a car.

How could she have been so stupid, so blind, that she couldn't see that Nick's pride and ego were on the line? Now she had hurt him, simply by being unaware. Somehow she had to straighten out this mess her life had become. Then she had to start making amends.

Steadier, she rose, carefully locked the door, then walked to her car.

She hated police stations—had from the first. Fingering her plastic visitor's badge, she walked down the corridor. It had been scrubbed recently, and she caught the scent of pine cleaner over the ever-present aroma of coffee.

Phones rang. An incessant, strident, whirl of sound punctuated by voices raised to a shout or lowered to a grumble. Cilla turned into a doorway, to the heart of the noise, and scanned the room.

It was different from the cramped quarters where her mother had worked. And died. There was more space, less grime, and there was the addition of several computer work stations. The clickety-clack of keyboards was an underlying rhythm.

There were men and women, jackets off, shirts limp with sweat, though it was a windy fifty-five outside.

On a nearby bench, a woman rocked a fretful baby while a cop tried to distract it by jiggling a pair of handcuffs. Across the room, a young girl, surely just a teenager, related information to a trim woman cop in jeans and a sweatshirt. Silent tears coursed down the girl's face.

And Cilla remembered.

She remembered sitting in a corner of a squad room, smaller, hotter, dingier, than the one she stood in now. She had been five or six, and the baby-sitter had canceled because she'd been suffering from stomach flu. Cilla's mother had taken her to work—something about a report that couldn't wait to be written. So Cilla had sat in a corner with a doll and a Dr. Seuss book, listening to the phones and the voices. And waiting for her mother to take her home.

There had been a water cooler, she remembered. And a ceiling fan. She had watched the bubbles glug in the water and the blades whirl sluggishly. For hours. Her mother had forgotten her. Until, suffering from the same bug as her sitter, Cilla had lost her breakfast all over the squad room floor.

Shaky, Cilla wiped a hand over her damp brow. It was an old memory, she reminded herself. And not all of it. After she had been sick, her mother had cleaned her up, held her, taken her home and pampered her for the rest of the day. It wasn't fair to anyone to remember only the unhappy side.

But as she stood there she could feel all too clearly the dragging nausea, the cold sweat, and the misery of being alone and forgotten.

Then she saw him, stepping from another room. His T-shirt was damp down the front. Jackson was behind him, his hat in place, his face sheened with sweat and nerves. Flanking him was Althea.

Jackson saw her first. He took a hesitant step toward her, then stopped and shrugged. Cilla didn't hesitate. She walked to him to take his hand in both of hers.

"You okay?"

"Sure." Jackson shrugged again, but his fingers held tight on hers. "We just had to clear some things up. No big deal."

"I'm sorry. Look, if you need to talk, you can wait for me."

"No, I'm okay. Really." He lifted a hand to adjust his cap. "I guess if you screw up once you've got to keep paying for it."

"Oh, Jim."

"Hey, I'm handling it." He gave her a quick smile. "I'll catch you tonight."

"Sure."

"We appreciate your cooperation, Mr. Jackson," Althea put in.

"I told you, anything I can do to help Cilla, I'll do. I owe you," he said to Cilla, cutting her off before she could shake her head. "I owe you," he repeated, then crossed the room into the corridor.

"I could have told you that you were wasting your time with him," Cilla stated.

Boyd only nodded. "You could have told us a lot of things."

"Maybe." She turned back to him. "I need to talk to you, both of you."

"All right." Boyd gestured toward the conference room. "It's a little quieter in here."

"You want something cold?" Althea began before they settled. "I think they've finally fixed the furnace, but it's still like an oven in here."

"No, thanks. This won't take long." She sat, Althea across from her, Boyd at the table's head. She wanted to choose her words carefully. "Can I ask why you brought Jackson in?"

"You worked together in Richmond." Boyd shoved a file aside. "He had a drinking problem that got him fired, and you took over his job. He wasn't too happy about it at the time."

"No, he wasn't."

"Why didn't you tell us about it, Cilla?"

"I didn't think of it." She lifted a hand. "I honestly didn't think of it. It was a long time ago, and Jackson's come a long way. I'm sure he told you he's been in AA for over three years. He made a point of coming to see me when I was doing my run in Chicago. He wanted me to know he didn't blame me for what had happened. He's been putting his life back together."

"You got him the job at KHIP," Boyd added.

"I put in a good word for him," she said. "I don't do the hiring. He was a friend, he needed a break. When he's sober, Jackson's one of the best. And he wouldn't hurt a fly."

"And when he's drunk, he breaks up bars, threatens women and drives his car into telephone poles."

"That was a long time ago," Cilla said, struggling for calm. "And the point is, he is sober. There are some things you have to forgive and forget."

"Yes." He watched her carefully. "There are."

She thought of her mother again, and of that painful memory of the squad room. "Actually, I didn't come here to talk to you about Jackson. I got another call at home."

"We know." Althea's voice was brisk and professional. "They relayed the information to us here."

"Then you know what he said." Finding Althea's cool gaze unsympathetic, Cilla turned to Boyd. "He wants to hurt you now. He knows you're involved with me, and he's dragged you into whatever sick plans he has."

"They traced the call to another phone booth, just a couple of blocks from your house," Boyd began.

"Didn't you hear me?" Cilla slapped a fist on the table. Pencils jumped. "He's going to try to kill you, too."

He didn't reach for her hand to soothe her. At the moment, he thought, she needed him more professionally than personally. "Since I'm protecting you, he would have had to try all along. Nothing's changed."

"Everything's changed," she burst out. "It doesn't matter to him if you're with the police or not, it only matters that you're with me. I want you off the case. I want you reassigned. I don't want you anywhere near me until this is over."

Boyd crushed a disposable cup in his hand and tossed it in a wastebasket. "Don't be ridiculous."

"I'm not being ridiculous. I'm being practical." She turned to Althea, her eyes full of pleas. "Talk to him. He'll listen to you."

"I'm sorry," she said after a moment. "I agree with him. We both have a job to do, and at the moment you're it."

Desperate, Cilla whipped back to Boyd. "I'll go to your captain myself."

"He already knows about the call."

She sprang up. "I'll tell him I'm sleeping with you."

"Sit down, Cilla."

"I'll insist he take you off the case."

"Sit down," Boyd repeated. His voice was still mild, but this time she relented and dropped back in her chair. "You can go to the captain and request another officer. You can demand one. It won't make any difference. If he takes me off the case, I'll just turn in my badge."

Her head snapped up at that. "I don't believe you."

"Try me."

He was too calm, Cilla realized. And too determined. Like a brick wall, she thought in despair. Going head-to-head with him when he was like this was futile. "Boyd, don't you realize I couldn't handle it if anything happened to you?"

"Yes," he said slowly. "I think I do. Then you should realize I'm just as vulnerable where you're concerned."

"That's the whole point." She broke down enough to take his hands. "You are vulnerable. Listen to me."

Desperate, she pulled his hand to her cheek. "For eight years I've wondered if it had been anyone else in the room with my mother that day, anyone else but my father, would she have been sharper, would she have been quicker. Would her concentration have been more focused. Don't make me have to ask that same question about you for the rest of my life."

"Your mother wasn't prepared. I am."

"Nothing I say is going to change your mind."

"No. I love you, Cilla. One day soon you're going to have to learn to accept that. In the meantime, you're going to have to trust me."

She took her hand away to drop it into her lap. "Then there's nothing more to say."

"There's this." He pulled a file closer. She was already upset, he mused. Already on edge. But they couldn't afford to wait. "John McGillis."

Her head aching, Cilla pressed the heels of her hands to her eyes. "What about him?"

"He's dead."

Slowly she lowered her hands. "Dead?" she repeated dully. "But he was just a kid. Are you sure? Are you sure it's the same one?"

"Yes." The man wished he could spare her this. The cop knew he couldn't. "He committed suicide about five months ago."

For a moment she only stared. The blood drained out of her face, inch by inch, until it was bone white. "Oh, God. Oh, dear God. He— He threatened, but I didn't believe—"

"He was unstable, Cilla. He'd been in and out of therapy since he was fourteen. Trouble with his mother, in school, with his contemporaries. He'd already attempted suicide twice before."

"But he was so quiet. He tried so hard to make me—" She stopped, squeezing her eyes shut. "He killed himself after I left Chicago to come here. Just as he said he would."

"He was disturbed," Althea said gently. "Deeply disturbed. A year before he contacted you, he was involved with a girl. When she broke things off, he swallowed a fistful of barbiturates. He was in a clinic for a while. He'd only been out for a few weeks when he made the connection with you."

"I was cruel to him." Cilla turned her purse over and over on her lap. "Really cruel. At the time I thought it was the best way to handle it. I thought he would be hurt, maybe hate me for a little while, then find some nice girl and… But he won't."

"I'm not going to tell you it wasn't your fault, because you're smart enough to know that yourself." Boyd's voice was deliberately devoid of sympathy. "What McGillis did, he did to himself. You were just an excuse."

She gave a quick, involuntary shudder. "It's not as easy for me. I don't live with death the way you do."

"It's never easy, not for anyone." He opened the file. "But there are priorities here, and mine is to make the connection between McGillis and the man we're after."

"You really think John's the reason I'm being threatened?"

"It's the only thing that fits. Now I want you to tell us everything you remember about him."

She released her death grip on the bag, then carefully folded her hands on the table. As clearly as possible, she repeated everything she'd already told him.

"Did you ever see him with anyone?" Boyd asked. "Did he ever talk about his friends, his family?"

"He was always alone. Like I told you, he used to call the station. I didn't meet him face-to-face for weeks. After I did, all he really talked about was the way he felt about me. The way he wanted us to be together." Her fingers twisted together. "He used to send me notes, and flowers. Little presents. It isn't that unusual for a fan to develop a kind of fantasy relationship with a jock. But then I began to see that it wasn't—" she cleared her throat "—it wasn't the normal kind of weird, if you know what I mean."

Boyd nodded and continued to write on the pad. "Go on."

"The notes became more personal. Not sexual so much as emotional. The only time he got out of hand was when he showed me his tattoo. He had these knives tattooed on his chest. It seemed so out of character for him, and I told him I thought it was foolish for him to mark up his body that way. We were out in the parking lot. I was tired and annoyed, and here was this kid pulling open his shirt to show me this stupid tattoo. He was upset that I didn't like it. Angry, really. It was the only time I saw him angry. He said that if it was good enough for his brother, it was good enough for him."

"His brother?" Boyd repeated.

"That's right."

"He didn't have a brother."

She stopped twisting her fingers. "Yes, he did. He mentioned him a couple of times."

"By name?"

"No." She hesitated, tried to think. "No," she repeated, more certain now. "He just mentioned that his brother was living out in California. He hadn't seen him for a couple of months. He wanted me to meet him. Stuff like that."

"He didn't have a brother." Althea turned the file around to skim the top sheet again. "He was an only child."

Cilla shook her head. "So he made it up."

"No." Boyd sat back, studying his partner and Cilla in turn. "I don't think the man we're after is a figment of John McGillis's imagination."

Chapter 11

Her head was pounding in a dull, steady rhythm that made her ears ring. It was too much to absorb all at once. The phone call, Nick's visit, the reminders at the station house. John McGillis's suicide.

For the first time in her life, Cilla was tempted to shut herself in her room, lock the door and escape into a drugged sleep. She wanted peace, a few hours of peace, without guilt, without dreams, without fears.

No, she realized. More than that, much more than that, she wanted control over her life again. She'd taken that control for granted once, but she would never do so again.

She could think of nothing to say to Boyd as he followed her into the house. She was much too tired to argue, particularly since she knew the argument would be futile on her side. He wouldn't take himself off the case. He wouldn't believe her when she told him they could have no future. He refused to understand that in both instances she was looking out for his best interests.

Going to the kitchen, she went directly to the cupboard above the sink. From a bottle she shook out three extra-strength aspirin.

Boyd watched her fill a glass from the tap and swallow the pills. Her movements were automatic and just a little jerky. As she rinsed the glass, she stared out the window at the backyard.

There were daffodils, their yellow blooms still secreted in the protective green. Along the low fence they sprang up like slender spears, promising spring. She hadn't known they were there when she'd bought the house.

She wished they were blooming now so that she could see those cheerful yellow trumpets waving in the breeze. How bad could life be if you could look through your own window and see flowers blooming?

"Have you eaten?" he asked her.

"I don't remember." She folded her arms and looked out at the trees. There was the faintest hint of green along the branches. You had to look hard to see it. She wondered how long it would take for the leaves to unfurl and make shade. "But I'm not hungry. There's probably something around if you are."

"How about a nap?" He brought his hands to her shoulders and massaged them gently.

"I couldn't sleep yet." On a quiet sigh, she lifted a hand up to lay it over his. "In a few weeks I'll have to cut the grass. I think I'll like that. I've never had a lawn to mow before."

"Can I come over and watch?"

She smiled, as he'd wanted her to. "I love it here,"

she murmured. "Not just the house, though it means a lot to stand here, just here, and look out at something that belongs to me. It's this place. I haven't really felt at home anywhere since I left Georgia. It wasn't even something I realized until I came here and felt at home again."

"Sometimes you find what you want without looking."

He was talking of love, she knew. But she was afraid to speak of it.

"Some days the sky is so blue that it hurts your eyes. If you're downtown on one of those days when the wind has swept through and cleared everything, the buildings look painted against the sky. And you can see the mountains. You can stand on the corner in the middle of rush hour and see the mountains. I want to belong here."

He turned her to him. "You do."

"I never really believed that things could last. But I was beginning to, before this. I'm not sure I can belong here, or anywhere, until I can stop being afraid. Boyd." She lifted her hands to his face. Intense, she studied him, as if to memorize every plane, every angle. "I'm not just talking about belonging to a place, but to a person. I care for you more than I've cared for anyone in my life but Deborah. And I know that's not enough."

"You're wrong." He touched his lips to hers. "It's exactly enough."

She gave him a quick, frustrated shake of her head. "You just won't listen."

"Wrong again. I listen, Cilla. I just don't always agree with what you say."

"You don't have to agree, you just have to accept."

"Tell you what—when this is over, you and I will have a nice, long talk about what we both have to accept."

"When this is over, you might be dead." On impulse, she gripped him harder. "Do you really want to marry me?"

"You know I do."

"If I said I'd marry you, would you take yourself off the case? Would you let someone else take over and go up to your cabin until it's done?"

He struggled against a bitter anger. "You should know better than to try to bribe a public servant."

"I'm not joking."

"No." His eyes hardened. "I wish you were."

"I'll marry you, and I'll do my best to make you happy if you do this one thing for me."

He set her aside and stepped back. "No deal, O'Roarke."

"Damn it, Boyd."

He jammed his hands into his pockets before he exploded. "Do you think this is some kind of trade-off? What you want for what I want? Damn you, we're talking about marriage. It's an emotional commitment and a legal contract, not a bartering tool. What's next?" he demanded. "I give up my job and you agree to have my child?"

Shock and shame robbed her of speech. She held up both hands, palms out. "I'm sorry. I'm sorry," she managed. "I didn't mean for it to sound like that. I just keep thinking of what he said today. How he said it. And I can imagine what it would be like if you weren't here." She shut her eyes. "It would be worse than dying."

"I am here." He reached for her again. "And I'm going to stay here. Nothing's going to happen to either of us."

She pulled him close, pressed her face to his throat. "Don't be angry. I just haven't got a good fight in me right now."

He relented and lifted a hand to her hair. "We'll save it for later, then."

She didn't want to think about later. Only now. "Come upstairs," she whispered. "Make love with me."

Hand in hand they walked through the empty house, up the stairs. In the bedroom she closed the door, then locked it. The gesture was a symbol of her need to lock out everything but him for this one moment in time.

The sun came strong through the windows, but she felt no need for dim lights or shadows. There would be no secrets between them here. With her eyes on his, she began to unbutton her shirt.

Only days before, she thought, she would have been afraid of this. Afraid she would make the wrong move, say the wrong word, offer too much, or not enough. He had already shown her that she had only to hold out a hand and be willing to share.

They undressed in silence, not yet touching. Did he sense her mood? she wondered. Or did she sense his? All she knew was that she wanted to look, to absorb the sight of him.

There was the way the light streamed through the window and over his hair—the way his eyes darkened as they skimmed over her. She wanted to savor the line of his body, the ridges of muscle, the smooth, taut skin.

Could she have any idea how exciting she was? he wondered. Standing in the center of the room, her clothes pooled at her feet, her skin already flushed with anticipation, her eyes clouded and aware?

He waited. Though he wanted to touch her so badly his fingers felt singed, he waited.

She came to him, her arms lifted, her lips parted. Slim, soft, seductive, she pressed against him. Still, he waited. His name was a quiet sigh as she brought her mouth to his.

Home. The thought stirred inside her, a trembling wish. He was home to her. The strength of his arms, the tenderness of his hands, the unstinting generosity of his heart. Tears burned the backs of her lids as she lost herself in the kiss.

He felt the change, the slow and subtle yielding. It aroused unbearably. Strong, she was like a flame, smoldering and snapping with life and passion. In surrender, she was like a drug that seeped silently into his blood.

Lured by, lost in, her total submission, he lowered her to the bed. Her body was his. And so for the first time, he felt, was her mind, and her heart. He was careful to treat each gently.

So sweet, she thought dreamily. So lovely. The patient stroke of his fingers, the featherbrush of his lips, turned the bright afternoon into the rich secrets of midnight. Now that she knew where he could take her, she craved the journey all the more.

No dark thoughts. No nagging fears. Like flowers on the verge of blooming, she wanted to celebrate life, the simplicity of being alive and capable of love.

He aroused her thoroughly, thoughtfully, torturously. Her answering touch and her answering kiss were just as generous. What she murmured to him were not demands, but promises she desperately wanted to keep.

They knelt together in the center of the bed, lips curved as they touched, bodies almost painfully in tune. Her hair flowed through his fingers. His skin quivered at her light caress.

Soft, quiet sighs.

Heart-to-heart, they lowered again. Mouth teased mouth. Their eyes were open when he slid into her. Joined, they held close, absorbing a fresh riot of sensation. When they moved, they moved together, with equal wonder.

The booth seemed like another world. Cilla sat at the console, studying the controls she knew so well. Both her mind and body were sluggish. The clear-sighted control she had felt for a short time with Boyd that afternoon had vanished. She wanted only for the night to be over.

He had mentioned going to Chicago the next day. She intended to encourage him. If she couldn't convince him to be reassigned, at least she would have the satisfaction of knowing he would be miles away for a day or two. Away from her, and safe, she thought.

He, whoever he was, was closing in. She could feel it. When he struck, she wanted Boyd far away.

If this man was determined to punish her for what had happened to John McGillis, she would deal with it. Boyd had been right, to a point. She didn't blame herself for John's suicide. But she did share in the responsibility. And she couldn't keep herself from grieving for a young, wasted life.

The police would protect her, she thought as she cued up the next song. And she would protect herself. The new fear, the grinding fear, came from the fact that she didn't know how to protect Boyd.

"You're asleep at the switch," Boyd commented.

She shook herself. "No, just resting between bouts." She glanced at the clock. It was nearly midnight. Nearly time for the request line.

Once again the station was locked. There was only the two of them.

"You're nearly halfway home," he pointed out. "Look, why don't you come back to my place tonight? We can listen to my Muddy Waters records."

She decided to play dumb, because she knew it amused him. "Who?"

"Come on, O'Roarke."

It helped, a great deal, to see him grin at her. It made everything seem almost normal. "Okay, I'll listen to Muddy Whatsis—"

"Waters."

"Right—if you can answer these three music trivia questions."

"Shoot."

"Hold on." She set the next record, did a quick intro. She ruffled through her papers. "Okay, you've got three-ten to come up with them. Number one, what was the first British rock group to tour the States?"

"Ah, a trick question. The Dave Clark Five. The Beatles were the second."

"Not bad for an amateur. Number two. Who was the last performer at Woodstock?"

"Jimi Hendrix. You'll have to do better, O'Roarke."

"I'm just lulling you into complacency. Number three, and this is the big one, Fletcher. What year was Buddy Holly and the Crickets' hit 'That'll Be the Day' released?"

"Going back a ways, aren't you?"

"Just answer the question, Slick."

"Fifty-six."

"Is that 1956?"

"Yeah, that's 1956."

"Too bad. It was '57. You lose."

"I want to look it up."

"Go ahead. Now you'll have to come back to my place and listen to a Rolling Stones retrospective." She yawned hugely.

"If you stay awake that long." It pleased him that she had taken a moment out to play. "Want some coffee?"

She shot him a grateful look. "Only as much as I want to breathe."

"I'll get it."

The station was empty, he thought. Since Nick Peters had gotten his ego bruised and quit, there had been no one around to brew that last pot of the evening. He, too, glanced at the clock. He wanted to have it done and be back beside her before the phones started to ring.

He'd grab her a doughnut while he was at it, Boyd decided as he checked the corridor automatically. A little sugar would help her get through the night.

Before going to the lounge, he moved to the front of the building to check the doors. The locks were in place, and the alarm was engaged. His car was alone on the lot. Satisfied, he walked through the building and gave the same careful check to the rear delivery doors before he turned into the lounge.

It wasn't going to go on much longer. With the Mc-Gillis lead, Boyd had every confidence they would tie someone to the threats in a matter of days. It would be good to see Cilla without those traces of fear in her eyes, that tension in the set of her shoulders.

The restlessness would remain, he thought. And the

energy. They were as much a part of her as the color of her hair.

He added an extra scoop of coffee to the pot and listened to her voice over the speaker as she segued from one record to the next.

That magic voice, he thought. He'd had no idea when he first heard it, when he was first affected by it, that he would fall in love with the woman behind it.

It was Joan Jett now, blasting out "I Love Rock and Roll." Though the lounge speaker was turned down to little more than a murmur, the feeling gritted out. It should be Cilla's theme song, he mused. Though he'd learned in their two days in his cabin that she was just as easily fascinated by the likes of Patsy Cline or Ella Fitzgerald.

What they needed was a good solid week in the mountains, he decided. Without any outside tensions to interfere.

He took an appreciative sniff of the coffee as it began to brew and hoped that he could get to Chicago, find the answers he needed and make the trip back quickly.

He whirled, disturbed by some slight sound in the corridor. A rustle. A creak of a board. His hand was already on the butt of his weapon. Drawing it, turning his back to the side wall, he took three careful strides to the doorway, scanning.

Getting jumpy, he told himself when he saw nothing but the empty halls and the glare of security lights. But instinct had him keeping the gun in his hand. He'd taken the next step when the lights went out.

Cursing under his breath, he moved fast. Though he held his weapon up for safety, he was prepared to use it. Above, from the speakers, the passionate music continued to throb. Up ahead he could see the faint glow of lights from the booth. She was there, he told himself. Safe in those lights. Keeping his back to the wall, skimming his gaze up and down the darkened hallway, he moved toward her.

As he rounded the last turn in the hallway before the booth, he heard something behind him. He saw the storeroom door swing open as he whirled. But he never saw the knife.

"That was Joan Jett and the Blackhearts coming at you. It's 11:50, Denver, and a balmy forty-two degrees." Cilla frowned at the clock and wondered why Boyd was taking so long. "A little reminder that you can catch KHIP's own Wild Bob tomorrow at the Brown Palace Hotel downtown on 17th. And hey, if you've never been there, it's a very classy place. Tickets are still available for the banquet benefiting abused children. So open your wallets. It's twenty dollars stag, forty if you take your sweetie. The festivities start at seven o'clock, and Wild Bob will be spinning those discs for you." She potted up the next song. "Now get ready for a double-header to take you to midnight. This is Cilla O'Roarke. We've got the news, then the request line, coming up."

She switched off her mike. Shrugging her shoulders to loosen them, she slipped off the headphones. She was humming to herself as she checked the program director's hot clock. A canned ad was next, then she'd *seg* into the news at the top of the hour. She pushed away from the console to set up for the next segment.

It was then that she saw that the corridor beyond the glass door was dark. At first she only stared, baffled. Then the blood rushed to her head. If the security lights were out, the alarm might be out, as well.

He was here. Sweat pearled cold on her brow as she gripped the back of her chair. There would be no call tonight, because he was here. He was coming for her.

A scream rose in her throat to drown in a flood of panic.

Boyd. He had also come for Boyd.

Propelled by a new terror, she hit the door at a run.

"Boyd!" She shouted for him, stumbling in the dark. Her forward motion stopped when she saw the shadow move toward her. Though it was only a shape, formless in the darkened corridor, she knew. Groping behind her, she stepped back. "Where's Boyd? What have you done with him?" She stepped back again. The lights from the booth slanted through the glass and split the dark in two.

She started to speak again, to beg, then nearly fainted with relief. "Oh, God, it's you. I didn't know you were here. I thought everyone had left."

"Everyone's gone," he answered. He moved fully into the light. And smiled. Cilla's relief iced over. He held a knife, a long-bladed hunting knife already stained with blood.

"Boyd," she said again.

"He can't help you now. No one can. We're all alone. I've waited a long time for us to be alone."

"Why?" She was beyond fear now. It was Boyd's blood on the blade, and grief left no room for fear. "Why, Billy?"

"You killed my brother."

"No. No, I didn't." She stepped back, into the booth. Hot hysteria bubbled in her throat. A cold chill sheened her skin. "I didn't kill John. I hardly knew him."

"He loved you." He limped forward, the knife in

front of him, his eyes on hers. His feet were bare. He wore only camouflage pants and a dark stocking cap pulled low over his graying hair and brows. Though he had smeared his face and chest and arms with black, she could see the tattoo over his heart. The twin to the one she had seen over John McGillis's.

"You were going to marry him. He told me."

"He misunderstood." She let out a quick gasp as he jabbed with the knife. Her chair toppled with a crash as she fell back against the console.

"Don't lie to me, you bitch. He told me everything, how you told him you loved him and wanted him." His voice lowered, wavered, whispered, like the voice over the phone, and had her numbed heart racing. "How you seduced him. He was so young. He didn't understand about women like you. But I do. I would have protected him. I always protected him. He was good." Billy wiped his eyes with the hand holding the knife, then drew a gun out of his pocket. "Too good for you." He fired, ramming a bullet into the board above the controls. Cilla pressed both hands to her mouth to hold back a scream. "He told me how you lied, how you cheated, how you flaunted yourself."

"I never wanted to hurt John." She had to stay calm. Boyd wasn't dead. She wouldn't believe he was dead. But he was hurt. Somehow she had to get help. Bracing herself on the console, she reached slowly behind her and opened her mike, all the while keeping her eyes on his face. "I swear, Billy, I never wanted to hurt your brother."

"Liar," he shouted, lifting the knife to her throat. She arched back, struggling to control her shuddering.

"You don't care about him. You never cared. You just used him. Women like you love to use."

"I liked him." She sucked in her breath as the knife nicked her throat. Blood trickled warm along her skin. "He was a nice boy. He—he loved you."

"I loved him." The knife trembled in his hand, but he pulled it back an inch. Cilla let out a long, quiet breath. "He was the only person I ever loved, who ever loved me. I took care of him."

"I know." She moistened her dry lips. Surely someone would come. Someone was listening. She didn't dare take her eyes from his to glance around to the phone, where the lights were blinking madly.

"He was only five when they sent me to that house. I would have hated it there, like I'd hated all the other places they'd sent me. But John lived there. He looked up to me. He cared. He needed me. So I stayed until I was eighteen. It was only a year and a half, but we were brothers."

"Yes."

"I joined the Army. When I'd have leave he'd sneak out to see me. His pig of a mother didn't want him to have anything to do with me, 'cause I'd gotten in some trouble." He fired again, randomly, and shattered the glass in the top of the door. "But I liked the Army. I liked it fine, and John liked my uniform."

His eyes glazed over a moment, as he remembered. "They sent us to Nam. Messed up my leg. Messed up my life. When we came back, people wanted to hate us. But not John. He was proud of me. No one else had ever been proud of me."

"I know."

"They tried to put him away. Twice." Again he

squeezed the trigger. A bullet plowed into the reel-to-reel six inches from Cilla's head. Sweaty fear dried to ice on her skin. "They didn't understand him. I went to California. I was going to find us a nice place there. I just needed to find work. John was going to write poetry. Then he met you." The glaze melted away from his eyes, burned away by hate. "He didn't want to come to California anymore. He didn't want to leave you. He wrote me letters about you, long letters. Once he called. He shouldn't have spent his money, but he called all the way to California to tell me he was getting married. You wanted to get married at Christmas, so he was going to wait. I was coming back for it, because he wanted me there."

She could only shake her head. "I never agreed to marry him. Killing me isn't going to change that," she said when he leveled the gun at her. "You're right, he didn't understand me. And I guess I didn't understand him. He was young. He imagined I was something I wasn't, Billy. I'm sorry, terribly sorry, but I didn't cause his death."

"You killed him." He ran the flat of the blade down her cheek. "And you're going to pay."

"I can't stop you. I won't even try. But please, tell me what you've done with Boyd."

"I killed him." He smiled a sweet, vacant smile that made the weapons he carried incongruous.

"I don't believe you."

"He's dead." Still smiling, he held the knife up to the light. "It was easy. Easier than I remembered. I was quick," he assured her. "I wanted him dead, but I didn't care if he suffered. Not like you. You're going to suffer. I told you, remember? I told you what I was going to do."

"If you've killed Boyd," she whispered, "you've already killed me."

"I want you to beg." He laid the knife against her throat again. "I want you to beg the way John begged."

"I don't care what you do to me." She couldn't feel the knife against her flesh. She couldn't feel anything. From a long way off came the wail of sirens. She heard them without emotion, without hope. They were coming, but they were coming too late. She looked into Billy's eyes. She understood that kind of pain, she realized. It came when the person who meant the most was taken from you.

"I'm sorry," she said, prepared to die. "I didn't love him."

On a howl of rage, he struck her a stunning blow against the temple with the knife handle. He had planned and waited for weeks. He wouldn't kill her quickly, mercifully. He wouldn't. He wanted her on her knees, crying and screaming for her life.

She landed in a heap, driven down by the explosive pain. She would have wept then, with her hands covering her face and her body limp. Not for herself, but for what she had lost.

They both turned as Boyd staggered to the doorway.

Seconds. It took only seconds. Her vision cleared, her heart almost burst. Alive. He was alive.

Her sob of relief turned to a scream of terror as she saw Billy raise the gun. Then she was on her feet, struggling with him. Records crashed to the floor and were crushed underfoot as they rammed into a shelf.

His eyes burned into hers. She did beg. She pleaded even as she fought him.

Boyd dropped to his knees. The gun nearly slipped out of his slickened fingers. Through a pale red mist he could see them. He tried to shout at her, but he couldn't drag his voice through his throat. He could only pray as he struggled to maintain a grip on consciousness and the gun. He saw the knife come up, start its vicious downward sweep. He fired.

She didn't hear the crashing glass or the clamor of feet. She didn't even hear the report as the bullet struck home. But she felt the jerk of his body as the knife flew out of his hand. She lost her grip on him as he slammed back into the console.

Wild-eyed, she whirled. She saw Boyd swaying on his knees, the gun held in both hands. Behind him was Althea, her weapon still trained on the figure sprawled on the floor. On a strangled cry, Cilla rushed over as Boyd fell.

"No." She was weeping as she brushed the hair from his eyes, as she ran a hand down his side and felt the blood. "Please, no." She covered his body with hers.

"You've got to move back." Althea bit down on panic as she urged Cilla aside.

"He's bleeding."

"I know." And badly, she thought. Very badly. "There's an ambulance coming."

Cilla stripped off her shirt to make a pressure bandage. Kneeling in her chemise, she bent over Boyd. "I'm not going to let him die."

Althea's eyes met hers. "That makes two of us."

Chapter 12

There had been a sea of faces. They seemed to swim inside Cilla's head as she paced the hospital waiting room. It was so quiet there, quiet enough to hear the swish of crepe-soled shoes on tile or the whoosh of the elevator doors opening, closing. Yet in her head she could still hear the chaos of sirens, voices, the crackle of static on the police cruisers that had nosed together in the station's parking lot.

The paramedics had come. Hands had pulled her away from Boyd, pulled her out of the booth and into the cool, fresh night.

Mark, she remembered. It was Mark who had held her back as she'd run the gamut from hysteria to shock. Jackson had been there, steady as a rock, pushing a cup of some hot liquid into her hand. And Nick, white-faced, mumbling assurances and apologies.

There had been strangers, dozens of them, who had

heard the confrontation over their radios. They had crowded in until the uniformed police set up a barricade.

Then Deborah had been there, racing across the lot in tears, shoving aside cops, reporters, gawkers, to get to her sister. It was Deborah who had discovered that some of the blood on Cilla was her own.

Now, dully, Cilla looked down at her bandaged hand. She hadn't felt the knife slice into it during the few frantic seconds she had fought with Billy. The scratch along her throat where the blade had nicked her was more painful. Shallow wounds, she thought. They were only shallow wounds, nothing compared to the deep gash in her heart.

She could still see how Boyd had looked when they had wheeled him out to the ambulance. For one horrible moment, she'd been afraid he was dead. So white, so still.

But he was alive. Althea had told her. He'd lost a lot of blood, but he was alive.

Now he was in surgery, fighting to stay that way. And she could only wait.

Althea watched her pace. For herself, she preferred to sit, to gather her resources and hold steady. She had her own visions to contend with. The jolt when Cilla's voice had broken into the music. The race from the precinct to the radio station. The sight of her partner kneeling on the floor, struggling to hold his weapon. He had fired only an instant before her.

She'd been too late. She would have to live with that.

Now her partner, her friend, her family, was lying on an operating table. And she was helpless.

Rising, Deborah walked across the room to put

an arm around her sister. Cilla stopped pacing long enough to stare out the window.

"Why don't you lie down?" Deborah suggested.

"No, I can't."

"You don't have to sleep. You could just stretch out on the couch over there."

Cilla shook her head. "So many things are going through my mind, you know? The way he'd just sit there and grin after he'd gotten me mad. How he'd settle down in the corner of the booth with a book. The calm way he'd boss me around. I spent most of my time trying to push him away, but I didn't push hard enough. And now he's—"

"You can't blame yourself for this."

"I don't know who to blame." She looked up at the clock. How could the minutes go by so slowly? "I can't really think about that now. The cause isn't nearly as important as the effect."

"He wouldn't want you to take this on, Cilla."

She nearly smiled. "I haven't made a habit of doing what he wanted. He saved my life, Deb. How can I stand it if the price of that is his?"

There seemed to be no comfort she could offer. "If you won't lie down, how about some coffee?"

"Sure. Thanks."

She crossed to a pot of stale coffee resting on a hot plate. When Althea joined her, Deborah poured a second cup.

"How's she holding up?" Althea asked.

"By a thread." Deborah rubbed her gritty eyes before she turned to Althea. "She's blaming herself." Studying Althea, she offered the coffee. "Do you blame her, too?"

Athlea hesitated, bringing the coffee to her lips first.

She'd long since stopped tasting it. She looked over to the woman still standing by the window. Cilla wore baggy jeans and Mark Harrison's tailored jacket. She wanted to blame Cilla, she realized. She wanted to blame her for involving Boyd past the point of wisdom. She wanted to blame her for being the catalyst that had set an already disturbed mind on the bloody path of revenge.

But she couldn't. Neither as a cop nor as a woman.

"No," she said with a sigh. "I don't blame her. She's only one of the victims here."

"Maybe you could tell her that." Deborah passed the second cup to Althea. "Maybe that's what she needs to hear."

It wasn't easy to approach Cilla. They hadn't spoken since they had come to the waiting room. In some strange way, Althea realized, they were rivals. They both loved the same man. In different ways, perhaps, and certainly on different levels, but the emotions were deep on both sides. It occurred to her that if there had been no emotion on Cilla's part, there would have been no resentment on hers. If she had remained an assignment, and only an assignment, Althea would never have felt the need to cast blame.

It seemed Boyd had not been the only one to lose his objectivity.

She stopped beside Cilla, stared at the same view of the dark studded with city lights. "Coffee?"

"Thanks." Cilla accepted the cup but didn't drink. "They're taking a long time."

"It shouldn't be much longer."

Cilla drew in a breath and her courage. "You saw the wound. Do you think he'll make it?"

I don't know. She almost said it. They both knew she'd thought it. "I'm counting on it."

"You told me once he was a good man. You were right. For a long time I was afraid to see that, but you were right." She turned to face Althea directly. "I don't expect you to believe me, but I would have done anything to keep him from being hurt."

"I do believe you. And you did what you could." Before Cilla could turn away again, Althea put a hand on her arm. "Opening your mike may have saved his life. I want you to think about that. With a wound as serious as Boyd's, every second counted. With the broadcast, you gave us a fix on the situation, so there was an ambulance on the scene almost as quickly as we were. If Boyd makes it, it's partially due to your presence of mind. I want you to think about that."

"Billy only went after him because of me. I have to think about that, as well."

"You're trying to logic out an irrational situation. It won't work." The sympathy vanished from her voice. "If you want to start passing out blame, how about John McGillis? It was his fantasy that lit the fuse. How about the system that allowed someone like Billy Lomus to bounce from foster home to foster home so that he never knew what it was like to feel loved or wanted by anyone but a young, troubled boy? You could blame Mark for not checking Billy's references closely enough. Or Boyd and me for not making the connection quicker. There's plenty of blame to pass around, Cilla. We're all just going to have to live with our share."

"It doesn't really matter, does it? No matter who's at fault, it's still Boyd's life on the line."

"Detective Grayson?"

Althea snapped to attention. The doctor who entered was still in surgical greens damped down the front with sweat. She tried to judge his eyes first. They were a clear and quiet gray and told her nothing.

"I'm Grayson."

His brow lifted slightly. It wasn't often you met a police detective who looked as though she belonged on the cover of *Vogue*. "Dr. Winthrop, chief of surgery."

"You operated on Boyd, Boyd Fletcher?"

"That's right. He's your partner?"

"Yes." Without conscious thought on either side, Althea and Cilla clasped hands. "Can you tell us how he is?"

"I can tell you he's a lucky man," Winthrop said. "If the knife had gone a few inches either way, he wouldn't have had a chance. As it is, he's still critical, but the prognosis is good."

"He's alive." Cilla finally managed to force the words out.

"Yes." Winthrop turned to her. "I'm sorry, are you a relative?"

"No, I… No."

"Miss O'Roarke is the first person Boyd will want to see when he wakes up." Althea gave Cilla's hand a quick squeeze. "His family's been notified, but they were in Europe and won't be here for several hours yet."

"I see. He'll be done in Recovery shortly. Then we'll transfer him to ICU. O'Roarke," he said suddenly. "Of course. My son's a big fan." He lifted her bandaged hand gently. "I've already heard the story. If you were my patient, you'd be sedated and in bed."

"I'm fine."

Frowning, he studied her pupils. "To put it in un-professional terms, not by a long shot." His gaze skimmed down the long scratch on her throat. "You've had a bad shock, Miss O'Roarke. Is there someone who can drive you home?"

"I'm not going home until I see Boyd."

"Five minutes, once he's settled in ICU. Only five. I can guarantee he won't be awake for at least eight hours."

"Thank you." If he thought she would settle for five minutes, he was very much mistaken.

"Someone will come by to let you know when you can go down." He walked out rubbing the small of his back and thinking about a hot meal.

"I need to call the captain." It infuriated Althea that she was close to tears. "I'd appreciate it if you'd come back for me after you've seen him. I'd like a moment with him myself."

"Yes, of course. Thea." Letting her emotions rule, Cilla wrapped her arms around Althea. The tears didn't seem to matter. Nor did pride. They clung together and held on to hope. They didn't speak. They didn't have to. When they separated, Althea walked away to call her captain. Cilla turned blindly to the window.

"He's going to be okay," Deborah murmured be-side her.

"I know." She closed her eyes. She did know. The dull edge of fear was gone. "I just need to see him, Deb. I need to see him for myself."

"Have you told him you love him?"

She shook her head.

"Now might be a good time."

"I was afraid I wouldn't get the chance, and now... I don't know."

"Only a fool would turn her back on something so special."

"Or a coward." Cilla pressed her fingers to her lips. "Tonight, all night, I've been half out of my mind thinking he might die. Line of duty." She turned to face her sister. "In the line of duty, Deborah. If I let myself go, if I don't turn my back, how many other times might I stand here wondering if he'll live or die?"

"Cilla—"

"Or open the door one day and have his captain standing there, waiting to tell me that he was already gone, the way Mom's captain came to the door that day."

"You can't live your life waiting for the worst, Cilla. You have to live it hoping for the best."

"I'm not sure I can." Weary, she dragged her hands through her hair. "I'm not sure of anything right now except that he's alive."

"Miss O'Roarke?" Both Cilla and Deborah turned toward the nurse. "Dr. Winthrop said to bring you to ICU."

"Thank you."

Her heart hammered in her ears as she followed the nurse toward the corridor. Her mouth was dry, and her palms were damp. She tried to ignore the machines and monitors as they passed through the double doors into Intensive Care. She wanted to concentrate on Boyd.

He was still so white. His face was as colorless as the sheet that covered him. The machines blipped and hummed. A good sound, she tried to tell herself. It meant he was alive. Only resting.

Tentatively she reached out to brush at his hair. It was so warm and soft. As was his skin when she traced the back of her knuckles over his cheek.

"It's all over now," she said quietly. "All you have to do is rest and get better." Desperate for the contact, she took his limp hand in hers, then pressed it to her lips. "I'm going to stay as close as they'll let me. I promise." It wasn't enough, not nearly enough. She brushed her lips over his hair, his cheek, his mouth. "I'll be here when you wake up."

She kept her word. Despite Deborah's arguments, she spent the rest of the night on the couch in the waiting room. Every hour they allowed her five minutes with him. Every hour she woke and took what she was given.

He didn't stir.

Dawn broke, shedding pale, rosy light through the window. The shifts changed. Cilla sipped coffee and watched the night staff leave for home. New sounds began. The clatter of the rolling tray as breakfast was served. Bright morning voices replaced the hushed tones of night. Checking her watch, she set the coffee aside and walked out to sit on a bench near the doors of ICU. It was almost time for her hourly visit.

While she waited to be cleared, a group of three hurried down the hall. The man was tall, with a shock of gray hair and a lean, almost cadaverous face. Beside him was a trim woman, her blond hair ruffled, her suit wrinkled. They were clutching hands. Walking with them was another woman. The daughter, Cilla thought with dazed weariness. She had her father's build and her mother's face.

There was panic in her eyes. Even through the fatigue Cilla saw it and recognized it. Beautiful eyes. Dark green, just like... Boyd's.

"Boyd Fletcher," the younger woman said to the nurse. "We're his family. They told us we could see him."

The nurse checked her list. "I'll take you. Only two at a time, please."

"You go." Boyd's sister turned to her parents. "I'll wait right here."

Cilla wanted to speak, but as the woman sat on the opposite end of the bench she could only sit, clutching her hands together.

What could she say to them? To any of them? Even as she searched for words, Boyd's sister leaned back against the wall and shut her eyes.

Ten minutes later, the Fletchers came out again. There were lines of strain around the woman's eyes, but they were dry. Her hand was still gripping her husband's.

"Natalie." She touched her daughter's shoulder. "He's awake. Groggy, but awake. He recognized us." She beamed a smile at her husband. "He wanted to know what the hell we were doing here when we were supposed to be in Paris." Her eyes filled then, and she groped impatiently for a handkerchief. "The doctor's looking at him now, but you can see him in a few minutes."

Natalie slipped an arm around her mother's waist, then her father's. "So what were we worried about?"

"I still want to know exactly what happened." Boyd's father shot a grim look at the double doors. "Boyd's captain has some explaining to do."

"We'll get the whole story," his wife said soothingly.

"Let's just take a few minutes to be grateful it wasn't worse." She dropped the handkerchief back in her purse. "When he was coming around, he asked for someone named Cilla. That's not his partner's name. I don't believe we know a Cilla."

Though her legs had turned to jelly, Cilla rose. "I'm Cilla." Three pairs of eyes fixed on her. "I'm sorry," she managed. "Boyd was…he was hurt because…he was protecting me. I'm sorry," she said again.

"Excuse me." The nurse stood by the double doors again. "Detective Fletcher insists on seeing you, Miss O'Roarke. He's becoming agitated."

"I'll go with you." Taking charge, Natalie steered Cilla through the doors.

Boyd's eyes were closed again, but he wasn't asleep. He was concentrating on reviving the strength he'd lost in arguing with the doctor. But he knew the moment she entered the room, even before she laid a tentative hand on his. He opened his eyes and looked at her.

"Hi, Slick." She made herself smile. "How's it going?"

"You're okay." He hadn't been sure. The last clear memory was of Billy holding the knife and Cilla struggling.

"I'm fine." Deliberately she put her bandaged hand behind her back. Natalie noted the gesture with a frown. "You're the one hooked up to machines." Though her voice was brisk, the hand that brushed over his cheek was infinitely tender. "I've seen you looking better, Fletcher."

He linked his fingers with hers. "I've felt better."

"You saved my life." She struggled to keep it light, keep it easy. "I guess I owe you."

"Damn right." He wanted to touch her, but his arms felt like lead. "When are you going to pay up?"

"We'll talk about it. Your sister's here." She glanced across the bed at Natalie.

Natalie leaned down and pressed a kiss to his brow. "You jerk."

"It's nice to see you, too."

"You just couldn't be a pushy, uncomplicated business shark, could you?"

"No." He smiled and nearly floated off again. "But you make a great one. Try to keep them from worrying."

She sighed a little as she thought of their parents. "You don't ask for much."

"I'm doing okay. Just keep telling them that. You met Cilla."

Natalie's gaze skimmed up, measuring. "Yes, we met. Just now."

"Make her get the hell out of here." Natalie saw the shocked hurt in Cilla's eyes, saw her fingers tighten convulsively on the bedguard.

"She doesn't have to make me go." With her last scrap of pride, she lifted her chin. "If you don't want me around, I'll—"

"Don't be stupid," Boyd said in that mild, slightly irritated voice that made her want to weep. He looked back at his sister. "She's dead on her feet. Last night was rough. She's too stubborn to admit it, but she needs to go home and get some sleep."

"Ungrateful slob," Cilla managed. "Do you think you can order me around even when you're flat on your back?"

"Yeah. Give me a kiss."

"If I didn't feel sorry for you, I'd make you beg."
She leaned close to touch her lips to his. At the moment of contact she realized with a new panic that she was going to break down. "Since you want me to clear out, I will. I've got a show to prep for."

"Hey, O'Roarke."

She got enough of a grip on control to look over her shoulder. "Yes?"

"Come back soon."

"Well, well…" Natalie murmured as Cilla hurried away.

"Well, well…" her brother echoed. He simply could not keep his eyes open another moment. "She's terrific, isn't she?"

"I suppose she must be."

"As soon as I can stay awake for more than an hour at a time, I'm going to marry her."

"I see. Maybe you should wait until you can actually stand up for an hour at a time."

"I'll think about it. Nat." He found her hand again. "It is good to see you."

"You bet," she said as he fell asleep.

Cilla was almost running when she hit the double doors. She didn't pause, not even when Boyd's parents both rose from the bench. As her breath hitched and her eyes filled, she hurried down the hall and stumbled into the ladies' room.

Natalie found her there ten minutes later, curled up in a corner, sobbing wretchedly. Saying nothing, Natalie pulled out a handful of paper towels. She dampened a few, then walked over to crouch in front of Cilla.

"Here you go."

"I hate to do this," Cilla said between sobbing breaths.

"Me, too." Natalie wiped her own eyes, and then, without a thought to her seven-hundred-dollar suit, sat on the floor. "The doctor said they'd probably move him to a regular room by tomorrow. They're hoping to downgrade his condition from critical to serious by this afternoon."

"That's good." Cilla covered her face with the cool, wet towel. "Don't tell him I cried."

"All right."

There was silence between them as each worked on control.

"I guess you'd like to know everything that happened," Cilla said at length.

"Yes, but it can wait. I think Boyd had a point when he told you to go home and get some sleep."

With very little effort she could have stretched out on the cool tile floor and winked out like a light. "Maybe."

"I'll give you a lift."

"No, thanks. I'll call a cab."

"I'll give you a lift," Natalie repeated, and rose.

Lowering the towel, Cilla studied her. "You're a lot like him, aren't you?"

"So they say." Natalie offered a hand to help Cilla to her feet. "Boyd told me you're getting married."

"So he says."

For the first time in hours, Natalie laughed. "We really will have to talk."

She all but lived in the hospital for the next week. Boyd was rarely alone. Though it might have frustrated him from time to time that he barely had a moment for a private word with her, Cilla was grateful.

His room was always filled with friends, with family, with associates. As the days passed and his condition improved, she cut her visits shorter and kept them farther apart.

They both needed the distance. That was how she rationalized it. They both needed time for clear thinking. If she was to put the past—both the distant past and the near past—behind her, she needed to do it on her own.

It was Thea who filled her in on Billy Lomus. In his troubled childhood, the only bright spot had been John McGillis. As fate would have it, they had fed on each other's weaknesses. John's first suicide attempt had occurred two months after Billy left for Vietnam. He'd been barely ten years old.

When Billy had returned, bitter and wounded, John had run away to join him. Though the authorities had separated them, they had always managed to find each other again. John's death had driven Billy over the fine line of reason he had walked.

"Delayed stress syndrome," Althea said as they stood together in the hospital parking lot. "Paranoid psychosis. Obsessive love. It doesn't really matter what label you put on it."

"Over these past couple of weeks, I've asked myself dozens of times if there was anything I could have done differently with John McGillis." She took in a deep breath of the early spring air. "And there wasn't. I can't tell you what a relief it is to finally be sure of that."

"Then you can put it behind you."

"Yes. It's not something I can forget, but I can put

it behind me. Before I do, I'd like to thank you for everything you did, and tried to do."

"It was my job," Althea said simply. "We weren't friends then. I think maybe we nearly are now."

Cilla laughed. "Nearly."

"So, as someone who's nearly your friend, there's something I'd like to say."

"Okay."

"I've been watching you and Boyd since the beginning. Observation's also part of the job." Her eyes, clear and brown and direct, met Cilla's. "I still haven't decided if I think you're good for Boyd. It's not really my call, but I like to form an opinion."

Cilla looked out beyond the parking lot to a patch of green. The daffodils were blooming there, beautifully. "Thea, you're not telling me anything I don't already know."

"My point is, Boyd thinks you're good for him. That's enough for me. I guess the only thing you've got to decide now is if he's good for you."

"He thinks he is," she murmured.

"I've noticed." In an abrupt change of mood, Althea looked toward the hospital. "I heard he was getting out in a couple of days."

"That's the rumor."

"You've already been up, I take it."

"For a few minutes. His sister's there, and a couple of cops. They brought in a flower arrangement shaped like a horseshoe. The card read Tough break, Lucky. They tried to tell him they'd confiscated it from some gangster's funeral."

"Wouldn't surprise me. Funny thing about cops. They usually have a sense of humor, just like real people." She gave Cilla an easy smile. "I'm going to go up. Should I tell him I ran into you and you're coming back later?"

"No. Not this time. Just—just tell him to listen to the radio. I'll see if I can dig up 'Dueling Banjos.'"

"'Dueling Banjos'?"

"Yeah. I'll see you later, Thea."

"Sure." Althea watched Cilla walk to her car and was grateful, not for the first time, not to be in love.

Though the first couple of nights in the booth after the shooting had been difficult, Cilla had picked up her old routine. She no longer got a flash of Boyd bleeding as he knelt by the door, or of Billy, his eyes wild, holding a knife to her throat.

She'd come to enjoy the request line again. The blinking lights no longer grated on her nerves. Every hour she was grateful that Boyd was recovering, and so she threw herself into her work with an enthusiasm she had lost for too long.

"Cilla."

She didn't jolt at the sound of her name, but swiveled easily in her chair and smiled at Nick. "Hey."

"I, ah, decided to come back."

She kept smiling as she accepted the cup of coffee he offered. "I heard."

"Mark was real good about it."

"You're an asset to the station, Nick. I'm glad you changed your mind."

"Yeah, well…" He let his words trail off as he studied the scar on the palm of her hand. The stitches had come out only days earlier. "I'm glad you're okay."

"Me, too. You want to get me the Rocco's Pizza commercial?"

He nearly jumped for it, sliding it out of place and handing it to her. Cilla popped the tape in, then potted it up.

"I wanted to apologize," he blurted out.

"You don't have to."

"I feel like a jerk, especially after I heard…well, the whole story about Billy and that guy from Chicago."

"You're nothing like John, Nick. And I'm flattered that you were attracted to me—especially since you have a class with my incredibly beautiful sister."

"Deborah's nice. But she's too smart."

Cilla had her first big laugh of the month. "Thanks a lot, kid. Just what does that make me?"

"I didn't mean—" He broke off, mortally embarrassed. "I only meant—"

"Don't bury yourself." Giving him a quick grin, she turned on her mike. "Hey, Denver, we're going to keep it rocking for you for the next quarter hour. It's 10:45 on this Thursday night, and I'm just getting started." She hit them with a blast of Guns 'n' Roses. "Now that's rock and roll," she said to herself. "Hey, Nick, why don't you…" Her words trailed off when she saw Boyd's mother in the doorway. "Mrs. Fletcher." She sprang up, nearly strangling herself with her headphones.

"I hope I'm not disturbing you." She smiled at Cilla, nodded to Nick.

"No, no, of course not." Cilla brushed uselessly at her grimy jeans. "Um… Nick, why don't you get Mrs. Fletcher a cup of coffee?"

"No, thank you, dear. I can only stay a moment."

Nick made his excuses and left them alone.

"So," Mrs. Fletcher said after a quick study. She blinked at the posters on the wall and examined the equipment. "This is where you work?"

"Yes. I'd, ah...give you a tour, but I've got—"

"That's perfectly all right." The lines of strain were no longer around her eyes. She was a trim, attractive and perfectly groomed woman. And she intimidated the hell out of Cilla. "Don't let me interrupt you."

"No, I... I'm used to working with people around."

"I missed you at the hospital the past few days, so I thought I'd come by here and say goodbye."

"You're leaving?"

"Since Boyd is on the mend, we're going back to Paris. It's business, as well as pleasure."

Cilla made a noncommittal noise and cued up the next record. "I know you must be relieved that Boyd... well, that he's all right. I'm sure it was dreadful for you."

"For all of us. Boyd explained it all to us. You've had a horrible ordeal."

"It's over now."

"Yes." She lifted Cilla's hand and glanced at the healing wound. "Experiences leave scars. Some deeper than others." She released Cilla's hand to wander around the tiny booth. "Boyd tells me you're to be married."

"I..." She shook off the shock, cleared her throat. "Excuse me a minute." Turning to the console she segued into the next record, then pushed another switch. "It's time for our mystery record," she explained. "The roll of thunder plays over the song, then people call in. The first caller who can give me the name of the song, the artist and the year of the recording wins a pair of concert tickets. We've got Madonna coming in at the end of the month."

"Fascinating." Mrs. Fletcher smiled, a smile precisely like Boyd's. "As I was saying, Boyd tells me you're to be married. I wondered if you'd like any help with the arrangements."

"No. That is, I haven't said... Excuse me." She pounced on a blinking light. "KHIP. No, I'm sorry, wrong answer. Try again." She struggled to keep her mind clear as the calls came through. The fourth caller's voice was very familiar.

"Hey, O'Roarke."

"Boyd." She sent his mother a helpless look. "I'm working."

"I'm calling. You got a winner yet?"

"No, but—"

"You've got one now. 'Electric Avenue,' Eddy Grant, 1983."

She had to smile. "You're pretty sharp, Slick. Looks like you've got yourself a couple of concert tickets. Hold on." She switched on her mike. "We've got a winner."

Patient, Mrs. Fletcher watched her work, smiling as she heard her son's voice over the speakers.

"Congratulations," Cilla said after she'd potted up a new record.

"So, are you going to the concert with me?"

"If you're lucky. Gotta go."

"Hey!" he shouted before she could cut him off. "I haven't heard 'Dueling Banjos' yet."

"Keep listening." After a long breath, she turned back to his mother. "I'm very sorry."

"No problem, no problem at all." In fact, she'd found the interlude delightful. "About the wedding?"

"I don't know that there's going to be a wedding. I mean, there isn't a wedding." She dragged a hand through her hair. "I don't think."

"Ah, well…" That same faint, knowing smile hovered around her mouth. "I'm sure you or Boyd will let us know. He's very much in love with you. You know that?"

"Yes. At least I think I do."

"He told me about your parents. I hope you don't mind."

"No." She sat again. "Mrs. Fletcher—"

"Liz is fine."

"Liz. I hope you don't think I'm playing some sort of game with Boyd. I wouldn't ask him to change. I could never ask him to change, and I just don't know if I can live with what he does."

"Because you're afraid of his being a policeman? Afraid he might die and leave you, as your parents did?"

Cilla looked down at her hands, spread her fingers. "I guess when you trim away all the fat, that's it."

"I understand. I worry about him," she said quietly. "I also understand he's doing what he has to do."

"Yes, it is what he has to do. I've given that a lot of thought since he was hurt." Cilla looked up again, her eyes intense. "How do you live with it?"

Liz took Cilla's restless hand in hers. "I love him."

"And that's enough?"

"It has to be. It's always difficult to lose someone you love. The way you lost your parents was tragic— and, according to Boyd, unnecessary. My mother died when I was only six. I loved her very much, though I had little time with her."

"I'm sorry."

"She cut herself in the garden one day. Just a little nick on the thumb she paid no attention to. A few weeks later she was dead of blood poisoning. All from a little cut on the thumb with a pair of rusty garden shears. Tragic, and unnecessary. It's hard to say how and when a loved one will be taken from us. How sad it would be not to allow ourselves to love because we were afraid to lose." She touched a hand to Cilla's cheek. "I hope to see you again soon."

"Mrs. Fletcher—Liz," Cilla said as she stopped at the door. "Thank you for coming."

"It was my pleasure." She glanced at a poster of a bare-chested rock star with shoulder-length hair and a smoldering sneer. "Though I do prefer Cole Porter."

Cilla found herself smiling as she slipped in another tape. After the ad, she gave her listeners fifteen uninterrupted minutes of music and herself time to think.

When the request line rolled around, she was as nervous as a cat, but her mind was made up.

"This is Cilla O'Roarke for KHIP. It's five minutes past midnight and our request lines are open. Before I take a call, I've got a request of my own. This one goes to Boyd. No, it's not 'Dueling Banjos,' Slick. You're just going to have to try a new memory on for size. It's an old one by the Platters. 'Only You.' I hope you're listening, because I want you to know—" For the first time in her career, she choked on the air. "Oh, boy, it's a lot to get out. I guess I want to say I finally figured out it's only you for me. I love you, and if the offer's still open, you've got a deal."

She sent the record out and, with her eyes closed, let the song flow through her head.

Struggling for composure, she took call after call. There were jokes and questions about Boyd, but none of the callers *was* Boyd. She'd been so certain he would phone.

Maybe he hadn't even been listening. The thought of that had her dropping her head in her hands. She had finally dragged out the courage to tell him how she felt, and he hadn't been listening.

She got through the next two hours step-by-step. It had been a stupid move, she told herself. It was unbelievably foolish to announce that you loved someone over the radio. She'd only succeeded in embarrassing herself.

The more she thought about it, the angrier she became. She'd told him to listen, damn it. Couldn't he do anything she asked him to do? She'd told him to go away, he'd stayed. She'd told him she wasn't going to marry him, he'd told everyone she was. She'd told him to listen to the radio, he'd shut it off. She'd bared her soul over the public airwaves for nothing.

"That was a hell of a request," Jackson commented when he strolled into the booth just before two.

"Shut up."

"Right." He hummed to himself as he checked the programmer's clock for his shift. "Ratings should shoot right through the roof."

"If I wanted someone to be cheerful in here, I'd have brought along Mickey Mouse."

"Sorry." Undaunted, he continued to hum.

With her teeth on edge, Cilla opened her mike. "That's all for tonight, Denver. It's 1:58. I'm turning you over to my man Jackson. He'll be with you until six in the a.m. Have a good one. And remember, when you dream of me, dream good." She kicked her chair out of the way. "And if you're smart," she said to Jackson, "you won't say a word."

"Lips are sealed."

She stalked out, snatching up her jacket and digging for her keys as she headed for the door. She was going to go home and soak her head. And if Deborah had been listening and was waiting up, it would just give her someone to chew out.

Head down, hands in her pockets, she stomped to her car. She had her hand on the door handle before she saw that Boyd was sitting on the hood.

"Nice night," he said.

"What—what the hell are you doing here?" Anger forgotten, she rushed around the car. "You're supposed to be in the hospital. They haven't released you yet."

"I went over the wall. Come here."

"You jerk. Sitting out here in the night air. You were nearly dead two weeks ago, and—"

"I've never felt better in my life." He grabbed her by the front of her jacket and hauled her against him for a kiss. "And neither have you."

"What?"

"You've never felt better in my life, either."

She shook her head to clear it and stepped back. "Get in the car. I'm taking you back to the hospital."

"Like hell." Laughing, he pulled her against him again and devoured her mouth.

She went weak and hot and dizzy. On a little sigh, she clung to him, letting her hands rush over his face, into his hair. Just to touch him, to touch him and know he was whole and safe and hers.

"Lord, do you know how long it's been since you've kissed me like that?" He held her close, waiting for his heart rate to level. His side was throbbing in time with it. "Those chaste little pecks in the hospital weren't enough."

"We were never alone."

"You never stayed around long enough." He pressed his lips to the top of her head. "I liked the song."

"What song? Oh." She stepped back again. "You were listening."

"I liked the song a lot." He took her hand and pressed his mouth to the scar. "But I liked what you said before it even better. How about saying it again, face-to-face?"

"I..." She let out a huff of breath.

Patient, he cupped her face in his hands. "Come on, O'Roarke." He smiled. "Spit it out."

"I love you." She said it so quickly, and with such obvious relief, that he laughed again. "Damn it, it's not funny. I really love you, and it's your fault for making it impossible for me to do anything else."

"Remind me to pat myself on the back later. You've got a hell of a voice, Cilla." He wrapped his arms around her, comfortably. "And you've never sounded better than tonight."

"I was scared."

"I know."

"I guess I'm not anymore." She rested her head against his shoulder. "It feels right."

"Yeah. Just right. The offer still holds, Cilla. Marry me."

She took her time, not because she was afraid, but because she wanted to savor it. She wanted to remember every second. The moon was full, the stars were out. She could just catch the faintest drift of those fragile spring flowers.

"There's one question I have to ask you first."

"Okay."

"Can we really hire a cook?"

He laughed and lowered his mouth to hers. "Absolutely."

"Then it's a deal."

* * * * *

NIGHT MOVES

To the mountains I live in,
and the people who love them

Chapter 1

"What the hell are you doing in a place like this?"

Maggie, on her hands and knees, didn't look up. "C.J., you're playing the same old song."

C.J. pulled down the hem of his cashmere sweater. He was a man who made worry an art, and he worried about Maggie. Someone had to. Frustrated, he looked down at the sable-brown hair twisted untidily into a knot on top of her head. Her neck was slender, pale, her shoulders curved slightly forward as she rested her weight on her forearms. She had a delicate build, with the kind of fragility C.J. had always associated with nineteenth-century English aristocratic ladies. Though perhaps they, too, had possessed endless stores of strength and endurance under frail bones and porcelain skin.

She wore a T-shirt and jeans that were both faded and slightly damp from perspiration. When he looked at her hands, fine-boned, elegant hands, and saw they were grimy, he shuddered. He knew the magic they were capable of.

A phase, he thought. She was just going through a phase. After two marriages and a few affairs, C.J. understood that women went through odd moods from time to time. He brushed at his trim, sandy mustache with one finger. It was up to him to guide her back, gently, to the real world.

As he glanced around at nothing but trees and rocks and isolation, he wondered, fleetingly, if there were bears in the woods. In the real world, such things were kept in zoos. Keeping a nervous lookout for suspicious movements, he tried again.

"Maggie, just how long are you going to go on this way?"

"What way is that, C.J.?" Her voice was low, husky, as if she'd just been awakened. It was a voice that made most men wish they'd awakened her.

The woman was infuriating. C.J. tugged a hand through his carefully styled, blow-dried hair. What was she doing three thousand miles from L.A., wasting herself on this dirty work? He had a responsibility to her and, damn it, to himself. C.J. blew out a long breath, an old habit he had whenever he met with opposition. Negotiations were, after all, his business. It was up to him to talk some sense into her. He shifted his feet, careful to keep his polished loafers out of the dirt. "Babe, I love you. You know I do. Come home."

This time Maggie turned her head, looking up with a flash of a smile that involved every inch of her face— the mouth that stopped just short of being too wide, the chin a bit pointed, the sweep of cheekbones that gave her face a diamond shape. Her eyes, big, round and shades darker than her hair, added that final spark of animation. It wasn't a stunning face. You'd tell yourself that while you tried to focus in on the reason you were stunned. Even now, without makeup, with a long streak of topsoil across one cheek, the face involved you. Maggie Fitzgerald involved you because she was exactly what she seemed. Interesting. Interested.

Now she sat back on her haunches, blowing a wisp of hair out of her eyes as she looked up at the man who was frowning at her. She felt a tug of affection, a tug of amusement. Both had always come easily to her. "C.J., I love you, too. Now stop acting like an old woman."

"You don't belong here," he began, more exasperated than insulted. "You shouldn't be grubbing around on your hands and knees—"

"I like it," she said simply.

It was the very simplicity of the tone that told him he had a real problem. If she'd shouted, argued, his chances of turning her around would've been all but secured. But when she was like this, calmly stubborn, changing her mind would be like climbing Mount Everest. Treacherous and exhausting. Because he was a clever man, C.J. changed tactics.

"Maggie, I can certainly understand why you might like to get away for a while, rest a bit. No one deserves it more." That was a nice touch, he thought, because it was true. "Why don't you take a couple weeks in Cancún, or go on a shopping spree in Paris?"

"Mmm." Maggie shifted on her knees and fluffed up the petals of the pansies she was planting. They looked, she decided, a bit sick. "Hand me that watering can, will you?"

"You're not listening."

"Yes, I am." Stretching over, she retrieved the can herself. "I've been to Cancún, and I have so many clothes now I left half of them in storage in L.A."

Without breaking stride, C.J. tried a different turn. "It's not just me," he began again, watching as she drenched the pansies. "Everyone who knows you, who knows about this, thinks you've—"

"Slipped a gear?" Maggie supplied. Overdid the water, she decided as the saturated blossoms drooped. She had a lot to learn about the basics of country life. "C.J., instead of nagging me and trying to talk me into doing something I've no intention of doing, why don't you come down here and give me a hand?"

"A hand?" His voice held the slightly appalled note it might have if she'd suggested he dilute prime scotch with tap water. Maggie chuckled.

"Pass me that flat of petunias." She stuck the small spade in the ground again, fighting the rocky soil. "Gardening's good for you. It gets you back in touch with nature."

"I've no desire to touch nature."

This time she laughed and lifted her face to the sky. No, the closest C.J. would come to nature would be a chlorinated pool—solar-heated. Up to a few months ago she'd barely gotten much closer herself. She'd certainly never attempted to. But now she'd found something— something she hadn't even been looking for. If she hadn't come to the East Coast to collaborate on the score for a new musical, if she hadn't taken an impulsive drive south after the long, grueling sessions had ended, she never would've happened on the sleepy little town tucked into the Blue Ridge.

Do we ever know where we belong, Maggie wondered, unless we're lucky enough to stumble onto our own personal space? She only knew that she'd been heading nowhere in particular and she'd come home.

Maybe it had been fate that had led her into Morganville, a cluster of houses cupped in the foothills that boasted a population of 142. From the town proper, it spread out into farms and isolated mountain homes. If fate had taken her to Morganville, it had again taken her past the sign that listed the sale of a house and twelve acres. There'd been no moment of indecision, no quibbling over the price, no last-minute doubts. Maggie had met the terms and had had the deed in her hand within thirty days.

Looking up at the three-story frame house, with shutters still hanging crooked, Maggie could well imagine her friends and colleagues wondering about her mental state. She'd left her Italian-marble entrance hall and mosaic-tiled pool for rusty hinges and rocks. She'd done it without a backward glance.

Maggie patted the dirt around the petunias, then sat back. They looked a bit more spritely than her pansies. Maybe she was beginning to get the hang of it. "What do you think?"

"I think you should come back to L.A. and finish the score."

"I meant the flowers." She brushed off her jeans as she rose. "In any case, I am finishing the score—right here."

"Maggie, how can you work here?" C.J. exploded. He tossed out both arms in a gesture she'd always admired for its unapologetic theatrics. "How can you live here? This place isn't even civilized."

"Why? Because there's no health club and boutique on every other corner?" Wanting to temper the words, she tucked a hand through C.J.'s arm. "Go ahead, take a deep breath. The clean air won't hurt you."

"Smog's underrated," he mumbled as he shifted his feet again. Professionally he was her agent, but personally C.J. considered himself her friend, perhaps her best friend since Jerry had died. Thinking of that, he changed his tone again. This time it was gentle. "Look, Maggie, I know you've been through some rough times. Maybe L.A. has too many memories for you to deal with right now. But you can't bury yourself."

"I'm not burying myself." She put her hands on his forearms, squeezing for both emphasis and support. "And I buried Jerry nearly two years ago. That was another part of my life, C.J., and has nothing to do with this. This is home. I don't know how else to explain it." She slid her hands down to his, forgetting hers were smeared with earth. "This is my mountain now, and I'm happier here, more settled, than I ever was in Los Angeles."

He knew he was beating his head against a wall, but opted to give it one more shot. "Maggie." He slipped an arm around her shoulder, as if, she thought ruefully, she was a small child needing guidance. "Look at that place." He let the silence hang a moment while they both studied the house on the rise above. He noticed that the porch was missing several boards and that the paint on the trim was peeling badly. Maggie saw the sun reflecting off the window glass in rainbows. "You can't possibly be serious about living there."

"A little paint, a few nails." She shrugged it away. Long ago she'd learned that surface problems were best ignored. It was the problem simmering under the surface, not quite visible, that had to be dealt with. "It has such possibilities, C.J."

"The biggest one is that it'll fall down on your head."

"I had the roof fixed last week—a local man."

"Maggie, I'm not at all convinced there are any local men, or women, within ten miles. This place doesn't look fit for anything but elves and gnomes."

"Well, he might've been a gnome." Her sense of fun spurred her on as she stretched her back muscles. "He was about five foot five, stocky as a bull and somewhere around a hundred and two. His name was Bog."

"Maggie—"

"He was very helpful," she went on. "He and his boy are coming back to deal with the porch and some of the other major repairs."

"All right, so you've got a gnome to do some hammering and sawing. What about this?" He swept his hand around to take in the surrounding land. It was rocky, uneven and overgrown with weeds and thickets. Not even a dedicated optimist could've considered any part of it a lawn. A burly tree slanted dangerously toward the house itself, while thorny vines and wildflowers scrambled for space. There was a pervading smell of earth and green.

"Like Sleeping Beauty's castle," Maggie murmured. "I'll be sorry in a way to hack it down, but Mr. Bog has that under control, too."

"He does excavation work, too?"

Maggie tilted her head and arched her brows. It was a look that made anyone over forty remember her mother. "He recommended a landscaper. Mr. Bog assures me that Cliff Delaney is the best man in the county. He's coming by this afternoon to take a look at the place."

"If he's a smart man, he'll take one look at that gully you call a road leading up here and keep on going."

"But you brought your rented Mercedes all the way up." Turning, she threw her arms around his neck and kissed him. "Don't think I don't appreciate that or the fact that you flew in from the Coast or that you care enough to be concerned. I appreciate all of it. I appreciate you." She ruffled his hair, something no one else would've gotten away with. "Trust my judgment on this, C.J. I really do know what I'm doing. Professionally, my work can't do anything but improve here."

"That's yet to be seen," he muttered, but lifted a hand to touch her cheek. She was still young enough to have foolish dreams, he thought. Still sweet enough to believe in them. "You know it's not your work I'm worried about."

"I know." Her voice softened, and with it her eyes, her mouth. She was not a woman who guided her emotions, but one who was guided by them. "I need the peace here. Do you know, this is the first time in my life I've gotten off the merry-go-round? I'm enjoying the solid ground, C.J."

He knew her well and understood that there was no moving her, for the moment, from the position she'd taken. He understood, too, that from birth her life had been ribboned with the stuff of fantasies—and of nightmares. Perhaps she did need to compensate, for a time.

"I've got a plane to catch," he grumbled. "As long as you insist on staying here, I want you to call me every day."

Maggie kissed him again. "Once a week," she countered. "You'll have the completed score for *Heat Dance* in ten days." With her arm around his waist, she led him to the end of the uneven, overgrown path where his Mercedes sat in incongruous splendor. "I love the film, C.J. It's even better than I thought it would be when I first read the script. The music's all but writing itself."

He only grunted and cast one look behind him at the house. "If you get lonely—"

"I won't." With a quick laugh, Maggie nudged him into the car. "It's been enlightening discovering how self-sufficient I can be. Now, have a nice trip back and stop worrying about me."

Fat chance, he thought, automatically reaching in his briefcase to make certain his Dramamine was there. "Send me the score, and if it's sensational, I might stop worrying…a little."

"It is sensational." She backed off from the car to give him room to turn around. "*I'm* sensational!" she shouted as the Mercedes began to inch around. "Tell everyone back on the Coast that I've decided to buy some goats and chickens."

The Mercedes stopped dead. "Maggie…"

Laughing, she waved at him and backed down the path. "Not yet…but maybe in the fall." She decided it was best to reassure him, or else he might get out and start again. "Oh, and send me some Godiva chocolates."

That was more like it, C.J. thought, and put the car in gear again. She'd be back in L.A. in six weeks. He glanced in his rearview mirror as he started to drive away. He could see her, small and slender, still laughing, against the backdrop of the overgrown land, greening trees and dilapidated house. Once again he shuddered, but this time it wasn't from an offense of his sensibilities. This time it was from something like fear. He had a sudden flash of certainty that she wasn't safe there.

Shaking his head, C.J. reached in his pocket for his antacids as the car bumped noisily over a rock. Everyone told him he worried too much.

Lonely, Maggie thought as she watched the Mercedes bump and wind its way down her excuse for a lane. No, she wasn't lonely. She was as certain as she'd ever been about anything that she'd never be lonely here. She felt an unexpected sense of foreboding that she shrugged off as ridiculous.

Wrapping her arms around herself, she turned in two slow circles. Trees rose up out of the rocky hillside. The leaves were hardly more than buds now, but in a few weeks they would grow and spread, turning the woods into a lush cover of green. She liked to imagine it that way and to try to picture it in the dead of winter—white, all white and black with ice clinging to the branches and shimmering on the rocks. In the fall there'd be a tapestry outside every window. She was far from lonely.

For the first time in her life, she had a chance to put her own stamp on a place. It wouldn't be a copy of anything she'd had before or anything that'd been given to her. It was hers, absolutely, and so were any mistakes she made here, any triumphs. There'd be no press to compare this isolated spot in western Maryland with her mother's mansion in Beverly Hills or her father's villa in the south of France. If she was lucky, very, very lucky, Maggie thought with a satisfied sigh, there'd be no press at all. She could make her music and live her life in peace and solitude.

If she stood very still, if she closed her eyes and

didn't move, she could hear the music all around her. Not birdsong but the ruffle of air through branches and tiny leaves. If she concentrated, she could hear the faint trickle of the narrow creek that ran along the other side of the lane. The quality of silence was rich, flowing over her like a symphony.

There was a place for glitz, she mused, and for glamour. She simply didn't want that place any longer. The truth was she hadn't wanted that place for a very long time but hadn't known the way out. When your birth had been celebrated by the international press, your first step, your first words, cataloged for the public, it was natural to forget there was another way of life.

Her mother had been one of the greatest blues and ballad singers in America, her father a child actor turned successful film director. Their courtship and marriage had been followed religiously by fans around the world. The birth of their daughter had been an event treated like the birth of royalty. And Maggie had lived the life of a pampered princess. Gold carousels and white fur coats. She'd been lucky because her parents had adored her, and each other. That had compensated for the make-believe, often hard-edged world of show business, with all its demands and inconstancy. Her world had been cushioned by wealth and love, rippled continually with publicity.

The paparazzi haunted her on dates through her teenage years—to her amusement but often to the boys' frustration. Maggie had accepted the fact that her life was public domain. It had never been otherwise.

And when her parents' private plane had crashed into the Swiss Alps, the press had frozen her grief in glossies and newsprint. She hadn't tried to stop it; she'd realized that the world had mourned with her. She'd been eighteen when the fabric of her world had torn.

Then there had been Jerry. First friend, then lover, then husband. With him, her life had drifted into more fantasy, and more tragedy.

She wouldn't think of any of that now, Maggie told herself as she picked up her spade and began to fight the tough soil again. All that was really left of that portion of her life was her music. That she would never give up. She couldn't have if she'd tried. It was part of her the way her eyes and ears were part of her. She composed words and music and twined them together, not effortlessly, as it sometimes seemed from the fluid finished result, but obsessively, wonderingly, constantly. Unlike her mother, she didn't perform but fed other performers with her gift.

At twenty-eight, she had two Oscars, five Grammies and a Tony. She could sit at the piano and play any song she'd ever written from memory. The awards were still in the packing boxes that had been shipped from L.A.

The little flower plot she was planting in a spot perhaps no one would see but herself was a labor of love with no guarantee of success. It was enough that it gave her pleasure to add her own peculiar spot of color to the land she'd claimed as hers. Maggie began to sing as she worked. She'd completely forgotten her former feeling of apprehension.

Normally he didn't do the estimating and initial planning on a job himself. Not anymore. For the past six years Cliff Delaney had been in the position of being able to send one or two of his best men out on the first stage of a project; then he would fine-tune.

If the job was interesting enough, he would visit the site while work was in progress, perhaps handle some of the grading and planting himself. He was making an exception.

He knew the old Morgan place. It had been built by a Morgan, even as the tiny community a few miles away had been named after one. For ten years, since William Morgan's car had crashed into the Potomac, the house had stood empty. The house had always been stern, the land formidable. But with the right touch, the right insight, Cliff knew, it could be magnificent. He had his doubts that the lady from L.A. had the right insight.

He knew of her. Naturally he knew of her. Anyone who hadn't spent the last twenty-eight years in a cave knew Maggie Fitzgerald. At the moment, she was the biggest news in Morganville—all but eclipsing the hot gossip of Lloyd Messner's wife running off with the bank manager.

It was a simple town, the kind that moved slowly. The kind of town where everyone took pride in the acquisition of a new fire engine and the yearly Founder's Day parade. That's why Cliff chose to live there after he'd reached a point where he could live anywhere he chose. He'd grown up there and understood the people, their unity and their possessiveness. He understood their failings. More, perhaps much more, than that, he understood the land. He had serious doubts that the glamorous songwriter from California would understand either.

C.J. had estimated six weeks before she flew back. Cliff, without ever setting eyes on her, cut that in half. But perhaps before Maggie Fitzgerald grew bored with her shot at rural living, he could put his own mark on the land.

He turned off the paved road onto the quarter-mile lane that cut through the Morgan property. It had been years since he'd been on it, and it was worse than he remembered. Rain and neglect had worn ruts in the dirt. From both sides of the lane, branches reached out to whip at the truck. The first order of business would be the lane itself, Cliff thought as his small pickup bounced over ruts. It would be graded, leveled, filled. Drainage ditches would have to be dug, gravel spread.

He went slowly, not for the truck's sake but because the land on either side of the lane appealed to him. It was wild and primitive, timeless. He'd want to work with that, incorporate his own talents with the genius of nature. If Maggie Fitzgerald wanted blacktop and hothouse plants, she'd come to the wrong place. He'd be the first one to let her know.

If he had a distrust of outsiders, Cliff considered he'd come by it honestly. They came, often from the rich suburbs of D.C., and wanted their lawns flat and free of the poplar and oak that had first claim. They wanted neat little flowers in orderly rows. Lawns should be even, so that their mowers could handle the weekly cutting effortlessly. What they wanted, Cliff thought derisively, was to say they lived *in the country* while they brought city attitudes and city tastes with them. By the time he rounded the last bend, he was already out of patience with Maggie Fitzgerald.

Maggie heard the truck coming before it was in sight. That was something else she liked about her new home. It was quiet—so quiet that the sound of a truck, which would have been ignored in the city, brought her to attention. Halfheartedly brushing her hands on the seat of her pants, she rose from her planting, then shielded her eyes against the sun.

While she watched, the truck rounded the curve and parked where the Mercedes had been only an hour before. A bit dusty from the road, with its chrome dull rather than gleaming, the truck looked much more comfortable than the luxury car had. Though she couldn't yet see the driver through the glare of sun on windshield, Maggie smiled and lifted a hand in greeting.

The first thing Cliff thought was that she was smaller than he'd expected, more delicate in build. The Fitzgeralds had always been larger than life. He wondered, with a quick grunt, if she'd want to raise orchids to match her style. He got out of the truck, convinced she was going to annoy him.

Perhaps it was because she'd been expecting another Mr. Bog that Maggie felt a flutter of surprise when Cliff stepped out of the truck. Or perhaps, she thought with her usual penchant for honesty, it was because he was quite simply a magnificent example of manhood. Six-two, Maggie decided, with an impressive breadth of shoulders. Black hair that had been ruffled by the wind through the open truck windows fell over his forehead and ears in loose waves. He didn't smile, but his mouth was sculpted, sensual. She had a fleeting regret that he wore dark glasses so that his eyes were hidden. She judged people from their eyes.

Instead, Maggie summed him up from the way he moved—loosely, confidently. Athletic, she concluded, as he strode over the uneven ground. Definitely self-assured. He was still a yard away when she got the unmistakable impression that he wasn't particularly friendly.

"Miss Fitzgerald?"

"Yes." Giving him a neutral smile, Maggie held out a hand. "You're from Delaney's?"

"That's right." Their hands met, briefly, hers soft, his hard, both of them capable. Without bothering to identify himself, Cliff scanned the grounds. "You wanted an estimate on some landscaping."

Maggie followed his gaze, and this time her smile held amusement. "Obviously I need something. Does your company perform miracles?"

"We do the job." He glanced down at the splash of color behind her, wilted pansies and soggy petunias. Her effort touched something in him that he ignored, telling himself she'd be bored long before it was time to pull the first weeds. "Why don't you tell me what you have in mind?"

"A glass of iced tea at the moment. Look around while I get some—then we'll talk about it." She'd been giving orders without a second thought all her life. After giving this one, Maggie turned and climbed the rickety steps to the porch. Behind the tinted glasses, Cliff's eyes narrowed.

Designer jeans, he thought with a smirk as he watched the graceful sway of hips before the screen door banged shut at her back. And the solitaire on the thin chain around her neck had been no less than a carat. Just what game was little Miss Hollywood playing? She'd left a trace of her scent behind, something soft and subtle that would nag at a man's senses. Shrugging, he turned his back on the house and looked at the land.

It could be shaped and structured without being tamed. It should never lose its basic unruly sense by being manicured, though he admitted the years of neglect had given the rougher side of nature too much of an advantage. Still, he wouldn't level it for her. Cliff had turned down more than one job because the client had insisted on altering the land's personality. Even with that, he wouldn't have called himself an artist. He was a businessman. His business was the land.

He walked farther away from the house, toward a grove of trees overrun with tangling vines, greedy saplings and thistles. Without effort he could see it cleared of undergrowth, richly mulched, naturalized perhaps with jonquils. That one section would personify peace, as he saw it. Hitching his thumbs in his back pockets, Cliff reflected that from the reams that had been written about Maggie Fitzgerald over the years, she didn't go in much for peace.

Jet-setting, the fast lane, glitter and glitz. What the hell had she moved out here for?

Before he heard her, Cliff caught a fresh whiff of her perfume. When he turned, she was a few paces behind him, two glasses in her hand. She watched him steadily with a curiosity she didn't bother to hide. He learned something more about her then as she stood with her eyes on his face and the sun at her back. She was the most alluring woman he'd ever met, though he'd be damned if he knew why.

Maggie approached him and offered a glass of frosty tea. "Want to hear my ideas?"

The voice had something to do with it, Cliff decided. An innocent question, phrased in that sultry voice, conjured up a dozen dark pleasures. He took a slow sip.

"That's what I'm here for," he told her with a curtness he'd never shown any potential client.

Her brow lifted at the tone, the only sign that she'd noticed his rudeness. With that attitude, she thought, he wouldn't have the job for long. Then again, he didn't strike her as a man who'd work for someone else. "Indeed you are, Mr....?"

"Delaney."

"Ah, the man himself." That made more sense, she decided, if his attitude didn't. "Well, Mr. Delaney, I'm told you're the best. I believe in having the best, so..." Thoughtfully, she ran a fingertip down the length of her glass, streaking the film of moisture. "I'll tell you what I want, and you tell me if you can deliver."

"Fair enough." He didn't know why her simple statement should annoy him any more than he could understand why he was just noticing how smooth her skin was and how compelling were those large velvet eyes. Like a doe's, Cliff realized. He wasn't a man who hunted but a man who watched. "I'll tell you up front that my company has a policy against destroying the natural terrain in order to make the land into something it's not. This is rough country, Miss Fitzgerald. It's supposed to be. If you want an acre or two of manicured lawn, you've bought the wrong land and called the wrong landscaper."

It took a great deal to fire up her temper. Maggie had worked long and hard to control a natural tendency toward quick fury in order to block the label of temperamental daughter of temperamental artists. "Decent of you to point it out," she managed after three long, quiet breaths.

"I don't know why you bought the place," he began.

"I don't believe I've offered that information."

"And it's none of my business," Cliff finished with an acknowledging nod. "But this—" he indicated the property with a gesture of his hand "—is my business."

"You're a bit premature in condemning me, aren't you, Mr. Delaney?" To keep herself in check, Maggie took a sip of tea. It was cold, with a faint bite of lemon. "I've yet to ask you to bring on the bulldozers and chain saws." She ought to tell him to haul his buns into his truck and take off. Almost before she could wonder why she didn't, the answer came. Instinct. Instinct had brought her to Morganville and to the property she now stood on. It was instinct that told her he was indeed the best. Nothing else would do for her land. To give herself a moment to be sure she didn't do anything rash, Maggie took another sip from her glass.

"That grove there," she began briskly. "I want it cleared of undergrowth. It can't be enjoyed if you have to fight your way through thorns and thickets to walk in it." She shot him a look. "Don't you want to take notes?"

He watched her, consideringly. "No. Go on."

"All right. This stretch right here, in front of the porch—I imagine that was a lawn of sorts at one time." She turned, looking at the knee-high weeds. "It should be again, but I want enough room to plant, I don't know, some pines, maybe, to keep the line between lawn and woods from being too marked. Then there's the way the whole thing just sort of falls away until it reaches the lane below."

Forgetting her annoyance for the moment, Maggie made her way across the relatively flat land to where it sloped steeply down. Weeds, some of them as tall as she, grew in abundance wherever the rocks would permit. "It's certainly too steep for grass to be practical," she said half to herself. "But I can't just let all these weeds have their way. I'd like some color, but I don't want uniformity."

"You'll want some evergreens," he said from behind her. "Some spreading junipers along the bottom edge of the whole slope, a few coming farther up over there, with some forsythia mixed in. Here, where the grade's not so dramatic, you'd want some low ground cover." He could see phlox spilling and bumping over the rocks. "That tree's got to come down," he went on, frowning at the one that leaned precariously toward her roof. "And there's two, maybe three, on the rise behind the house that've got to be taken down before they fall down."

She was frowning now, but she'd always believed in letting an expert set the plan. "Okay, but I don't want you to cut down anything that doesn't have to be cleared."

Maggie could only see her own reflection in his glasses when he faced her. "I never do." He turned and began to walk around the side of the house. "That's another problem," Cliff continued without checking to see if she was following. "The way that dirt wall's eroding down from the cliff here. You're going to end up with a tree or a boulder in your kitchen when you least expect it."

"So?" Maggie tilted her head so she could scan the ridge behind her house. "You're the expert."

"It'll need to be recut, tapered back some. Then I'd put up a retaining wall, three, maybe four, feet high. Crown vetch'd hold the dirt above that. Plant it along the entire slope. It's hardy and fast."

"All right." It sounded reasonable. He sounded more

reasonable, Maggie decided, when he was talking about his business. A man of the land, she mused, and wished again she could see beyond the tinted glass to his eyes. "This part behind the house has to be cleared." She began to fight her way through the weeds and briars as she talked. "I think if I had a walkway of some kind from here to the lane, I could have a rockery…here." A vague gesture of her hands indicated the spot she had in mind. "There're plenty of rocks," she muttered, nearly stumbling over one. "Then down here—"

Cliff took her arm before she could start down the slope on the far side of the house. The contact jolted both of them. More surprised than alarmed, Maggie turned her head.

"I wouldn't," Cliff said softly, and she felt a tiny trickle, an odd excitement, sprint up her spine.

"Wouldn't what?" Her chin automatically tilted, her eyes challenged.

"Walk down there." Her skin was soft, Cliff discovered. With his hand wrapped around her arm, he could touch his fingertips to his thumb. Small and soft, he mused, enjoying the feel of his flesh against hers. Too small and soft for land that would fight back at you.

Maggie glanced down to where he held her. She noticed the tan on the back of his hand; she noticed the size and the strength of it. When she noticed her pulse wasn't quite steady, she lifted her gaze again. "Mr. Delaney—"

"Snakes," he said simply, and had the satisfaction of seeing her take two quick steps back. "You're almost sure to have some down in a spot like that. In fact, with the way this place is overgrown, you're likely to have them everywhere."

"Well, then—" Maggie swallowed and made a Herculean effort not to shudder "—maybe you can start the job right away."

For the first time, he smiled, a very slight, very cautious, curving of lips. They'd both forgotten he still held her, but they were standing much closer now, within a hand span of touching. She certainly hadn't reacted the way he'd expected. He wouldn't have been surprised if she'd screeched at the mention of snakes, then had dashed into the house, slamming and locking the door. Her skin was soft, Cliff mused, unconsciously moving his thumb over it. But apparently she wasn't.

"I might be able to send a crew out next week, but the first thing that has to be dealt with is your road."

Maggie dismissed this with a shrug. "Do whatever you think best there, excluding asphalt. It's only a means of getting in and out to me. I want to concentrate on the house and grounds."

"The road's going to run you twelve, maybe fifteen, hundred," he began, but she cut him off again.

"Do what you have to," she told him with the unconscious arrogance of someone who'd never worried about money. "This section here—" She pointed to the steep drop in front of them, making no move this time to go down it. At the base it spread twenty feet wide, perhaps thirty in length, in a wicked maze of thorny vines and weeds as thick at the stem as her thumb. "I want a pond."

Cliff brought his attention back to her. "A pond?"

She gave him a level look and stood her ground. "Allow me one eccentricity, Mr. Delaney. A small one," she continued before he could comment. "There's certainly enough room, and it seems to me that this section here's the worst. It's hardly more than a hole in the ground in a very awkward place. Do you have an objection to water?"

Instead of answering, he studied the ground below them, running through the possibilities. The truth was, she couldn't have picked a better spot as far as the lay of the land and the angle to the house. It could be done, he mused. It wouldn't be an easy job, but it could be done. And it would be very effective.

"It's going to cost you," he said at length. "You're going to be sinking a lot of cash into this place. If you're weighing that against resale value, I can tell you, this property won't be easy to sell."

It snapped her patience. She was tired, very tired, of having people suggest she didn't know what she was doing. "Mr. Delaney, I'm hiring you to do a job, not to advise me on real estate or my finances. If you can't handle it, just say so and I'll get someone else."

His eyes narrowed. The fingers on her arm tightened fractionally. "I can handle it, Miss Fitzgerald. I'll draw up an estimate and a contract. They'll be in the mail tomorrow. If you still want the job done after you've looked them over, call my office." Slowly, he released her arm, then handed her back the glass of tea. He left her there, near the edge where the slope gave way to gully as he headed back toward his truck. "By the way," he said without turning around, "you overwatered your pansies."

Maggie let out one long, simmering breath and dumped the tepid tea on the ground at her feet.

Chapter 2

When she was alone, Maggie went back inside, through the back door, which creaked ominously on its hinges. She wasn't going to think about Cliff Delaney. In fact, she doubted if she'd see him again. He'd send crews out to deal with the actual work, and whatever they had to discuss would be done via phone or letter. Better that way, Maggie decided. He'd been unfriendly, abrupt and annoying, though his mouth had been attractive, she reflected, even kind.

She was halfway through the kitchen when she remembered the glasses in her hand. Turning back, she crossed the scarred linoleum to set them both in the sink, then leaned on the windowsill to look out at the rise behind her house. Even as she watched, a few loose stones and dirt slid down the wall. A couple of hard rains, she mused, and half that bank would be at her back door. A retaining wall. Maggie nodded. Cliff Delaney obviously knew his business.

There was just enough breeze to carry a hint of spring to her. Far back in the woods a bird she couldn't see sang out as though it would never stop. Listening, she forgot the eroding wall and the exposed roots of trees that were much too close to its edge. She forgot the rudeness, and the attraction, of a stranger. If she looked up, far up, she could see where the tops of the trees met the sky.

She wondered how this view would change with the seasons and found herself impatient to experience them all. Perhaps she'd never realized how badly she'd needed a place to herself, time to herself, until she'd found it.

With a sigh, Maggie moved away from the window. It was time to get down to work if she was to deliver the finished score as promised. She walked down the hall, where the wallpaper was peeling and curled, and turned into what had once been the back parlor. It was now her music room.

Boxes she hadn't even thought of unpacking stood in a pile against one wall. A few odd pieces of furniture that had come with the house sat hidden under dust-covers. The windows were uncurtained, the floor was uncarpeted. There were pale squares intermittently on the walls where pictures had once hung. In the center of the room, glossy and elegant, stood her baby grand. A single box lay open beside it, and from this Maggie took a sheet of staff paper. Tucking a pencil behind her ear, she sat.

For a moment she did nothing else, just sat in the silence while she let the music come and play in her head.

She knew what she wanted for this segment—something dramatic, something strong and full of power. Behind her closed eyelids she could see the scene from the film sweep by. It was up to her to underscore, to accentuate, to take the mood and make it music.

Reaching out, she switched on the cassette tape and began.

She let the notes build in strength as she continued to visualize the scene her music would amplify. She only worked on films she had a feeling for. Though the Oscars told her she excelled in this area of work, Maggie's true affection was for the single song—words and music.

Maggie had always compared the composing of a score to the building of a bridge. First came the blueprint, the overall plan. Then the construction had to be done, slowly, meticulously, until each end fit snugly on solid ground, a flawless arch in between. It was a labor of precision.

The single song was a painting, to be created as the mood dictated. The single song could be written from nothing more than a phrasing of words or notes. It could encapsulate mood, emotion or a story in a matter of minutes. It was a labor of love.

When she worked, she forgot the time, forgot everything but the careful structuring of notes to mood. Her fingers moved over the piano keys as she repeated the same segment again and again, changing perhaps no more than one note until her instincts told her it was right. An hour passed, then two. She didn't grow weary or bored or impatient with the constant repetition. Music was her business, but it was also her lover.

She might not have heard the knock if she hadn't

paused to rewind the tape. Disoriented, she ignored it, waiting for the maid to answer before she recalled where she was.

No maids, Maggie, she reminded herself. *No gardener, no cook. It's all up to you now.* The thought pleased her. If there was no one to answer to her, she had no one to answer to.

Rising, she went back into the hall and down to the big front door. She didn't have to develop the country habit of leaving the doors unlocked. In L.A., there'd been servants to deal with bolts and chains and security systems. Maggie never gave them a thought. Taking the knob in both hands, she twisted and tugged. She reminded herself to tell Mr. Bog about the sticking problem as the door swung open.

On the porch stood a tall, prim-looking woman in her early fifties. Her hair was a soft, uniform gray worn with more tidiness than style. Faded blue eyes studied Maggie from behind rose-framed glasses. If this was the welcome wagon lady, Maggie thought after a glance at the unhappy line of the woman's mouth, she didn't seem thrilled with the job. Much too used to strangers' approaches to be reserved, Maggie tilted her head and smiled.

"Hello, can I help you?"

"You are Miss Fitzgerald?" The voice was low and even, as subdued and inoffensive as her plain, pale coatdress.

"Yes, I am."

"I'm Louella Morgan."

It took Maggie a moment; then the name clicked. Louella Morgan, widow of William Morgan, former owner of the house that was now hers. For an instant

Maggie felt like an intruder; then she shook the feeling away and extended her hand. "Hello, Mrs. Morgan. Won't you come in?"

"I don't want to disturb you."

"No, please." As she spoke, she opened the door a bit wider. "I met your daughter when we settled on the house."

"Yes, Joyce told me." Louella's gaze darted around and behind Maggie as she stepped over the threshold. "She never expected to sell so quickly. The property had only been on the market a week."

"I like to think it was fate." Maggie put her weight against the door and pushed until she managed to close it. Definitely a job for Bog, she decided.

"Fate?" Louella turned back from her study of the long, empty hall.

"It just seemed to be waiting for me." Though she found the woman's direct, unsmiling stare odd, Maggie gestured toward the living room. "Come in and sit down," she invited. "Would you like some coffee? Something cold?"

"No, thank you. I'll stay only a minute." Louella did wander into the living room, and though there was a single sofa piled with soft, inviting pillows, she didn't accept Maggie's invitation to sit. She looked at the crumbling wallpaper, the cracked paint and the windows that glistened from Maggie's diligence with ammonia. "I suppose I wanted to see the house again with someone living in it."

Maggie took a look at the almost-empty room. Maybe she'd start stripping off the wallpaper next week. "I guess it'll be a few weeks more before it looks as though someone is."

Louella didn't seem to hear. "I came here as a new-lywed." She smiled then, but Maggie didn't see anything happy in it. The eyes, she thought, looked lost, as if the woman had been lost for years. "But then, my husband wanted something more modern, more convenient to town and his business. So we moved, and he rented it out."

Louella focused on Maggie again. "Such a lovely, quiet spot," she murmured. "A pity it's been so neglected over the years."

"It is a lovely spot," Maggie agreed, struggling not to sound as uncomfortable as she felt. "I'm having some work done on both the house and the land..." Her voice trailed off when Louella wandered to the front window and stared out. *Heavens*, Maggie thought, searching for something more to say, *what have I got here?* "Ah, of course I plan to do a lot of the painting and papering and such myself."

"The weeds have taken over," Louella said with her back to the room.

Maggie's brows lifted and fell as she wondered what to do next. "Yes, well, Cliff Delaney was out this afternoon to take a look around."

"Cliff." Louella's attention seemed to focus again as she turned back. The light coming through the uncurtained windows made her seem more pale, more insubstantial. "An interesting young man, rather rough-and-ready, but very clever. He'll do well for you here, for the land. He's a cousin of the Morgans, you know." She paused and seemed to laugh, but very softly. "Then, you'll find many Morgans and their kin scattered throughout the county."

A cousin, Maggie mused. Perhaps he'd been unfriendly because he didn't think the property should've been sold to an outsider. Resolutely, she tried to push Cliff Delaney aside. He didn't have to approve. The land was hers.

"The front lawn was lovely once," Louella murmured.

Maggie felt a stirring of pity. "It will be again. The front's going to be cleared and planted. The back, too." Wanting to reassure her, Maggie stepped closer. Both women stood by the window now. "I'm going to have a rock garden, and there'll be a pond where the gully is on the side."

"A pond?" Louella turned and fixed her with another long stare. "You're going to clear out the gully?"

"Yes." Uncomfortable again, Maggie shifted. "It's the perfect place."

Louella ran a hand over the front of her purse as if she were wiping something away. "I used to have a rock garden. Sweet william and azure Adams. There was wisteria beneath my bedroom window, and roses, red roses, climbing on a trellis."

"I'd like to have seen it," Maggie said gently. "It must've been beautiful."

"I have pictures."

"Do you?" Struck with an idea, Maggie forgot her discomfort. "Perhaps I could see them. They'd help me decide just what to plant."

"I'll see that you get them. You're very kind to let me come in this way." Louella took one last scan of the room. "The house holds memories." When she walked out into the hall, Maggie went with her to tug open the front door again. "Goodbye, Miss Fitzgerald."

"Goodbye, Mrs. Morgan." Her pity stirred again,

and Maggie reached out to touch the woman's shoulder. "Please, come again."

Louella looked back, her smile very slight, her eyes very tired. "Thank you."

While Maggie watched, she walked to an old, well-preserved Lincoln, then drove slowly down the hill. Vaguely disturbed, Maggie went back into the music room. She hadn't met many residents of Morganville yet, she mused, but they were certainly an interesting bunch.

The noise brought Maggie out of a sound sleep into a drowsy, cranky state. For a moment, as she tried to bury her head under the pillow, she thought she was in New York. The groan and roar sounded like a big, nasty garbage truck. But she wasn't in New York, she thought as she surfaced, rubbing her hands over her eyes. She was in Morganville, and there weren't any garbage trucks. Here you piled your trash into the back of your car or pickup and hauled it to the county dump. Maggie had considered this the height of self-sufficiency.

Still, something was out there.

She lay on her back for a full minute, staring up at the ceiling. The sunlight slanted, low and thin, across her newly purchased quilt. She'd never been a morning person, nor did she intend to have country life change that intimate part of her nature. Warily, she turned her head to look at the clock: 7:05 a.m. Good heavens.

It was a struggle, but she pushed herself into a sitting position and stared blankly around the room. Here, too, boxes were piled, unopened. There was a precariously stacked pile of books and magazines on decorating and landscaping beside the bed. On the wall were three fresh strips of wallpaper, an ivory background with tiny violets, that she'd hung herself. More rolls and paste were pushed into a corner. The noise outside was a constant, irritating roar.

Resigned, Maggie got out of bed. She stumbled over a pair of shoes, swore, then went to the window. She'd chosen that room as her own because she could see out over the rolling pitch of what would be her front yard, over the tops of the trees on her own property to the valley beyond.

There was a farmhouse in the distance with a red roof and a smoking chimney. Beside it was a long, wide field that had just been plowed and planted. If she looked farther still, she could see the peaks of mountains faintly blue and indistinct in the morning mist. The window on the connecting wall would give her a view of the intended pond and the line of pines that would eventually be planted.

Maggie pushed the window up the rest of the way, struggling as it stuck a bit. The early-spring air had a pleasant chill. She could still hear the constant low sound of a running engine. Curious, she pressed her face against the screen, only to have it topple out of the window frame and fall to the porch below. One more thing for Mr. Bog to see to, Maggie thought with a sigh as she leaned through the opening. Just then the yellow bulk of a bulldozer rounded the bend in her lane and broke into view.

So, she thought, watching it inch its way along, leveling and pushing at rock and dirt, Cliff Delaney was a man of his word. She'd received the promised estimate and contract two days after his visit. When she'd called his office, Maggie had spoken to an efficient-sounding woman who'd told her the work would begin the first of the week.

And it's Monday, she reflected, leaning her elbows on the sill. Very prompt. Narrowing her eyes, she looked more closely at the man on top of the bulldozer. His build was too slight, she decided, his hair not quite dark enough. She didn't have to see his face to know it wasn't Cliff. Shrugging, she turned away from the window. Why should she have thought Cliff Delaney would work his own machines? And why should she have wanted it to be him? Hadn't she already decided she wouldn't see him again? She'd hired his company to do a job; the job would be done, and she'd write out a check. That was all there was to it.

Maggie attributed her crankiness to the early awakening as she snatched up her robe and headed for the shower.

Two hours later, fortified with the coffee she'd made for herself and the bulldozer operator, Maggie was on her knees on the kitchen floor. Since she was up at a barbaric hour, she thought it best to do something physical. On the counter above her sat her cassette tape player. The sound of her score, nearly completed, all but drowned out the whine of machinery. She let herself flow with it while words to the title song she'd yet to compose flitted in and out of her mind.

While she let her thoughts flow with the music she'd created, Maggie chipped away at the worn tile on the kitchen floor. True, her bedroom had only one wall partially papered, and only the ceiling in the upstairs bath was painted, *and* there were two more steps to be stripped and lacquered before the main stairway was finished, but she worked in her own way, at her own speed. She found herself jumping from project to project, leaving one partially done and leaping headlong into the next. This way, she reasoned, she could watch the house come together piece by piece rather than have one completed, out-of-place room.

Besides, she'd gotten a peek at the flooring beneath the tile when she'd inadvertently knocked an edge off a corner. Curiosity had done the rest.

When Cliff walked to the back door, he was already annoyed. It was ridiculous for him to be wasting time here, with all the other jobs his firm had in progress. Yet he was here. He'd knocked at the front door for almost five minutes. He knew Maggie was inside, her car was in the driveway, and the bulldozer operator had told him she'd brought out coffee an hour or so before. Didn't it occur to her that someone usually knocked when they wanted something?

The music coming through the open windows caught his attention, and his imagination. He'd never heard the melody before. It was compelling, sexy, moody. A lone piano, no backdrop of strings or brass, but it had the power of making the listener want to stop and hear every note. For a moment he did stop, both disturbed and moved.

Shifting the screen he'd found into his other hand, Cliff started to knock. Then he saw her.

She was on her hands and knees, prying up pieces of linoleum with what looked like a putty knife. Her hair was loose, falling over one shoulder so that her face was hidden behind it. The deep, rich sable brown picked up hints of gold from the sunlight that streamed through the open door and window.

Gray corduroys fit snugly over her hips, tapering

down to bare ankles and feet. A vivid red suede shirt was tucked into the waist. He recognized the shirt as one sold in exclusive shops for very exclusive prices. Her wrists and hands looked impossibly delicate against it. Cliff was scowling at them when Maggie got too enthusiastic with the putty knife and scraped her knuckle against a corner of the tile.

"What the hell are you doing?" he demanded, swinging the door open and striding in before Maggie had a chance to react. She'd barely put the knuckle to her mouth in an instinctive move when he was crouched beside her and grabbing her hand.

"It's nothing," she said automatically. "Just a scratch."

"You're lucky you didn't slice it, the way you're hacking at that tile." Though his voice was rough and impatient, his hand was gentle. She left hers in it.

Yes, his hand was gentle, though rough-edged, like his voice, but this time she could see his eyes. They were gray; smoky, secret. Evening mists came to her mind. Mists that were sometimes dangerous but always compelling. That was the sort of mist she'd always believed had cloaked Brigadoon for a hundred years at a time. Maggie decided she could like him, in a cautious sort of way.

"Who'd be stupid enough to put linoleum over this?" With the fingers of her free hand, she skimmed over the hardwood she'd exposed. "Lovely, isn't it? Or it will be when it's sanded and sealed."

"Get Bog to deal with it," Cliff ordered. "You don't know what you're doing."

So everyone said. Maggie withdrew a bit, annoyed

by the phrase. "Why should he have all the fun? Besides, I'm being careful."

"I can see that." He turned her hand over so that she saw the scrape over her thumb. It infuriated him to see the delicacy marred. "Doesn't someone in your profession have to be careful with their hands?"

"They're insured," she tossed back. "I think I can probably hit a few chords, even with a wound as serious as this." She pulled her hand out of his. "Did you come here to criticize me, Mr. Delaney, or did you have something else in mind?"

"I came to check on the job." Which wasn't necessary, he admitted. In any case, why should it matter to him if she was careless enough to hurt her hand? She was just a woman who had touched down in his territory and would be gone again before the leaves were full-blown with summer. He was going to have to remember that, and the fact that she didn't interest him personally. Shifting, he picked up the screen he'd dropped when he'd taken her hand. "I found this outside."

It wasn't often her voice took on that regal tone. He seemed to nudge it out of her. "Thank you." She took the screen and leaned it against the stove.

"Your road'll be blocked most of the day. I hope you weren't planning on going anywhere."

Maggie gave him a level look that held a hint of challenge. "I'm not going anywhere, Mr. Delaney."

He inclined his head. "Fine." The music on the tape player changed tempo. It was more hard-driving, more primitive. It seemed something to be played on hot, moonless nights. It drew him, pulled at him. "What is that?" Cliff demanded. "I've never heard it before."

Maggie glanced up at the recorder. "It's a movie score I'm composing. That's the melody for the title song." Because it had given her a great deal of trouble, she frowned at the revolving tape. "Do you like it?"

"Yes."

It was the most simple and most direct answer he'd given her thus far. It wasn't enough for Maggie.

"Why?"

He paused a moment, still listening, hardly aware that they were both still on the floor, close enough to touch. "It goes straight to the blood, straight to the imagination. Isn't that what a song's supposed to do?"

He could have said nothing more perfect. Her smile flashed, a quick, stunning smile that left him staring at her as though he'd been struck by lightning. "Yes. Yes, that's exactly what it's supposed to do." In her enthusiasm she shifted. Their knees brushed. "I'm trying for something very basic with this. It has to set the mood for a film about a passionate relationship—an intensely passionate relationship between two people who seem to have nothing in common but an uncontrollable desire for each other. One of them will kill because of it."

She trailed off, lost in the music and the mood. She could see it in vivid colors—scarlets, purples. She could feel it, like the close, sultry air on a hot summer night. Then she frowned, and as if on cue, the music stopped. From the tape came a sharp, pungent curse, then silence.

"I lost something in those last two bars," she muttered. "It was like—" she gestured with both hands, bringing them up, turning them over, then dropping them again "—something came unmeshed. It has to build to desperation, but it has to be more subtle than that. Passion at the very edge of control."

"Do you always write like that?" Cliff was studying her when she focused on him again, studying her as he had her land—thoroughly, with an eye both for detail and an overview.

She sat back on her haunches, comfortable now with a conversation on her own turf. He could hardly frustrate her in a discussion of music. She'd lived with it, in it, all her life. "Like what?" she countered.

"With the emphasis on mood and emotions rather than notes and timing."

Her brows lifted. With one hand, she pushed back the hair that swept across her cheek. She wore an amethyst on her finger, wine-colored, square. It caught the light, holding it until she dropped her hand again. As she thought it over, it occurred to her that no one, not even her closest associates, had ever defined her style so cleanly. It pleased her, though she didn't know why, that he had done so. "Yes," she said simply.

He didn't like what those big, soft eyes could do to him. Cliff rose. "That's why your music is good."

Maggie gave a quick laugh, not at the compliment, but at the grudging tone with which he delivered it. "So, you can say something nice, after all."

"When it's appropriate." He watched her stand, noting that she moved with the sort of fluidity he'd always associated with tall, willowy women. "I admire your music."

Again, it was the tone, rather than the words, that spoke to her. This time it touched off annoyance, rather than humor. "And little else that has to do with me."

"I don't know you," Cliff countered.

"You didn't like me when you drove up that hill the other day." With her temper rising, Maggie put her hands on her hips and faced him squarely. "I get the impression you didn't like me years before we met."

That was direct, Cliff decided. Maggie Fitzgerald, glamour girl from the Coast, didn't believe in evasions. Neither did he. "I have a problem with people who live their lives on silver platters. I've too much respect for reality."

"Silver platters," Maggie repeated in a voice that was much, much too quiet. "In other words, I was born into affluence, therefore, I can't understand the real world."

He didn't know why he wanted to smile. Perhaps it was the way color flooded her face. Perhaps it was because she stood nearly a foot beneath him but gave every appearance of being ready to Indian-wrestle and win. Yet he didn't smile. Cliff had the impression that if you gave an inch to this lady, you'd soon be begging to give a mile. "That about sums it up. The gravel for the lane'll be delivered and spread by five."

"Sums it up?" Accustomed to ending a conversation when she chose, Maggie grabbed his arm as he started to turn for the door. "You're a narrow-minded snob, and you know nothing about my life."

Cliff looked down at the delicate hand against his tanned muscled arm. The amethyst glowed up at him. "Miss Fitzgerald, everyone in the country knows about your life."

"That is one of the most unintelligent statements I've ever heard." She made one final attempt to control her temper, then forgot it. "Let me tell you something, Mr. Delaney—" The phone interrupted what would have been a stream of impassioned abuse. Maggie ended up swearing. "You stay there," she ordered as she turned to the wall phone.

Cliff's brows lifted at the command. Slowly, he leaned against the kitchen counter. He'd stay, he decided. Not because she'd told him to, but because he'd discovered he wanted to hear what she had to say.

Maggie yanked the receiver from the wall and barked into it. "Hello."

"Well, it's nice to hear that country life's agreeing with you."

"C.J." She struggled to hold down her temper. She wanted neither questions nor I-told-you-sos. "Sorry, you caught me in the middle of a philosophical discussion." Though she heard Cliff's quick snort of laughter, she ignored it. "Something up, C.J.?"

"Well, I hadn't heard from you in a couple of days—"

"I told you I'd call once a week. Will you stop worrying?"

"You know I can't."

She had to laugh. "No, I know you can't. If it relieves your mind, I'm having the lane fixed even as we speak. The next time you visit, you won't have to worry about your muffler falling off."

"It doesn't relieve my mind," C.J. grumbled. "I have nightmares about that roof caving in on your head. The damn place is falling apart."

"The place is not falling apart." She turned, inadvertently kicking the screen and sending it clattering across the floor. At that moment, her eyes met Cliff's. He was still leaning against the counter, still close enough to the back door to be gone in two strides. But now he was grinning. Maggie looked at the screen, then back at Cliff, and covered her mouth to smother a giggle.

"What was that noise?" C.J. demanded.

"Noise?" Maggie swallowed. "I didn't hear any noise." She covered the mouth of the receiver with her hand when Cliff laughed again. "Shh," she whispered, smiling. "C.J.," she said back into the phone, knowing she needed to distract him, "the score's nearly finished."

"When?" The response was immediate and predictable. She sent Cliff a knowing nod.

"For the most part, it's polished. I'm a little hung up on the title song. If you let me get back to work, the tape'll be in your office next week."

"Why don't you deliver it yourself? We'll have lunch."

"Forget it."

He sighed. "Just thought I'd try. To show you my heart's in the right place, I sent you a present."

"A present? The Godiva?"

"You'll have to wait and see," he said evasively. "It'll be there by tomorrow morning. I expect you to be so touched you'll catch the next plane to L.A. to thank me in person."

"C.J.—"

"Get back to work. And call me," he added, clever enough to know when to retreat and when to advance. "I keep having visions of you falling off that mountain."

He hung up, leaving her, as he often did, torn between amusement and annoyance. "My agent," Maggie said as she replaced the receiver. "He likes to worry."

"I see."

Cliff remained where he was; so did she. That one silly shared moment seemed to have broken down a barrier between them. Now, in its place, was an awkwardness neither of them fully understood. He was suddenly aware of the allure of her scent, of the slender line of her throat. She was suddenly disturbed by his basic masculinity, by the memory of the firm, rough feel of his palm. Maggie cleared her throat.

"Mr. Delaney—"

"Cliff," he corrected.

She smiled, telling herself to relax. "Cliff. We seem to've gotten off on the wrong foot for some reason. Maybe if we concentrate on something that interests us both—my land—we won't keep rubbing each other the wrong way."

He found it an interesting phrase, particularly since he was imagining what it would feel like to run his hands over her skin. "All right," he agreed as he straightened from the counter. He crossed to her, wondering who he was testing, himself or her. When he stopped, she was trapped between him and the stove.

He didn't touch her, but both of them could sense what it would be like. Hard hands, soft skin. Warmth turning quickly to heat. Mouth meeting mouth with confidence, with knowledge, with passion.

"I consider your land a challenge." He said it quietly, his eyes on hers. She didn't think of mists now but of smoke—of smoke and fire. "Which is why I've decided to give this project quite a bit of my personal attention."

Her nerves were suddenly strung tight. Maggie didn't back away, because she was almost certain that was what he wanted. Instead, she met his gaze. If her eyes weren't calm, if they'd darkened with the first traces of desire, she couldn't prevent it. "I can't argue with that."

"No." He smiled a little. If he stayed, even moments longer, he knew he'd find out how her lips tasted. That might be the biggest mistake he'd ever make. Turning, he went to the back door. "Call Bog." He tossed this over his shoulder as he pushed the screen door open. "Your fingers belong on piano keys, not on putty knives."

Maggie let out a long, tense breath when the screen door slammed. Did he do that on purpose? she wondered as she pressed a hand to her speeding heart. Or was it a natural talent of his to turn women into limp rags? Shaking her head, she told herself to forget it. If there was one thing she had experience in, it was in avoiding and evading the professional lothario. She was definitely uninterested in going a few rounds with Morganville's leading contender.

With a scowl, she dropped back to her knees and picked up the putty knife. She began to hack at the tile with a vengeance. Maggie Fitzgerald could take care of herself.

Chapter 3

For the third morning in a row, Maggie was awakened by the sound of men and machinery outside her windows. It occurred to her that she'd hardly had the chance to become used to the quiet when the chaos had started.

The bulldozer had been replaced by chain saws, industrial weed eaters and trucks. While she was far from getting used to the early risings, she was resigned. By seven-fifteen she had dragged herself out of the shower and was staring at her face in the bathroom mirror.

Not so good, she decided, studying her own sleepy eyes. But then she'd been up until two working on the score. Displeased, she ran a hand over her face. She'd never considered pampering her skin a luxury or a waste of time. It was simply something she did routinely, the same way she'd swim twenty laps every morning in California.

She'd been neglecting the basics lately, Maggie decided, squinting at her reflection. Had it been over two months since she'd been in a salon? Ruefully, she tugged at the bangs that swept over her forehead. It was showing, and it was time to do something about it.

After wrapping her still-damp hair in a towel, she pulled open the mirrored medicine-cabinet door. The nearest Elizabeth Arden's was seventy miles away. There were times, Maggie told herself as she smeared on a clay mask, that you had to fend for yourself.

She was just rinsing her hands when the sound of quick, high-pitched barking reached her. C.J.'s present, Maggie thought wryly, wanted his breakfast. In her short terry-cloth robe, which was raveled at the hem, her hair wrapped in a checked towel and the clay mask hardening on her face, she started downstairs to tend to the demanding gift her agent had flown out to her. She had just reached the bottom landing when a knock on the door sent the homely bulldog puppy into a frenzy.

"Calm down," she ordered, scooping him up under one arm. "All this excitement and I haven't had my coffee yet. Give me a break." The pup lowered his head and growled when she pulled on the front door. Definitely city-oriented, she thought, trying to calm the pup. She wondered if C.J. had planned it that way. The door resisted, sticking. Swearing, Maggie set down the dog and yanked with both hands.

The door swung open, carrying her a few steps back with the momentum. The pup dashed through the closest doorway, poking his head around the frame and snarling as if he meant business. Cliff stared at Maggie as she stood, panting, in the hall. She blew out a breath, wondering what could happen next. "I thought country life was supposed to be peaceful."

Cliff grinned, tucking his thumbs in the front pockets of his jeans. "Not necessarily. Get you up?"

"I've been up for quite some time," she said loftily.

"Mmm-hmm." His gaze skimmed over her legs, nicely exposed by the brief robe, before it lingered on the puppy crouched in the doorway. Her legs were longer, he mused, than one would think, considering the overall size of her. "Friend of yours?"

Maggie looked at the bulldog, which was making fierce sounds in his throat while keeping a careful distance. "A present from my agent."

"What's his name?"

Maggie sent the cowering puppy a wry look. "Killer."

Cliff watched the pup disappear behind the wall again. "Very apt. You figure to train him as a guard dog?"

"I'm going to teach him to attack music critics." She lifted a hand to push it through her hair—an old habit—and discovered the towel. Just as abruptly, she remembered the rest of her appearance. One hand flew to her face and found the thin layer of hardened clay. "Oh, my God," Maggie murmured as Cliff's grin widened. "Oh, damn." Turning, she raced for the stairs. "Just a minute." He was treated to an intriguing glimpse of bare thighs as she dashed upstairs.

Ten minutes later, she walked back down, perfectly composed. Her hair was swept back at the side with mother-of-pearl combs; her face was lightly touched with makeup. She'd pulled on the first thing she'd come to in her still-unpacked trunk. The tight black jeans proved an interesting contrast to the bulky white sweatshirt. Cliff sat on the bottom landing, sending the cowardly puppy into ecstasy by rubbing his belly. Maggie frowned down at the crown of Cliff's head.

"You weren't going to say a word, were you?"

He continued to rub the puppy, not bothering to look up. "About what?"

Maggie narrowed her eyes and folded her arms under her breasts. "Nothing. Was there something you wanted to discuss this morning?"

He wasn't precisely sure why that frosty, regal tone appealed to him. Perhaps he just liked knowing he had the ability to make her use it. "Still want that pond?"

"Yes, I still want the pond," she snapped, then gritted her teeth to prevent herself from doing so again. "I don't make a habit of changing my mind."

"Fine. We'll be clearing out the gully this afternoon." Rising, he faced her while the puppy sat expectantly at his feet. "You didn't call Bog about the kitchen floor."

Confusion came and went in her eyes. "How do you—"

"It's easy to find things out in Morganville."

"Well, it's none of your—"

"Hard to keep your business to yourself in small towns," Cliff interrupted again. It amused him to hear her breath huff out in frustration. "Fact is, you're about the top news item in town these days. Everybody wonders what the lady from California's doing up on this mountain. The more you keep to yourself," he added, "the more they wonder."

"Is that so?" Maggie tilted her head and stepped closer. "And you?" she countered. "Do you wonder?"

Cliff knew a challenge when he heard one, and knew he'd answer it in his own time. Impulsively, he cupped her chin in his hand and ran his thumb over her jawline.

She didn't flinch or draw back, but became very still. "Nice skin," he murmured, sweeping his gaze along the path his thumb took. "Very nice. You take good care of it, Maggie. I'll take care of your land."

With this, he left her precisely as she was—arms folded, head tilted back, eyes astonished.

By ten, Maggie decided it wasn't going to be the quiet, solitary sort of day she'd moved to the country for. The men outside shouted above the machinery to make themselves heard. Trucks came and went down her newly graveled lane. She could comfort herself that in a few weeks that part of the disruption would be over.

She took three calls from the Coast from friends who wondered how and what she was doing. By the third call, she was a bit testy from explaining she was scraping linoleum, papering walls, painting woodwork and enjoying it. She left the phone off the hook and went back to her putty knife and kitchen floor.

More than half of the wood was exposed now. The progress excited her enough that she decided to stick with this one job until it was completed. The floor would be beautiful, and, she added, thinking of Cliff's comments, she'd have done it herself.

Maggie had barely scraped off two more inches when there was a knock behind her. She turned her head, ready to flare if it was Cliff Delaney returned to taunt her. Instead, she saw a tall, slender woman of her own age with soft brown hair and pale blue eyes. As Maggie studied Joyce Morgan Agee, she wondered why she hadn't seen the resemblance to Louella before.

"Mrs. Agee." Maggie rose, brushing at the knees

of her jeans. "Please, come in. I'm sorry." Her sneakers squeaked as she stepped on a thin layer of old glue. "The floor's a bit sticky."

"I don't mean to disturb your work." Joyce stood uncertainly in the doorway, eyeing the floor. "I would've called, but I was on my way home from Mother's."

Joyce's pumps were trim and stylish. Maggie felt the glue pull at the bottom of her old sneakers. "We can talk outside, if you don't mind." Taking the initiative, Maggie walked out into the sunshine. "Things are a little confused around here right now."

"Yes." They heard one of the workers call to a companion, punctuating his suggestion with good-natured swearing. Joyce glanced over in their direction before she turned back to Maggie. "You're not wasting any time, I see."

"No." Maggie laughed and eyed the crumbling dirt wall beside them. "I've never been very patient. For some reason, I'm more anxious to have the outside the way I want it than the inside."

"You couldn't have picked a better company," Joyce murmured, glancing over at one of the trucks with *Delaney's* on the side.

Maggie followed her gaze but kept her tone neutral. "So I'm told."

"I want you to know I'm really glad you're doing so much to the place." Joyce began to fiddle with the strap of her shoulder bag. "I can hardly remember living here. I was a child when we moved, but I hate waste." With a little smile, she looked around again and shook her head. "I don't think I could live out here. I like being in town, with neighbors close by and other children for my children to play with. Of course, Stan, my husband, likes being available all the time."

It took Maggie a moment; then she remembered. "Oh, your husband's the sheriff, isn't he?"

"That's right. Morganville's a quiet town, nothing like Los Angeles, but it keeps him busy." She smiled, but Maggie wondered why she sensed strain. "We're just not city people."

"No." Maggie smiled, too. "I guess I've discovered I'm not, either."

"I don't understand how you could give up—" Joyce seemed to catch herself. "I guess what I meant was, this must be such a change for you after living in a place like Beverly Hills."

"A change," Maggie agreed. Was she sensing undercurrents here, too, as she had with Louella's dreaminess? "It was one I wanted."

"Yes, well, you know I'm glad you bought the place, and so quickly. Stan was a little upset with my putting it on the market when he was out of town, but I couldn't see it just sitting here. Who knows, if you hadn't come along so fast, he might've talked me out of selling it."

"Then we can both be grateful I saw the sign when I did." Mentally, Maggie was trying to figure out the logistics of the situation. It seemed the house had belonged exclusively to Joyce, without her husband or her mother having any claim. Fleetingly, she wondered why Joyce hadn't rented or sold the property before.

"The real reason I came by, Miss Fitzgerald, is my mother. She told me she was here a few days ago."

"Yes, she's a lovely woman."

"Yes." Joyce looked back toward the men working, then took a deep breath. Maggie no longer had to wonder if she was sensing undercurrents. She was sure of it. "It's more than possible she'll drop in on you again. I'd like to ask you a favor, that is, if she begins to bother you, if you'd tell me instead of her."

"Why should she bother me?"

Joyce let out a sound that was somewhere between fatigue and frustration. "Mother often dwells on the past. She's never completely gotten over my father's death. She makes some people uncomfortable."

Maggie remembered the discomfort she'd felt on and off during Louella's brief visit. Still, she shook her head. "Your mother's welcome to visit me from time to time, Mrs. Agee."

"Thank you, but you will promise to tell me if— well, if you'd like her to stay away. You see, she'd often come here, even when the place was deserted. I don't want her to get in your way. She doesn't know who you are. That is—" Obviously embarrassed, Joyce broke off. "I mean, Mother doesn't understand that someone like you would be busy."

Maggie remembered the lost eyes, the unhappy mouth. Pity stirred again. "All right, if she bothers me, I'll tell you."

The relief in Joyce's face was quick and very plain. "I appreciate it, Miss Fitzgerald."

"Maggie."

"Yes, well…" As if only more uncertain of her ground, Joyce managed a smile. "I understand that someone like you wouldn't want to have people dropping by and getting in the way."

Maggie laughed, thinking how many times the phone calls from California had interrupted her that morning. "I'm not a recluse," she told Joyce, though she was no longer completely sure. "And I'm not really very temperamental. Some people even consider me normal."

"Oh, I didn't mean—"

"I know you didn't. Come back when I've done something with that floor, and we'll have some coffee."

"I'd like to, really. Oh, I nearly forgot." She reached into the big canvas bag on her shoulder and pulled out a manila envelope. "Mother said you wanted to see these. Some pictures of the property."

"Yes." Pleased, Maggie took the envelope. She hadn't thought Louella would remember or bother to put them together for her. "I hoped they might give me some ideas."

"Mother said you could keep them as long as you liked." Joyce hesitated, fiddling again with the strap of her bag. "I have to get back. My youngest gets home from kindergarten at noon, and Stan sometimes comes home for lunch. I haven't done a thing to the house. I hope I see you sometime in town."

"I'm sure you will." Maggie tucked the envelope under her arm. "Give my best to your mother."

Maggie started back into the house, but as she put her hand on the doorknob, she noticed Cliff crossing to Joyce. Curiosity had her stopping to watch as Cliff took both the brunette's hands in his own. Though she couldn't hear the conversation over the din of motors, it was obvious that they knew each other well. There was a gentleness on Cliff's face Maggie hadn't seen before, and something she interpreted as concern. He bent down close, as if Joyce were speaking very softly, then touched her hair. The touch of a brother? Maggie wondered. Or a lover?

As she watched, Joyce shook her head, apparently fumbling with the door handle before she got into the car. Cliff leaned into the window for a moment. Were they arguing? Maggie wondered. Was the tension she sensed real or imaginary? Fascinated with the silent scene being played out in her driveway, Maggie watched as Cliff withdrew from the window and Joyce backed out to drive away. Before she could retreat inside, Cliff turned, and their gazes locked.

There were a hundred feet separating them, and the air was full of the sounds of men and machines. The sun was strong enough to make her almost too warm in the sweatshirt, yet she felt one quick, unexpected chill race up her spine. Perhaps it was hostility she felt. Maggie tried to tell herself it was hostility and not the first dangerous flutters of passion.

There was a temptation to cross those hundred feet and test both of them. Even the thought of it stirred her blood. He didn't move. He didn't take his eyes from her. With fingers gone suddenly numb, Maggie twisted the handle and went inside.

Two hours later, Maggie went out again. She'd never been one to retreat from a challenge, from her emotions or from trouble. Cliff Delaney seemed connected with all three. While she'd scraped linoleum, Maggie had lectured herself on letting Cliff intimidate her for no reason other than his being powerfully male and sexy.

And different, she'd admitted. Different from most of the men she'd encountered in her profession. He didn't fawn—far from it. He didn't pour on the charm. He wasn't impressed with his own physique, looks or sophistication. It must have been that difference that had made her not quite certain how to handle him.

A very direct, very frank business approach, she decided as she circled around the back of the house. Maggie paused to look at the bank fronting her house.

The vines, briars and thick sumac were gone. Piles of rich, dark topsoil were being spread over what had been a tangled jungle of neglect. The tree that had leaned toward her house was gone, stump and all. Two men, backs glistening with sweat, were setting stone in a low-spreading wall where the edge of the slope met the edge of the lawn.

Cliff Delaney ran a tight ship, Maggie concluded, and made her way through the new dirt toward the side yard. Here, too, the worst had been cleared out. An enormous bearded man in bib overalls sat atop a big yellow backhoe as easily as another might sit in an armchair. At the push of a lever, the digger went down into the gully, bit into earth and rock and came up full.

Maggie shaded her eyes and watched the procedure while the puppy circled her legs and snarled at everything in sight. Each time the digger would open its claws to drop its load, the dog would send up a ruckus of barks. Laughing, Maggie crouched down to scratch his ears and soothe him.

"Don't be a coward, Killer. I won't let it get you."

"I wouldn't get any closer," Cliff said from behind her.

She turned her head, squinting against the sun. "This is close enough." Disliking the disadvantage of looking up and into the sun, Maggie stood. "You seem to be making progress."

"We need to get the plants in and the wall of this thing solid—" he gestured toward the gully "—before the rain hits. Otherwise, you'll have a real mess on your hands."

"I see." Because he wore the frustratingly tinted glasses again, she turned from him to watch the backhoe work. "You certainly have a large staff."

Cliff's thumbs went into his pockets. "Large enough." He'd told himself he'd imagined that powerful sexual pull hours before. Now, feeling it again, he couldn't deny it.

She wasn't what he wanted, yet he wanted her. She wasn't what he would have chosen, yet he was choosing her. He could turn away logic until he'd learned what it was like to touch her.

Maggie was very aware of how close they stood. The stirring she'd felt hours before began to build again, slowly, seductively, until she felt her whole body tense with it. She understood that you could want someone you didn't know, someone you passed on the street. It all had to do with chemistry, but her chemistry had never reacted this way before. She had a wild urge to turn into his arms, to demand or offer the fulfillment, or whatever it was, that simmered between them. It was something that offered excitement and pleasure she had only glimpsed before. So she did turn, completely uncertain as to what she would say.

"I don't think I like what's happening here."

Cliff didn't pretend to misunderstand her. Neither of their minds was on the pond or the machine. "Do you have a choice?"

Maggie frowned, wishing she was more certain of her moves. He wasn't like the men she'd known before; therefore, the standard rules didn't apply. "I think so. I moved here because it was where I wanted to live, where I wanted to work. But I also moved here because I wanted to be on my own. I intend to do all those things."

Cliff studied her a moment, then gave the backhoe driver an absent wave as he shut off the machine to take his lunch break. "I took this job because I wanted to work this land. I intend to do it."

Though she didn't feel the slightest lessening of tension, Maggie nodded. "Then we understand each other."

As she started to turn away, Cliff put a hand on her shoulder, holding her still. "I think we both understand quite a bit."

The muscles in her stomach tightened and loosened like a nervous fist. With his fingers so light on the bulky sweatshirt, she shouldn't have felt anything. But hundreds of pulses sprang to life in her body. The air seemed to grow closer, hotter, the sounds of men more distant. "I don't know what you mean."

"Yes, you do."

Yes, she did. "I don't know anything about you," Maggie managed.

Cliff caught the tips of her hair in his fingers. "I can't say the same."

Maggie's temper flared, though she knew when she was being baited. "So, you believe everything you read in the tabloids and glossies." She tossed her head to free her hair from his fingers. "I'm surprised that a man who's obviously so successful and talented could be so ignorant."

Cliff acknowledged the hit with a nod. "I'm surprised a woman who's obviously so successful and talented could be so foolish."

"Foolish? What the hell's that supposed to mean?"

"It seems foolish to me to encourage the press to report every area of your life."

She clenched her teeth and tried deep breathing. Neither worked. "I don't encourage the press to do anything."

"You don't discourage them," Cliff countered.

"Discouragement *is* encouragement," she tossed back. Folding her arms under her breasts as she'd done earlier, she stared out over the open gully. "Why am I defending myself?" she muttered. "You don't know anything about it. I don't need you to know anything about it."

"I know you gave an interview about yourself and your husband weeks after his death." He heard her quick intake of breath even as he cursed himself for saying something so personal, and so uncalled-for.

"Do you have any idea how the press hammered at me during those weeks?" Her voice was low and strained, and she no longer looked at him. "Do you know all the garbage they were printing?" Her fingers tightened on her own arms. "I chose a reporter I could trust, and I gave the most honest, most straightforward interview I could manage, knowing it was my only chance to keep things from sinking lower. That interview was for Jerry. It was the only thing I had left to give him."

He'd wanted to prod, perhaps even to prick, but he hadn't wanted to hurt. "I'm sorry." Cliff put his hand on her shoulder again, but she jerked away.

"Forget it."

This time he took both of her shoulders, turning

her firmly to face him. "I don't forget blows below the belt, especially when I'm the one doing the punching."

She waited to speak until she was certain she had some control again. "I've survived hits before. My advice to you is not to criticize something you have no capacity for understanding."

"I apologized." He didn't release her shoulders when she tried to draw away. "But I'm not very good at following advice."

Maggie became still again. Somehow they had gotten closer, so that now their thighs brushed. The combination of anger and desire was becoming too strong to ignore. "Then you and I don't have any more to say to each other."

"You're wrong." His voice was very quiet, very compelling. "We haven't begun to say all there is to say."

"You work for me—"

"I work for myself," Cliff corrected.

She understood that kind of pride, admired it. But admiration wouldn't remove his hands from her shoulders. "I'm paying you to do a job."

"You're paying my company. That's business."

"It's going to be our only business."

"Wrong again," he murmured, but released her.

Maggie opened her mouth to hurl something back at him, but the dog began to bark in quick, excited yelps. She decided turning her back on him to investigate her pet was a much grander insult than the verbal one she'd planned. Without a word, she began to make her way around the slope of the gully to the pile of earth and rock and debris the backhoe had dumped.

"All right, Killer." The going was so rough that she swore under her breath as she stumbled over stones.

"You'll never find anything worthwhile in that pile, anyway."

Ignoring her, the puppy continued to dig, his barking muffled as his nose went farther in, his backside wriggling with either effort or delight in the new game.

"Cut it out." She bent to pull him out of the heap and ended up sitting down hard. "Damn it, Killer." Staying as she was, she grabbed the dog with one hand, dragging him back and unearthing a small avalanche of rock.

"Will you be careful?" Cliff shouted from above her, knowing she'd been lucky not to have one of the rocks bounce off her shin.

"It's the stupid dog!" Maggie shouted back as she lost her grip on him again. "God knows what he thinks is so fascinating about this mess. Nothing but dirt and rocks," she muttered, pushing at the pile that had landed near her hip.

"Well, grab him and get back up here before you're both hurt."

"Yeah," she muttered under her breath. "You're a big help." Disgusted, she started to struggle up when her fingers slid into the worn, rounded rock her hand had rested on. Hollow, she thought curiously. Her attention torn between the gully and the dog's unrelenting barks, Maggie glanced down.

Then she began to scream, loud and long enough to send the puppy racing for cover.

Cliff's first thought as he raced down the slope to her was snakes. When he reached her, he dragged her up and into his arms in an instinctive move of protection. She'd stopped screaming, and though her breathing was shallow, Maggie grabbed his shirt before he could carry her back up the slope. "Bones," she whispered. Closing her eyes, she dropped her head on his shoulder. "Oh, my God."

Cliff looked down and saw what the machine and dog had unearthed. Mixed with the rock and debris was a pile of what might have been mistaken for long white sticks layered with dirt.

But lying on the bones, inches from where Maggie had sat, was a human skull.

Chapter 4

"I'm all right." Maggie sat at the kitchen table and gripped the glass of water Cliff had handed her. When the pain in her fingers finally registered, she relaxed them a bit. "I feel like an idiot, screaming that way."

She was still pale, he noted. Though the hands on the glass were steady now, they were still white at the knuckles. Her eyes were wide and shocked, suddenly too big for the rest of her face. He started to stroke her hair, then stuck his own hands in his pockets. "A natural enough reaction."

"I guess." She looked up and managed a shaky smile. She was cold, but prayed she wouldn't begin to shiver in front of him. "I've never found myself in that sort of...situation before."

Cliff lifted a brow. "Neither have I."

"No?" Somehow she'd wanted to think it had happened before. If it had, it might make it less horrible—

and less personal. She looked down at the floor, not realizing until that moment that the dog lay across her feet, whimpering. "But don't you dig up a lot of—" She hesitated, not sure just how she wanted to phrase it. "Things—" Maggie decided weakly "—in your line of work?"

She was reaching, Cliff thought, and whether she knew it or not, those big brown eyes were pleading with him for some sort of easy explanation. He didn't have one to give her. "Not that kind of thing."

Their gazes held for one long, silent moment before Maggie nodded. If there was one thing she'd learned in the hard, competitive business she'd chosen, it was to handle things as they came. "So, neither of us has a tidy explanation." The little expulsion of breath was the last sign of weakness she intended to show him. "I guess the next step is the police."

"Yeah." The more determined she became to be calm, the more difficult it became for him. She was weakening something in him that he was determined to keep objective. His hands were balled into fists inside his pockets in his struggle not to touch her. Distance was the quickest defense. "You'd better call," Cliff said briskly. "I'll go out and make sure the crew keeps clear of the gully."

Again, her answer was a nod. Maggie watched as he crossed to the screen door and pushed it open. There he hesitated. He'd have cursed if he'd understood what it was he wanted to swear at. When he looked back, she saw the concern on his face she'd seen when he'd spoken to Joyce. "Maggie, are you all right?"

The question, and the tone, helped her to settle. Perhaps it had something to do with her knowing just what it was like to be pressured by another's weakness. "I will be. Thanks." She waited until the screen door banged shut behind him before she dropped her head on the table.

Good heavens, what had she walked into here? People didn't find bodies in their front yard. C.J. would've said it was totally uncivilized. Maggie choked back a hysterical giggle and straightened. The one unarguable fact she had to face was that she had found one. Now she had to deal with it. Taking deep breaths, she went to the phone and dialed the operator.

"Get me the police," she said quickly.

A few minutes later, Maggie went outside. Though she'd hoped the practical routine of reporting what she'd found would calm her, it hadn't worked. She didn't go near the gully, but she found she couldn't sit inside, waiting alone. Circling around the front of the house, she found a convenient rock and sat. The puppy stretched out in the patch of sunlight at her feet and went to sleep.

She could almost believe she'd imagined what she'd seen in that pile of dirt and rock. It was too peaceful here for anything so stark. The air was too soft, the sun too warm. Her land might be unruly, but it held a serenity that blocked out the harsher aspects of life.

Was that why she'd chosen it, Maggie wondered. Because she wanted to pretend there wasn't any real madness in the world? Here she could cocoon herself from so many of the pressures and demands that had threaded through her life for so long. Was this spot the home she'd always wanted, or was it in reality just an escape for her? She squeezed her eyes shut. If that were true, it made her weak and dishonest, two things she couldn't tolerate. Why had it taken this incident to make her question what she hadn't questioned before? As she tried to find her tranquillity again, a shadow fell over her. Opening her eyes, Maggie looked up at Cliff.

For some reason it toughened her. She wouldn't admit to him that she'd begun to doubt herself or her motives. No, not to him.

"Someone should be here soon." She linked her folded hands over one knee and looked back into the woods.

"Good." Several minutes passed while they both remained silent, looking into the trees.

Eventually, Cliff crouched down beside her. Funny, but he thought that she looked more apt to fall apart now than she had when he'd carried her into her kitchen. Reaction, he decided, had different speeds for different people. He wanted to hold her again, hard and close, as he'd done all too briefly before. The contact had made something strong and sultry move through him. Like her music—something like her music.

He wished like hell he'd turned down the job and had walked away the first time he'd seen her. Cliff looked past her to the slope that led to the gully.

"You talked to Stan?"

"Stan?" Blankly, Maggie stared at Cliff's set profile. At that moment, he was close enough to reach but seemed miles away. "Oh, the sheriff." She wished he'd touch her, just for a moment. Just a hand on her. "No, I didn't call him. I called the operator and asked for the police. She connected me with the state police in Hagerstown." She lapsed into silence, waiting for him to make some comment on her typical city response.

"Probably for the best," Cliff murmured. "I let the crew go. It'll be less confusing."

"Oh." She must've been in a daze not to notice that the trucks and men were gone. When she forced herself to look, she saw that the backhoe remained, sitting on the rise above the gully, big and yellow and silent. The sun was warm on her back. Her skin was like ice. Time to snap out of it, Maggie told herself, and straightened her shoulders. "Yes, I'm sure you're right. Should I call your office when the police say it's all right to start work again?" Her voice was businesslike. Her throat was dry with the thought of being left alone, completely alone, with what was down by the gully.

Cliff turned his head. Without speaking, he took off his sunglasses so that their eyes met. "Thought I'd hang around."

Relief washed over her. Maggie knew it must've shown in her face, but she didn't have the will to put pride first. "I'd like you to. It's stupid, but—" She glanced over in the direction of the gully.

"Not stupid."

"Maybe *weak*'s a better word," she mumbled, try-ing to smile.

"Human." Despite his determination not to, Cliff reached out and took her hand. The touch, one designed to comfort, to reassure her, set off a chain reaction of emotion too swift to stop.

It ran through her head that she should rise swiftly and go inside. He might stop her, or he might let her go. Maggie didn't ask herself which she wanted, nor did she move. Instead, she sat where she was, meet-ing his gaze and letting the sensation of torrid, liquid heat flow through her. Nothing else existed. Nothing else mattered.

She felt each of his fingers tense individually on her

hand. There was a sense of power there; whether it was his or hers, she wasn't sure. Perhaps it was the melding of both. She saw his eyes darken until the irises were only shades lighter than the pupils. It was as if he were looking through her, into her chaotic thoughts. In the quiet of midafternoon, she heard each breath he drew in and expelled. The sound stirred the excitement that vibrated in the air between them.

Together they moved toward each other until mouth molded itself to mouth.

Intensity. She hadn't known anything between two people could be so concentrated, such pure sensation. She understood that if years passed, if she was blind and deaf, she would know this man just by the touch of his lips. In one instant she became intimate with the shape of his mouth, the taste and texture of his tongue. Her mouth was on his, his hand on hers, and they touched nowhere else. In that moment there was no need to.

There was an aggressiveness, even a harshness, to the kiss that Maggie hadn't expected. It held none of the sweetness, the hesitation, that first kisses often do, yet she didn't back away from it. Perhaps it was all part of the attraction that had begun the moment he'd stepped from the truck. Different, yes, he was different from the other men who'd touched her life—different still from the man she'd shared her body with. She'd known that from the first encounter. Now, with his mouth stirring her senses, she found herself grateful for it. She wanted nothing to be the same as it had been, no reminders of what she'd had once and lost. This man wouldn't pamper or worship. He was strong enough to want strength in return. She felt his tongue tangle with hers, probing deeper. Maggie reveled in the demands.

It was easy, almost too easy, to forget her delicate build, her fragile looks, when her mouth was so ardent on his. He should've known there'd be deep, restless passion in a woman who created music with such sexuality. But how could he have known that passion would call to him as though he'd been waiting for years?

It was much too easy to forget she wasn't the kind of woman he wanted in his life when her taste was filling him. Again, he should have known she'd have the power to make a man toss aside all logic, all intellect. Her lips were warm, moist, the taste as pungent as the scent of newly turned earth around them. The urge rose to take her in his arms and fulfill, there under the clear afternoon sun, all the needs that welled inside him. Cliff drew back, resisting that final painful twist of desire.

Breathless, throbbing, Maggie stared at him. Could that one searing meeting of lips have moved him as it had moved her? Were his thoughts swimming as hers were? Was his body pulsing with wild, urgent needs? She could tell nothing from his face. Though his eyes were fixed on hers, their expression was unreadable. If she asked, would he tell her that he, too, had never known a wave of passion so overwhelming or so mesmerizing? She would ask, and would know, as soon as she had the voice to question. As she sat, struggling to catch her breath, the events of the day came flashing back into her mind. Abruptly, Maggie sprang to her feet.

"God, what are we doing?" she demanded. With a hand that shook, she pushed the hair away from her face. "How can we sit here like this when that—that thing's only a few yards away?"

Cliff took her arm, turning her back to face him. "What does one have to do with the other?"

"Nothing. I don't know." With her insides churning, she looked up at him. Her emotions had always been too dominant. Though she knew it, Maggie had never been able to change it. It had been years since she'd really tried. Confusion, distress, passion, radiated from her as tangible things. "What we found, it's dreadful, unbelievably dreadful, and a few moments ago I was sitting there wondering what it would be like to make love with you."

Something flashed in his eyes, quickly controlled. Unlike Maggie, Cliff had learned long ago to channel his emotions and keep them to himself. "You obviously don't believe in evading the issue."

"Evasions take too much time and effort." After letting out a long breath, Maggie managed to match his even, casual tone. "Listen, I didn't expect that sort of—eruption," she decided. "I suppose I'm wound up over all of this, and a bit too susceptible."

"Susceptible." Her choice of words made him smile. Somehow, when she became cool and calm, he became tempted to prod. Deliberately, he lifted a hand and ran his fingertips down her cheek. Her skin was still warm with desire. "I wouldn't have described you that way. You seem to be a woman who knows what she wants and how to get it."

If he'd wanted to fire her up, he'd found the perfect key. "Stop it." In one sharp move, she pushed his hand from her face. "I've said it before—you don't know me. Every time we're together, I become more certain that I don't want you to. You're a very attractive man, Cliff. And very unlikable. I stay away from people I don't like."

It occurred to him that he'd never gone out of his way to argue with anyone before. A lot of things were changing. "In a small community like this, it's hard to stay away from anyone."

"I'll put more effort into it."

"Nearly impossible."

She narrowed her eyes and fought to keep her lips from curving. "I'm very good when I put my mind to something."

"Yeah." He put his sunglasses back on. When he grinned, the deliberate cockiness was almost too appealing to resist. "I bet you are."

"Are you trying to be smart, or are you trying to be charming?"

"I never had to try to be either one."

"Think again." Because she was having trouble controlling the grin, Maggie turned away. As luck would have it, she found herself staring out over the gully. A chill raced up her spine. Swearing, she folded her arms under her breasts. "I can't believe it," she muttered. "I can't believe I'm standing here having a ridiculous conversation when there's a—" She found she couldn't say it and detested herself. "I think the whole world must be going mad."

He wasn't going to let her get shaky on him again. When she was vulnerable, she was much more dangerous. "What's down there's been there for a long time." His voice was brisk, almost hard. "It doesn't have anything to do with you."

"It's my land," Maggie tossed back. She whirled

around, eyes glowing, chin angled. "So it has everything to do with me."

"Then you better stop shaking every time you think about it."

"I'm not shaking."

Without a word, he drew her hand away from her elbow so they could both see the tremor. Furious, Maggie snatched it away again. "When I want you to touch me, I'll let you know," she said between her teeth.

"You already have."

Before she could think of an appropriate response, the dog scrambled up and began to bark furiously. Seconds later, they both heard the sound of an approaching car.

"He might make you a decent watchdog, after all," Cliff said mildly. The pup bounded around in circles like a mad thing, then hid behind the rock. "Then again…"

As the official car came into sight, he bent down to pat the dog on the head before he walked toward the end of the drive. Maggie hurried to keep pace. Her land, her problem, her responsibility, she told herself. *She'd* do the talking.

A trooper climbed out of the car, adjusted his hat, then broke into a grin. "Cliff, didn't expect to see you out here."

"Bob." Because the greeting didn't include a handshake, Maggie assumed the men knew each other well and saw each other often. "My company's handling the landscaping."

"The old Morgan place." The trooper looked around with interest. "Been a while since I was back here. You dig up something we should know about?"

"So it seems."

"It's the Fitzgerald place now," Maggie cut in briskly.

The trooper touched the brim of his hat and started to make a polite comment. His eyes widened when he took his first good look at her. "Fitzgerald," he repeated. "Hey, aren't you Maggie Fitzgerald?"

She smiled, though the recognition, with Cliff beside her, made her uncomfortable. "Yes, I am."

"I'll be damned. You look just like your pictures in all the magazines. I guess there isn't a song you've written I can't hum. You bought the Morgan place."

"That's right."

He pushed the hat back on his head in a gesture that made her think of cowboys. "Wait till I tell my wife. We had 'Forever' played at our wedding. You remember, Cliff. Cliff was best man."

Maggie tilted her head to look at the man beside her. "Really?"

"If you've finished being impressed," Cliff said mildly, "you might want to take a look at what's down by the gully."

Bob grinned again, all amiability. "That's why I'm here." They began to walk toward the gully together. "You know, it isn't easy to tell what's from a human and what's from an animal just by looking. Could be, ma'am, that you uncovered a deer."

Maggie glanced over at Cliff. She could still feel the way her hand had slid into the hollow opening of what she'd taken for a rock. "I wish I could think so."

"Down here," Cliff said without acknowledging the look. "The going's rough." In a smooth, calculated move, he blocked Maggie's way before she could start down. It forced her to pull up short and grab his arm for support. "Why don't you wait here?"

It would've been easy to do so. Much too easy. "It's my land," Maggie said, and, brushing by him, led the way down herself. "The dog started digging in this pile." She heard the nerves in her own voice and fought against them. "I came down to pull him away, and that's when I saw…" Trailing off, she pointed.

The trooper crouched down, letting out a low whistle. "Holy hell," he murmured. He turned his head, but it was Cliff he looked at, not Maggie. "It doesn't look like you dug up any deer."

"No." In a casual move, Cliff shifted so that he blocked Maggie's view. "What now?"

Bob rose. He wasn't smiling now, but Maggie thought she detected a gleam of excitement. "I'll have to call the investigation section. Those boys are going to want to take a look at this."

Maggie didn't speak when they climbed up the slope again. She waited in silence while the trooper went to his car to radio in his report. When she did speak, she deliberately avoided the reason they were all standing outside in the middle of the afternoon.

"So you two know each other," she commented as though it were any normal remark made on any normal day.

"Bob and I went to school together." Cliff watched a big black crow swoop over the trees. He was remembering the look on Maggie's face the moment before she'd begun to scream. "He ended up marrying one of my cousins a couple of years ago."

Bending over, she plucked a wildflower and began to shred it. "You have a lot of cousins."

He shrugged. The crow landed and was still. "Enough."

"A few Morgans."

That caught his attention. "A few," he said slowly. "Why?"

"I wondered if it was your connection with them that made you resent my having this land."

Cliff wondered why, when he normally respected candor, it annoyed him from her. "No."

"But you did resent it," Maggie insisted. "You resented me before you even saw me."

He had, and perhaps the resentment had grown since he'd had a taste of her. "Joyce had the right to sell this property whenever, and to whomever, she wanted."

Maggie nodded, looking down to where the puppy scrambled in the new dirt. "Is Joyce a cousin, too?"

"What are you getting at?"

Lifting her head, Maggie met his impatient look. "I'm just trying to understand small towns. After all, I'm going to be living here."

"Then the first thing you should learn is that people don't like questions. They might volunteer more information than you want to hear, but they don't like to be asked."

Maggie acknowledged this with a lift of a brow. "I'll keep that in mind." Rather pleased that she'd annoyed him, Maggie turned to the trooper as he approached.

"They're sending out a team." He glanced from her to Cliff, then over his friend's shoulder toward the gully. "Probably be here for a while, then take what they find with them."

"What then?"

Bob brought his attention back to Maggie. "Good

question." He shifted his feet as he considered it. "To tell you the truth, I've never been in on anything like this before, but my guess would be they'd ship everything off to the medical examiner in Baltimore. He'd have to check the, ah, everything out before they could start an investigation."

"Investigation?" she repeated, and felt something tighten in her throat. "What kind of investigation?"

The trooper ran his thumb and forefinger down his nose. "Well, ma'am, as far as I can see, there's no reason for anything like that to be buried down in that gully unless—"

"Unless someone buried it there," Cliff finished.

Maggie stared out into the peaceful spread of greening wood across the lane. "I think we could all use some coffee," she murmured. Without waiting for an acknowledgment, she went back toward the house.

Bob took off his hat and wiped at the sweat on his forehead. "This is one for the books."

Cliff followed his friend's long look at the woman climbing the rickety front steps. "Which? Her or that?" With one hand he gestured toward the gully.

"Both." Bob took out a pack of gum and carefully unwrapped a piece. "First place, what's a woman like her, a celebrity, doing holed up here in the woods?"

"Maybe she decided she likes trees."

Bob slipped the gum into his mouth. "Must be ten, twelve acres of them here."

"Twelve."

"Looks to me like she bought more than she bargained for. Holy hell, Cliff, we haven't had anything like this down in this end of the county since crazy Mel Stickler set those barn fires. Now, in the city—"

"Taken to the fast pace, have you?"

Bob knew Cliff well enough to catch both the dig and the humor. "I like some action," he said easily. "Speaking of which, the lady songwriter smells like heaven."

"How's Carol Ann?"

Bob grinned at the mention of his wife. "Just fine. Look, Cliff, if a man doesn't look, and appreciate, he'd better see a doctor. You're not going to tell me you haven't noticed just how nice that lady's put together."

"I've noticed." He glanced down at the rock beside him. She'd sat there when he'd kissed her. It wouldn't take any effort to remember each separate sensation that had run through him in that one moment. "I'm more interested in her land."

Bob let out a quick laugh. "If you are, you've done a lot of changing since high school. Remember when we used to come up here—those blond twins, the cheerleaders whose parents rented the place for a while? That old Chevy of yours lost its muffler right there on that turn."

"I remember."

"We had some interesting walks up there in the woods," Bob reminisced. "They were the prettiest girls in school till their daddy got transferred and they moved away."

"Who moved in after that?" Cliff wondered, half to himself. "That old couple from Harrisburg—the Faradays. They were here a long time, until the old man died and she went to live with her kids." Cliff narrowed his eyes as he tried to remember. "That was a couple months before Morgan ran off the bridge. Nobody's lived here since."

Bob shrugged; then both of them looked toward the gully. "Guess it's been ten years since anybody lived here."

"Ten years," Cliff repeated. "A long time."

They both looked over at the sound of a car. "The investigators," Bob said, adjusting his hat again. "They'll take over now."

From the corner of the porch, Maggie watched the proceedings. She'd decided that if the police crew needed her, they'd let her know. It appeared to her that they knew their business. She would just be in the way down there, Maggie reasoned as she drank another cup of black coffee.

She watched them shovel, sift and systematically bag what they'd come for. Maggie told herself that once it was off her property, she'd forget it. It would no longer concern her. She wished she could believe it. What was now being transferred into plastic bags had once been a living being. A man or a woman who'd had thoughts and feelings had lain, alone, only yards from what was now her home. No, she didn't believe she'd be able to forget that.

Before it was over, she'd have to know who that person had been, why they had died and why their grave had been on her land. She'd have to have the answers if she were to live in the home she'd chosen. She finished the last swallow of coffee as one of the police crew broke away from the group and came toward the porch. Maggie went to the steps to meet him.

"Ma'am." He nodded to her but, to her relief, didn't offer his hand. Instead, he took out a badge, flashing the cover up briefly. "I'm Lieutenant Reiker."

She thought he looked like a middle-aged accountant and wondered if he carried a gun under his jacket. "Yes, Lieutenant."

"We're just about finished up. Sorry for the inconvenience."

"That's all right." She gripped her hands together over the cup and wished she could go inside, to her music.

"I've got the trooper's report, but I wonder if you could tell me how you happened to find the remains."

Remains, Maggie thought with a shudder. It seemed a very cold word. For the second time, she related her story of the puppy's digging. She did so calmly now, without a tremor.

"You just bought the place?"

"Yes, I only moved in a few weeks ago."

"And you hired Delaney to do some landscaping."

"Yes." She looked down to where Cliff stood talking to another of the team. "The handyman I hired recommended him."

"Mmm-hmm." In a very casual way, the investigator took notes. "Delaney tells me you wanted the gully there dug out for a pond."

Maggie moistened her lips. "That's right."

"Nice place for one," he said conversationally. "I'd like to ask you to hold off on that for a while, though. We might need to come back and take another look around."

Maggie's hands twisted on the empty cup. "All right."

"What we'd like to do is block off that area." He hitched at his belt, then settled one foot on the step above the other. "Some chicken wire," he said easily, "to keep your dog and any other stray animal from digging around in there."

And people, Maggie thought, deciding it didn't take a genius to read between the lines. Before the day was over, this would be the biggest news flash in the county. She was learning fast. "Do whatever you need to do."

"We appreciate the cooperation, Miss Fitzgerald." He twirled the pen in his fingers, hesitating.

"Is there something else?"

"I know it's a bad time," he said with a sheepish smile, "but I can't pass it up. Would you mind signing my pad? I was a big fan of your mother's, and I guess I know most all of your songs, too."

Maggie laughed. It was far better to laugh. The day had been a series of one ludicrous event after another. "Of course." She took the offered pad and pen. "Would you like me to say anything special?"

"Maybe you could just write—to my good friend Harvey."

Before she could oblige, she glanced up and caught Cliff's eyes on her. She saw his lips twist into something between a sneer and a smile. With a silent oath, she signed the pad and handed it back.

"I don't know much about this kind of thing," she began briskly, "but I'd appreciate it if you kept me informed on whatever's being done."

"We'll have the medical examiner's report in a few days." Pocketing his pad, the investigator became solidly professional again. "We'll all know more then. Thanks for your time, Miss Fitzgerald. We'll be out of your way as soon as we can."

Though she felt Cliff's gaze still on her, Maggie didn't look over. Instead, she turned and walked back into the house. Moments later, music could be heard through the open windows.

Cliff remained where he was, though he'd answered all the questions that he could answer. His thoughts were focused on the sounds coming from the music room. It wasn't one of her songs, he concluded, but something from the classics, something that required speed, concentration and passion. Therapy, he wondered, frowning up at the window. With a shrug, he started toward his car. It wasn't his concern if the lady was upset. Hadn't she told him she'd moved back here to be on her own?

Turning his head, he saw the investigators preparing to leave. Within moments, he reflected, she'd be alone. The music pouring out of the windows was tense, almost desperate. Swearing, Cliff stuffed his keys back in his pocket and strode toward the steps.

She didn't answer his knock. The music played on. Without giving it a second thought, he pushed open the front door. The house vibrated with the storm coming from the piano. Following it into the music room, he watched her from the doorway.

Her eyes were dark, her head was bent, though he didn't think she even saw the keys. Talent? There was no denying it, any more than there could be any denying her tension or her vulnerability. Later, he might ask himself why all three made him uncomfortable.

Perhaps he did want to comfort her, he told himself. He'd do the same for anyone, under the circumstances. She didn't have to mean anything to him for him to want to offer a diversion. Strays and wounded birds had always been weaknesses of his. Dissatisfied with his own logic, Cliff waited until she'd finished.

Maggie looked up, startled to see him in the doorway. Damn her nerves, she thought, carefully folding her hands in her lap. "I thought you'd gone."

"No. They have."

She tossed the hair out of her eyes and hoped she looked composed. "Was there something else?"

"Yeah." He walked over to run a finger over the piano keys. No dust, he noted, in a house nearly choked with it. Her work was obviously of first importance.

When he didn't elaborate, Maggie frowned. Cliff preferred the impatience he saw in her eyes now. "What?"

"I had a steak in mind."

"I beg your pardon?"

The cool response made his lips curve. Yes, he definitely preferred her this way. "I haven't eaten."

"Sorry." Maggie began to straighten her sheet music. "I don't happen to have one handy."

"There's a place about ten miles out of town." He took her arm to draw her to her feet. "I have a feeling they'd treat a steak better than you would, anyway."

She pulled away, stood her ground and studied him. "We're going out to dinner?"

"That's right."

"Why?"

He took her arm again, so that he wouldn't ask himself the same question. "Because I'm hungry," Cliff said simply.

Maggie started to resist, though he didn't appear to notice. Then it struck her how much she wanted to get out, to get away, just for a little while. Sooner or later, she'd have to be alone in the house, but right then— No, right then, she didn't want to be alone anywhere.

He knew, understood, and whatever his approach, Cliff was offering her exactly what she needed.

Though their thoughts weren't particularly calm, neither of them spoke as they walked through the door together.

Chapter 5

Maggie set aside the next day to complete the title song for the movie score. She made a conscious effort to forget everything that had happened the day before. Everything. She wouldn't think of what had been buried and unearthed so close to her house, nor would she think of police or investigators or medical examiners.

In exactly the same way, she refused to think of Cliff, of the one wildly exciting kiss or of the oddly civilized dinner they'd shared. It was difficult to believe that she'd experienced both with the same man.

Today, she was Maggie Fitzgerald, writer of songs, creator of music. If she thought of only that, *was* only that, perhaps she could convince herself that everything that had happened yesterday had happened to someone else.

She knew there were men outside spreading seed, planting. There were shrubs going in, mulch being laid, more brush being cleared. If the landscape timbers she'd seen brought in that morning meant what she thought, construction was about to begin on her retaining wall.

None of that concerned her. The score demanded to be completed, and she'd complete it. The one form of discipline she understood perfectly was that a job had to be done no matter what went on around you. She'd seen her father direct a movie when his equipment had broken down and his actors had thrown tantrums. She'd known her mother to perform while running a fever. Much of her life might have been lived in a plush, make-believe world, but she'd learned responsibility.

The score came first today, and the title song would be written. Perhaps she'd even add some clever little aside to C.J. at the end of the tape before she mailed it off.

It certainly wouldn't do to mention what was going on in her side yard, Maggie thought as she meticulously copied notes onto staff paper. C.J. wouldn't be able to find enough antacids in L.A. to handle it for him. Poor man, she mused, he'd been worried about the roof caving in on her. In a totally unexpected way, it certainly had. If he knew there'd been policemen swarming over her land with plastic bags, he'd catch the next plane and drag her back to L.A.

She wondered if Cliff would've dragged her from the house the night before if she hadn't gone voluntarily. Fortunately, it hadn't been an issue, because Maggie thought him perfectly capable of it. Yet he'd been the ideal dinner companion. While she hadn't expected consideration from him, he'd been considerate. She hadn't expected subtle kindness, but it had been there. Finding both had made it difficult to remember she considered him an unlikable man.

They hadn't spoken of what had been found on her property that day, nor had there been any speculation on the whys and hows. They hadn't discussed his work or hers, but had simply talked.

Looking back, Maggie couldn't say precisely what they'd talked about, only that the mood had been easy. So easy, she had almost forgotten the passion they'd pulled from each other in the quiet afternoon sunlight. Almost forgotten. The memory had been there, quietly nagging at her throughout the evening. It had made her blood move a little faster. It had made her wonder if he'd felt it, too.

Maggie swore and erased the last five notes she'd copied down. C.J. wouldn't appreciate the fact that she was mixing her bass and tenor. She was doing exactly what she'd promised herself she wouldn't do, and as she'd known it would, the upheaval of yesterday was affecting her work. Calmly, she took deep breaths until her mind was clear again. The wisest course was to switch the recorder back on to play and start from the beginning. Then the knock on the front door disrupted her thoughts. Quiet country life. She asked herself where she'd ever heard that expression as she went to answer.

The gun on the man's hip made her stomach twist. The little badge pinned to the khaki shirt told her he was the sheriff. When she took her gaze up to his face, she was surprised by his looks. Blond, tanned, with blue eyes fanned by lines that spoke of humor or sun. For a moment, she had the insane notion that C.J. had sent him out from central casting.

"Miss Fitzgerald?"

She moistened her lips as she tried to be rational. C.J. worried too much for practical jokes. Besides, the gun looked very, very real. "Yes."

"I'm Sheriff Agee. Hope you don't mind me dropping by."

"No." She tried a polite smile, but found it strained. Guns and badges and official vehicles. Too many police in too short a time, Maggie told herself.

"If it wouldn't put you out too much, I'd like to come in and talk to you for a few minutes."

It did put her out. She wanted to say it did, then close the door on him and everything he wanted to talk about. *Coward*, she told herself, and stepped back to let him in. "I suppose you're here about what we found yesterday." Maggie put her shoulder to the door to shut it. "I don't know what I can tell you."

"I'm sure it was a nasty experience, Miss Fitzgerald, and one you'd just as soon forget." His voice held just the right trace of sympathy mixed with professionalism. She decided he knew his business. "I wouldn't feel I was doing my duty as sheriff or as a neighbor if I didn't give you whatever help I can."

Maggie looked at him again. This time her smile came a bit more easily. "I appreciate that. I can offer you coffee, if you don't mind the mess in the kitchen."

He smiled and looked so solid, so pleasant, Maggie almost forgot the gun at his hip. "I never turn down coffee."

"The kitchen's down here," she began, then laughed. "I don't have to tell you, do I? You'd know this house as well as I do."

He fell into step beside her. "Tell you the truth, I've

been around the outside, hacking at the weeds now and again or hunting, but I've only been inside a handful of times. The Morgans moved out when Joyce was still a kid."

"Yes, she told me."

"Nobody's lived here for more'n ten years. Louella just let it go after the old man died." He glanced up at the cracked ceiling paint. "She held it in trust till Joyce inherited it at twenty-five. You probably heard I held Joyce off from selling."

"Well…" Uncertain how to respond, Maggie busied herself at the stove.

"Guess I thought we'd fix it up eventually, rent it out again." To her, he sounded like a man who knew about dreams but never found the time for them. "But a big old place like this needs a lot of time and money to put right. Joyce probably did the right thing, selling out."

"I'm glad she did." After switching on the coffee-maker, Maggie indicated a chair.

"With Bog handling repairs and Delaney working on the grounds, you picked the right men." When Maggie just looked at him, the sheriff grinned again. "Nothing travels fast in small towns but news."

"No, I suppose not."

"Look, what happened yesterday…" He paused, clearing his throat. "I know it must be rough on you. I gotta tell you, Joyce was worked up about it. A lot of people who'd find something like that a stone's throw from their house would just pull up stakes and take off."

Maggie reached in the cabinets for cups. "I'm not going anywhere."

"Glad to hear it." He was silent a moment, watching

her pour the coffee. Her hands looked steady enough. "I understand Cliff was here yesterday, too."

"That's right. He was overseeing some of the work."

"And your dog dug up—"

"Yes." Maggie set both cups on the table before she sat down. "He's just a puppy. Right now he's asleep upstairs. Too much excitement."

The sheriff waved away her offer of cream, sipping the coffee black. "I didn't come to press you for details. The state police filled me in. I just wanted to let you know I was as close as the phone if you needed anything."

"I appreciate that. I'm not really familiar with the procedure, but I suppose I should've called you yesterday."

"I like to take care of my own territory," he said slowly, "but with something like this—" He shrugged. "Hell, I'd've had to call in the state, anyway." She watched his wedding ring gleam dully in the sunlight. Joyce had had a matching one, Maggie recalled. Plain and gold and solid. "Looks like you're redoing this floor."

Maggie looked down blankly. "Oh, yes, I took up the old linoleum. I've got to get to the sanding."

"You call George Cooper," the sheriff told her. "He's in the book. He'll get you an electric sander that'll take care of this in no time. Just tell him Stan Agee gave you his name."

"All right." She knew the conversation should've eased her mind, but her nerves were jumping again. "Thank you."

"Anything else you need, you just give us a call.

Joyce'll want to have you over for dinner. She bakes the best ham in the county."

"That'd be nice."

"She can't get over someone like you moving here to Morganville." He sipped at his coffee while Maggie's grew cold. While he leaned back in the chair, relaxed, she sat very straight with tension. "I don't keep up with music much, but Joyce knows all of your songs. She reads all those magazines, too, and now somebody's who's in them's living in her old house." He glanced idly at the back door. "You ought to speak to Bog about putting some dead bolts on."

She looked over at the screen, remembering the hinges needed oiling. "Dead bolts?"

With a laugh, he finished off his coffee. "That's what happens when you're sheriff. You're always thinking of security. We've got a nice, quiet community, Miss Fitzgerald. Wouldn't want you to think otherwise. But I'd feel better knowing you had some good solid locks on the doors, since you're back here alone." Rising, he tugged absently at his holster. "Thanks for the coffee. You just remember to call if you need anything."

"Yes, I'll remember."

"I'll go on out this way and let you get back to work. You call George Cooper, now."

"All right." Maggie walked to the back door with him. "Thank you, Sheriff."

For a moment she just stood there by the door, her head resting against the jamb. She hated knowing she could be so easily worked up. The sheriff had come to reassure her, to show her that the community she'd chosen to live in had a concerned, capable law enforcer. Now her nerves were raw from talking to so many police. So many police, Maggie mused, just as it had been when Jerry died. All the police, all the questions. She thought she'd been over it, but now everything was coming back again, much too clearly.

"Your husband drove off the road, Mrs. Browning. We haven't located his body yet, but we're doing everything we can. I'm sorry."

Yes, there'd been sympathy at first, Maggie remembered. She'd had sympathy from the police, from her friends, Jerry's friends. Then questions: "Had your husband been drinking when he left the house?" "Was he upset, angry?" "Were you fighting?"

God, hadn't it been enough that he'd been dead? Why had they picked and pulled at all the reasons? How many reasons could there be for a twenty-eight-year-old man to turn his car toward a cliff and drive over it?

Yes, he'd been drinking. He'd done a lot of drinking since his career had started to skid and hers had kept climbing. Yes, they'd been fighting, because neither of them had understood what had happened to the dreams they'd once had. She'd answered their questions; she'd suffered the press until she had thought she'd go mad.

Maggie squeezed her eyes tight. That was over, she told herself. She couldn't bring Jerry back and solve his problems now. He'd found his own solution. Turning from the door, she went back to the music room.

In her work she found the serenity and the discipline she needed. It had always been that way for her. She could escape into the music so that her emotions found their outlet. She could train her mind on timing and structure. Her drive had always been to release the emotions, hers by the creation of a song and the listener's by hearing it. If she was successful in that, she needed no other ambition.

Talent wasn't enough in itself, she knew. It hadn't been enough for Jerry. Talent had to be harnessed by discipline; discipline, guided by creativity. Maggie used all three now.

As time passed, she became absorbed in the music and in the goal she'd set. The title song had to be passionate, full of movement and sexuality, as the title itself suggested. When it was played, she wanted it to stir the senses, touch off needs, build longings.

No one had been signed to perform it yet, so she was free to use whatever style she chose. She wanted something bluesy, and in her mind she could hear the moan of a sax. Sexy, sultry. She wanted the quiet wail of brass and the smoky throb of bass. Late the night before, when she'd been restless, she'd written down a few phrases. Now she experimented with them, twining words to music.

Almost at once she knew she'd found the key. The key was unexplained passion, barely controlled. It was desire that promised to rip aside anything civilized. It was the fury and heat that a man and woman could bring to each other until both were senseless from it. She had the key now, Maggie thought as her pulse began to pound with the music, because she'd experienced it herself. Yesterday, on the rise, in the sun, with Cliff.

Madness. That was the word that streamed through her mind. Desire was madness. She closed her eyes as words and melody flowed through her. Hadn't she felt that madness, the sweetness and the ache of it, when his mouth had moved on hers? Hadn't she wanted to feel him against her, flesh to flesh? He'd made her think of dark nights, steamy, moonless nights when the air was so thick you'd feel it pulse on your skin. Then she hadn't thought at all, because desire was madness.

She let the words come, passionate, wanton promises that simmered over the heat of the music. Seductive, suggestive, they poured out of her own needs. Lovers' words, desperate words, were whispered out in her low, husky voice until the room was charged with them. No one who heard would be unmoved. That was her ambition.

When she was finished, Maggie was breathless and moved and exhilarated. She reached up to rewind the recorder for playback when, for the second time, she saw Cliff standing in the doorway.

Her hand froze, and her pulse, already fast, went racing. Had she called him with the song? she wondered frantically. Was the magic that strong? When he said nothing, she switched off the recorder and spoke with studied calm. "Is it an accepted habit in the country for people to walk into homes uninvited?"

"You don't seem to hear the door when you're working."

She acknowledged this with an inclination of her head. "That might mean I don't like to be disturbed when I'm working."

"It might." Disturbed. The word almost made him laugh. Perhaps he had disturbed her work, but that was nothing compared to what the song had done to him—to what watching her sing had done to him. It had taken every ounce of his control not to yank her from the piano stool and take her on the littered, dusty floor. He came closer, knowing before it reached him that her scent would be there to add to her allure.

"I lost quite a bit of time yesterday." Maggie swallowed whatever was trying to block her voice. Her body was still throbbing, still much too vulnerable from the passion she'd released. "I have a deadline on this score."

He glanced down at her hands. He wanted to feel them stroke over him with the same skill she'd used on the piano keys. Slowly, he took his gaze up her arms, over the curve of her shoulder to her face. For both of them, it was as if he'd touched her.

Her breath wasn't steady; her eyes weren't calm. That was as he wanted it now. No matter how often or how firmly he told himself to back off from her, Cliff knew he was reaching a point when it would be impossible. She wasn't for him—he could convince himself of that. But they had something that had to be freed and had to be tasted.

"From what I heard," he murmured, "you seem to be finished."

"That's for me to decide."

"Play it back." It was a challenge. He saw from her eyes that she knew it. A challenge could backfire on either of them. "The last song—I want to hear it again."

Dangerous. Maggie understood the danger. As she hesitated, his lips curved. It was enough. Without a word, she punched the rewind button. The song was a fantasy, she told herself as the tape hurried backward. It was a fantasy, just as the film was a fantasy. The song was for the characters in a story and had nothing, absolutely nothing, to do with her. Or with him. She flicked the recorder to play.

She'd listen objectively, Maggie decided as the music began to spill into the room. She'd listen as a musician, as a technician. That was what her job demanded. But she found, as her own voice began to tempt her, that she was listening as a woman. Rising, she walked to the window and faced out. When a hunger was this strong, she thought, distance could mean everything.

> Wait for night when the air's
> hot and there's madness
> I'll make your blood swim
> Wait for night when passion rises like
> a flood in the heat dance
> Desire pours over the rim

He listened, as he had before, and felt his system respond to the music and the promises that low voice made. He wanted all that the song hinted at. All that, and more.

When Cliff crossed the room, he saw her tense. He thought he could feel the air snap, hissing with the heat the song had fanned. Before he reached her, Maggie turned. The sun at her back shot a nimbus around her. In contrast, her eyes were dark. Like night, he thought. Like her night music. The words she'd written filled the room around them. It seemed those words were enough.

He didn't speak, but circled the back of her neck with his hand. She didn't speak, but resisted, forcing her body to stiffen. There was anger in her eyes now, as much for herself as for him. She'd taken herself to this point by allowing her own needs and fantasies to clear the path. It wasn't madness she wanted, Maggie told herself as she drew back. It was stability. It wasn't the wild she sought, but serenity. He wouldn't offer those things.

His fingers only tightened as she pulled back. That surprised them both. He'd forgotten the rules of a civilized seduction, just as he'd forgotten he'd only come there to see how she was. The music, the words, made the vulnerability that had concerned him a thing of the past. Now he felt strength as his fingers pressed into her skin. He saw challenge in her stance, and a dare, mixed with the fury in her eyes. Cliff wanted nothing less from her.

He stepped closer. When she lifted a hand in protest, he took her wrist. The pulse throbbed under his hand as intensely as the music throbbed on the air. Their eyes met, clashed, passion against passion. In one move, he pulled her against him and took her mouth.

She saw the vivid colors and lights she'd once imagined. She tasted the flavor of urgent desire. As her arms pulled him yet closer to her, Maggie heard her own moan of shuddering pleasure. The world was suddenly honed down to an instant, and the instant went on and on.

Had she been waiting for this? This mindless, melting pleasure? Were these sensations, these emotions, what she'd poured out into music for so long? She could find no answers, only more needs.

He'd stopped thinking. In some small portion of his brain, Cliff knew he'd lost the capacity to reason. She made him feel, outrageously, so that there was no room for intellect. His hands sought her, skimming under her shirt to find the soft, heated skin he knew he'd dreamed about. She strained against him, offering more. Against his mouth, he felt her lips form his name. Something wild burst inside him.

He wasn't gentle, though as a lover he'd never been rough before. He was too desperate to touch to realize that he might bruise something more fragile than he. The kiss grew savage. He knew he'd never be able to draw enough from her to satisfy him. More, and still more, he wanted, though her mouth was as crazed and demanding as his.

He was driving her mad. No one had ever shown her a need so great. Hunger fueled hunger until she ached with it. She knew it could consume her, perhaps both of them. With a fire so hot, they could burn each other out and be left with nothing. The thought made her moan again, and cling. She wanted more. Yet she feared to take more and find herself empty.

"No." His lips at her throat were turning her knees to water. "No, this is crazy," she managed.

He lifted his head. His eyes were nearly black now, and his breathing was unsteady. For the first time, Maggie felt a twinge of fear. What did she know of this man? "You called it madness," he murmured. "You were right."

Yes, she'd been right, and it had been him she'd thought of when she'd written the words. Yet she told herself it was sanity she needed. "It's not what either of us should want."

"No." His control was threatening to snap completely. Deliberately, he ran a hand down her hair. "But it's already too far along to stop. I want you, Maggie, whether I should or not."

If he hadn't used her name— Until then she hadn't realized that he could say her name and make her weak.

As needs welled up again, she dropped her head on his chest. It was that artless, unplanned gesture that cleared his frenzied thoughts and tugged at something other than desire.

This was the kind of woman who could get inside a man. Once she did, he'd never be free of her. Knowing that, he fought back the overwhelming need to hold her close again. He wanted her, and he intended to have her. That didn't mean he'd get involved. They both knew that what had ignited between them would have to be consummated sooner or later. It was basic; it was simple. And they'd both walk away undamaged.

Whereas the arousal he'd felt hadn't worried him, the tenderness he was feeling now did. They'd better get things back on the right road. He took her by the shoulders and drew her back.

"We want each other." It sounded simple when he said it. Cliff was determined to believe it could be.

"Yes." She nodded, almost composed again. "I'm sure you've learned, as I have, that you can't have everything you want."

"True enough. But there's no reason for either of us not to have what we want this time."

"I can think of a few. The first is that I barely know you."

He frowned as he studied her face. "Does that matter to you?"

Maggie jerked away so quickly his hands fell to his sides. "So, you do believe everything you read." Her voice was brittle now, and her eyes were cold. "Los Angeles, land of sinning and sinners. I'm sorry to disappoint you, Cliff, but I haven't filled my life with nameless, faceless lovers. This fills my life." She slapped her hand down on the piano so that papers slid off onto the floor. "And since you read so much, since you know so much about me, you'll know that up to two years ago I was married. I had a husband, and as ridiculous as it sounds, was faithful for six years."

"My question didn't have anything to do with that." His voice was so mild in contrast to hers that she stiffened. Maggie had learned to trust him the least when he used that tone. "It was more personal, as in you and me."

"Then let's just say I have a rule of thumb not to hop into bed with men I don't know. You included."

He crossed the room, then laid his hand over hers on the piano. "Just how well do you have to know me?"

"Better, I think, than I ever will." She had to fight the urge to snatch her hand away. She'd made a fool of herself enough for one day. "I have another rule about steering clear of people who don't like who and what I am."

He looked down at the hand beneath his. It was pale, slender and strong. "Maybe I don't know who and what you are." His gaze lifted to lock on hers. "Maybe I intend to find out for myself."

"You'll have to have my cooperation for that, won't you?"

He lifted a brow, as if amused. "We'll see."

Her voice became only more icy. "I'd like you to leave. I've a lot of work to do."

"Tell me what you were thinking about when you wrote that song."

Something fluttered over her face so quickly he couldn't be certain if it was panic or passion. Either would have suited him.

"I said I want you to leave."

"I will—after you tell me what you were thinking of."

She kept her chin angled and her eyes level. "I was thinking of you."

He smiled. Taking her hand, he brought her palm to his lips. The unexpected gesture had thunderbolts echoing in her head. "Good," he murmured. "Think some more. I'll be back."

She closed her fingers over her palm as he walked away. He'd given her no choice but to do as he'd asked.

It was late, late into the night, when she woke. Groggy, Maggie thought it had been the dream that had disturbed her. She cursed Cliff and rolled onto her back. She didn't want to dream of him. She certainly didn't want to lie awake in the middle of the night, thinking of him.

Staring up at the ceiling, she listened to the quiet. At times like this, it struck her how alone she was. There were no servants sleeping downstairs, as there had been all her life. Her closest neighbor was perhaps a quarter of a mile away through the woods. No all-night clubs or drugstores, she mused. So far, she'd yet to even deal with getting an outside antenna for television. She was on her own, as she'd chosen.

Then why, Maggie wondered, did her bed suddenly seem so empty and the night so long? Rolling to her side, she struggled to shake off the mood and her thoughts of Cliff.

Overhead, a board creaked, but she paid no attention. Old houses made noises at night. Maggie had learned that quickly. Restless, she shifted in bed and lay watching the light of the waning moon.

She didn't want Cliff there, with her. Even allowing herself to think that she did was coming too close to dangerous ground. It was true her body had reacted to him, strongly. A woman couldn't always control the needs of her body, but she could control the direction of her thoughts. Firmly, she set her mind on the list of chores for the next day.

When the sound came again, she frowned, glancing automatically at the ceiling. The creaks and groans rarely disturbed her, but then, she'd always slept soundly in this house. Until Cliff Delaney, she thought, and determinedly shut her eyes. The sound of a door shutting quietly had them flying open again.

Before panic could register or reason overtake it, her heart was lodged in her throat, pounding. She was alone, and someone was in the house. All the nightmares that had ever plagued a woman alone in the dark loomed in her mind. Her fingers curled into the sheets as she lay stiffly, straining to hear.

Was that a footstep on the stairs, or was it all in her imagination? As terror flowed into her, she thought of the gully outside. She bit down on her lip to keep herself from making a sound. Very slowly, Maggie turned her head and made out the puppy sleeping at the foot of the bed. He didn't hear anything. She closed her eyes again and tried to even her breathing.

If the dog heard nothing that disturbed him, she reasoned, there was nothing to worry about. Just boards settling. Even as she tried to convince herself, Maggie heard a movement downstairs. A soft squeak, a gentle scrape. The kitchen door? she asked herself as the panic buzzed in her head. Fighting to move slowly and quietly, she reached for the phone beside the bed. As she held it to her ear, she heard the buzz that reminded her she'd left the kitchen extension off the hook earlier so as not to be disturbed. Her phone was as good as dead. Hysteria bubbled and was swallowed.

Think, she ordered herself. *Stay calm and think.* If she was alone, with no way to reach help, she had to rely on herself. How many times in the past few weeks had she stated that she could do just that?

She pressed a hand against her mouth so that the sound of her own breathing wouldn't disturb her concentrated listening. There was nothing now, no creaks, no soft steps on wood.

Careful to make no sound, she climbed out of bed and found the fireplace poker. Muscles tense, Maggie propped herself in the chair, facing the door. Gripping the poker in both hands, she prayed for morning.

Chapter 6

After a few days, Maggie had all but forgotten about the noises in her house. As early as the morning after the incident, she'd felt like a fool. She'd been awakened by the puppy licking her bare feet while she sat, stiff and sore from the night in the chair. The fireplace poker had lain across her lap like a medieval sword. The bright sunlight and birdsong had convinced her she'd imagined everything, then had magnified every small noise the way a child magnifies shadows in the dark. Perhaps she wasn't quite as acclimated to living alone as she'd thought. At least she could be grateful she'd left the downstairs extension off the hook. If she hadn't, everyone in town would know she was a nervous idiot.

If she had nerves, Maggie told herself, it was certainly understandable under the circumstances. People digging up skeletons beside her house, the local sheriff suggesting she lock her doors, and Cliff Delaney, Maggie added, keeping her up at night. The only good thing to come out of the entire week was the completed score. She imagined that C.J. would be pleased enough with the finished product not to nag her about coming back to L.A., at least for a little while.

Maggie decided the next constructive thing to do was to take the tape and sheet music she'd packaged to the post office and mail it off. Perhaps later she'd celebrate her first songs written in her new home.

She enjoyed the trip to town and took it leisurely. The narrow little roads were flanked by trees that would offer a blanket of shade in a few short weeks. Now the sun streamed through the tiny leaves to pour white onto the road. Here and there the woods were interrupted by fields, brown earth turned up. She could see farmers working with their tractors and wondered what was being planted. Corn, hay, wheat? She knew virtually nothing of that aspect of the home she'd chosen. Maggie thought it would be interesting to watch things grow until the summer or autumn harvest.

She saw cows with small calves nursing frantically. There was a woman carrying a steel bucket to what must have been a chicken coop. A dog raced along a fenced yard, barking furiously at Maggie's car.

Her panic of a few nights before seemed so ridiculous she refused to think of it.

She passed a few houses, some of them hardly more than cabins, others so obviously new and modern they offended the eyes. She found herself resenting the pristine homes on lots where trees had been cleared. Why hadn't they worked with what was there, instead of spoiling it? Then she laughed at herself. She was sounding too much like Cliff Delaney. People had a right to live where and how they chose, didn't they? But she couldn't deny that she preferred the old weathered brick or wood homes surrounded by trees.

As she drove into Morganville, she noted the homes were closer together. That was town life, she decided. There were sidewalks here, and a few cars parked along the curb. People kept their lawns trimmed. Maggie decided that from the look of it, there was quite a bit of pride and competition among the flower gardens. It reminded her to check her own petunias.

The post office was on the corner, a small redbrick building with a two-car parking lot. Beside it, separated by no more than a two-foot strip of grass, was the Morganville bank. Two men stood beside the outside mailbox, smoking and talking. They watched as Maggie pulled into the lot, as she stepped out of the car and as she walked toward the post office. Deciding to try her luck, she turned her head and flashed them a smile.

"Good morning."

"Morning," they said in unison. One of them pushed back his fishing cap. "Nice car."

"Thank you."

She walked inside, pleased that she had had what could pass for a conversation.

There was one woman behind the counter already engaged in what appeared to be casual gossip with a younger woman who toted a baby on her hip. "No telling how long they've been there," the postmistress stated, counting out stamps. "Nobody's lived out there since the Faradays, and that's been ten years last month. Old lady Faraday used to come in for a dollar's worth of stamps once a week, like clockwork. 'Course, they were cheaper then." She pushed the stamps across the counter. "That's five dollars' worth, Amy."

"Well, I think it's spooky." The young mother jiggled the baby on her hip while he busied himself gurgling at Maggie. Gathering up the stamps, she stuffed them into a bag on her other shoulder. "If I found a bunch of old bones in my yard, I'd have a For Sale sign up the next day." Hearing the words, Maggie felt some of her pleasure in the day fade. "Billy said some drifter probably fell in that gully and nobody ever knew about it."

"Could be. Guess the state police'll figure it out before long." The postmistress closed the conversation by turning to Maggie. "Help you?"

"Yes." Maggie stepped up to the counter. The young woman gave her one long, curious look before she took her baby outside. "I'd like to send this registered mail."

"Well, let's see what it weighs." The postmistress took the package and put it on the scale. "You want a return receipt?"

"Yes, please."

"Okay." She took the pencil from behind her ear to run the tip along a chart taped to the scale. "Cost you a bit more, but you'll know it got there. Let's see, it's going to zone—" She broke off as she caught the return address on the corner of the package. Her gaze lifted, focusing sharply on Maggie, before she began to fill out the form. "You're the songwriter from California. Bought the Morgan place."

"That's right." Because she wasn't sure what to say after the conversation she'd overheard, Maggie left it at that.

"Nice music." The postmistress wrote in meticulously rounded letters. "Lot of that stuff they play I can't even understand. I got some of your mama's records. She was the best. Nobody else comes close."

Maggie's heart warmed, as it always did when someone spoke of her mother. "Yes, I think so, too."

"You sign this here." As she obeyed, Maggie felt the postmistress's eyes on her. It occurred to her that this woman saw every piece of correspondence that came to or from her. Though it was an odd feeling, she found it wasn't unpleasant. "Big old house, the Morgan place." The woman figured the total on a little white pad. "You settling in all right out there?"

"Bit by bit. There's a lot to be done."

"That's the way it is when you move into a place, 'specially one's been empty so long. Must be a lot different for you."

Maggie lifted her head. "Yes. I like it."

Perhaps it was the direct eyes or perhaps it was the simple phrasing, but the postmistress seemed to nod to herself. Maggie felt as though she'd found her first full acceptance. "Bog'll do well by you. So will young Delaney."

Maggie smiled to herself as she reached for her wallet. Small towns, she thought. No secrets.

"You had a shock the other day."

Because she'd been expecting some kind of comment, Maggie took it easily. "I wouldn't care to have another like it."

"Nope, guess nobody would. You just relax and enjoy that old house," the postmistress advised. "It was a showcase in its day. Louella always kept it fine. Let the police worry about the rest of it."

"That's what I'm trying to do." Maggie pocketed her change. "Thank you."

"We'll get this off for you right away. You have a nice day."

Maggie was definitely feeling pleased with herself when she walked back outside. She took a deep breath of soft spring air, smiled again at the two men still talking beside the mailbox, then turned toward her car. The smile faded when she saw Cliff leaning against the hood.

"Out early," he said easily.

He'd told her it was difficult to avoid anyone in a town that size. Maggie decided it was his accuracy that annoyed her. "Shouldn't you be working somewhere?"

He grinned and offered her the bottle of soda he held. "Actually, I just came off a job site and was on my way to another." When she made no move to take the soda, he lifted the bottle to his lips again and drank deeply. "You don't see too many of these in Morganville." He tapped a finger against the side of her Aston Martin.

She started to move around him to the driver's door. "If you'll excuse me," she said coolly, "I'm busy."

He stopped her effortlessly with a hand on her arm. Ignoring her glare, as well as the interested speculation of the two men a few yards away, Cliff studied her face. "You've shadows under your eyes. Haven't you been sleeping?"

"I've been sleeping just fine."

"No." He stopped her again, but this time he lifted a hand to her face, as well. Though she didn't seem to know it, every time her fragile side showed, he lost ground. "I thought you didn't believe in evasions."

"Look, I'm busy."

"You've let that business in the gully get to you."

"Well, what if I have?" Maggie exploded. "I'm human. It's a normal reaction."

"I didn't say it wasn't." The hand on her face tilted her chin back a bit farther. "You fire up easily these days. Is it just that business that has you tense, or is there something else?"

Maggie stopped trying to pull away and stood very still. Maybe he hadn't noticed the men watching them, or the postmistress in the window, but she had. "It's none of your business whether I'm tense or not. Now, if you'll stop making a scene, I have to go home and work."

"Do scenes bother you?" Amused now, he drew her closer. "I wouldn't have thought so, from the number of times you've had your picture snapped."

"Cliff, cut it out." She put both hands on his chest. "For heaven's sake, we're standing on Main Street."

"Yeah. And we've just become the ten-o'clock bulletin."

A laugh escaped before she even knew it was going to happen. "You get a real kick out of that, don't you?"

"Well…" He took advantage of her slight relaxing and wrapped his arms around her. "Maybe. I've been meaning to talk to you."

A woman walked by with a letter in her hand. Maggie noticed that she took her time putting it into the box. "I think we could find a better place." At his snort of laughter, she narrowed her eyes. "I didn't mean that. Now, will you let go?"

"In a minute. Remember when we went out to dinner the other night?"

"Yes, I remember. Cliff—" She turned her head and saw that the two men were still there, still watching. Now the woman had joined them. "This really isn't funny."

"Thing is," he continued easily, "we have this custom around here. I take you out to dinner, then you reciprocate."

Out of patience, she wriggled against him and found that only made her blood pressure rise. "I haven't the time to go out to dinner right now. I'll get back to you in a few weeks."

"I'll take potluck."

"Potluck?" she repeated. "At *my* house?"

"Good idea."

"Wait a minute. I didn't say—"

"Unless you can't cook."

"Of course I can cook," she tossed back.

"Fine. Seven o'clock?"

She aimed her most deadly, most regal stare. "I'm hanging wallpaper tonight."

"You have to eat sometime." Before she could comment, he kissed her, briefly but firmly enough to make a point. "See you at seven," he said, then strolled over to his truck. "And, Maggie," he added through the open window, "nothing fancy. I'm not fussy."

"You—" she began, but the roar of the truck's engine drowned her out. She was left standing alone, fuming, in the center of the parking lot. Knowing there were at least a dozen pair of eyes on her, Maggie kept her head high as she climbed into her own car.

She cursed Cliff repeatedly, and expertly, on the three-mile drive back to her house.

Maggie expected the men from Cliff's crew to be

there when she returned. The discreet black car at the end of her driveway, however, was unexpected. She discovered as she pulled alongside it that she wasn't in the mood for visitors, not for neighbors calling to pay their respects or for curiosity-seekers. She wanted to be alone with the sander she'd rented from George Cooper.

As she stepped from the car, she spotted the rangy man with the salt-and-pepper hair crossing her front yard from the direction of the gully. And she recognized him.

"Miss Fitzgerald."

"Good morning. Lieutenant Reiker, isn't it?"

"Yes, ma'am."

What was the accepted etiquette, Maggie wondered, when you came home and found a homicide detective on your doorstep? Maggie decided on the practical, marginally friendly approach. "Is there something I can do for you?"

"I'm going to have to ask for your cooperation, Miss Fitzgerald." The lieutenant kept his weight on one foot, as if his hips were troubling him. "I'm sure you'd like to get on with all your landscaping plans, but we want you to hold off on the pond a while longer."

"I see." She was afraid she did. "Can you tell me why?"

"We've received the medical examiner's preliminary report. We'll be investigating."

It might've been easier not to ask, not to know. Maggie wasn't certain she could live with herself if she took the coward's way out that she was obviously being offered. "Lieutenant, I'm not sure how much you're at liberty to tell me, but I do think I have a right to know certain things. This is my property."

"You won't be involved to any real extent, Miss Fitzgerald. This business goes back a long way."

"As long as my land's part of it, I'm involved." She caught herself worrying the strap of her bag, much as Joyce had done on her visit. She forced her hands to be still. "It'd be easier for me, Lieutenant, if I knew what was going on."

Reiker rubbed his hand over his face. The investigation was barely under way, and he already had a bad taste in his mouth. Maybe things that'd been dead and buried for ten years should just stay buried. Some things, he decided grimly. Yes, some things.

"The medical examiner determined that the remains belonged to a Caucasian male in his early fifties."

Maggie swallowed. That made it too real. Much too real. "How long—" she began, but had to swallow again. "How long had he been there?"

"The examiner puts it at about ten years."

"As long as the house has been empty," she murmured. She brought herself back, telling herself that it wasn't personal. Logically, practically, it had nothing to do with her. "I don't suppose they could determine how he died?"

"Shot," Reiker said flatly, and watched the horror fill her eyes. "Appears to've been a thirty-gauge shotgun, probably at close range."

"Good God." Murder. Yet hadn't she known it, sensed it almost from the first instant? Maggie stared out into the woods and watched two squirrels race up the trunk of a tree. How could it have happened here? "After so many years—" she began, but had to swallow yet again. "After so many years, wouldn't it be virtually impossible to identify the—him?"

"He was identified this morning." Reiker watched as she turned to him, pale, her eyes almost opaque. It gave him a bad feeling. He told himself it was because, like every other man in the country, he'd had a fantasy love affair with her mother twenty years before. He told himself it was because she was young enough to be his daughter. At times like this, he wished he'd chosen any other line of work.

"We found a ring, too, an old ring with a lot of fancy carving and three small diamond chips. An hour ago, Joyce Agee identified it as her father's. William Morgan was murdered and buried in that gully."

But that was wrong. Maggie dragged a hand through her hair and tried to think. No matter how bluntly, how practically, Reiker put it, it was wrong. "That can't be. I was told that William Morgan had an accident—something about a car accident."

"Ten years ago, his car went through the guardrail of the bridge crossing into West Virginia. His car was dragged out of the Potomac, but not his body. His body was never found…until a few days ago."

Through the rail, into the water, Maggie thought numbly. Like Jerry. They hadn't found Jerry's body, either, not for nearly a week. She'd lived through every kind of hell during that week. As she stood, staring straight ahead, she felt as though she were two people in two separate times. "What will you do now?"

"There'll be an official investigation. It has nothing to do with you, Miss Fitzgerald, other than we need for you to keep that section of your property clear. There'll be a team here this afternoon to start going over it again, just in case we missed something."

"All right. If you don't need anything else—"

"No, ma'am."

"I'll be inside."

As she walked across the lawn toward the house, she told herself that something that had happened ten years before had nothing to do with her. Ten years before, she'd been dealing with her own tragedy, the loss of her parents. Unable to resist, she looked back over her shoulder at the gully as she climbed the steps to the porch.

Joyce Agee's father, Maggie thought with a shudder. Joyce had sold her the house without knowing what would be discovered. She thought of the pretty, tense young woman who had been grateful for a simple kindness to her mother. Compelled, Maggie went to the pad scrawled with names and numbers beside the phone. Without hesitating, she called the number for Joyce Agee. The voice that answered was soft, hardly more than a whisper. Maggie felt a stab of sympathy.

"Mrs. Agee—Joyce, this is Maggie Fitzgerald."

"Oh… Yes, hello."

"I don't want to intrude." Now what? Maggie asked herself. She had no part of this, no link other than a plot of land that had lain neglected for a decade. "I just wanted you to know that I'm terribly sorry, and if there's anything I can do… I'd like to help."

"Thank you, there's nothing." Her voice hitched, then faltered. "It's been such a shock. We always thought—"

"Yes, I know. Please, don't think you have to talk to me or be polite. I only called because somehow—" She broke off, passing a hand over her hair. "I don't know. I feel as though I've set it all off."

"It's better to know the truth." Joyce's voice became

suddenly calm. "It's always better to know. I worry about Mother."

"Is she all right?"

"I'm not— I'm not sure." Maggie sensed fatigue now, rather than tears. She understood that form of grief, as well. "She's here now. The doctor's with her."

"I won't keep you, then. Joyce, I understand we hardly know each other, but I would like to help. Please let me know if I can."

"I will. Thank you for calling."

Maggie replaced the receiver. That accomplished nothing, she reflected. It accomplished nothing, because she didn't know Joyce Agee. When you grieved, you needed someone you knew, the way she'd needed Jerry when her parents had been killed. Though she knew Joyce had a husband, Maggie thought of Cliff and the way he'd taken the woman's hands, the look of concern on his face, when he'd spoken to her. He'd be there for her, Maggie mused, and wished she knew what they meant to each other.

To give her excess energy an outlet, she switched on the rented sander.

The sun was low, the sky rosy with it, when Cliff drove toward the old Morgan property. His mind was full of questions. William Morgan murdered. He'd been shot, buried on his own property; then someone had covered the trail by sending his car into the river.

Cliff was close enough to the Morgans and to the people of Morganville to know that every other person in town might've wished William Morgan dead. He'd been a hard man, a cold man, with a genius for making money and enemies. But could someone who

Cliff knew, someone he'd talk to on the street any day
of the week, have actually murdered him?

In truth, he didn't give a damn about the old man,
but he worried about Louella and Joyce—especially
Joyce. He didn't like to see her the way she'd been that
afternoon, so calm, so detached, with nerves snagged
at the edge. She meant more to him than any other
woman he'd known, yet there seemed to be no way to
help her now. That was for Stan, Cliff thought, down-
shifting as he came to a corner.

God knew if the police would ever come up with
anything viable. He didn't have much faith in that after
ten years. That meant Joyce would have to live with
knowing that her father had been murdered and that
his murderer still walked free. Would she, Cliff mused,
look at her neighbors and wonder?

Swearing, Cliff turned onto the lane that led to the
Morgan place. There was someone else he worried
about, he thought grimly, though he didn't have the
excuse of a long, close friendship with this woman.

Damned if he wanted to worry about Maggie
Fitzgerald. She was a woman from another place,
who liked glittery parties and opening nights. Where
he'd choose solitude, she'd choose crowds. She'd want
champagne; he, cold beer. She'd prefer trips to Europe;
he, a quiet ride down the river. She was the last person
he needed to worry about.

She'd been married to a performer who'd flamed
like a comet and who'd burned out just as quickly. Her
escorts had been among the princes of the celebrity
world. Tuxedos, silk scarves and diamond cuff links,
he thought derisively. What the hell was she doing in

the middle of a mess like this? And what the hell, he asked himself, was she doing in his life?

He pulled up behind her car and stared broodingly at her house. Maybe with all that was going on she'd decide to go back West. He'd prefer it that way. Damned if he didn't want to believe he would. She had no business crashing into his thoughts the way she had lately. That music. He let out a long stream of curses as he remembered it. That night music. Cliff knew he wanted her the way he'd wanted no woman before. It was something he couldn't overcome. Something he could barely control.

So why was he here? Why had he pushed his way into a meeting she hadn't wanted? Because, he admitted, when he thought of the way it had been between them, he didn't want to overcome it. Tonight he didn't want control.

As he walked toward the front door, he reminded himself that he was dealing with a woman who was different from any he'd known. Approach with caution, he told himself, then knocked at the front door.

From the other side, Maggie gripped the knob with both hands and tugged. It took two tries before she opened the door, and by that time Killer was barking nonstop.

"You should have Bog take care of that," Cliff suggested. He bent down to ruffle the dog's fur. Killer flopped on his back, offering his belly.

"Yeah." She was glad to see him. Maggie told herself she would've been glad to see anyone, but when she looked at him, she knew it was a lie. All through the afternoon she'd waited. "I keep meaning to."

He saw tension in the way she stood, in the way one

hand still gripped the doorknob. Deliberately, he gave her a cocky smile. "So, what's for dinner?"

She let out a quick laugh as some of the nerves escaped. "Hamburgers."

"Hamburgers?"

"You did invite yourself," she reminded him. "And you did say not to fuss."

"So I did." He gave Killer a last scratch behind the ears, then rose.

"Well, since it's my first dinner party, I thought I'd stick with my speciality. It was either that or canned soup and cold sandwiches."

"If that's been your staple since you moved in, it's no wonder you're thin."

Frowning, Maggie glanced down at herself. "Do you realize you make a habit of criticizing?"

"I didn't say I didn't like thin women."

"That's not the point. You can come back and complain while I cook the hamburgers."

As they walked down the hall, Cliff noticed a few bare spots where she'd removed strips of wallpaper. Apparently she was serious about taking on the overwhelming job of redoing the house. When they passed the music room, he glanced in at her piano and wondered why. She was in the position of being able to hire a fleet of decorators and craftsmen. The job could be done in weeks, rather than the months, even years, it promised to take this way. The freshly sanded floor in the kitchen caught his eye.

"Nice job." Automatically, he crouched down to run his fingers over the floor's surface. The dog took this as an invitation to lick his face.

Maggie lifted a brow. "Well, thank you."

Catching the tone, he looked up at her. He couldn't deny that he'd been giving her a hard time from the outset. He had his reasons. The primary one as Cliff saw it now was her effect on him. "The question is," he said, rising again, "why you're doing it."

"The floor needed it." She turned to the counter to begin making patties.

"I meant why *you're* doing it."

"It's my house."

He wandered over to stand beside her. Again, he found himself watching her hands. "Did you sand your own floors in California?"

"No." Annoyed, she set the patties under the broiler. "How many can you eat?"

"One'll do. Why are you sanding floors and hanging wallpaper?"

"Because it's my house." Maggie grabbed a head of lettuce from the refrigerator and began to shred it for salad.

"It was your house in California, too."

"Not the way this is." She dropped the lettuce and faced him. Impatience, annoyance, frustration—the emotions were plainly on the surface for him to see. "Look, I don't expect you to understand. I don't *care* if you understand. This house is special. Even after everything that's happened, it's special."

No, he didn't understand, but he discovered he wanted to. "The police have contacted you, then."

"Yes." She began to shred lettuce with a vengeance. "That investigator, Lieutenant Reiker, was here this morning." Her fingers dug into the cold, wet leaves. "Damn it, Cliff, I feel gruesome. I called Joyce and felt like an idiot, an intruder. There was nothing I could say."

"Did you?" he murmured. Strange that Joyce hadn't said anything about it, he thought. Then again, Joyce had said very little to him. "There isn't anything for you to say." He put his hands on her shoulders and felt the tension ripple. "This is something Joyce and her mother and the police have to deal with. It's nothing to do with you."

"I tell myself that," she said quietly. "Intellectually, I know it's true, but—" She turned, because she needed someone. Because, she admitted, she needed him. "It happened right outside. I'm involved, connected, whether I want to be or not. A man was murdered a few yards from my house. He was killed in a spot where I'd planned to put a nice quiet pond, and now—"

"And now," Cliff said, interrupting, "it's ten years later."

"Why should that matter?" she demanded. "My parents were killed ten years ago— Time doesn't make any difference."

"That," he countered, less gently than he'd intended, "had everything to do with you."

With a sigh, she allowed herself the weakness of resting her head against him. "I know how Joyce is feeling now. Everywhere I look, something draws me into this."

The more Maggie talked of Joyce, the less Cliff thought of the quiet brunette, and the more he thought of Maggie. His fingers tangled in her hair. It wasn't desire he felt now, but an almost fierce, protective urge he'd never expected. Perhaps there was something he could do, he decided, drawing her away.

"You didn't know William Morgan."

"No, but—"

"I did. He was a cold, ruthless man who didn't believe in words like *compassion* or *generosity*." Deliberately, he set Maggie aside and tended to the meat under the broiler himself. "Half the town would've cheered ten years ago if it hadn't been for Louella. She loved the old man. Joyce loved him, too, but both of them feared him every bit as much. The police won't have an easy time proving who killed him, and the town won't care. I detested him myself, for a lot of reasons."

She didn't like knowing that he could speak of a man's murder so calmly, so coldly. But then, as she'd told him herself before, they really didn't understand each other. To keep her hands busy, Maggie went back to the salad. "Joyce?" she asked casually.

He glanced at her sharply, then leaned on the counter again. "Yeah, for one. Morgan believed in discipline. Old-fashioned discipline. Joyce was like my kid sister. When I caught Morgan going at her with a belt when she was sixteen, I threatened to kill him myself."

He said it so casually Maggie's blood froze. He saw the doubts and the questions in her eyes when she looked at him.

"And so," Cliff added, "as the stories go, did half the population of Morganville. No one grieved when they fished William Morgan's car out of the river."

"No one has the right to take a life," Maggie said in a shaky voice. "Not their own or anyone else's."

He remembered that they had fished her husband's car out of the water, too. He remembered that the final verdict had been suicide. "You'd be better off not making comparisons," he said roughly.

"They seem to make themselves."

"What happened to Jerry Browning was a tragic waste of a life and of a talent. Do you plan on taking the blame for that, too?"

"I never took the blame," Maggie said wearily.

"Did you love him?"

Her eyes were eloquent, but her voice was steady. "Not enough."

"Enough to be faithful to him for six years," Cliff countered.

She smiled as her own words came back to her. "Yes, enough for that. Still, there's more to love than loyalty, isn't there?"

His hand was gentle again when he touched her face. "You said you hadn't taken the blame."

"Responsibility and blame are different things."

"No." He shook his head. "There's no responsibility or blame this time, either. Don't you think it's the height of egotism to feel responsible for someone else's actions?"

She started to snap at him, but the words hit home. "Maybe. Maybe it is." It wasn't easy, but she shook off the mood and smiled. "I think the hamburgers are done. Let's eat."

Chapter 7

Maggie found the kitchen cozy with the smell of hot food and the patter of raindrops that had just begun to strike the windows. When she thought of it, she decided she'd never really experienced coziness before. Her parents had lived on a grand scale: huge, elegant rooms and huge, elegant parties; boisterous, eccentric friends. With her own home in Beverly Hills, Maggie had followed the same pattern. Extravagance might've been what she needed during that phase of her life, or it might've been a habit. She wasn't sure when it had begun to wear on her, any more than she was certain if she'd ever been as relaxed as she was at that moment, eating in her half-finished kitchen with a man she wasn't quite sure of.

He was strong, she mused. Perhaps she'd never allowed a strong man into her life. Her father had been strong, Maggie remembered. He'd been the type of man who could do and get precisely what he wanted simply because he wanted it. The strength hadn't been a physical one, but one of personality and will. But then, her mother had matched him with her own combination of grit and exuberance. Maggie had never seen a more perfect relationship than theirs.

Theirs had been an all-consuming, enduring love, with qualities of practicality, compassion and fire. They'd never competed, never envied each other's success. Support, she thought. Perhaps that had been the real key to the quality and lasting power of their relationship. Unquestioning mutual support. She hadn't found that in her own marriage, and she'd come to think her parents had been unique.

Something had happened to the balance in her relationship with Jerry. As he'd grown weaker, she'd grown stronger. Eventually, they'd come to a point where all the support had been on her side and all the need on his. Yet she'd stayed, because it had been impossible to forget that they'd been friends. Friends don't break promises.

She wondered, as she studied Cliff, what sort of friend he would be. And she wondered, though she tried not to, what he would be like as a lover.

"What're you thinking of?"

The question came so abruptly that Maggie almost overturned her glass. Quickly, she sorted out her thoughts and chose the least personal. She could hardly tell him what had been the last thing on her mind. "I was thinking," she began, picking up her wine again, "how cozy it is eating here in the kitchen. I'll probably demote the dining room to the last thing on my list."

"That's what you were thinking?" By the way he

held her gaze, she knew he sensed there'd been other things.

"More or less." A woman who'd been interviewed and questioned all her life knew how to evade and dodge. Lifting the bottle, she filled Cliff's glass again. "The Bordeaux's another present from my agent. Or another bribe," she added.

"Bribe?"

"He wants me to give up this mad scheme of camping out in the wilderness and come back to civilization."

"He thinks he can persuade you with puppies and French wine?"

With a bubbling laugh, Maggie sipped. "If I weren't so attached to this place, either one might've worked."

"Is that what you are?" Cliff asked thoughtfully. "Attached?"

At the question, her eyes stopped laughing, and her soft, wide mouth sobered. "In your business you should know that some things root quickly."

"Some do," he agreed. "And some that do can't acclimate to the new territory."

She tapped the side of her glass with a fingertip, wishing she understood why his doubts dug at her so deeply. "You don't have much faith in me, do you?"

"Maybe not." He shrugged as if to lighten a subject he wasn't so certain of any longer. "In any case, I'm finding it interesting to watch you make the adjustments."

She decided to go with his mood. "How'm I doing?"

"Better than I'd thought." He lifted his glass in a half toast. "But it's early yet."

She laughed, because arguing seemed like a waste

of time. "Were you born cynical, Cliff, or did you take lessons?"

"Were you born an optimist?"

Both brows lifted to disappear under the fringe of sable bangs. *"Touché,"* Maggie said. No longer interested in the meal, she studied him, finding that while his face was very much to her liking, she still couldn't judge him by his eyes. Too much control, she thought. A person would only get inside his head if he or she was invited. "You know," she began slowly, "after I'd stopped being annoyed, I decided I was glad you were coming by this evening." Now she grinned. "I don't know when I might've opened the wine otherwise."

This time he grinned. "I annoy you?"

"I think you're well aware of that," Maggie returned dryly. "And that for your own personal reasons it pleases you to do so."

Cliff tasted the wine again. It was warm and rich, reminding him of her mouth. "Actually, I do."

He said it so easily that Maggie laughed again. "Is it just me, or is annoying people a hobby of yours?"

"Just you." Over the rim of his glass, he studied her. She'd pinned her hair up in a loose Gibson style that accentuated her delicate, old-fashioned features. She wore some dark contouring shadow that made her eyes seem even larger, but her mouth was naked. This was a woman, Cliff thought, who knew how to accentuate her own looks to the best advantage, subtly, so that a man would be caught before he analysed what was Maggie and what was illusion. "I like your reactions," Cliff continued after a moment. "You don't like to lose your temper."

"So you like to provoke me until I do."

"Yeah." He smiled again. "That about sizes it up."

"Why?" she demanded in a voice filled with exasperated amusement.

"I'm not immune to you," Cliff said, so quietly her fingers tightened on the stem of her glass. "I wouldn't like to think you were immune to me."

She sat for a moment, stirred and baffled. Before her emotions could rise any closer to the surface, she stood and began to clear the table. "No, I'm not. Would you like more wine or some coffee?"

His hands closed over hers on the dishes. Slowly, he rose, his gaze fixed on her face. Maggie felt as though the kitchen had shrunk in size. Like Alice in the rabbit hole, she thought confusedly, unsure whether to sample that tempting little bottle or not. The patter of rain outside seemed to grow to a roar.

"I want to make love with you."

She wasn't a child, Maggie told herself. She was an adult, and men had wanted her before. She'd resisted temptations before. But had any ever been quite so alluring? "We've already been through this."

His hands tightened on hers when she tried to turn away. "But we never resolved it."

No, she couldn't turn away, or run away, from a man like this, Maggie realized. She'd have to stand her ground. "I was sure we had. Perhaps coffee would be best, since you have to drive this evening and I have to work."

Cliff took the dishes and set them back on the table. With her hands empty, Maggie found herself at a loss. She folded her arms under her breasts, a habit Cliff had discovered she used whenever she was upset or disturbed. At the moment, he didn't care which she was, as long as she wasn't unmoved.

"We haven't resolved it," he repeated, and plucked a pin from her hair. "We haven't begun to resolve it."

Though her eyes remained steady, she backed up when he stepped closer. It made him feel as though he were stalking her, an odd and thrilling sensation. "I really thought I'd made myself clear," Maggie managed, in what sounded to her like a firm, dismissive tone.

"It's clear when I touch you." Cliff backed her up against the counter, then pulled another pin from her hair. "It's clear when you look at me like you're looking at me now."

Maggie's heart began to pound at the base of her throat. She was weakening; she felt it in the heaviness of her limbs, the lightness in her head. Desire was temptation, and temptation a seduction in itself. "I didn't say I didn't want you—"

"No, you didn't," Cliff interrupted. When he drew out the next pin, her hair fell heavily to her shoulders and lay there, dark and tousled. "I don't think lying comes easily to you."

How could she have been so relaxed a few moments before and so tense now? Every muscle in her body was taut in the effort to combat what seemed to be inevitable. "No, I don't lie." Her voice was lower, huskier. "I said I didn't know you. I said you didn't understand me."

Something flashed into him. Perhaps it was rage; perhaps it was need. "I don't give a damn how little we know each other or how little we understand each other. I know I want you." He gathered her hair in one hand. "I only have to touch you to know you want me."

Her eyes grew darker. Why did it always seem her desire was mixed with anger and, though she detested it, a certain weakness she couldn't control? "Can you really believe it's that simple?"

He had to. For the sake of his own survival, Cliff knew, he had to keep whatever was between them purely physical. They'd make love through the night until they were exhausted. In the morning, the need and the bond would be gone. He had to believe it. Otherwise... He didn't want to dwell on otherwise. "Why should it be complicated?" he countered.

The anger and the longing flowed through her. "Why indeed?" Maggie murmured.

The room had lost its cozy ambience. Now she felt she'd suffocate if she didn't escape it. Her eyes were stormy, his almost brutally calm, but she kept her gaze level on his while her thoughts raged. Why should she feel the need to rationalize, to romanticize? she asked herself. She wasn't an innocent young girl with misty dreams, but an adult, a widow, a professional woman who'd learned to live with reality. In reality, people took what they wanted, then dealt with the consequences. Now so would she.

"The bedroom's upstairs," she told him, and, brushing by him, walked out of the kitchen.

Disturbed, Cliff frowned after her. This was what he wanted, he thought. The lack of complications. Yet her abrupt acceptance had been so unexpected, so cool. No, he realized as he started after her, that wasn't what he wanted.

Maggie was at the base of the steps before he caught up with her. When she looked over her shoulder, he saw the fury in her eyes. The moment he took her arm, he felt the tension. This, he discovered, was what he wanted. He didn't want her cool, emotionless agreement or a careless acquiescence. He wanted to build that fury and tension until the passion that spawned them broke through. Before the night was over, he'd draw it all from her and purge himself, as well.

In silence, they climbed the stairs to the second floor.

The rain fell, strong and steady, against the windows and the newly seeded earth below. The sound made Maggie think of the subtle rhythmic percussion she'd imagined in the arrangement of the song she'd just completed. There was no moon to guide the way, so she moved from memory. Darkness was deep and without shadows. She didn't look when she entered the bedroom, but she knew Cliff was still beside her.

What now? she thought with sudden panic. What was she doing, bringing him here, to the single spot she considered purely private? He might learn more than she wanted before he left again, yet she might learn nothing more than she already knew. They wanted each other; it was unexplainable. It was undeniable.

As her nerves stretched tighter, Maggie was grateful for the dark. She didn't want him to see the doubts that would be clear on her face. As the need grew stronger, she knew she wouldn't have been able to conceal that, either. Darkness was better, she told herself, because it was anonymous. When he touched her, her body went rigid with a dozen conflicting emotions.

Feeling it, Cliff ran his hands over the slope of her shoulders, down to her lower back. He found he didn't want her to be too relaxed, to be too yielding. Not yet.

He wanted to know she struggled against something deeper, something unnamed, even as he did.

"You don't want to give in to this," Cliff said quietly. "Or to me."

"No." Yet she felt the tremor, not fear but pleasure, course through her body when he slipped his hands under her thin wool sweater. "No, I don't."

"What choice is there?"

She could see his face through the gloom of darkness, close, very close, to hers. "Damn you," she whispered. "There's none at all."

He slid his hands up her naked back, through the neck opening of her sweater, until his fingers found her hair. "No, not for either of us."

His body was firm against hers. His voice, soft and low, was faintly edged with anger. She caught the scent of soap, sharp, unrepentantly male, that lingered on his skin. His face was mysterious, indistinct in the darkness. He might've been anyone. As Maggie felt the next fierce pull of desire, she almost wished he was.

"Make love with me," she demanded. A decision made quickly, freely, would leave no room for regrets. "Take me now. It's all either of us wants."

Was it? The question had barely formed in his mind when his mouth was on hers. Then there were no questions, just flame and flash and power. Understanding, if there had been any before, dimmed. Reason vanished. Sensation, and only sensation, ruled. While perhaps both of them had expected it, they were caught in a maelstrom in which neither of them had any control. Racked by it, they fell together onto the bed and let the fire rage.

He could find no gentleness to give her, but it

seemed she neither demanded nor expected any. He wanted her naked but not vulnerable, soft but not yielding. If he had spoken the needs aloud, she could have been no more than what he'd asked for. As she arched against him, her lips clung in a wild, urgent kiss that was only a prelude to passion. He pulled at her clothes, forgetting finesse, then caught his breath when, in an equal frenzy, she began to strip him.

Clothes were tossed aside as if they were meaningless. Her scent rose up from her skin, from her hair, clouding whatever logic he might have tried to regain. The mattress swayed and dipped as they rolled over it, mindless now of the rain, of the dark, of time and place.

Then they were naked, heated flesh to heated flesh. The desperation grew in each to have all there could be of the other. Whispered demands, labored breathing, moans and sighs of pleasure, drowned out the sound of falling rain. Her body was small and supple and surprisingly strong. All three aspects combined to drive him mad.

This was what it meant to be consumed. Maggie knew it as his hands skimmed over her, inciting thrill after thrill. She hungered, no, starved, for each new demand. Greedy for what pleasure he would give and what pleasure she would take, she allowed him whatever he wanted. She felt no shame, no hesitation, in tasting, in touching, in asking for more or in taking it.

If his body had been designed to her wish, it could have been no more perfect. She reveled in the leanness, the cords of muscle, the long, narrow bones that ran along his hips. Wherever, whenever, she touched, she could almost feel the blood throb under his skin.

She wanted to know he had no more control than

she. She wanted to know they were both victims of their own combined power. The fuse that had been lit between them with a look was burning quickly. Desire was madness, and if the words she'd written were true, she'd cast aside her reason for it.

With a savageness they both craved, they came together, fighting to prolong an outrageous passion, greedy to capture that final flash of pleasure. She thought of whirlpools and high winds and the bellow of thunder. She felt the spin, the speed and heard the roar. Then both her mind and body shuddered from the last violent surge.

Love? Maggie thought some dim time later, when her thoughts began to clear again. If this was making love, she'd been innocent all her life. Could something with so gentle a name have such a violent effect on the body? Hers was pulsing and throbbing as if she'd raced up one side of a mountain and fallen off the other. She'd written songs about love, songs about passion, yet she'd never fully understood her own words until now.

Until now, she thought, when the man who lay beside her had dared her to live her own fantasies. With him she'd found the answer to the dark, driving needs that gave the grit, or the wistfulness, to most of her music. She understood, but understanding opened the door to dozens of questions.

Maggie ran a hand up her own body, astonished at the lingering sense of power and of wonder. How long had she been waiting for this night to come? Perhaps it was possible for passion to lie dormant, unexplored, until it was triggered by a certain person at a certain time.

Maggie thought of the film her music would score. It had been that way for the female character. She'd been content with life, almost smug, until one day a man had entered it, a man she'd shared little common ground with, a man who'd ignited a spark that had changed everything. It hadn't mattered that the woman was intelligent, successful, independent. The man, merely by existing, had altered the scope and pattern of her life.

If the same thing was happening to her, there was still time to stop it before she, too, became so consumed by needs, so ruled by desire, that nothing would ever be the same again.

In the film, the relationship had spawned violence. Instinct told her that there was something between her and Cliff that could do the same. There was little moderation in either of them. It was extremes, she knew, that played havoc with human nature.

Maybe fate had brought her to this serene little plot of land with its undertones of violence. The same fate might have brought her to this taciturn, physical man who seemed connected with both the tranquillity and the danger. The question now was whether she was strong enough to deal with the consequences of each.

What, Maggie asked herself while she stared into the darkness, would happen next?

Because nothing was as he'd expected it, Cliff was silent. He'd wanted passion, but he'd never imagined the scope of it. He'd wanted what her song had whispered of, but the reality had been much more dramatic than any words or any melody. He'd been certain that once the tension between them had been released, once the lure had been accepted, the needs would lessen.

It was true his body was sated with a pleasure more

intense than anything he'd known, but his mind— Cliff closed his eyes, wishing his mind would rest as easy. But it was too full of her. So full that he knew even a touch would set his body raging again. That kind of need was a shade too close to dependence for comfort. They had nothing to offer each other, he reminded himself, nothing but outrageous mutual desire.

And suddenly he remembered a line from her song. "Desire is madness."

If he could have stopped himself, he wouldn't have touched her again. He was already reaching for her.

"You're cold," he murmured, automatically drawing her against him to warm her.

"A bit." There was an awkwardness she didn't know how to alleviate and a need she didn't know how to explain.

"Here." He tugged the tangled spread over her, then pulled her close again. "Better?"

"Yes." Her body relaxed against his, even as her thoughts continued to race.

They lapsed into silence again, neither knowing quite how to deal with what had flared between them. Cliff listened to the rain beat against the window glass, adding to the sense of isolation. Even on a clear night, he knew, you would see no light from a neighboring house. "Are you having trouble staying out here alone?"

"Trouble?" Maggie hedged. She wanted to stay exactly as she was, wrapped close around him, warm and safe and untroubled. She didn't want to think now of staying in the big house alone, of sleeping alone.

"This place is more isolated than most around here." How soft she was, he thought. It brought him an odd sort of contentment to feel her hair lie against his shoulder. "A lot of people, even if they were raised here, would have trouble being this far back and alone, especially after everything that's happened."

No, she didn't want to talk about it. Maggie closed her eyes, reminding herself that she'd come here determined to take care of herself, to deal with whatever came. She drew a deep breath, but when she started to shift away, Cliff held her still.

"You are having trouble."

"No. No, not really." Her biggest problem at the moment was to keep her mind and body from wanting more of him. Opening her eyes again, she stared at the rain-drenched window. "I'll admit I've had a couple of restless nights since—well, since we started to dig the pond. It isn't easy knowing what happened in that gully ten years ago, and I have a very active imagination."

"Part of the job?" He turned toward her a bit more, so that her leg slid casually between his. Her skin was smooth as polished glass.

"I suppose." She laughed, but he thought he detected nerves in it. "One night I was certain I heard someone in the house."

He stopped stroking her hair, drawing her back far enough to see her eyes. "In the house?"

"Just my imagination," she said with a shrug. "Boards creaking in the attic, stealthy footsteps on the stairs, doors opening and closing. I worked myself up into quite a state."

He didn't like the sound of it, even in her dismissive tone of voice. "Don't you have a phone in this room?" Cliff demanded.

"Well, yes, but—"

"Why didn't you call the police?"

Maggie sighed and wished she'd never mentioned anything about it. He sounded like a cranky older brother scolding his scatterbrained sister. "Because I'd left the kitchen extension off the hook. I'd been trying to work that afternoon, and—" The word scatterbrained flowed back into her head. Embarrassed, she trailed off. "Anyway, it's better that I didn't call. I felt like an idiot in the morning in any case."

Imagination or not, Cliff reflected, she was still a woman alone, isolated, and everyone in a ten-mile radius knew it. "Are you locking your doors?"

"Cliff—"

"Maggie." He rolled until she was on her back and he was looking down at her. "Are you locking your doors?"

"I wasn't," she said, annoyed. "But after the sheriff came by, I—"

"Stan was here?"

A breath hissed out between her teeth. "Damn it, do you know how often you cut me off in the middle of a sentence?"

"Yes. When did Stan come by?"

"The day after the state police were here. He wanted to reassure me." She wasn't cold now, not with the way his body was pressed against hers. Desire began to stir again, not too quiet, not too slow. "He seems to know his job."

"He's been a good sheriff."

"But?" Maggie prompted, sensing more.

"Just a personal thing," Cliff murmured, shifting away again. Maggie felt the chill return immediately.

"Joyce," she said flatly, and started to rise. Cliff's arm came out to pin her down.

"You have a habit of saying little and implying a lot." His voice was cool now, his hold firm. "It's quite a talent."

"It seems we have little to say to each other."

"I don't have to explain myself to you."

She lay stiff and still. "I'm not asking you to."

"The hell you aren't." Angry, he sat up, drawing her with him so that the cover dropped away. Her skin was pale, her hair like a flood of night over her shoulders. Despite a strong will and a keen sense of privacy, he felt compelled to clarify. "Joyce's been like my sister. When she married Stan, I gave her away. I'm godfather to her oldest girl. It might be difficult for you to understand that kind of friendship."

It wasn't. It had been like that between herself and Jerry. The friendship had gradually deteriorated during marriage, because the marriage had been a mistake. "No, I understand it," Maggie said quietly. "I don't understand why you seem so concerned about her."

"That's my business."

"It certainly is."

He swore again. "Look, Joyce has been going through a difficult time. She never wanted to stay in Morganville. When she was a kid, she'd had ideas about going to the city and studying to be an actress."

"She wanted to act?"

"Pipe dreams, maybe." Cliff moved his shoulders. "Maybe not. She let them go when she married Stan, but she's never been happy staying in Morganville. One of the reasons she sold the house was so they'd have enough money to move. Stan won't budge."

"They could compromise."

"Stan doesn't understand how important it is to her

to get away from here. She was eighteen when she married. Then she had three children over the next five years. She spent the first part of her life following her father's rules, the second caring for her children and her mother. A woman like you wouldn't understand that."

"I'm sick of that!" Maggie exploded, jerking away from him. "I'm sick to death of you putting me in some category. Pampered celebrity with no conception of how real people feel or live." Anger rocketed through her, so quick and powerful she never thought to repress it. "What kind of man are you, going to bed with a woman you haven't an ounce of respect for?"

Stunned by the sudden, passionate outburst, he watched her spring from the bed. "Wait a minute."

"No, I've made enough mistakes for one evening." She began to search for her clothes among those scattered on the floor. "You had your dinner and your sex," she said in a brittle tone. "Now get out."

Fury rose so that he had to fight it back. She was right, Cliff told himself. He'd come to take her to bed; that was all. Intimacy didn't always equal closeness. He wasn't interested in being close to her or in becoming involved with anything more than her body. Even as he thought it, the emptiness of it washed over him. The contentment he'd felt so briefly vanished. He could hear her unsteady breathing as she pulled on her sweater. Reaching for his clothes, he tried to concentrate on the sound of the rain instead.

"We're not finished, you and I," he murmured.

"Aren't we?" Enraged, aching, Maggie turned. She could feel the tears well in her eyes, but felt secure in the darkness. The sweater skimmed her thighs, leaving the length of her legs naked. She knew what he thought of her, and this time would give him the satisfaction of believing he was right. "We went to bed, and it was good for both of us," she said easily. "Not all one-night stands are as successful. You get a high rating as a lover, Cliff, if that helps your ego."

This time there was no controlling the temper that roared into him. Grabbing both her arms, he pulled her toward him. "Damn you, Maggie."

"Why?" she tossed back. "Because I said it first? Go home and curl up with your double standard, Cliff. I don't need it."

Everything she said hit home, and hit hard. If he stayed, he wasn't certain what he might do. Throttle her? It was tempting. Drag her back to bed and purge himself of the angry desire that pounded in him? More temptation. As he held her, he wasn't sure if it was he who was shaking or her, but he knew if he stayed, something volatile, perhaps irrevocable, would burst.

Dropping his hands, he walked from the room. "Lock your doors," he called out, and cursed her as he strode down the stairs.

Maggie wrapped her arms around herself and let the tears overflow. It was much too late for locks, she thought.

Chapter 8

For the next few days, Maggie worked like a Trojan. Her kitchen floor was sealed, making it her first fully and successfully completed project. She added three fresh strips of wallpaper to her bedroom, found a rug for the music room and cleaned the trim in the downstairs hall.

In the evenings, she worked at her piano until she was too tired to see the keys or hear her own music. She kept her phone off the hook. All in all, she decided, the life of a recluse had its advantages. She was productive, and no one interfered with the flow of her days. It became almost possible to believe that was what she wanted and no more.

Perhaps she was pushing herself. She might admit that, but she wouldn't admit she did so to prevent herself from thinking about her night with Cliff. That had been a mistake. It wasn't wise to dwell on mistakes.

She saw no one, spoke to no one, and told herself she was content to go on that way indefinitely.

But of course complete solitude lasts only so long. Maggie was painting the window trim in the music room when she heard the sound of an approaching car. She debated whether she might just ignore the caller until he or she went away again. As a beginning recluse, it was certainly her right. Then she recognized the old Lincoln. Setting the paint bucket on the drop cloth at her feet, Maggie went to the front door to meet Louella Morgan.

She looked even more frail this time, Maggie mused. Her skin seemed almost translucent against the tidy white hair. It was an odd, somewhat eerie combination of youth and age. As Maggie watched, Louella looked over toward the gully. For a moment she seemed like a statue, unmoving, unblinking, unbreathing. When Maggie saw her take a step toward the fenced-off section, she walked outside.

"Good morning, Mrs. Morgan."

Louella glanced up, her eyes focusing slowly. The hand she lifted to pat at her hair shook lightly. "I wanted to come."

"Of course." Maggie smiled and hoped she was doing the right thing. "Please come in. I was about to fix some coffee."

Louella walked up the sagging steps Maggie had yet to contact Bog about. "You've made some changes."

Unsure which route to take, she decided on light, cheerful chatter. "Yes, inside and out. The landscapers work faster than I do." Killer stood in the doorway, snarling and backing up. Maggie hushed him as they went inside.

"This wallpaper was here when we moved in,"

Louella murmured, looking around the hall. "I always meant to change it."

"Did you?" Maggie led her gently toward the living room as she spoke. "Perhaps you could give me some suggestions. I haven't quite made up my mind yet."

"Something warm," Louella said softly. "Something warm, with subtle color, so people would feel welcome. That's what I wanted."

"Yes, I'm sure that's just what it needs." She wanted to put her arm around the woman and tell her she understood. Perhaps it was kinder not to.

"A house like this should smell of lemon oil and flowers."

"It will," Maggie told her, wishing she could change the scent of dust and paint.

"I always felt it should be filled with children." She gazed around the room with the kind of misty concentration that made Maggie think she was seeing it as it had been more than twenty years before. "Children give a house its personality, you know, more than its decorating. They leave their mark on it."

"You have grandchildren, don't you?" Maggie steered her toward the sofa.

"Yes, Joyce's children. The baby's in school now. Time goes so quickly for the young. You've looked at the pictures?" Louella asked suddenly.

"The pictures?" Maggie's brow creased, then cleared. "Oh, yes, I've really only had a chance to glance at them. I've been a bit tied up." Remembering, she walked to the mantel and retrieved the envelope. "Your roses looked beautiful. I'm not sure I'd have that kind of talent."

Louella took the envelope and stared down at it. "Roses need love and discipline. Like children."

Maggie decided against another offer of coffee. Instead, she sat down beside Louella. "Perhaps if we looked at them together it would help."

"Old pictures." Louella opened the flap and drew them out. "There's so much to see in old pictures if you know where to look. Early spring," she murmured, looking down at the first snapshot. "You see, the hyacinths are blooming, and the daffodils."

Maggie studied the square, pristine black and white, but it was the man and small girl who caught her attention rather than the flowers. He was tall, broad in the chest, with a sharp-boned, lantern-jawed face. The suit he wore was severe and proper. Beside him, the little girl wore a frilly dress, ribboned at the waist with black strap shoes and a flowered bonnet.

It must've been Easter, Maggie concluded. The little girl smiled determinedly at the camera. Joyce would've been around four then, Maggie calculated, and perhaps a bit uncomfortable in the organdy and flounces. William Morgan didn't look cruel, she thought as she studied his set, unreadable face. He simply looked untouchable. She fought back a shudder and spoke lightly.

"I want to plant some bulbs myself. Things should be a little more settled by fall."

Louella said nothing as she turned over the next picture. This time Maggie was looking at a young Louella. The style of hair and dress told her the picture was more than twenty years old. The lopsided angle of the shot made her suspect that Joyce had taken it as a child.

"The roses," Louella murmured, running a finger

over the picture where they grew in profusion. "Gone now, with no one to care for them."

"Do you have a garden now?"

"Joyce does." Louella set the picture aside and took up another. "I tend it now and then, but it isn't the same as having your own."

"No, it's not, but Joyce must be grateful for your help."

"She's never been easy in town," Louella said, half to herself. "Never easy. A pity she took after me rather than her father."

"She's lovely," Maggie told her, searching for something to say. "I hope to see more of her. Her husband suggested that we have dinner."

"Stan's a good man. Solid. He's always loved her." The sad, elusive smile touched her lips. "He's been kind to me."

When she turned over the next picture, Maggie felt her stiffen. She saw the smile freeze rather than fade. Looking down, she saw William Morgan and a young, perhaps teenaged Stan Agee. This more recent photo was in color, and the trees in the background were vibrant with fall. The two men were dressed in flannel shirts and caps, and each wore a drab-colored vest with what looked to Maggie like small weights around the hem. Each carried a shotgun.

Shells, not weights, Maggie realized as she looked at the vests again. They must've been hunting. And they stood, she noted, near the slope of the gully. Disturbed, she looked at the trees again, at the tapestry she wanted to see for herself.

"Joyce would've taken this," Louella murmured. "She hunted with her father. He taught her how to handle guns before she was twelve. It didn't matter that she hated them—she learned to please him. William looks pleased," Louella continued, though Maggie couldn't see it. "He liked to hunt this land. Now we know he died here. Here," she repeated, placing a palm over the picture. "Not three miles away, in the river. He never left his land. Somehow I think I always knew."

"Mrs. Morgan." Maggie set the pictures aside and laid a hand on her arm. "I know this must be difficult for you; it must be like going through it all over again. I wish there was something I could do."

Turning her head, Louella fixed Maggie with a long, unsmiling stare. "Put in your pond," she said flatly. "Plant your flowers. That's as it should be. The rest is over."

When she started to rise, Maggie found herself more disturbed by the emotionless reply than she would've been with a bout of tears. "Your pictures," she began helplessly.

"Keep them." Louella walked to the doorway before she turned. "I've no need for them anymore."

Should she have been depressed? Maggie wondered as she listened to the car drive away. Was her reaction normal empathy for another's tragedy, or was she allowing herself to become personally involved again? Over the last few days, she'd nearly convinced herself that the Morgan business had nothing to do with her. Now, after one brief contact, it was beginning again.

Yet it was more than a sense of involvement, Maggie admitted as she rubbed her arms to bring back warmth. There'd been something eerie in the way Louella had looked at the pictures. As if, Maggie reflected, she'd been putting the people in them to rest, though only one was dead.

Imagination again, she scolded herself. An overactive one. Yet hadn't there been something odd in the way Louella had studied that last snapshot? It had been as if she'd been searching for details, looking for something. With a frown, Maggie walked over and sifted through the pictures herself, stopping when she came to the color print.

There was William Morgan again, his hair a bit thinner, his eyes a bit sterner than they'd been in the Easter photo. Sheriff Agee stood beside him, hardly more than a boy, his build not quite filled out, his hair a little shaggy. He'd looked even more like a beachcomber in his youth, Maggie decided, though he held the gun as if he were very familiar with firearms. Looking at him, Maggie could easily see why Joyce had fallen for him hard enough to give up dreams of fame and fortune. He was young, handsome, with a trace of cocky sexuality around his mouth.

She could understand, too, why Joyce had feared and obeyed and struggled to please the man beside him. William Morgan looked straight at the camera, legs spread, the gun held in both hands. Cliff had described him as a hard, cold man. Maggie had no trouble believing him, but it didn't explain why Louella had been so disturbed by this one picture. Or why, Maggie added, she herself became uneasy when she looked at it.

Annoyed by her own susceptibility, she started to study the picture more closely when the rumble outside warned of another approaching vehicle.

When it rains it pours, she thought bad-temperedly. Tossing the picture carelessly on top of the others, she walked to the window. When Cliff's pickup came into view, the flare of excitement left her shaken. *Oh, no*, Maggie warned herself. *Not again. A woman who makes the same mistake twice deserves what she gets.* Determined, she picked up her brush and began to paint in long, hard strokes. Let him knock all he wanted, she thought with an angry toss of her head. She had work to do.

Minutes passed, but he didn't come to her door. Maggie continued to paint, telling herself it didn't matter to her what he was doing outside. When she tried to lean closer to the window to look through, paint smeared from the sill to her jeans. Swearing, she wiped at it and made it worse.

She didn't give a damn about Cliff Delaney, Maggie told herself. But she did care about having people wander around on her land. It was her right to go out and see what he was up to and order him away, she told herself as she set down her brush. If he were only checking on how her grass was growing, she fumed as she headed for the door, he should still have the courtesy to announce himself. By not announcing himself, he was denying her the satisfaction of ignoring him.

She yanked open the door but didn't, as she'd expected, see him bending over the little green sprouts that had begun to shoot up through the topsoil. Neither was he looking out over the plugs of phlox or the juniper shrubs on her front bank. Perhaps, Maggie thought with a frown, he'd gone around to check on the last project to be completed, the crown vetch on her eroding rear bank.

Annoyed that she hadn't thought of that in the first place, she started to turn back into the house when a movement near the gully caught her eye. For an instant, basic, primitive fear that slept in her awoke. She thought of ghouls and phantoms and legends of shades that never rest. In the next instant she recognized Cliff. As infuriated as she was embarrassed by her own reaction, she went to confront him.

As she drew closer, Maggie saw the willow, slender, small and tenderly green. Cliff was setting the ball of roots into a hole he'd dug out of the rocky soil with a pick and shovel. He stood perhaps six feet from the slope of the gully, his shirt tossed carelessly on the ground. She could see the muscles in his back ripple as he began to shovel dirt back into the hole. The twinge of her stomach told her that her reaction to him was no less powerful now than it had been before they'd made love.

Maggie straightened her shoulders and angled her chin. "What're you doing?"

Because he continued to shovel without breaking rhythm, she decided he'd known she was coming. "Planting a tree," Cliff said easily.

Her eyes narrowed dangerously. "I can see that. As far as I remember, I didn't order a willow from you."

"No." He knelt down to mound and smooth the dirt at the base of the tree. She watched his hands, knowing now what they could do on her body. It seemed he had the same talent with soil. "No charge."

Impatient with his nonanswers and with her own growing arousal, she folded her arms. "Why are you planting a tree I didn't buy?"

Satisfied that the willow was secure, he rose. Leaning casually on the shovel, he studied her. No, he hadn't gotten her out of his system, Cliff decided. Seeing her again didn't relieve the knots of tension he'd been living with for days. Somehow he'd known it wouldn't, but he'd had to try. "Some people might call it a peace offering," he told her at length, then watched her mouth open and close again.

Maggie looked at the tree. It was so young, so fragile, but one day she would see it in full sweep, spreading over her pond, and— She stopped, realizing that it was the first time she'd thought of going through with the pond since the discovery. He must have known that, just as he'd known the willow might be enough to make her see the beauty and serenity again. Most of her anger had drained before she remembered to hold on to any of it.

"A peace offering," she repeated, running a finger down one delicate leaf. "Is that what you call it?"

Her voice had been cool, but he saw that her eyes had already started to warm. He wondered how many strong men she'd slain with that one look. "Maybe." He sliced the shovel into the ground where it stood, tilting slightly to the left. "Got anything cold in there to drink?"

It was an apology, Maggie decided, perhaps the only kind a man like him could give. It only took her five seconds to decide to accept it. "Maybe," she said in an equal tone, then turned to walk back toward the house. A smile curved her lips when he fell into step beside her. "Your men did an excellent job," she continued while they circled around toward the rear of the house. "I'm anxious to see how the stuff over the retaining wall's going to look."

"Crown vetch," Cliff supplied before he stopped to check the job, as she'd suspected he would. "You should see something come through in four or five more days. It'll spread fast enough to cover this bank before summer's over." He kept his hands in his back pockets as he studied the work his men had done and thought of the woman beside him. "You've been busy?"

Maggie lifted a brow. "I suppose so. The house needs a lot of attention."

"Seen the paper?"

"No," she said, puzzled. "Why?"

Cliff shrugged, then walked ahead to the screen door to open it. "There was a big story on finding William Morgan buried on his old land. Land," he continued when Maggie moved by him into the kitchen, "recently purchased by a celebrated songwriter."

She turned sharply. "They had my name?"

"Yeah, it was mentioned—several times."

"Damn," she whispered, and, forgetting he'd asked for a drink, she dropped into a chair. "I'd wanted to avoid that." Half hopefully, she glanced up. "The local paper?"

Helping himself, Cliff went to the refrigerator and searched out a soda. "Morganville doesn't have a paper. There were stories in the *Frederick Post* and the *Herald Mail*." As he twisted off the top, he nodded toward the phone sitting off the hook. "If you hadn't done that, you'd have already answered a flood of calls from reporters." And from himself, Cliff thought silently. In the past twenty-four hours, he'd called her a dozen times. He'd vacillated between being frantic and furious every time he'd gotten a busy signal. What kind of woman left her phone off the hook for hours at a time? One who was independent of the outside world, he mused, or one who was hiding from it. Lifting the bottle, he drank. "That your escape route these days?"

In defense, Maggie rose and slammed the receiver back in place. "I don't need to escape from anything. You said yourself that this whole business doesn't have anything to do with me."

"So I did." He examined the liquid left in the bottle. "Maybe you were escaping from something else." He shifted his gaze until it locked on hers. "Were you hiding from me, Maggie?"

"Certainly not." She swept over to the sink and began to scrub the paint splatters from her hands. "I told you, I've been busy."

"Too busy to answer the phone?"

"The phone's a distraction. If you want to start an argument, Cliff, you can just take your peace offering and—" The phone shrilled behind her so that she ended her suggestion with an oath. Before she could answer it herself, Cliff had picked up the phone.

"Yes?" He watched the fury spring into her eyes as he leaned on the counter. He'd missed that, he discovered, just as he'd missed the subtle sexiness of the scent she wore. "No, I'm sorry, Miss Fitzgerald isn't available for comment." He replaced the receiver while Maggie wiped her damp hands on her jeans.

"I can screen my own calls, thank you. When I want a liaison, I'll let you know."

He drank from the bottle again. "Just saving you some aggravation."

"I don't want you or anyone to save me aggravation," she fumed. "It's my aggravation, and I'll do whatever I want with it." He grinned, but before she could think of any retaliation, the phone rang again. "Don't you dare," she warned. Shoving him aside, she answered herself.

"Hello."

"Damn it, Maggie, you've been leaving the phone off the hook again."

She let out a huff of breath. A reporter might've been easier to deal with. "Hello, C.J. How are you?"

"I'll tell you how I am!"

Maggie drew the phone back from her ear and scowled at Cliff. "There's no need for you to hang around."

He took another long sip from the bottle before he settled back comfortably. "I don't mind."

"Maggie!" C.J.'s voice vibrated in her ear. "Who the hell are you talking to?"

"Nobody," she mumbled, deliberately turning her back on Cliff. "You were going to tell me how you were."

"For the past twenty-four hours I've been frantic trying to get through to you. Maggie, it's irresponsible to leave your phone off the hook when people're trying to reach you."

There was a bag of cookies on the counter. Maggie dug into it, then bit into one with a vengeance. "Obviously I left it off the hook so I couldn't be reached."

"If I hadn't gotten you this time, I was going to send a telegram, and I'm not even sure they deliver telegrams in that place. What the hell have you been doing?"

"I've been working," she said between her teeth. "I can't work when the phone's ringing off the wall and people are forever coming by. I moved out here to be alone. I'm still waiting for that to happen."

"That's a nice attitude," he tossed back. In Los Angeles, C.J. searched through his desk drawer for a roll of antacids. "You've got people all over the country worried about you."

"Damn it, people all over the country don't have to worry about me. I'm fine!"

"You sound fine."

With an effort, Maggie controlled her precarious temper. When she lost it with C.J., she invariably lost the bout, as well. "I'm sorry I snapped at you, C.J., but I'm tired of being criticized for doing what I want to do."

"I'm not criticizing you," he grumbled over the peppermint-flavored pill. "It's just natural concern. For God's sake, Maggie, who wouldn't be concerned after that business in the paper?"

She tensed and, without thinking, turned back to face Cliff. He was watching her intently, the neck of the bottle held loosely in his fingers. "What business in the paper?"

"About that man's—ah, what was left of that man being dug up on your property. Good God, Maggie, I nearly had a heart attack when I read it. Then, not being able to reach you—"

"I'm sorry." She dragged a hand through her hair. "I'm really sorry, C.J. I didn't think it would hit the papers, at least not out there."

"So what I didn't know wouldn't hurt me?"

She smiled at the offended tone of voice. "Yes, something like that. I'd've called you with the details if I'd realized the news would get that far."

"Get this far?" he retorted, unappeased. "Maggie, you know that anything with your name in it's going to hit the press on both sides of the Atlantic."

She began to rub one finger slowly up and down

her right temple. "And you know that was one of the reasons I wanted to get out."

"Where you live isn't going to change that."

She sighed. "Apparently not."

"Besides, that doesn't have anything to do with what's happened now," C.J. argued. He pressed a hand to his nervous stomach and wondered if a glass of Perrier would calm him. Maybe scotch would be a better idea.

"I haven't seen the paper," Maggie began in an even tone, "but I'm sure the whole thing was blown out of proportion."

"Blown out of proportion?" Again, she had to move the receiver back from her ear. A few steps away, Cliff heard C.J.'s voice clearly. "Did you or did you not stumble over a pile of—of bones?"

She grimaced at the image. "Not exactly." She had to concentrate harder on keeping her voice calm. "Actually, it was the dog that found them. The police came right out and took over. I really haven't been involved." She saw Cliff lift a brow at her final statement but made no comment.

"Maggie, it said that man had been murdered and buried right there, only yards from your house."

"Ten years ago." She pressed her fingers more firmly against her temple.

"Maggie, come home."

She closed her eyes, because his voice held the kind of plea that was hard to resist. "C.J., I am home."

"Damn it, how am I supposed to sleep at night thinking of you alone out in the middle of nowhere? For God's sake, you're one of the most successful, wealthiest, most celebrated women in the world, and you're living in Dogpatch."

"If I'm successful, wealthy and celebrated, I can live wherever I want." She struggled against temper again. However he phrased it, whatever his tone, the concern was real. It was better to concentrate on that. "Besides, C.J., I have the vicious guard dog you sent me." She looked down to where Killer was sleeping peacefully at Cliff's feet. When she lifted her gaze, she found herself smiling into Cliff's face. "I couldn't be safer."

"If you hired a bodyguard—"

Now she laughed. "You're being an old woman again. The last thing I need's a bodyguard. I'm fine," she went on quickly before he could comment. "I've finished the score, I've a dozen ideas for new songs running around in my head, and I'm even considering another musical. Why don't you tell me how brilliant the score was?"

"You know it's brilliant," he mumbled. "It's probably the best thing you've done."

"More," she insisted. "Tell me more. My ego's starving."

He sighed, recognizing defeat. "When I played it for the producers, they were ecstatic. It was suggested that you come out and supervise the recording."

"Forget it." She began to pace to the sink and back again.

"Damn it, we'd come to you, but there's no studio in Hicksville."

"Morganville," she corrected mildly. "You don't need me for the recording."

"They want you to do the title song."

"What?" Surprised, she stopped her restless pacing.

"Now listen to me before you say no." C.J. straightened in his chair and put on his best negotiator's voice. "I realize you've always refused to perform or record, and I've never pressed you. But this is something I really think you should consider. Maggie, that song's dynamite, absolute dynamite, and nobody's going to be able to put into it what you did. After I played the tape, everyone in the room needed a cold shower."

Though she laughed, Maggie couldn't quite put the idea aside. "I can think of a half-dozen artists who could deliver that number, C.J. You don't need me."

"I can think of a dozen who could deliver it," he countered. "But not like you. The song needs you, Maggie. At least you could think about it."

She told herself she'd already refused him enough for one day. "Okay, I'll think about it."

"You let me know in a week."

"C.J.—"

"Okay, okay, two weeks."

"All right. And I'm sorry about the phone."

"You could at least get one of those hateful answering machines."

"Maybe. Take care of yourself, C.J."

"I always do. Just take your own advice."

"I always do. Bye." She hung up, heaving a long sigh. "I feel like I've just been taken to task by the school principal."

Cliff watched her pick up a folded dish towel, crumple it, then set it down again. "You know how to handle him."

"I've had plenty of practice."

"What's C.J. stand for?"

"Constant Jitters," she murmured, then shook her head. "No, to tell you the truth, I haven't any idea."

"Does he always give you a hard time?"

"I suppose." She picked up the dish towel again. "It seems the news hit the papers on the Coast. Then, when he couldn't reach me…" She trailed off, frowning out the window.

"You're tense."

She dropped the cloth over the edge of the sink. "No."

"Yes," Cliff corrected. "I can see it." Reaching out, he ran his hand down the side of her neck to the curve of her shoulder. "I can feel it."

The brush of his fingers made her skin hum. Slowly, she turned her head. "I don't want you to do that."

Deliberately, he took his other hand on a like journey, so that he could knead at the tension in both of her shoulders. Was it her nerves he sought to soothe or his own? "To touch you?" he said quietly. "It's difficult not to."

Knowing she was already weakening, Maggie lifted her hands to his wrists. "Put some effort into it," she advised as she tried to push him aside.

"I have for the past few days." His fingers pressed into her skin and released, pressed and released, in a rhythm that caused her bones to liquefy. "I decided it was a misdirection of energy when I could put the same effort into making love to you."

Her mind was starting to haze, her breath beginning to tremble. "We've nothing to give each other."

"We both know better than that." He lowered his head so that his lips could brush along the temple he'd seen her stroke while on the phone.

A sigh escaped before she stopped it. This wasn't

what she wanted—it was everything she wanted. "Sex is—"

"A necessary and enjoyable part of life," Cliff finished before he moved his lips down to tease hers.

So this was seduction, Maggie thought as her mind began to float. This was arousal without will. She knew she wasn't resisting, but yielding, melting, submitting, just as she knew that when surrender was complete, her bridges would be in flames behind her.

"We'll only be two people sharing a bed," she murmured. "There's nothing else."

Whether it was a question or a statement, Cliff tried to believe it was true. If there was more, it wouldn't end, and he'd find himself tangled around a woman he barely understood for the rest of his life. If there were only needs, he could relinquish his control and race with them. If there was only desire, he could take whatever he wanted with no consequences. When she was softening and heating in his arms, what did he care for consequences?

"Let me feel you," he murmured against her lips. "I want your skin under my hands, smooth and hot, your heart pounding."

Anything, she thought dizzily. She'd give him anything, as long as he stayed close like this, as long as his mouth continued that dark, desperate, delirious seduction of her senses. He tugged her T-shirt over her head, then ran his hands down her sides, up again, so that the friction had her nearly mad for more. His shirt scraped against her taut nipples until his hands came between them to possess.

He could feel her heart beat now, and she could hear it pounding in her own head. Her thighs pressed against his with only two layers of thin, soft denim between. She could remember every slope and plane of his body, how it had felt warm and urgent and naked on hers.

He smelled of work and the outdoors, traces of sweat and turned earth. As the scent raced through her senses, she took her lips over his face and throat to draw in the taste.

Uncivilized, like the land that held them both. Alluring and not quite tamed, like the thick woods that surrounded them. If she thought at all, this was how she thought of the need that burned between them. There was danger in both, and pleasure and wonder. Throwing aside all reason, Maggie gave herself to it.

"Now," she demanded huskily. "I want you now."

With no sense of time or place, no hesitation, they lowered onto the floor. The struggle with clothes only added to the aura of desperation and unrelenting desire that sprang back whenever they touched. Warmth against warmth, they found each other.

When the phone shrilled on the wall beside them, neither heard. Whether it was by choice or the will of fate, there was nothing for either of them but each other.

A tremble, a moan, a rough caress, the scent and fury of passion; that was their world. Urgently and more urgently, they sought the taste and touch of each other, as if the hunger would never abate, as if neither would allow it to. The floor was hard and smooth beneath them. They rolled over it as if it were layered with feathers. Sunlight streamed in, falling over them. They explored all the secrets of the night.

Man for woman, woman for man—time had no place and place no meaning. Hot and open, his mouth found hers, and finding it, he burned with the need to possess her completely. His fingers dug into her hips as he shifted her on top of him so that her skin slid tantalizingly over his. He felt her throb, just as he felt the flood of passion beat against the weakened dam of his control. At the moment of joining, her body arched back in stunned pleasure. The pace was frenetic, leaving them both helpless and raging. On and on they drove each other, mercilessly, ruthlessly.

Through half-closed eyes, Cliff saw her shudder with the speed of the crest. Then he was swept up with her in the power of the ultimate heat dance.

Chapter 9

Had hours passed, or was his sense of time still distorted? Cliff tried to gauge the hour by the slant of the sun through the window, but couldn't be sure. He felt more than rested; he felt vitalized. Turning his head, he watched Maggie as she slept beside him. Though his own actions were vague in his mind, like a half dream that blurs on awakening, he could remember carrying her upstairs where they'd tumbled into bed. Wrapped around each other, they'd fallen into an exhausted sleep. Yes, that part was vague, he mused, but the rest—

On the kitchen floor. He ran a hand over his face, uncertain if he was pleased or astonished. Cliff discovered he was both.

He'd made love to her on the kitchen floor like a frantic teenager in the first spin of desire. By the time a man of experience had reached his thirties, he should be able to show a bit more control, use a bit more finesse. Yet he'd had neither both times he'd made love with her. Cliff wasn't certain that would change if he'd loved her a hundred times. She had some power over him that went deep and triggered frenzy rather than style. And yet... Because she was asleep and unaware, he brushed the hair from her cheek so that he could see more of her face. Looking at her was becoming a habit he wasn't sure could be easily broken. Yet when they lay quiet like this, he was overwhelmed by a sense of protective tenderness. As far as he could remember, no other woman had elicited either response from him before. The knowledge wasn't comfortable.

Perhaps it was because when she slept as she did now, she looked frail, defenseless, small. He'd never been able to resist fragility. When she was in his arms, she was all fire and flare, with a power so potent she seemed indestructible. Challenges were something else he'd never been able to resist.

Just who was Maggie Fitzgerald? Cliff wondered while he traced the shape of her mouth with a fingertip. He wouldn't have said she was beautiful, yet her face had the power to both stun and haunt a man. He hadn't expected her to be kind or compassionate, yet he'd seen the qualities in her. He hadn't expected her to be self-sufficient, yet she was proving to be just that under an uneasy set of circumstances.

He frowned and unconsciously drew her closer. Maggie murmured but slept on. Though he'd told her that she had no connection with what had happened there ten years before, Cliff didn't like knowing she was alone in the big, remote house. Knowing Morganville was a quiet, settled town didn't change that. Even the quiet, the settled, had undercurrents. That had been made plain in the past two weeks.

Whoever had killed William Morgan had gone unpunished for a decade. Whoever had murdered him had probably walked the streets of town, chatted outside the bank, cheered at Little League games. It wasn't a pleasant thought. Nor was it pleasant to conclude that whoever had killed once might do anything necessary to go on living a quiet, settled life in a town where everyone knew your name and your history. It might be a cliché about the murderer returning to the scene of the crime, but—

She woke up alone, her mind still disoriented. Was it morning? she wondered groggily. When she shifted, lifting both hands to push back her hair, she felt the sweet heaviness in her limbs that came from lovemaking. Abruptly awake, she looked over to see the bed beside her empty.

Perhaps she'd been dreaming. But when she felt the sheets beside her, they were still warm, and when she turned her face into the pillow, his scent lingered on the case.

They'd made love on the kitchen floor, she remembered with a reaction that directly paralleled Cliff's. But she also remembered quite clearly the sensation of being carried up the stairs, gently, as if she'd been something precious. It was a warm memory, different from the erotic scene that had preceded it. A memory like that was something she could hold on to during some long, restless night in the future.

But he'd left, saying nothing.

Grow up, Maggie, she ordered herself. *Be sensible.*

From the beginning she'd known this wasn't romance but desire. The only thing she'd gain from dwelling on the first was pain. Romance was for the impractical, the vulnerable, the naive. Hadn't she spent a great deal of her time training herself to be none of those things?

He didn't love her; she didn't love him. There was a twinge in her stomach at the second denial that had her biting her lip. No, she insisted, she didn't love him. She couldn't afford to.

He was a hard man, though she'd seen some softer aspects of him. He was intolerant, impatient and more often rude than not. A woman didn't need to fix her heart on a man like that. In any case, he'd made it clear that he wanted her body, and her body only. Twice she'd made the decision to give it to him, so she had no right to regrets, even though he'd left without a word.

Maggie flung her arms over her eyes and refused to acknowledge the growing fear that she'd already given him more than her body, without either of them being aware of it.

Then she heard it, the soft creak directly overhead. Slowly, she lowered her arms, then lay still. When it came the second time, the panic fluttered in her throat. She was awake, it was midafternoon, and the sounds came from the attic, not her imagination.

Though she was shaking, she climbed quietly out of bed. This time she wouldn't cower in her room while someone invaded her home. This time, she thought, moistening her lips as she slipped into her T-shirt, she'd find out who it was and what they wanted. Cold and clearheaded, she took the poker from the fireplace and slipped into the hallway.

The attic stairs were to her right. When she saw

that the door at the top was open, fear sliced through her again. It hadn't been opened since she'd moved in. Shaking, determined, she took a firmer grip on the poker and started up the stairs.

At the doorway, she paused, hearing the faint whisper of movement inside. She pressed her lips together, swallowed, then stepped inside.

"Damn it, Maggie, you could hurt someone with that thing."

She jumped back, banging smartly into the doorjamb. "What are you doing up here?" she demanded as Cliff scowled back at her.

"Just checking. When's the last time you were up here?"

She expelled a breath, releasing pent-up tension. "Never. It's far down on my lists of priorities, so I haven't been up since I moved in."

He nodded, taking another glance around. "Someone has."

For the first time, she looked into the room. As she'd suspected, it contained little more than dust and cobwebs. It was high enough that Cliff could stand upright with an inch or so to spare, though at the sides it sloped down with the pitch of the roof. There was an old rocker that might prove interesting after refinishing, a sofa that was hopeless, two lamps without shades and a large upright traveling chest.

"It doesn't look as though anyone's been up here for years."

"More like a week," Cliff corrected. "Take a look at this."

He walked toward the chest, and making a face at the layer of dust on the floor, Maggie padded after him in her bare feet. "So?" she demanded. "Joyce mentioned that there were some things up here she didn't have any use for. I told her not to bother with them, that I'd take care of hauling them out when I was ready."

"I'd say someone already took something out." Cliff crouched in front of the dust-covered chest, then pointed.

Annoyed, stifling the urge to sneeze, Maggie bent toward the dust-covered chest. Then she saw it. Just near the lock, and very faint, was the imprint of a hand. "But—"

Cliff grabbed her wrist before she could touch the imprint herself. "I wouldn't."

"Someone was here," she murmured. "I didn't imagine it." Struggling for calm, she looked back at Cliff. "But what could anyone have wanted up here, in this thing?"

"Good question." He straightened, but kept her hand in his.

She wanted to play it light. "How about a good answer?"

"I think we might see what the sheriff thinks."

"You think it has something to do with—the other thing."

Her voice was steady enough, but with his fingers on her wrist, he knew her pulse wasn't. "I think it's odd that everything's happening at once. Coincidences are curious things. You wouldn't be smart to let this one go."

"No." This wasn't ten years ago, she thought. This was now. "I'll call the sheriff."

"I'll do it."

She stopped in the doorway, bristling. "It's my house," she began.

"It certainly is," Cliff agreed mildly, then stunned her by running both hands up her naked thighs to her hips. "I don't mind looking at you half dressed, but it's bound to distract Stan."

"Very funny."

"No, very beautiful." While she stared, wide-eyed, he lowered his head and kissed her with the first true gentleness he'd shown. She didn't move or speak when he lifted his head again. Her eyes were still open. "I'll call the sheriff," Cliff said roughly. "You get some pants on."

Without waiting for her reply, he was heading down the steps, leaving her staring after him. Dazed, Maggie lifted a finger to trace over her own lips. That, she decided, had been as unexpected and as difficult to explain as anything else that had happened between them.

Utterly confused, Maggie left the poker tilted against the door and went back to her room. She couldn't have known he could kiss like that—tenderly, exquisitely. If she couldn't have known that, she couldn't have known that her heart could stop beating and her lungs could choke up. The totally different kiss had brought on a totally different reaction. This reaction, she knew, had left her without any form of defense.

A passionate, aggressive demand she could meet with passion and aggression of her own. There they were equal, and if she had no control, neither did he. Urgency would be met with urgency, fire with fire, but tenderness... What would she do if he kissed her like that again? And how long would she have to wait until he did? A woman could fall in love with a man who kissed like that.

Maggie caught herself. Some women, she corrected, hastily dragging on her jeans. Not her. She wasn't going to fall in love with Cliff Delaney. He wasn't for her. He wanted no more than—

Then she remembered that he hadn't left without a word. He hadn't left at all.

"Maggie!"

The voice from the bottom of the stairs had her jolting. "Yes." She answered him while she stared at her own astonished face in the mirror.

"Stan's on his way."

"All right, I'm coming down." In a minute, she added silently, in just a minute. Moving like someone who wasn't sure her legs could be trusted, she sat on the bed.

If she was falling in love with him, she'd better admit it now, while there was still time to do something about it. Was there still time? It washed over her that her time had been up days before, perhaps longer. Perhaps it had been up the moment he'd stepped out of his truck onto her land.

Now what? she asked herself. She'd let herself fall for a man she hardly knew, barely understood and wasn't altogether sure she liked a great deal of the time. He certainly didn't understand her and didn't appear to want to.

Yet he'd planted a willow in her yard. Perhaps he understood more than either of them realized. Of course, there couldn't be anything between them, really, she reminded herself hastily. They were poles apart in attitude. Still, for the moment, she had no choice but to follow her heart and hope that her mind would keep her somewhat level. As she rose, Maggie remembered fatalistically that it never had before.

It was quiet downstairs, but as soon as she came to the landing, she smelled coffee. She stood there a moment, wondering if she should be annoyed or pleased that Cliff was making himself at home. Unable to decide, she walked back to the kitchen.

"Want a cup?" Cliff asked as she entered. He was already leaning against the counter in his habitual position, drinking one of his own.

Maggie lifted a brow. "As a matter of fact, I would. Have any trouble finding what you needed?"

He ignored the sarcasm and reached in a cupboard for another cup. "Nope. You haven't eaten lunch."

"I generally don't." She came up behind him to pour the cup herself.

"I do," he said simply. With a naturalness Maggie thought bordered on arrogance, he opened the refrigerator and began to search through it.

"Just help yourself," she muttered before she scalded her tongue on the coffee.

"You'd better learn to stock up," Cliff told her when he found her supplies discouragingly slim. "It isn't unusual to get snowed in on a back road like this for a week at a time in the winter."

"I'll keep that in mind."

"You eat this stuff?" he asked, pushing aside a carton of yogurt.

"I happen to like it." She strode over, intending to slam the refrigerator door whether his hand was inside or not. Cliff outmaneuvered her by plucking out a single chicken leg, then stepping aside. "I'd just like to mention you're eating my dinner."

"Want a bite?" Apparently all amiability, he held out the drumstick. Maggie concentrated on keeping her lips from curving.

"No."

"Funny." Cliff took a bite and chewed thoughtfully. "Just coming into this kitchen seems to work up my appetite."

She shot him a look, well aware that she was now standing on the spot where they'd made wild love only a short time before. If he was trying to get a rise out of her, he was succeeding. If he was trying to distract her from what they'd discovered in the attic, he was succeeding, as well. Either way, Maggie found she couldn't resist him.

Deliberately, she took a step closer, running her hands slowly up his chest. It was time, she decided, to give him back a bit of his own. "Maybe I'm hungry, after all," she murmured, and, rising on her toes, brushed her lips teasingly over his.

Because he hadn't expected the move from her, Cliff did nothing. From the start he'd stalked and seduced. She was the lady, the crown princess with the wanton passion men often fantasize about on long, dark nights. Now, looking into those deep, velvet eyes, he thought her more of a witch. And who, he wondered as his blood began to swim, had been stalked and seduced?

She took his breath away—just the scent of her. She made his reason cloud—just the touch of her. When she looked at him like this, her eyes knowing, her lips parted and close, she was the only woman he wanted, the only woman he knew. At times like this, he wanted her with a fire that promised never to be banked. Quite suddenly and quite clearly, she terrified him.

"Maggie." He put a hand up to ward her off, to draw her closer; he'd never know, for the dog began to bark, and the rumble of a car laboring up the lane sounded from outside. Cliff dropped the hand to his side again. "That'll be Stan."

"Yes." She studied him with an open curiosity he wasn't ready to deal with.

"You'd better get the door."

"All right." She kept her gaze direct on his for another moment, rather pleased with the uncertainty she saw there. "You coming?"

"Yeah. In a minute." He waited until she had gone, then let out a long, uneasy breath. That had been too close for comfort. Too close to what, he wasn't certain, but he was certain he didn't like it. With his appetite strangely vanished, Cliff abandoned the drumstick and picked up his coffee. When he noticed his hands weren't quite steady, he downed the contents in one swallow.

Well, she certainly had enough to think about, Maggie mused as she walked down the hall. The sheriff was at her door again, Cliff was standing in her kitchen looking as though he'd been struck with a blunt instrument, and her own head was so light from a sense of—was it power?—that she didn't know what might happen next. Her move to the country certainly hadn't been quiet. She'd never been more stimulated in her life.

"Miss Fitzgerald."

"Sheriff." Maggie scooped Killer up in one arm to quiet his barking.

"Quite a beast you've got there," he commented. Then, holding out a hand, he allowed the puppy to sniff it cautiously. "Cliff gave me a call," he continued. "Said it looked like somebody's broken into the house."

"That seems to be the only explanation." Maggie stepped back to struggle with both the puppy and the door. "Although it doesn't make any sense to me. Apparently someone was in the attic last week."

"Last week?" Stan took care of the door himself, then rested his hand lightly, it seemed negligently, on the butt of his gun. "Why didn't you call before?"

Feeling foolish, Maggie set the dog down, giving him an impatient nudge on the rear that sent him scampering into the music room. "I woke up sometime in the middle of the night and heard noises. I admit it panicked me at the time, but in the morning..." She trailed off and shrugged. "In the morning, I thought it'd been my imagination, so I more or less forgot the whole thing."

Stan listened, and his nod was both understanding and prompting. "And now?"

"I happened to mention it to Cliff this...ah...this morning," she finished. "He was curious enough to go up into the attic."

"I see." Maggie had the feeling he saw everything, very well.

"Stan." Cliff strode down the hall from the kitchen, looking perfectly at ease. "Thanks for coming by."

I should've said that, Maggie thought, but before she could open her mouth again, the men were talking around her.

"Just part of the job," Stan stated. "You're doing quite a job yourself on the grounds outside."

"They're coming along."

Stan gave him a crooked, appealing smile. "You've always liked a challenge."

They knew each other well enough that Cliff understood he referred to the woman, as well as her land. "Things would be dull without them," he said mildly.

"Heard you found something in the attic."

"Enough to make me think someone's been poking around."

"I'd better have a look."

"I'll show you," Maggie said flatly, then, sending Cliff a telling look, led the way upstairs.

When they came to the attic door, Stan glanced down at the poker still leaning against it. "Somebody could trip over that," he said mildly.

"I must have left it there before." Ignoring Cliff's grin, she picked it up and held it behind her back.

"Doesn't look like anyone's been up here in a long time," Stan commented as he brushed a cobweb away from his face.

"I haven't been up at all until today." Maggie shivered as a large black spider crawled sedately up the wall to her left. She hadn't admitted to anyone yet that the prospect of insects and mice was primarily what had kept her out. "There's been so much else to do in the house." Deliberately, she stepped farther away from the wall.

"Not much up here." Stan rubbed a hand over his chin. "Joyce and I cleared out everything we were interested in when she first inherited. Louella already had everything she wanted. If you haven't been up," he continued, peering slowly around, "how do you know anything's missing?"

"I don't. It's this." For the second time, Maggie crossed the dusty floor to the trunk. This time it was she who crouched down and pointed.

Stan bent down over her, close enough that she could smell the simple department-store aftershave he wore. She recognized it and, on a wave of nostalgia, remembered her mother's driver had worn it, too. For no other reason, her sense of trust in him was confirmed.

"That's curious," Stan murmured, careful not to smear the faint outline. "Did you open this?"

"Neither of us touched it," Cliff said from behind.

With another nod, Stan pushed the button on the latch. His other hand came up automatically, stopping just short of gripping the trunk in the same spot the handprint was. "Looks like somebody did." Cautiously, he put his hand on the closure and tugged. "Locked." Sitting back on his haunches, he frowned at the trunk. "Damn if I can remember what's in this thing or if there's a key. Joyce might know—more'n likely Louella, though. Still…" With a shake of his head, he straightened. "It doesn't make much sense for somebody to break in and take something out of this old trunk, especially now that the house is occupied for the first time in ten years." He looked back at Maggie. "Are you sure nothing's missing from downstairs?"

"No—that is, I don't think so. Almost everything I shipped out's still in crates."

"Wouldn't hurt to take a good look."

"All right." She started back toward the second floor, realizing she hoped something would be missing. That would make sense; that would be tangible. The faint handprint on the trunk and no explanation gave her a queasy feeling in the stomach. A cut-and-dried burglary would only make her angry.

With the two men following, she went into her bedroom, checking her jewelry first. Everything was exactly as it should've been. In the next bedroom were crates that at a glance she could see were untouched and unopened.

"That's all up here. There's more crates downstairs and some paintings I haven't had reframed yet."

"Let's take a look."

Going with the sheriff's suggestion, Maggie headed for the stairs again.

"I don't like it," Cliff said to Stan in an undertone. "And you don't think she's going to find anything missing downstairs."

"Only thing that makes sense is a burglary, Cliff."

"A lot of things haven't made sense since we started digging in that gully."

Stan let out a quiet breath, watching Maggie's back as she descended the steps. "I know, and a lot of times there just aren't any answers."

"Are you going to tell Joyce about this?"

"I might have to." Stan stopped at the base of the stairs, running a hand over the back of his neck as though there were tension or weariness there. "She's a strong woman, Cliff. I guess I didn't know just how strong until this business started. I know when we first got married, a lot of people thought I did it for her inheritance."

"Not anyone who knew you."

Stan shrugged. "Anyway, that died down after a while, died completely after I became sheriff. I guess there were times I wondered whether Joyce ever thought it."

"She'd have told me if she had," Cliff said bluntly.

With a half laugh, Stan turned to him. "Yes, she would've at that."

Maggie came back into the hall from the music room. "There's nothing missing in there, either. I've a few things in the living room, but—"

"Might as well be thorough," Stan told her, then strode across the hall and over the threshold. "Doing some painting?" he asked when he noticed the can and brush by the window.

"I'd planned to have all the trim done in here today," she said absently as she examined a few more packing boxes, "but then Mrs. Morgan stopped by, and—"

"Louella," Stan interrupted.

Because he was frowning, Maggie began to smooth it over. "Yes, though she didn't stay very long. We just looked over the pictures she'd lent me." Distracted, she picked up the stack. "Actually, I'd wanted to show these to you, Cliff. I wondered if you could tell me how to deal with getting some climbing roses like these started."

With the men flanking her, Maggie flipped through the snapshots.

"Louella certainly had a feel for making flowers look like they'd grown up on their own," she murmured. "I don't know if I have the talent for it."

"She always loved this place," Stan said. "She—" Then he stopped when she flipped to the color shot of himself and Morgan. "I'd forgotten about that one," he said after a moment. "Joyce took that the first day of deer season."

"Louella mentioned that she hunted."

"She did," Cliff put in, "because he wanted her to. Morgan had an—affection for guns."

And died by one, Maggie thought with a shudder. She turned the pictures facedown. "There's nothing missing anywhere that I can see, Sheriff."

He stared down at the pile of photos. "Well, then, I'll do a check of the doors and windows, see if anything's been forced."

"You can look," Maggie said with a sigh, "but I don't know if the doors were locked, and half the windows at least were open."

He gave her the look parents give children when they do something foolish and expected. "I'll just poke around, anyway. Never can tell."

When he'd gone out, Maggie flopped down on the sofa and lapsed into silence. As if he had nothing better to do, Cliff wandered to the clock on the mantel and began to wind it. Killer came out from under the sofa and began to dance around his legs. The tension in the room was palpable. Maggie had almost given up wondering if it would ever be resolved.

Why would anyone break into an old trunk that had been neglected for years? Why had Cliff been in on the discovery, just as he'd been in on the discovery in the gully? What had caused her to fall in love with him, and would this need between them fade, as flash fires had a habit of doing? If she could understand any of it, perhaps the rest would fall into place and she'd know what move to make.

"There doesn't seem to be any forced entry," Stan said as he came back into the room. "I'll go into town, file a formal report and get to work on this, but—" He shook his head at Maggie. "I can't promise anything. I'd suggest you keep your doors locked and give some more thought to those dead bolts."

"I'll be staying here for the next few days," Cliff announced, throwing Stan and Maggie into surprised silence. He continued as if he hadn't noticed the reaction his statement caused. "Maggie won't be alone, though it would seem that whatever was wanted in the house was taken."

"Yeah." Stan scratched his nose, almost concealing a grin. "I'd better get back. I'll just let myself out."

Maggie didn't rouse herself to say goodbye but stared at Cliff until the front door shut. "Just what do you mean, you'll be staying here?"

"We'll have to do some grocery shopping first. I can't live off what you keep in that kitchen."

"Nobody asked you to live off it," she said, springing to her feet. "And nobody asked you to stay here. I don't understand why I have to keep reminding you whose house and land this is."

"Neither do I."

"You told *him*," she continued. "You just as good as announced to the town in general that you and I—"

"Are exactly what we are," Cliff finished easily. "You'd better get some shoes on, if we're going to town."

"I'm not going to town, and you're not staying here."

He moved so quickly she was caught completely off guard. His hands closed over both her arms. "I'm not letting you stay here alone until we know exactly what's going on."

"I've told you before I can take care of myself."

"Maybe you can, but we're not putting it to the test right now. I'm staying."

She gave him a long stare. The truth was she didn't want to be alone. The truth was, she wanted him, perhaps too much for her own good. Yet he was the one insisting, she thought as her temper began to cool. Since he was insisting, perhaps he cared more than he was willing to admit. Maybe it was time she took a gamble on that.

"If I let you stay…" she began.

"I am staying."

"If I let you stay," she repeated coolly, "you have to cook dinner tonight."

He lifted a brow, and the grip on her arms relaxed slightly. "After sampling your cooking, you won't get any argument."

Refusing to be insulted, she nodded. "Fine. I'll get my shoes."

"Later." Before she knew what he was up to, they were tumbling back onto the sofa. "We've got all day."

Chapter 10

Maggie considered it ironic that she'd just begun to become accustomed to living alone and she was no longer living alone. Cliff made the transition unobtrusively. No fuss, no bother. A brisk, rather subtle sense of organization seemed to be a part of his makeup. She'd always respected organized people—from a safe distance.

He left early each morning, long before she considered it decent for a person to be out of his bed. He was quiet and efficient and never woke her. Occasionally, when she groped her way downstairs later in the morning, she'd find a scrawled note next to the coffeepot.

"Phone was off the hook again," it might say. Or "Milk's low. I'll pick some up."

Not exactly love letters, Maggie thought wryly. A man like Cliff wouldn't put his feelings down on paper the way she was compelled to. It was just one more area of opposition between them.

In any case, Maggie wasn't certain Cliff had any feelings about her other than impatience and an occasional bout of intolerance. Though there were times she suspected she touched some of his softer edges, he didn't act much like a lover. He brought her no flowers, but she remembered he'd planted a willow tree. He gave her no smooth, clever phrases, but she remembered the look she'd sometimes catch in his eyes. He wasn't a poet, he wasn't a romantic, but that look, that one long, intense look, said more than most women ever heard.

Perhaps, despite both of them, she was beginning to understand him. The more she understood, the more difficult it became to control a steadily growing love. He wasn't a man whose emotions could be pushed or channeled. She was a woman who, once her feelings were touched, ran with them in whatever direction they went.

Though she'd lived in the house outside of Morganville for only a month, Maggie understood a few basics of small-town life. Whatever she did became common knowledge almost before she'd done it. Whatever it was she did would draw a variety of opinions that would lead to a general consensus. There were a few key people whose opinion could sway that consensus. Cliff, she knew, was one of them, if he chose to bother. Stan Agee and the postmistress were others. It didn't take her long to discover that Bog was another whose opinion was sought and carefully weighed.

The politics in Morganville might've been on a smaller scale than those in Southern California's music industry, but Maggie saw that they ran in the same vein. In L.A., however, she'd been second-generation royalty, while here she was an outsider. An outsider, she knew, whose notoriety could be either scorned or accepted. To date, she'd been fortunate, because most of the key people had decided to accept. Thinking of small, close-knit towns, she realized she'd taken a chance on that acceptance by living with Cliff.

Not living with, Maggie corrected as she spread adhesive on her newly stripped bathroom floor. He wasn't living with her; he was staying with her. There was a world of difference between the two. He hadn't moved in, bag and baggage, nor had there been any discussion about the length of his stay. It was, she decided, a bit like having a guest whom you didn't feel obligated to entertain or impress.

Unnecessarily, and through his own choice, he'd opted to be her bodyguard. And at night, when the sun went down and the woods were quiet, her body was his. He accepted her passion, her hungers and desires. Perhaps, just perhaps, one day he might accept her emotions, which raged just as hot, and just as high. First he had to come to understand her as she was beginning to understand him. Without that, and the respect that went with it, emotions and desires would wither and die.

Maggie set the next square of tile into position, then sat back to judge the outcome. The stone-patterned ceramic was rustic and would leave her free to use an infinite range of color combinations. She wanted nothing in her home to be too restricted or regimented, just as she wanted to do most of the changes and improvements herself.

Looking at the six pieces of tile she'd installed, Maggie nodded. She was becoming quite handy these days. Though her pansies had never recovered, they were her only major failure.

Pleased and ready for more, Maggie debated whether to mix up another batch of adhesive or to start the next wall of paper in her bedroom. There was only a wall and a half left to cover, she remembered; then it would be time to make a decision on curtains. Priscillas, cafés, Cape Cods... Nothing monumental, most people would say, she mused, but then she'd always left such things up to decorators before. Now, if something didn't work, she had no one to blame but herself.

With a laugh, she reached into the box of tiles again, swearing halfheartedly as she scraped her finger against a sharp edge. The price of being your own handyman, Maggie decided, going to the sink to run water over the cut. Maybe it was time to turn in the tiles for wallpaper and paste.

When the dog began to bark, she knew that either project would have to wait. Resigned, she turned off the tap just as the sound of a car reached her. Going to the tiny latticed window, she watched Lieutenant Reiker pull around the last curve.

Why was he back? she wondered, frowning. There couldn't possibly be any more information she could give him. When he didn't approach the house immediately, Maggie stayed where she was. He walked along the path of flagstone Cliff's crew had set just that week. When he reached the end, he didn't turn toward the porch, but looked out over the gully. Slowly, he drew out a cigarette, then lit it with a short wooden match. For several moments he just stood there, smoking and watching the dirt and rocks as if they had the answers he wanted. Then, before she could react, he turned and looked directly up at the window where she stood. Feeling like an idiot, she started down to meet him.

"Lieutenant." Maggie went cautiously down the porch steps and onto the sturdy new flagstone.

"Miss Fitzgerald." He flipped the cigarette stub into the tangle of brush near the gully. "Your place is coming along. Hard to believe what it looked like a few weeks ago."

"Thank you." He looked so harmless, so pleasant. She wondered if he carried a gun in a shoulder holster under his jacket.

"Noticed you planted a willow over there." But he looked at her, not at the gully. "It shouldn't be much longer before you can have your pond put in."

Like Reiker, Maggie didn't look toward the gully. "Does that mean the investigation's almost over?"

Reiker scratched along the side of his jaw. "I don't know if I'd say that. We're working on it."

She bit back a sigh. "Are you going to search the gully again?"

"I don't think it's going to come to that. We've been through it twice now. Thing is—" He stopped, shifting his weight to ease his hip. "I don't like loose ends. The more we look into this thing, the more we find. It's hard to tie up ends that've been dangling for ten years."

Was this a social call or an official one? she wondered, trying not to be annoyed. Maggie could remember how embarrassed he'd been when he'd asked for her autograph. At the moment, she didn't need a fan. "Lieutenant, is there something I can do?"

"I wondered if you'd had anyone coming around, someone you know, maybe someone you don't know."

"Coming around?"

"The murder happened here, Miss Fitzgerald, and

the more we dig, the more people we find who had reason to kill Morgan. A lot of them still live in town."

She folded her arms under her breasts. "If you're trying to make me uneasy, Lieutenant, you're doing a good job."

"I don't want to do that, but I don't want to keep you in the dark, either." He hesitated, then decided to go with his instincts. "We discovered that Morgan withdrew twenty-five thousand cash from his bank account on the day he disappeared. His car was found, now his body's been found, but the money's never showed up."

"Twenty-five thousand," Maggie murmured. A tidy sum, even tidier ten years ago. "You're telling me you think the money was the motive for murder?"

"Money's always a motive for murder, and it's a loose end. We're checking a lot of people out, but it takes time. So far, nobody around here's ever flashed that kind of money." He started to reach for another cigarette, then apparently changed his mind. "I've got a couple of theories…"

She might've smiled if her head wasn't beginning to ache. "And you'd like to tell me?"

"Whoever killed Morgan was smart enough to cover his tracks. He might've been smart enough to know that coming up with twenty-five thousand dollars wouldn't go unnoticed in a town like this. Maybe, just maybe, he panicked and got rid of the money. Or maybe he hid it so he could wait a good long time, until any rumors about Morgan had died down—then it'd just be waiting for him."

"Ten years is a very long time, Lieutenant."

"Some people're more patient than others." He shrugged. "It's just a theory."

But it made her think. The attic, and the trunk and the handprint. "The other night—" she began, then stopped.

"Something happen the other night?" he prompted.

It was foolish not to tell him, to feel as though, if she did, she would be forging another link in the chain that bound her to everything that had happened. He was, after all, in charge of the investigation. "Well, it seems someone broke in and took something out of a trunk in the attic. I didn't realize it until days later— then I reported it to Sheriff Agee."

"That was the thing to do." His gaze lifted to the dormer window. "He come up with anything?"

"Not really. He did find a key. That is, his wife found one somewhere. He came back and opened the trunk, but it was empty."

"Would you mind if I had a look myself?"

She wanted it over, yet it seemed every step she took brought her in deeper. "No, I don't mind." Resigned, Maggie turned to lead him into the house. "It seems odd that anyone would hide money in the attic, then wait until someone was living here to claim it."

"You bought the place almost as soon as the sign was posted," Reiker reminded her.

"But it was nearly a month before I'd moved in."

"I heard Mrs. Agee kept quiet about the sale. Her husband didn't like the idea."

"You hear a lot of things, Lieutenant."

He gave her the slow, half-embarrassed smile he'd given her when he'd asked for her autograph. "I'm supposed to."

Maggie lapsed into silence until they reached the

second floor. "The attic's up here. For what it's worth, I haven't found anything missing in the house."

"How'd they get in?" he asked as he began to climb the steeper, more narrow staircase.

"I don't know," she mumbled. "I wasn't locking my doors."

"But you are now?" He looked back over his shoulder.

"Yes, I'm locking them."

"Good." He went directly to the trunk, and, crouching down, studied the lock. The handprint had faded back to dust. "You say Mrs. Agee had the key?"

"Yes, or one of them. It seems this trunk belonged to the last people who rented the house, an old couple. The woman left it here after her husband died. Apparently there were at least two keys, but Joyce could only find one of them."

"Hmm." Reiker opened the now-unlocked trunk and peered inside, much as he'd peered into the gully. And it, Maggie thought, was just as empty now.

"Lieutenant, you don't really think there's a connection between this and—what you're investigating?"

"I don't like coincidences," he muttered, echoing Cliff's earlier statement. "You say the sheriff's looking into it?"

"Yes."

"I'll talk to him before I head back. Twenty-five thousand doesn't take up much room," he said. "It's a big trunk."

"I don't understand why anyone would let it sit in one for ten years."

"People're funny." He straightened, grunting a little

with the effort. "Of course, it's just a theory. Another is that Morgan's mistress took the money and ran."

"His mistress?" Maggie repeated blankly.

"Alice Delaney," Reiker said easily. "She'd been having an affair with Morgan for five or six years. Funny how people'll talk once you get them started."

"Delaney?" Maggie said it quietly, hoping she'd heard incorrectly.

"That's right. As a matter of fact, it's her son who's been doing your landscaping. Coincidences," he repeated. "This business is full of them."

Somehow she managed to remain composed as they walked back downstairs. She spoke politely when he told her again how much he admired her music. Maybe she even smiled when she closed the door on him. When she was alone, Maggie felt her blood turn to ice, then drain.

Cliff's mother had been Morgan's mistress for years; then she'd disappeared, right after his death? Cliff would've known. Everyone would've known, she thought, and covered her face with both hands. What had she fallen into, and how would she ever get out again?

Maybe he was going crazy, but Cliff was beginning to think of the long, winding drive up the hill as going home. He'd never have believed he could consider the old Morgan place as home. Not with the way he'd always felt about William Morgan. Nor would he have believed the woman who lived there could make him think that way. It seemed a great deal was happening that he could neither stop nor harness. Yet staying with Maggie had been his own choice, just as leaving again would be—when he was ready. From time to time he found he needed to remind himself that he could and would leave again.

Yet when she laughed, the house was so warm. When she was angry, it was so full of energy. When she sang—when she worked in the music room in the evening, Cliff thought. When the woods were quiet, before the moon had risen, she'd play. She'd sing snatches of words, sentences, phrases, as she composed. Long before she'd finished, he'd find himself in a frenzy of need. He wondered how she worked hour after hour, day after day, with such passion and feeling driving her.

It was the discipline, Cliff decided. He'd never expected her to be so disciplined about her music. The talent he'd admired all along, but in the few days he'd lived with her, he'd learned that she drove herself hard in the hours she worked.

A contrast, Cliff decided. It was an implausible contrast to the woman who jumped sporadically from one project to another in that big, dusty house. She left walls half papered, ceilings half painted. There were crates and boxes everywhere, most of which hadn't been touched. Rolls of supplies were tucked into every corner. He'd say her work on the house was precise, even creative, to the point where she'd leave off for something new.

She wasn't like anyone he'd ever known, and he realized that somewhere along the way he'd begun to understand her. It had been easier when he could dismiss her as a spoiled Hollywood princess who'd bought a dilapidated country house on a whim or for a publicity stunt. He knew now that she'd bought the house for no other reason than she'd loved it.

Perhaps she was a bit spoiled. She tended to give orders a little too casually. When she didn't get her own way, she tended to bristle or to freeze up. Cliff grinned. The same could be said of himself, he admitted.

To give Maggie her due, she hadn't run from the trouble or unpleasantness that had begun so shortly after she'd moved in. If he'd seen another woman stick as Maggie was sticking, he'd have said she'd indeed taken root. Cliff still had his doubts. Perhaps he fostered them purposely, because if he believed Maggie Fitzgerald would stay in Morganville, he might have to admit he wanted her to. He might have to admit that coming home every night to a woman who made him laugh and fume and throb wasn't something he'd give up without a fight.

He drove the last few yards, then stopped at the edge of the drive. The phlox was blooming on the bank. The new grass was like a green shadow over the soil. Maggie's petunias were a splash of color.

They'd both put part of themselves into the land already, he realized. Perhaps that in itself was a bond that would be difficult to break. Even as he stepped out of the truck, he wanted her, just the scent, just the softness of her. There was nothing he could do to change it.

There was no music. Cliff frowned as he slowly climbed the front steps. Maggie was always at her piano at this time of day. There were times he'd come back earlier and work on the yard himself. He'd know it was five o'clock, because that's when the music would begin, and it would continue for no less than an hour, often longer. Cliff looked at his watch: 5:35 p.m. Uneasy, he turned the knob on the front door.

Of course it was unlocked, he thought, annoyed. He'd left her a note that morning, telling her none of his crew would be there that day and to keep the doors locked. Senseless woman, he thought as he shoved the door open. Why couldn't she get it through her head that she was completely isolated here? Too many things had happened, and simply by living in this house, she was in the center of them.

Quiet. Too damn quiet, Cliff realized as annoyance began to fade into anxiety. The dog wasn't barking. The house had that echoing, empty feeling almost everyone can sense but can't explain. Though instinct told him no one was there, he began to go from room to room, calling her. Her name bounced back off the walls in his own voice and taunted him.

Where the hell was she, Cliff demanded as he took the stairs two at a time to check the second floor. He didn't like to admit that he could feel panic at nothing more than coming home to an empty house, but panic was exactly what he felt. Every day that week he'd been sure he'd had a crew, or part of one, working outside until he'd been there. He hadn't wanted her left alone, but because he couldn't explain it, Cliff had broken the ritual that day. And now he couldn't find her.

"Maggie!" Desperately, he searched the second floor, not even certain what he expected, or wanted, to find. He'd never experienced this kind of raw, basic fear. He only knew the house was empty and his woman was gone. A pair of her shoes sat carelessly in the center of the bedroom rug. A blouse was tossed negligently over a chair. The earrings he'd watched her

take off the night before still lay on the dresser, beside
a silver-backed brush engraved with her mother's ini-
tials. The room held her scent; it always did.

When he saw the new tiles in the bathroom, he tried
to calm himself. In her helter-skelter way, she'd started
a new project. But where in the hell—

Then, in the bowl of the sink, he saw something
that stopped his heart. Against the pristine white porcelain were three drops of blood. He stared while panic
swirled through him, making his head swim and his
skin ice.

From somewhere outside, the dog began to bark
frantically. Cliff was racing down the steps, not even
aware that he called her name again and again.

He saw her as soon as he burst through the back
door. She was coming slowly through the woods to
the east, the dog dancing around her legs, leaping and
nipping. She had her hands in her pockets, her head
down. His mind took in every detail while the combination of fear and relief made his legs weak.

He ran toward her, seeing her head lift as he called
her again. Then he had her in his arms, holding tight,
closing his eyes and just feeling her, warm and whole
and safe. He was too overcome with emotions that had
no precedent to notice that she stood stiff and unyield-
ing against him.

He buried his face in the soft luxury of her hair.
"Maggie, where've you been?"

This was the man she'd thought she was beginning
to understand. This was the man she was beginning to
love. Maggie stared straight ahead over his shoulder to
the house beyond. "I went for a walk."

"Alone?" he demanded irrationally, drawing her back. "You went out alone?"

Everything turned cold; her skin, her manner, her eyes. "It's my land, Cliff. Why shouldn't I go out alone?"

He caught himself before he could rage that she should've left him a note. What was happening to him? "There was blood in the sink upstairs."

"I cut my finger on a tile."

He found he wanted to rage at her for that. She had no business hurting herself. "You're usually playing this time of day," he managed.

"I'm not locked into a routine any more than I'm locked into the house. If you want a placid little female who's waiting to fall at your feet every night when you come home, you'd better look somewhere else." Leaving him staring, she broke away and went into the house.

Calmer but more confused, Cliff went into the kitchen to see her pouring a drink. Scotch, he noted, another first. With his mind a bit clearer, he could see that the normal color was absent from her cheeks and that her shoulders were stiff with tension. This time he didn't go to her or touch her.

"What's happened?"

Maggie swirled the scotch once before she swallowed. She found it too warm, too strong, but she sipped again. "I don't know what you mean." The kitchen was too small. Maggie took the glass and went out. The air was warm and soft. Outside there were no walls or ceilings to make her feel closed in. Circling around, she sat down on the spread of new grass. She'd sit here in the summer, Maggie thought, and read—Byron, if that was her mood. She'd let the sun fall over her, the silence cloak her, and read until she slept. Maggie continued to look out over the woods when Cliff's shadow slanted over her.

"Maggie, what's wrong with you?"

"I'm having a mood," she said flatly. "You'd expect spoiled celebrities to have moods, wouldn't you?"

Keeping his temper in check, Cliff sat down beside her, then took her chin in his hand. He waited until their eyes had met and held. "What?"

She'd known she'd have to tell him. It was the not knowing what there would be afterward that left her insides cold and knotted. "Lieutenant Reiker was here today," she began, but carefully removed Cliff's hand from her face.

Cliff swore, cursing himself for leaving her alone. "What'd he want?"

Maggie shrugged and sipped at the scotch again. "He's a man who doesn't like loose ends. Apparently he's been finding quite a number. It seems William Morgan withdrew twenty-five thousand dollars from his bank account on the day he was murdered."

"Twenty-five thousand?"

He sounded surprised, Maggie noted. Genuinely surprised. She recognized his expression, that thoughtful, narrow-eyed look that meant he was considering all the details and angles. How could she be certain of anything any longer? "The money was never recovered. One of Reiker's theories is that the murderer hid it away, patiently waiting until people forgot about Morgan."

Cliff's eyes sharpened. Automatically, he turned his head and looked back to the house. "Here?"

"Possibly."

"Ten years is a damn long time to sit on twenty-five thousand," Cliff muttered. Still, he didn't care for loose ends, either. "Did you tell him about the trunk in the attic?"

"Yes, he had a look at it himself."

He touched her shoulder, just his fingertips, so lightly that the touch offered whatever support she might want to take. "It's upset you." Maggie said nothing, nor did she look at him. Tension began to work at his own muscles. "There's more."

"There's always more," Maggie said quietly. Now she looked at him; she had to. "He mentioned that Morgan's mistress had disappeared right after his death." She felt Cliff's fingers tighten convulsively on her shoulder just as she felt the waves of anger.

"She wasn't his mistress," Cliff said tightly. "My mother might've been foolish enough to fall in love with a man like Morgan, she might've been unwise enough to sleep with him, but she wasn't his mistress."

"Why didn't you tell me before?" Maggie demanded. "Why did you wait until I found out this way?"

"It doesn't have anything to do with you or with anything that's happened here." As restless anger swarmed in him, he rose.

"Coincidences," Maggie said quietly, but Cliff turned and stared down at her. "Weren't you the one who said not to trust coincidences?"

He was trapped, by an old anger and by a pair of depthless brown eyes. Again he found himself compelled to explain what he'd never explained before. "My mother was lonely and very vulnerable after my father died. Morgan knew how to exploit that. I was living outside of D.C. at the time. If I'd been here, I might've stopped it." Resentment welled up and was controlled. "He knew how to play on weaknesses, and he played on my mother's. When I found out they were lovers, I wanted to kill him."

He said it as he had once before, coldly, calmly. Maggie swallowed on a dry throat. "She was already too involved for anything to be done, deluded into believing she loved him, or maybe she did love him. Other intelligent women had. She'd been friends with Louella for years, but that didn't matter. When they found his car in the river, she snapped."

It was painful to look back on it, but Maggie's solemn brown eyes insisted he go on. "She didn't disappear—she came to me. She was frantic, and for the first time since she'd become involved with Morgan, she was seeing clearly again. Shame affects different people in different ways. My mother broke all ties with Morganville and everyone in it. She knew her relationship with Morgan wasn't a secret, and now that it was over, she simply couldn't face the gossip. She's still in D.C. She has a new life, and I don't want any of this to touch her."

Was he always so unflaggingly protective of the women in his life? Maggie wondered. Joyce, his mother... Where, she wondered, did she fit in? "Cliff, I understand how you feel. My mother was one of the most precious people in my life, too. But there might not be anything you can do about it. They're reconstructing what happened ten years ago, and your mother has a part in it."

But that wasn't all she was thinking, Cliff realized. Deliberately, he sat down beside her, struggling to keep the tension from his fingers when he took her shoulders. "You're wondering how much a part I might've had in it."

"Don't." She tried to stand, but he held her still.

"It's possible that I could've shot Morgan to end a destructive relationship with my mother."

"You hated him."

"Yes."

Her eyes never left his. They looked deep, searching. Logic might implicate him; his own temperament might make him suspect. Maggie stared into the smoky gray of his eyes and believed what she saw. "No," she murmured, drawing him against her. "No, I understand you too well."

Her faith—the warm flood of it—almost destroyed him. "Do you?"

"Maybe too well," she murmured. "I was so frightened before." Closing her eyes, she drew in the familiar scent of him. He was real, he was solid, and for as long as she could hold on, he was hers. "Not now, not now that you're here."

He could feel the pull, that slow, gentle pull. If he wasn't careful, he'd soon forget there was anything or anyone but her in his life. "Maggie." His fingers were already tangling in her hair. "You shouldn't trust without questions."

"It isn't trust with questions," she countered. She wanted it to be only the two of them, with the rest of the world locked out, forgotten. Framing his face with her hands, she drew his mouth down to hers.

She'd expected fire, aggression, but his lips were soft and sweet. Confused, moved, Maggie drew back to stare at him. The eyes that had fascinated her from the beginning held hers as seconds edged closer to a minute. She was lost in the mists and the smoke. Without a word, he brought her close again.

With his eyes on hers, he lightly traced the shape of her face with a fingertip. This, he discovered, was the only face he ever needed to see again. Lightly, he outlined the shape of her lips. These, he knew, were the only lips he'd ever need to taste. With a gentleness he'd shown to no other lover, he laid her back. This was the only body he ever wanted to possess.

Tenderness left her stunned, weak. His mouth lingered on hers, but with such poignancy, the kiss alone made her bones liquefy. The grass was cool beneath her, the sun warm. Swimming in emotion, Maggie closed her eyes while his lips traveled over her face.

Had she ever been touched like this before? As if she were spun glass, his hands stroked over her. As if she were the rarest of delicacies, his lips tasted. And she was helplessly caught in the silken web that was more love than passion.

"Cliff—"

She might've told him, if his lips hadn't captured hers with a sweetness that left her speechless.

He'd never felt a stronger need to savor. It was as if each moment could be stretched to an hour as long as they lay together in the fragrant spring grass. The color in her cheeks was delicate; the sunlight combed through her hair. The look in her eyes was one no man could resist. It told him as clearly as words that she was his. He had only to claim. Knowing it, he moved only more slowly and touched only more reverently.

He undressed her while his kisses continued to hold her in the honey-steeped prison of pleasure. When she was naked, he watched how the sun streamed over her skin. Her large, expressive eyes were half closed. He could feel the pliancy in her body when, with a sigh, she lifted her hands to help him undress.

The raw, primitive need she so often incited in him didn't rise up. Instead, she drew out the softer emotions he normally held back. He wanted only to please her.

Gently, he lowered his mouth to her breast. He could hear her heartbeat increase in pace as he lingered there with his tongue tracing, his teeth nibbling. The tip grew taut, so that when he drew it into his mouth, he heard her breath shudder out, then catch again. Her hand moved through his hair as she lay back, saturated with sensation.

Her body was like a treasure to be discovered and admired before possession. Slowly, almost leisurely, he took those moist kisses and gentle hands over it, stopping, lingering, when he felt her shuddering response. He knew she was steeped in that dim, heavy world where passions hover around the edges and desires lick temptingly, like tiny tongues of fire. He wanted to keep her there for hours or days or years.

Her thighs were slender and long and pearl-white. He loitered there, nudging them both closer, still closer to the edge. But not yet.

She'd forgotten where she was. Though her eyes were half opened, she saw nothing but mists and dreams. She could feel, oh, yes, she could feel each stroke of his hand, each warm brush of lips. She could hear gentle murmurs, quiet sighs that might've been his or hers. There was no reason to ever feel or hear anything else. She was slowly, inevitably, being drawn through the sweetness and into the heat. She began to crave it.

He felt the change in her body, heard the change in

the breaths that whispered through her lips. He swept his mouth farther up her thigh, but still he didn't hurry. She would have all he had to give before they were finished.

She arched, catapulted with the sudden intensity of pleasure. She crested, quickly, shatteringly, with an abandonment of self and will. He wanted, demanded, just that. Before she could settle, he drove her up again until the madness once more began to creep into both of them. Cliff held it off, almost delirious with the knowledge that he could give her what a woman might only dream of. Her body was alive with sensations only he could bring to her. Her mind was swirling with thoughts of only him.

Knowing it, reveling in it, he slipped into her, taking her with a tenderness that lasted and lasted and lasted.

Chapter 11

Saturday morning, Maggie decided she could lie there, half dozing, until it was Saturday afternoon. She could feel the weight of Cliff's arm across her waist, his warm breath fluttering over her cheek. Without opening her eyes, she snuggled closer, wallowing in lazy contentment.

If she'd been certain he could be so gentle, she'd have fallen in love with him willingly. But how satisfying it was to have discovered it after her heart had already been lost. He had such emotion in him. Perhaps he was cautious with it, but she could love him much more comfortably knowing it was there and that now and again, unexpectedly, it would reach out to her.

No, it wasn't flowery phrases she wanted, but his stability. She didn't need smooth charm. When a woman found a man who was capable of such passion and such tenderness, she'd be a fool to want to change him in any way. Maggie Fitzgerald, she thought with a little satisfied smile, was no fool.

"What're you smiling at?"

Opening her eyes, Maggie looked directly into Cliff's. Because his were alert and direct, she knew he'd been awake for some time. She tried to blink away the mists and smiled again. "It feels good," she murmured, snuggling even closer. "You feel good."

He ran a hand down her back, over her hip and thigh. Yes, it felt very good. "Soft," Cliff said quietly. "So soft and smooth." He wondered how he'd gone so many years without being able to touch her like this, when she was lazy and warm and naked. He felt no tension in her, none of the subtle little signs he'd grown so adept at spotting. The need was very strong in him to keep that tension away for as long as he could. She'd walked unwittingly into a whirlpool, and somehow he was connected with it. If it was only for a day, he'd keep the problems at bay.

He rolled, pressed her down into the mattress so that she laughingly murmured a complaint. "Are you going to cook breakfast?" he demanded.

Maggie pillowed her head on her hands, giving him arrogant look for arrogant look. "You don't like my cooking."

"I've decided to be tolerant this morning."

"Have you?" She arched a brow. "How lucky for me."

"Floppy bacon and sloppy eggs," he told her before he nuzzled at her neck.

She shifted, enjoying the rough feel of the night's growth of beard against her skin. "What?"

"I don't like my bacon too crisp—" he nipped at the pulse in her throat "—or my eggs too set."

With a sigh, she closed her eyes again. She wanted to bottle this moment, so that she could take it out again whenever she needed to feel content. "I like my bacon so crisp it crumbles, and I don't like eggs at all."

"They're good for you." Cliff took his lips up her throat to nibble at her ear. "Might put some meat on you." As he spoke, he took his hand down her side again.

"Complaining?"

"Uh-uh." He ran his hand back up again so that his fingers brushed the side of her breast. "Though you do tend toward the lean side. We could build you up with three square meals a day and some exercise."

"No one needs three meals a day," she began, a bit huffily. "And as for exercise—"

"Do you like to dance?"

"Yes, but I—"

"Not much muscle," he noted, pinching her arm. "How's your endurance?"

She gave him a saucy look. "You should know."

With a laugh, he pressed his lips to hers. "You've a very quick, very wicked mind."

"Thanks."

"Now, about dancing. Ever been in a contre line?"

"A what?"

"I thought so." He shook his head, then shifted so that he could look down at her with pity. "Country dancing, Maggie."

Her brows drew together. "Square dancing?"

"No." It was time to educate the lady, Cliff decided, and drew her up to a sitting position. Her hair flowed wildly over her shoulders, the way he liked it best. "Square dancing's more formal, more regimented, than country dancing, but there'd be traditional music and a caller."

Maggie ran a finger up his chest. "Swing your partner and do-si-do?"

He felt the little thrill inch along his skin behind the trail of her finger. Did she know it? he wondered. From the smile that hovered on her lips, he thought she knew it very well. "Among other things."

Maggie linked her hands around his neck and let her head fall back so that she could look at him from beneath lowered lashes. "I'm sure it's all very fascinating, but I don't know why we're doing all this talking when you could be kissing me."

For an answer he gave her a long, searing kiss that left her breathless and pleased. "Because," he said, and nipped at her ear, "I want to go dancing with you."

Sighing, content, Maggie enjoyed the sensation of feeling her own blood begin to sizzle. "Where and when?"

"Tonight, in the park outside of town."

"Tonight?" She opened one eye. "Dancing in the park?"

"It's a tradition." He laid her back again but kept himself propped up so that his hand was free to skim her body. "A sort of Founder's Day celebration combined with rites of spring. Most of the town'll show. There'll be dancing till midnight, then a potluck supper. Then…" He cupped her breast, enjoying the way her eyes clouded when he brushed a fingertip over the point. "There's dancing till dawn for anybody who can handle it."

"Until dawn?" Intrigued and already hopelessly aroused, Maggie arched under him.

"You've danced until dawn before, I imagine."

He'd said the wrong thing or used the wrong tone,

because her body stiffened. No, he didn't want to bring up their differences now. At the moment, he could hardly recognize them. He lay down beside her and cradled her in his arms. "We could watch the sun come up," he murmured. "And the stars go out."

She lay against him, but her mind was clear now. The doubts had returned. "You never mentioned this to me before."

"I didn't think you'd be much interested in country dances and potluck suppers. I guess I realized I was wrong."

It was another kind of apology. Maggie accepted this one as easily as she had the first. Smiling again, she tilted her head back from him. "Are you asking me for a date?"

He liked it when her eyes held that half teasing, half challenging light. "Looks like it."

"I'd love to."

"Okay." Her hair fell onto his shoulder. Absently, he twisted the end around his finger. "Now, about breakfast."

She grinned, lowering her mouth to his. "We'll have it for lunch."

She didn't know what she expected, but Maggie looked forward to an evening out, away from the house, an evening to spend with other people. After her brief stab at being a hermit, she'd discovered that she could indeed take total command of her own needs. Being able to live with herself for long periods of time simply showed her that she didn't always have to in order to prove her independence. Perhaps she hadn't been attempting to learn anything with the dramatic change in her lifestyle, but she'd learned something, anyway.

She could take charge of the tiny details of day-to-day living that she'd always left to others, but she didn't have to cut herself off from everyone to do it.

No, she didn't know what to expect, perhaps a quaint little festival with tinny music and warm lemonade in paper cups. She didn't expect to be particularly impressed. She certainly didn't expect to be enchanted.

The line of cars that sloped down the winding drive to the park surprised her. She'd thought most of the people in town would simply walk. When she mentioned it to Cliff, he shrugged and negotiated his pickup into a spot behind a yellow van.

"They come from all over the county, and from as far away as D.C. and Pennsylvania."

"Really?" Pursing her lips, she climbed out of the truck into the warm, clear night. There'd be a full moon, though the sun was just beginning to set. She wondered if the town had planned it that way or if it had been the luck of the draw. Either way, it was one more thing to be enjoyed. Putting her hand in Cliff's, she began to walk with him to the crest of the hill.

As she watched, the sun dropped lower behind the mountains in the west. She'd seen the sun sink gloriously into the sea and been awed by the colors and brilliance of sunsets in the snow-covered Alps. She'd seen the desert vibrate with color at dusk and cities glow with twilight. Somehow, watching the gold and mauve and pink layer over what were hardly more than foothills of a great range, she was more deeply affected. Perhaps it was foolish, perhaps it was fanciful, but she felt more a part of this place, more involved with the coming of this night, than she'd been of any other.

On impulse, she threw her arms around Cliff's neck and held on.

Laughing, he put his hands on her hips. "What's this for?"

"It feels good," she said, echoing her morning words.

Then with a bang that shattered the silence, the music burst out. As a musician, she recognized each individual instrument—violin, banjo, guitar, piano. As a music lover, she felt her excitement leap.

"It's fabulous!" she exclaimed, drawing quickly away. "Absolutely fabulous. Hurry, I have to see." Maggie grabbed his hand and raced the rest of the way up the hill.

Her first impression was of a maze of people, two hundred, perhaps two hundred fifty, crowded together in a covered pavilion. Then she saw they were in lines, six, no, eight, she realized after a quick count. There would be a line of men facing a line of women, and so on, until they simply ran out of room. And they were moving to the music in a system that looked both confusing and fluid.

Some of the women wore skirts that flared out as they dipped, swayed or spun. Others wore jeans. Men's attire was no more consistent and no more formal than the women's. Some of the dancers wore sneakers, while a great many more wore what seemed to be old-fashioned black leather shoes that tied and had thick, sturdy heels. Still others wore what looked like oriental slippers with a single strap across the instep. It didn't seem to matter what was worn; everyone moved. Petticoats flashed, heels stomped, laughter rang out.

A woman stood at the edge of a small wooden stage in front of the band and belted out instructions in a singsong voice. Maggie might not have understood most of the words, but she understood rhythm. Already she was itching to try it herself.

"But how do they know what to do?" she shouted over the music. "How do they understand her?"

"It's a sequence of moves repeated over and over," Cliff told her. "Once you've got the sequence down, you don't even need a caller; she just adds to it."

A sequence, Maggie mused and tried to find it. At first, she only saw bodies moving in what seemed a helter-skelter pattern, but gradually she began to see the repetition. Counting off the beats, she concentrated on one couple while trying to anticipate their next move. It pleased her to be able to find the sequence, just as the music pleased her ear and the swirling colors pleased her eye. She could smell a mixture of colognes, men's and women's, and the bursting fragrance of the spring flowers that skirted the pavilion.

As the sun dropped lower, the lights, strung overhead, spilled over the dancers. The floor vibrated under her feet so that she felt she was already dancing herself. With Cliff's arm around her, she watched with the undiluted fascination of discovering something new and exciting. She recognized the postmistress. The rather severe-looking middle-aged woman spun by like a dervish and flirted like a young girl.

Flirtation was part of it, Maggie realized as she began to watch faces instead of feet and bodies. Eye contact was essential, as were the saucy smiles she noted and the quick head tosses. It was, as perhaps dances had always been, a kind of mating ritual.

He hadn't thought she'd be fascinated or excited, but he recognized both in the look in her eyes. It gave Cliff overwhelming pleasure to know he'd brought that to her.

Her face was flushed, her body already moving to the beat, and her eyes were everywhere at once. She didn't make him think of Maggie Fitzgerald, star baby and glamorous celebrity, but of Maggie, a woman he could hold on to and dance with until the sun came up again.

When the music ended, Maggie burst into raucous applause with everyone else. Laughing, her face tilted back, she grabbed his hand. "I have to try the next one, even if I make a fool of myself."

"Just listen to the calls and follow the music," he said simply as the lines began to form again. "They always run through the dance once before the music starts."

She listened as the next dance sequence was explained by the caller. Though she didn't understand half of the terms, Maggie tried to link them in her mind with the moves that followed. As Cliff guided her slowly through the paces, she enjoyed the sense of camaraderie and the lack of inhibitions around her.

Though she could sense that she was being watched with speculation and interest, Maggie refused to be perturbed by it. They had a right to look, she decided. It was, after all, the first time she'd participated in a town function, and she was being partnered by a man everyone seemed to know.

"This one's called, 'Whiskey before Breakfast,'" the caller sang out. "If you've tried it, you know it ain't as good for you as dancing." She stomped her foot on the platform, one, two, three, and the music began.

The dance was fast and exuberant. Maggie was caught up in the moves before she'd fully registered them. Right, then left; join left hands with your corner and turn around twice. Pass through. Balance and swing.

The first time Cliff whirled her around, she felt the rush of air on her face and laughed.

"Watch my eyes," he warned. "Or you'll be too dizzy to stand up."

"I like it!" she tossed back, then "Whoops!" as she botched the next step and hurried to keep up with the rest of the line.

She didn't mind the sense of confusion or the crowd. Shoulders bumped, feet tangled, her waist was gripped, and she was whirled around by people she'd never met. Teenagers danced with grandmothers. Ladies in frilly dresses swirled with men in jeans with bandannas in their back pockets. Obviously anyone was welcome to line up and dance, and Maggie had already noticed that women picked men for partners just as often as men picked women. It was a free-for-all, and the rules were loose.

As the steps became more repetitive and more instinctive, she began to enjoy it even more. Her steps became more animated, her concentration less focused on the moves and more on the music. She could see why it drove people to dance. Feet couldn't be still with that rhythm jangling out. She knew, as Cliff grabbed her and swung her in fast circles, that she could've danced for hours.

"That's it," he said, laughing as she clung to him.

"Already?" She was breathless but not nearly finished. "It was wonderful, but too short. When do we do another?"

"Anytime you like."

"Now," she told him, sliding in as new lines formed.

She was fitting in as if she'd been to country dances in rural parks all her life. Perhaps he shouldn't have been surprised; she'd proved him wrong time and time again in his preconception of her. Yet in other ways, Cliff mused, he'd been right. She had an elegance that was too ingrained to be missed, whether she was scraping linoleum or lying in his arms. There was a polish that came from affluence and classy schools that set her apart from the other women around her. For days he'd been telling himself that it was that difference that attracted him as much as it put his back up. He couldn't explain the reason for either. He couldn't explain now, as he watched her begin the next dance as if she'd been moving to the call all her life, why she made him uneasy.

Circumstances, he told himself, and turned her back and around in a butterfly swing. The circumstances almost from the moment they'd met had been uneasy. That was bound to affect the way he felt when he looked at her—when he thought of her. And he thought of her, Cliff admitted, more often than he should; he looked at her less often than he wanted to.

Living with her for the past few days had given him the odd sensation of having something he hadn't known he'd wanted. There was something just a little too appealing about waking each morning with her warm beside him, about coming home to Maggie and her music. It would be wiser, much wiser, if he remembered those differences between them. No real common ground, he told himself again. But when she whirled into his arms, laughing, it was as though he'd been waiting for her.

The first few dances were a blur of color and sound and music. Maggie let herself go, realizing it had been weeks since she'd felt this free of tension and trouble. She'd danced in trendy clubs with celebrities, twirled in ballrooms with royalty, but she knew she'd never had as much simple fun as she was having now, following the caller and the fiddle.

As she turned to her next partner, she found her hand gripped by Stan Agee. Without his badge and gun, he might've been an attractive athlete in his prime. For a reason Maggie couldn't analyze, she tensed immediately on contact.

"Glad to see you're out, Miss Fitzgerald."

"Thank you." Determined not to give in to the mood, she smiled, lifting a hand to his shoulder as he began the spin. She caught his scent, the familiar department-store cologne, but it didn't soothe her.

"You catch on fast."

"It's wonderful. I can't believe I've missed it all my life." Out of the corner of her eye, she saw Cliff spinning with Joyce. The tension wouldn't dissolve.

"Save out a dance for me," he ordered before they whirled back to their original partners for the next step.

The moment he touched her, Cliff felt the rigidity of her muscles. "What's wrong?"

"Nothing." It was nothing, Maggie told herself, because she couldn't explain it. But now, as she swirled and turned from one pair of arms to another, it came to her that each time she danced with someone, she might be dancing with a murderer. How was she to know? It could be anyone—the real estate agent who'd sold her the house, the butcher who'd recommended the pork chops only the day before, the postmistress, the bank teller. How was she to know?

Maggie's mind began to whirl. For an instant, her eyes locked on Lieutenant Reiker's as he stood on the sidelines, watching. Why here? she asked herself as she was snatched up and spun again. Why would he come here? Perhaps he was watching her—but why? Protecting her—from what?

Then she was in Cliff's arms again, grateful that her feet could follow the mindless repetition of the dance while her thoughts raced in dozens of directions. Hadn't Cliff said people came from all over to this all-night festival? Maybe Reiker was a country-dance enthusiast. More likely, she thought grimly, he'd wanted to see all the townspeople together, observe, dissect. She shuddered. It was his job, she reminded herself. He was only doing his job. But how she wished he'd go away.

There was Louella, seeming to float through the dance. Rather than verve, she had a restrained dignity in her movements that was both lovely and uncomfortable to watch. Lovely, Maggie realized, because Louella had the grace of a natural dancer. Uncomfortable—though she wasn't able to put her finger on it, Maggie sensed there was something beneath the restraint that struggled for release.

Fanciful, she berated herself. She was being foolish and fanciful, imagining things that weren't there. But the feeling of discomfort was persistent. She was being watched, she knew. By Reiker? Stan Agee, Joyce, Louella? By everyone, Maggie thought. They all knew one another; they'd all known William Morgan. She was the outsider who'd uncovered what had been dead and buried for a decade. Logic indicated that at least one of them would resent her for that—perhaps all of them.

Suddenly, the music was too loud, the steps were too fast and the air was too full of scent.

Then she was caught up in Bog's short, wiry arms and spun at a breathless pace. "You're a good spinner, Miss Maggie," he told her, grinning and showing several gaps instead of teeth. "One helluva spinner."

Looking down into his homely, wrinkled face, she broke into a grin of her own. She was being ridiculous. No one resented her. Why should they? She wasn't involved in a tragedy that was ten years old. It was time she stopped looking beneath the surface and accepted things as she saw them. "I love to spin!" she shouted to Bog, leaning back into it. "I could spin for hours."

He gave a cackling laugh and released her for the next sequence. The music built, but it no longer seemed too loud. The tempo increased, but she could've danced faster and faster. When it was over, she had her hands linked around Cliff's neck and was laughing.

There was no tension in her now, but there had been. He thought he understood the reason. Deliberately, he steered her away from the Agees and Louella. "I could use a beer."

"Sounds perfect. I'd like to watch another one, anyway. It's the best show in town."

"You want a beer?"

Maggie glanced up, brow lifted. "Aren't I allowed?"

He shrugged and passed a man in overalls a dollar. "You just don't look like the beer type."

"You type too easily," Maggie countered, watching as beer was tapped from a wooden keg into paper cups.

"Maybe," he murmured as she sipped at the froth. "You're having a good time?"

"Yes." She laughed over the rim. The beer was lukewarm, but it was wet. Her foot was already tapping. They'd added a mandolin, she noticed. The sound was sweet and old-fashioned. "Didn't you think I would?"

"I thought you'd enjoy the music." He leaned against

the wall so that he could see her with the dancers at her back. "I thought you needed to get out. But I didn't expect you to take to all this as if you'd been born doing it."

She lowered her half-empty cup and gave him a solemn smile. "When are you going to stop putting me in that shiny glass cage, Cliff? I'm not a delicate hothouse flower or a spoiled Hollywood bitch. I'm Maggie Fitzgerald, and I write music."

The look held for a long time while the music pulsed around them. "I think I know who you are." Lifting a hand, he ran the back of it down her cheek. "I think I know Maggie Fitzgerald. It might've been safer for both of us with you in that glass cage."

She felt the heat rise. It only took a touch. "We'll have to see, won't we?" With one brow still lifted in question, she touched her cup to his. "To new understanding?"

"All right." He cradled her chin in his hand before he kissed her. "We'll give it a shot."

"Miss Fitzgerald?"

Maggie turned to see a short man in his early twenties running a felt hat around and around in his hands. Until that moment, she'd been so intent on Cliff that she hadn't noticed the music had stopped. "You're the piano player." Her eyes lit, and the smile that could stun so unexpectedly curved on her lips. "You're wonderful."

He'd been nervous before; now he was overwhelmed. "I just— Thank you," he managed, staring at her with his soul in his eyes.

She doesn't even know it, Cliff realized. She wasn't aware that she could make a man want to grovel. Sipping his beer, he watched the piano player try to find his voice again.

"I couldn't believe it when I heard you were here."

"I live here," she told him simply.

The way she said it, so matter-of-factly, had Cliff looking at her again. She'd said it before, countless times in countless ways, but he realized now he hadn't listened. Yes, she lived here. She'd chosen to live here just as he had. It hardly mattered where she'd lived or how she'd lived before. She was here now because she'd chosen to be. And she was staying. For the first time, he fully believed it.

"Miss Fitzgerald..." The piano player crushed the brim of his hat in his fingers, torn between pleasure and anxiety. "I just wanted you to know it's great having you here. We don't want to push you into anything, but if you'd like to play anything, anything at all—"

"Are you asking?" she interrupted.

The boy stumbled over uncertain ground. "We just wanted you to know that if you'd like—"

"I don't know any of the songs," she told him, taking a last sip of beer. "Do you trust me to improvise?"

His mouth dropped open. "Are you kidding?"

She laughed and handed her cup to Cliff. "Hang on to this."

He shook his head, leaning back against the wall as she walked to the stage with the piano player. She had a habit of giving orders, he mused. Then he thought of the look of stunned admiration in the boy's eyes. Maybe it was worth it.

She played for an hour. It was, she discovered, as much fun making the music as it was dancing to it. She enjoyed the challenge of the unfamiliar music and the freewheeling style. Before she'd gone through the second number, Maggie had decided to write one of her own.

From the vantage point of the stage, she could see the dancers. She saw Louella again, partnered by Stan. Automatically, she searched the crowd for Joyce and found her facing Cliff. As if she'd known he'd be there, her gaze was drawn to the left. Reiker leaned against a post, smoking, watching the dancers.

Who? Maggie wondered. Who is he watching? As the lines merged and shifted, she couldn't be sure, only that the direction of his gaze rested on where Stan danced with Louella and Cliff with Joyce.

If he saw one of them as a murderer, it didn't show in his eyes. They were calm and steady and made Maggie's stomach queasy. Deliberately, she turned her head and concentrated on the music.

"I didn't expect to lose my partner to a piano," Cliff said when the music paused again.

Maggie sent him an arch look. "You didn't appear to lack for any."

"A lone man's easy prey around here." Grabbing her hand, he drew her to her feet. "Hungry?"

"Is it midnight already?" Maggie pressed a hand to her stomach. "I'm starving."

They piled their plates high, though the light was so dim it was impossible to tell what they were eating until it was tasted. They sat on the grass under a tree and chatted easily to the people who passed by. It was easy, Maggie thought. They were just people drawn to one place by music. Again she felt a sense of camaraderie and connection. Leaning back, Maggie scanned the crowd.

"I don't see Louella."

"Stan would've taken her home," Cliff said between bites. "She never stays past midnight. He'll come back."

"Mmm." Maggie sampled what turned out to be Waldorf salad.

"Miss Fitzgerald."

Maggie set down her fork as Reiker crouched down beside her. "Lieutenant."

"I enjoyed your playing." He gave her the quiet smile that had her cursing her reaction to him. "I've listened to your music for years, but I never expected to be able to hear you play."

"I'm glad you liked it." She knew she should leave it at that, but felt compelled to go on. "I haven't noticed you dancing."

"Me?" The smile turned sheepish. "No, I don't dance. My wife, now, she likes to come."

Maggie felt herself relax. So the explanation had been a simple one, an innocent one. "Most people who appreciate music like to dance."

"I'd like to. My feet don't." His gaze shifted to Cliff. "I want to thank you for your cooperation. It might help us tie up a few loose ends."

"Whatever I can do," Cliff said briskly. "We'd all like this business tied up."

Reiker nodded, then, with some effort, rose. "I hope you'll play some more before the night's over, Miss Fitzgerald. It's a real pleasure listening to you."

When he was gone, Maggie let out a long breath. "It isn't fair that he makes me uncomfortable. He's only doing his job." She began to pick at her food again when Cliff remained silent. "What did he mean by cooperation?"

"I contacted my mother. She's coming up Monday to give a statement."

"I see. That must be difficult for her."

"No." Cliff shrugged it off. "It was ten years ago. It's behind her. It's behind all of us," he added quietly, "but one."

Maggie closed her eyes on a shudder. She wouldn't think of it now, not tonight. "Dance with me again," she insisted when the musicians began to tune. "There are hours yet before dawn."

She never tired, even after the moon began to set. The music and the movement gave her the release she needed for nervous energy. Some dancers faded; others became only more exuberant as the night grew later. The music never stopped.

As the sky began to lighten, there were no more than a hundred dancers left on their feet. There was something mystical, something powerful, in watching the sun rise from behind the mountains while the music poured onto the air. As the light grew rosy with the new day, the last waltz was called.

Cliff folded Maggie in his arms and circled the floor. He could feel the life vibrate from her—exciting, strong. Once she'd stopped, he thought as he gathered her closer, she'd sleep for hours.

She moved with him, snug against him. Her heartbeat was steady, her hair soft. He watched the colors spread over the mountains to the east. Then she tilted back her head and smiled at him.

And when he realized he was in love with her, Cliff was stunned and speechless.

Chapter 12

Maggie might've noticed Cliff's abrupt withdrawal if she hadn't been so full of the night and the music. "I can't believe it's over. I've hours more dancing in me."

"You'll be asleep before you're home," Cliff told her, but made certain he wasn't touching her. He must be crazy, falling in love with a woman like her. She couldn't decide whether to hang wallpaper or lay tile. She gave orders. She wore silk under her jeans. He must be crazy.

But she could dance with him through the night. There was a ridge of strength and courage under the delicate features. She made music that was part heaven and part sin. Hadn't he known, and hadn't he fought so hard, because he'd known almost from the first that she was a woman he'd never get out of his mind?

Now she was climbing into the cab of his pickup and resting her head against his shoulder as if it belonged there. It did belong there. Though the acceptance didn't come easily to him, Cliff put his arm around her, drawing her closer. She belonged there.

"I don't know when I've had such a good time." The energy was draining out of her swiftly. Through sheer will, Maggie kept her eyes open.

"The music's still running around in your head."

She tilted her head so that she could see his profile. "I think you are beginning to understand me."

"Some."

"Some's enough." She yawned hugely. "It was fun playing tonight. You know, I've always avoided performing, mainly because I knew it would only open the door for more comparisons. But tonight…"

Cliff frowned, not certain if he liked the drift. "You're thinking of performing?"

"No, not on a regular basis. If I'd had a drive to do it, I'd have done it long before this." She shifted into a more comfortable position. "But I've decided to take C.J.'s advice and do the title song for *Heat Dance*. It's a compromise, a recording rather than a performance. And I do feel rather personally toward that song."

"You decided this tonight?"

"I've been leaning toward it for quite a while. It seems foolish to live by rules so strict you can't do something you really want to do. I really want to do that song." As her head began to droop, she noticed they were turning into her lane. "It'll mean flying back to L.A. for a few days for the taping, which'll thrill C.J." She gave a sleepy laugh. "He'll pull out every trick in the book to keep me from coming back."

Cliff felt the panic in his chest. He pulled the truck

up at the end of the drive and set the brake. "I want you to marry me."

"What?" Half-asleep, Maggie shook her head, certain she'd misunderstood.

"I want you to marry me," Cliff repeated, but this time he took her shoulders so that she wasn't slumped down in the seat any longer. "I don't care if you record a dozen songs. You're going to marry me before you go back to California."

To say she was stunned would've been an immeasurable understatement. Maggie stared at him as if one of them had lost his mind. "I must be a little foggy at the moment," she said slowly. "Are you saying you want to marry me?"

"You know damn well what I'm saying." It was too much to know the fear of losing her just when he'd realized he couldn't live without her. He couldn't be calm; he couldn't be rational; he couldn't let her go without a pledge that she'd come back. "You're not going to California until you marry me."

Trying to clear her mind, Maggie drew back. "Are you talking about my doing a recording, or are we talking marriage? One has to do with my business, the other with my life."

Frustrated that she was calm when he couldn't be, Cliff dragged her back. "From now on, your life is my business."

"No." That sounded too familiar. "No, I don't want someone looking out for me, if that's what you mean. I won't take that kind of responsibility again, or that kind of guilt."

"I don't know what the hell you're talking about," Cliff exploded. "I'm telling you you're going to marry me."

"That's just it—you can't *tell* me!" She jerked away from him, and the sleepiness in her eyes had turned to fire. "Jerry told me we were getting married, and I went along because it seemed like the thing to do. He was my best friend. He'd helped me get over the death of my parents, encouraged me to write again. He wanted to take care of me." Maggie dragged a hand through her hair. "And I let him, until things started going downhill and he couldn't even take care of himself. I couldn't help him then. The pattern had been set, and I couldn't help him. Not again, Cliff. I won't be put in that glass cage again."

"This has nothing to do with your first marriage and nothing to do with cages," Cliff tossed back. "You can damn well take care of yourself, but you're going to marry me."

Her eyes narrowed into slits as she held down her own uncertain temper. "Why?"

"Because I'm telling you."

"Wrong answer." With a toss of her head, she was out of the truck and had slammed the door. "You can go cool off or go sleep it off or whatever you want," she told him coldly. "I'm going to bed." Turning on her heel, she strode up the shaky front steps to the door. As she turned the handle, she heard the sound of his truck descending the hill. *Let him go*, Maggie told herself before she could turn around and call him back. *You can't let yourself be pushed around that way.* When a man thinks he can order a woman to marry him, he deserves exactly what she'd given him, Maggie decided. A good swift kick in the ego. Imagine bringing up marriage out of the blue that way, she thought as she shoved open the front door. Marriage, not love. He dangled marriage at her as though it were a carrot at the end of a stick. She wasn't biting. If he wanted her, really wanted her, he'd have to do a hell of a lot better.

I love you. She leaned her head against the door and told herself she wouldn't cry. That's all it would've taken; that's all he'd needed to say. Understanding. No, she decided as she straightened again, they were still a long way from understanding each other.

Why wasn't the dog barking, she wondered grumpily as she pushed the door shut again. Terrific watchdog he'd turned out to be. Annoyed, she turned toward the steps, planning on a hot bath and a long sleep, when a scent stopped her. Candle wax, Maggie thought, puzzled. Roses? Odd, she thought. Her imagination was good, but not good enough to conjure up scents. She crossed toward the living room and stopped in the doorway.

Louella sat very straight and very prim in a high-backed chair. Her hands were neatly folded in the lap of the same misty-gray dress she'd worn for dancing. Her skin was so pale that the shadows under her eyes looked like bruises. The eyes themselves seemed to stare straight through Maggie. On the table beside her there were candles burning, the tapers hardly more than stubs now, with the wax pooled heavily on the base of the holders. A vase of fresh roses sat nearby, so that the breeze through the open window carried the scent through the room.

After the first shock, Maggie tried to bring her thoughts to order. It had been obvious from the first that Louella wasn't completely well. She'd have to be handled gently, Maggie thought, and so she approached her as one might a wounded bird.

"Mrs. Morgan," she said quietly, then cautiously touched a hand to her shoulder.

"I've always liked candlelight." Louella spoke in her calm, soft voice. "So much prettier than a lamp. I'd often burn candles in the evening."

"They're lovely." Maggie kept her tone gentle as she knelt beside her. "But it's morning now."

"Yes." Louella looked blankly at the sun-filled window. "I often sit up through the night. I like the sounds. The woods make such music at night."

Perhaps if she'd thought it through, Maggie wouldn't have questioned. She would simply have led Louella out to her car and driven her home. But she didn't think it through. "Do you often come here at night, Mrs. Morgan?"

"Sometimes I'll drive," she said dreamily. "Sometimes, if the night's as clear and warm as this, I'll walk. I used to walk a great deal as a girl. Joyce used to love to toddle on the paths in the woods when she was just a baby."

Maggie moistened her lips. "Do you come back here often, Mrs. Morgan, at night?"

"I know I should stay away. Joyce has told me so all along. But—" Louella sighed, and the small, sad smile touched her mouth. "She has Stan. Such a good man— they take care of each other. That's what marriage is, you know, loving and taking care of each other."

"Yes." Helplessly, Maggie watched as Louella's hands grew agitated in her lap.

"William wasn't a loving man. He just wasn't made that way. I wanted Joyce to have a loving man, like Stan." She lapsed into silence, closing her eyes and breathing shallowly so that Maggie thought she slept.

Deciding it was best to call the Agees, she started to rise, when Louella's hand closed over hers.

"I followed him here that night," she whispered. Now her eyes were intense, fully focused. Maggie's mouth went dry.

"Followed him?"

"I didn't want anything to happen. Joyce loved him so."

Maggie struggled to keep her voice low and even, her eyes steady. "You followed your husband here?"

"William was here," Louella told her. "He was here, and he had the money. I knew he was going to do something dreadful, something he'd have gotten away with because of who he was. There had to be an end to it." Her fingers tightened convulsively on Maggie's, then relaxed just as abruptly as her head fell back. "Of course, the money couldn't be buried with him. I thought, no, if they find him, they shouldn't find the money. So I hid it."

"Here," Maggie managed. "In the attic."

"In the old trunk. I forgot all about it," Louella said as fatigue washed through her voice. "Forgot until a few weeks ago, when they dug in the gully. I came and took the money out and burned it, as I should've burned it ten years ago."

Maggie looked down at the hand that lay limply on hers. It was frail, the blue veins showing sharply against the thin ivory skin. Could that hand have pulled a trigger, sending a bullet into a man? Maggie shifted her gaze to Louella's face and saw it was now serene in sleep.

What do I do? Maggie asked herself as she laid Louella's hand carefully back in her lap. Call the police? Maggie looked at the peacefully sleeping, fragile figure in the chair. No, she couldn't; she didn't have the steel for it. She'd call Joyce.

She went to the phone and asked the operator for Joyce's number. There was no answer at the Agee house. Maggie sighed and glanced over her shoulder into the living room at Louella, who was still sleeping. She hated to do it, but she had to call Lieutenant Reiker. When she couldn't get hold of him, either, she left a message with his office.

Coming back into the living room, Maggie gasped as a figure moved toward her. "Oh, you frightened me."

"Sorry." Stan looked with concern from Maggie to his mother-in-law. "I came in the back. The dog's sleeping pretty heavily in the kitchen. Looks like Louella might've given him part of a sleeping pill to keep him quiet."

"Oh." Maggie made an instinctive move toward the kitchen.

"He's all right," Stan assured her. "He'll just be a little groggy when he wakes up."

"Sheriff—Stan," she decided, hoping the lack of formality would make it easier for him. "I was just about to call you. I think Louella's been here most of the night."

"I'm sorry." He rubbed his own sleep-starved eyes. "She's been getting steadily worse since this business started. Joyce and I don't want to put her in a home."

"No." Concerned, she touched his arm. "But she told me she wanders at night, and—" Maggie broke off and circled the room. Could she tell him what Louella had said? He was her son-in-law, but he was still the sheriff. The badge and the gun he wore reminded her.

"I heard what she told you, Maggie."

She turned, her eyes filled with compassion and concern. "What should we do? She's so fragile. I can't bear to be a part of having her punished for something that happened so long ago. And yet, if she killed…" With her conscience tearing her in different directions, she turned again.

"I don't know." Stan looked at Louella while he rubbed the back of his neck. "What she told you doesn't have to be true."

"But it makes sense," Maggie insisted. "She knew about the money. If she'd hid it in the trunk, then forgotten about it, blocked it out because it reminded her—" Maggie shook her head and forced herself to continue. "Stan, it's the only explanation for the break-in here." She covered her face with her hands as her sense of right and wrong battled. "She needs help," Maggie said abruptly. "She doesn't need police or lawyers. She needs a doctor."

Relief ran over Stan's face. "She'll get one. The best one Joyce and I can find."

Shaky, uncertain, Maggie rested a hand on the table. "She's devoted to you," she murmured. "She always speaks so highly of you, of how you love Joyce. I think she'd do anything she could to keep both of you happy."

As she spoke, Maggie's gaze was drawn down to where her palm rested—on the color snapshot of Morgan and Stan, near the gully. It would all be laid to rest now, she thought as she stared down at the photo. Louella had suffered enough, been punished enough for—

Distracted, she narrowed her eyes and looked closer. Why it came to her now, Maggie would never know, but she remembered Reiker's words. "We found a ring, too, an old ring with a lot of fancy carving and three small diamond chips… Joyce Agee identified it as her father's."

But in the picture William Morgan wasn't wearing the ring. Stan Agee was.

She looked up, her eyes dry and clear with the knowledge.

He didn't have to look at the picture under her hand. He'd already seen. "You should've let it go, Maggie."

She didn't stop to think, to reason; she only reacted. In a dead run, she headed for the front door. The move was so unexpected, she was into the hall with her hand on the knob before he'd taken the first step. As the door stuck, she cursed it, cursed her own inefficiency for not having it seen to weeks before. As she started to tug a second time, Stan's hand closed over her arm.

"Don't." His voice was low and strained. "I don't want to hurt you. I have to think this through."

With her back to the door, Maggie stared at him. She was alone in the house with a murderer. Alone, she thought desperately, except for a fragile old woman who loved him enough to have shielded him for ten years. Maggie watched him rest his hand on the butt of his gun.

"We'd better sit down."

Cliff drank his second cup of coffee and wished it was bourbon. If he'd tried to make a fool of himself over a woman, he could've done no better. Drinking in the strong, bitter taste, he scowled down at the laminated counter in the café. The scent of frying eggs and sausage did nothing for his appetite.

How could he have botched it so badly? What woman in her right mind, he asked himself, would respond favorably to a shouted, angry proposal? Maggie had given him the heave-ho, and now that he'd cooled off a bit, he couldn't blame her.

Still, he wasn't one of the fancy crowd she'd run with in L.A., he reminded himself. He wasn't going to change his manners for her any more than he expected her to change for him. She'd chosen to change her life before he'd been a part of it.

Chosen, Cliff thought again, cursing himself. She'd chosen her home, and he'd never seen anyone put down roots so quickly. He shouldn't have panicked at the mention of the recording in L.A. She'd be back. The land was as important to her as it was to him. Perhaps that had been their first bond, though they both insisted they'd had no common ground.

She'd be back, Cliff told himself again. He'd been an idiot to think bullying her into marriage would assure that. Maggie wouldn't be bullied, and she was here to stay. Those were two of the reasons he loved her.

He should have told her that, he thought, pushing the unwanted coffee aside. He could have found the words to tell her he'd been in love with her for weeks and that at dawn, with the morning light spilling over her face, he'd realized it. It had taken his breath away, stolen his senses, made him weak. He could've found the words to tell her.

Straightening from the counter, he checked his watch. She'd had an hour's sleep. Cliff decided a woman didn't need any more than that for a proper proposal of marriage. He tossed the money on the counter and began to whistle.

He continued to whistle as he took the road through town, until Joyce dashed into the street and frantically hailed him.

"Oh, Cliff!"

Though he'd stopped the car in the middle of the street, he was halfway out of it as he spoke. "What is it, one of the kids?"

"No, no." Struggling for calm, Joyce gripped his arms. She, too, hadn't changed from the dance, but the hair she'd worn up was now escaping its pins and falling in clumps. "It's my mother," she managed after a moment. "She hasn't been in bed all night—and Stan, I can't find Stan anywhere."

"We'll find Louella." Cliff brushed the hair from her face as he'd done since she'd been a child. "She might have been restless and gone for a walk. With the excitement last night—"

"Cliff." Joyce gripped his arms tighter. "I think she went out to the old place. I'm dead sure of it—it wouldn't be the first time."

He thought of Maggie with a little ripple of unease. "Maggie's home," he said soothingly. "She'll look out for her."

"She's been getting worse." Joyce's breath began to shudder. "Oh, Cliff, I thought I was doing the right thing, the only thing."

"What're you talking about?"

"I lied to the police. I lied before I'd thought it through, but I know I'd do the same thing again." She pressed her fingers to her eyes briefly, then dropped them. When she looked at Cliff now, she looked at him with a surface calm that was deadly. "I know who killed my father. I've known for weeks. Mother—it seems Mother's known for ten years."

"Get in," he ordered. He was thinking of Maggie now, of Maggie alone in the house, surrounded by woods. "Tell me while we drive."

Maggie's back was stiff and straight as she sat on a low bench. Moving only her eyes, she watched Stan pace the room. She wanted to believe he wouldn't hurt her. But he'd killed once, ten years before. Now he'd have to deal with her or pay for it.

"I never wanted Joyce to sell this house." He paced to the window, then back to the center of the room. "I never wanted it. The money meant nothing to me. Her money—her father's money—never has. How could I've guessed she'd get it into her head to put it on the market when I was out of town?"

He ran a hand over his shirt and left faint streaks. He's sweating, Maggie noted. It didn't help her nerves.

"She lied to the police about the ring."

Maggie moistened her lips. "She loves you."

"She didn't know—I'd never told her all these years. Then, when I finally had to, she stood by me. A man can't ask for more than that." He paced again, so that the soles of his shoes hitting hardwood and rug were the only sounds. "I didn't murder him," Stan said flatly. When he looked at Maggie, his eyes were glazed with fatigue. "It was an accident."

She gripped that, clung to that. "Then if you go to the police and explain—"

"Explain?" Stan cut her off. "Explain that I killed a man, buried him and drove his car into the river?" He rubbed the heels of his hands over his face. "I was only twenty," he began. "Joyce and I'd been in love for two years. Morgan had already made it clear that there couldn't be anything between us, so we saw each other in secret. When Joyce found out she was pregnant, there couldn't be any more secrets."

He leaned against the window and stared into the room. "We should've known there was something wrong when he took it so well, but we were both so relieved, both so thrilled at the idea of being married and starting a family, that we never caught on. He told us to keep it quiet for a few weeks while he arranged for the wedding."

Maggie remembered the stern face from the photograph. "But he didn't mean it."

"No, both of us were too wrapped up in each other to remember what kind of man he was." Stan kept moving in the same line, to the window, back to the center of the room, to the window again. "He said he was having trouble with groundhogs up at his old place. I was young and eager to do anything to keep on the right side of him. I told him I'd bring my shotgun one evening after work and take care of them."

He saw Maggie shudder and glance at the pistol on his hip. "It was dusk when he drove up. I didn't expect him. When he got out of the car, I remember thinking he looked like an undertaker, all in black with shiny shoes. He was carrying a little metal box that he set down on the stump of a tree near the gully. He didn't waste any time," Stan continued. "He told me outright that he'd never let a small-town nobody like me marry his daughter. He said he was going to send her away. Sweden or somewhere. She'd have the baby and give it away. He didn't expect me to keep quiet for nothing. He told me he had twenty-five thousand in the box. I was to take it and disappear."

So the twenty-five thousand had been payoff money, blackmail. Yes, she could believe that the man in the photo had thought money would ensure anything.

"I got frantic. I couldn't believe he was threatening to take away everything I'd ever wanted. He could've done it, too." Stan wiped at the sweat that beaded on his upper lip. "He would've done it without a second thought. I shouted at him. I told him he wasn't going to take Joyce and our baby away from me. I told him we'd go away, we didn't need his filthy money. He opened the cash box and showed me all those bills, as if it would tempt me. I knocked it out of his hands."

His breath was coming quickly now, heavily, as if he were reliving that moment—the anger, the despair. Maggie felt her pity well up to tangle with her fear.

"He never lost his temper. Never once. He just bent down and scooped the money back in the box. He thought I wanted more. He never understood, wasn't capable of understanding. When it got to the point where he saw I wasn't going to take the money and go away, he picked up my gun just as calmly as he'd picked up the box. I knew, as sure as I'd ever know anything, that he'd kill me where I stood and he'd get away with it. Somehow he'd get away with it. All I could think was that I'd never see Joyce again, never hold our baby. I grabbed for the gun—it went off over my shoulder. We started struggling."

He was panting now, his eyes glazed. Maggie could visualize the struggle between man and boy as clearly as if it were happening in front of her eyes. She shut them. Then she saw the scene in the film she'd scored in which overpowering need had erupted into irrevocable violence. But this was real and needed no music to spark the drama.

"He was strong—that old man was strong. I knew I'd be dead if I didn't get the gun away. Somehow—" Stan dragged both his hands up his face and into his hair. "Somehow I had it in my hands and was falling back. I'll never forget—it was like a dream, a nightmare. I was falling back, and the gun went off."

She could picture it, all too clearly. Both sympathetic and afraid, Maggie dared to speak. "But it was
an accident, self-defense."

He shook his head as his hands dropped back to his
side, back, she noted with a tremor, near the gun on his
hip. "I was twenty, scraping pennies. I'd just killed the
most important man in town, and there was twenty-
five thousand dollars in a box next to his body. Who'd
have believed me? Maybe I panicked, maybe I did the
only sensible thing, but I buried him and his money in
the gully, then sent his car into the river."

"Louella…" Maggie began.

"I didn't know she'd followed me. I guess she knew
Morgan better than anyone and understood he'd never
let me marry Joyce. I didn't know she'd watched everything from the woods. Maybe if I had, things would've
been different. It seemed she never really came out of
the shock of losing her husband—now I understand
better. She'd seen it all—then, for some reason of her
own, she'd dug out the cash box and hidden it in the
house. I guess she was protecting me all these years."

"And Joyce?"

"She never knew." Stan shook his head and tugged at
the collar of his shirt as if it were too tight. "I never told
her. You have to understand. I love Joyce. I've loved
her since she was a girl. There's nothing I wouldn't
do for her if I could. If I'd told her everything, everything he'd threatened to do and what had happened,
she might have thought—she might not have believed
it was an accident. I couldn't have lived with that. For
years I've done everything I could to make up for what
happened in that gully. I dedicated myself to the law,

to the town. I've been the best father, the best husband, I know how to be."

He picked up the color snapshot and crushed it in his hand. "That damn picture. Damn ring. I was so wired up I didn't notice I'd lost it until days afterward. My grandfather's ring." He rubbed a hand over his temple. "Ten years later it's dug up with Morgan. Do you know how I felt when I learned that Joyce had identified it as her father's? She knew," he said passionately. "She knew it was mine, but she stood behind me. She never questioned me, and when I told her everything, she never doubted me. All these years—I've lived with it all these years."

"You don't have to live with it anymore." Maggie spoke calmly, though her heart was in her throat. He was strung so tight she couldn't gauge when he might snap or what he might do. "People respect you, know you. Louella saw everything. She'd testify."

"Louella's on the edge of a complete breakdown. Who knows if she'd be capable of making a coherent sentence if all this comes out? I have to think of Joyce, of my family, of my reputation." A muscle began to jerk in his cheek as he stared at Maggie. "There's so much at stake," he whispered. "So much to protect."

She watched his hand hover over the butt of his gun.

Cliff started up the steep lane at full speed, spitting gravel. Joyce's breathless story told him one vital thing. Maggie was caught in the middle of violence and passion that had simmered underground for ten years. If it erupted today, she'd be alone—alone because he'd been a fool. As he rounded the top curve, a man stepped into the path of the car, forcing him to brake. Swearing, Cliff stormed out of the car.

"Mr. Delaney," Reiker said mildly. "Mrs. Agee."

"Where's Maggie?" Cliff demanded, and would've moved past him if Reiker hadn't stopped him with a surprisingly strong grip.

"She's inside. At the moment, she's fine. Let's keep it that way."

"I'm going up."

"Not yet." He gave Cliff a long, steely look before he turned to Joyce. "Your mother's inside, Mrs. Agee. She's fine, sleeping. Your husband's in there, too."

"Stan." Joyce looked toward the house, taking an instinctive step forward.

"I've been keeping a close eye on things. Your husband told Miss Fitzgerald everything."

Cliff's blood iced. "Damn it, why haven't you gotten her out?"

"We're going to get her out. We're going to get them all out. Quietly."

"How do you know he won't hurt her?"

"I don't—if he's pushed. I want your help, Mrs. Agee. If your husband loves you as much as he says, you're the key." He looked toward the house. "He'd have heard the car. Better let him know you're here."

Inside the house, Stan had Maggie by the arm, holding her close as he stood at the window. She could feel his muscles jumping, hear his breath whistling. As terror washed over her, she closed her eyes and thought of Cliff. If he'd come back, everything would be all right. If he came back, the nightmare would end.

"Someone's out there." Stan jerked his head toward the open window, and his free hand opened and closed on the butt of his gun. "I can't let you talk to anyone. You have to understand. I can't risk it."

"I won't." His fingers dug into her arm so that the pain kept her head clear. "Stan, I want to help you. I swear I only want to help. If you hurt me, it'll never be over."

"Ten years," he muttered, straining to see any movement outside. "Ten years and he's still trying to ruin my life. I can't let him."

"Your life will be ruined if you do anything to me." *Be logical*, Maggie told herself as waves of panic threatened to overtake her. *Be calm*. "It wouldn't be an accident this time, Stan. This time you'd be a murderer. You'd never make Joyce understand."

His fingers tightened until she had to dig her teeth into her lower lip to keep from crying out. "Joyce stood behind me."

"She loves you. She believes in you. But if you hurt me, everything would change."

She felt him tremble. The grip on her arm loosened fractionally. As Maggie watched, Joyce walked up over the rise toward the house. At first, she thought she was hallucinating; then she heard Stan's breath catch. He saw her, too.

"Stan." Joyce's hand moved on her throat, as if she could make her voice stronger. "Stan, please come out."

"I don't want you involved in this." Stan's fingers were like iron on Maggie's arm again.

"I am involved. I've always been involved. I know everything you did you did for me."

"Damn it." He pressed his face against the window glass, pounding one fist steadily against the frame. "He can't ruin everything we've built."

"No, he can't." Joyce came closer to the house, measuring each step. In all the years she'd known her husband, she'd never heard despair in his voice. "Stan, he can't touch us now. We're together. We'll always be together."

"They'll take me away from you. The law." He squeezed his eyes tighter. "I've done my best by the law."

"Everyone knows that. Stan, I'll be with you. I love you. You're everything to me, my whole life. Please, please, don't do anything I'd be ashamed of."

Maggie felt him tense as he straightened from the window. The muscle was still working in his cheek. There was a line of sweat over his lip he no longer bothered to wipe away. He stared out the window, at Joyce, then over at the gully.

"Ten years," he whispered. "But it's still not over."

His fingers worked sporadically on Maggie's arm. Numb with fear, she watched as he drew the gun out of its holster. His eyes met hers, cold, clear blue, without expression. Perhaps she would've begged for her life, but she knew, as any prey knows, that mercy comes at the hunter's whim.

His expression never changed as he set the gun down on the sill and released her arm. Maggie felt her blood begin to pump again, fast and hot. "I'm going outside," Stan said flatly, "to my wife."

Weak with relief, Maggie sank down on the piano stool. Without even the energy to weep, she buried her face in her hands.

"Oh, Maggie." Then Cliff's arms were around her, and she could feel the hard, fast beat of his heart. "That was the longest ten minutes of my life," he murmured as he began to run wild kisses over her face. "The longest."

She didn't want explanations. He was here; that was enough. "I kept telling myself you'd come. It kept me sane."

"I shouldn't have left you alone." He buried his face in her hair and drew in the scent.

She held him tighter. "I told you I could take care of myself."

He laughed, because she was in his arms and nothing had changed. "Yes, you did. It's over now." He framed her face in his hands so that he could study it. Pale, he noticed. The eyes were shadowed but steady. His Maggie was a woman who could take care of herself. "Reiker was outside, long enough to get the drift of what was going on. He's taking all three of them."

She thought of Louella's pale face, Stan's anguished eyes, Joyce's trembling voice. "They've been punished enough."

"Maybe." He ran his hands up her arms, just to assure himself she was whole and safe. "If he'd hurt you—"

"He wouldn't have." She shook her head and clung again. "He couldn't have. I want the pond, Cliff," she said fiercely. "I want you to put in the pond quickly, and I want to see the willow draping over it."

"You'll have it." He drew her back again. "And me? Will you have me, Maggie?"

She took a deep breath, letting his fingers rest on her face again. Again, she thought. She would try again and see if he understood. "Why should I?"

His brows drew together, but he managed to swallow the oath that came to mind. Instead, he kissed her, hard and long. "Because I love you."

She let out a trembling breath. She was indeed home. "That was the right answer."

* * * * *